W9-CKR-636

# THE JASMINE TRADE

## Nominated for the Edgar, Anthony, Macavity, and Willa Awards

## BOOKS BY DENISE HAMILTON

*The Jasmine Trade*
*Sugar Skull*

T21140

# DENISE HAMILTON

# SUGAR SKULL

## AN EVE DIAMOND NOVEL

## POCKET STAR BOOKS
New York   London   Toronto   Sydney

This book is a work of fiction. Names, characters, places, and incidents either are products of the author's imagination or are used fictitiously. Any resemblance to actual events or locales or persons, living or dead, is entirely coincidental.

 A Pocket Star Book published by
POCKET BOOKS, a division of Simon & Schuster, Inc.
1230 Avenue of the Americas, New York, NY 10020

ISBN: 0-7434-8221-2

First Pocket Books printing February 2004

10  9  8  7  6  5  4  3  2  1

POCKET STAR BOOKS and colophon are registered trademarks
of Simon & Schuster, Inc.

Cover design by John Vairo Jr.
Photograph © Brad Cohen
Sugar Skulls provided by www.mexicansugarskull.com

Manufactured in the United States of America

For information regarding special discounts for bulk purchases,
please contact Simon & Schuster Special Sales at 1-800-456-6798
or business@simonandschuster.com.

For my wee ones, Adrian and Alexander

# SUGAR
# SKULL

# CHAPTER 1

*I* was sitting at the city desk, halfway through my first cup of cafeteria coffee, when I saw him. His jacket was flapping, his arms flailing, as he sprinted along the computer terminals and zigzagged past three-foot piles of newspapers, eyes trained on the prize—a big sign that said METRO, under which I sat, scanning the wires on a slow Saturday morning.

You might think that with all those deadline pressures, newsrooms would be kinetic places where people leapt and darted and yelled all day long. Maybe they do at other places, but here at the *Los Angeles Times,* the only place I've ever worked, such displays are considered a mark of poor breeding.

I'd never seen anyone run in the newsroom and wasn't sure what to make of it. But up he came, skidding to a stop before me, white bubbles foaming at the corners of his mouth. He wore a tweed cap, which he took off and ran along his forehead to swab up the sweat pearling at his hairline. Then he placed the cap over his chest like he was pledging allegiance.

"Miss, you've got to help me look for her. The police won't do anything until forty-eight hours have passed. But something's dreadfully wrong, I feel it here."

His cap flapped weakly against his chest.

"Look for who?" I cast around for someone who could wrestle him to the ground if it came down to that, but it wasn't yet eight o'clock and the newsroom was empty. How had he gotten past security downstairs?

"My daughter. Isabel," the man said. His face tightened, and he looked over his shoulder. "She's been missing since yesterday. I think I know where she is, but I don't want to go alone. The press should be there. Please, miss, are you a reporter? Will you come with me?"

He must have heard how unhinged he sounded, because he shoved his hand into his pants pocket, rooted around for a wallet, and pulled out his driver's license.

"Vincent Chevalier," he said, holding it up with a trembling hand. "I'm a sound engineer. Done all of Jackson Browne's records since *Late for the Sky*."

He looked at me. "Of course, you're too young to remember that one. I know what you're thinking. That I could be an ax murderer."

Damn straight, I thought, inching away my chair.

"I know I sound crazy, and I am—I'm crazed about what might be happening to my daughter. Please, miss, we have to hurry."

He craned his head again, and this time, I did too. We heard yelling and the pounding of feet.

"He went that way. There he is, get him."

For the second time in my career, I saw people running in the newsroom. This time it was two security guards, charging straight for the city desk. Was I going to be on the news myself tonight? The guards pounded up, each seizing one of Chevalier's arms.

"He flashed an ID at the door," one of them said, "but it didn't look right so I told him to wait. Then he ran up the stairs. I had to radio for backup before leaving my post."

The guard saw me staring at him, and then at the man he had apprehended much too late to save anyone. He shifted from one foot to the other and hooked his thumb into his thick black belt.

"We only have a skeleton crew on the weekends since budget cutbacks," he mumbled. "C'mon, you." He jerked the captive's arm roughly to show him who was boss. "Out we go."

An anguished howl leapt from Vincent Chevalier's throat. "Isabel," he bellowed. Then the fight went out of him and he began to weep. "And what if it was your daughter? Wouldn't you do everything you could?"

It wouldn't be my daughter, I thought, because I don't have a daughter. But if I did, I'd keep closer tabs on her than you obviously have. "Late for the Sky" indeed. But something about his tone got to me.

"Wait a minute," I said. "He came up here wanting to talk to a reporter. Let's hear what he has to say."

Reluctantly, the guards stepped back. Vincent Chevalier's face took on a cautious, cunning look. He knew he had one chance and he'd better not flub it.

"My daughter is only fifteen, but she's precocious. We live in a nice part of Pasadena, prep school and all that, but in the last year she's gotten restless. Started hanging out with an edgier crowd. Some of them are runaways, and she brings them food and warm clothes. They squat in abandoned buildings. There's a young man she's been trying to help. He gives me the creeps but I keep my mouth shut. I don't want to drive them closer. They've been on and off for months. Yesterday she said she was going to visit a girlfriend and would be home for dinner. She never showed."

He looked at us, anxiety mounting in his eyes. "I want someone to go to the squat with me."

"Why can't you check it out by yourself?" I asked.

Vincent Chevalier twitched his cap up and down against his fleecy sweater. He was slight and couldn't have stood more than five foot eight inches tall. "Last time I saw Finch, that's her squatter friend, he threatened me."

"Sounds like you need a bodyguard, not a puny girl reporter."

He stared at me. His silvery-black hair was curly and wet, plastered against his pale skull, except for one unruly lock that fell forward into his eyes.

"What I really need is the police, but they won't come. They've been there with me before, when she's run away. They don't take my calls seriously anymore. But if the press noses around, maybe they will. I don't want to go by myself. I want a witness."

"Where is this squat?"

Something about his story gnawed at me. His daughter had been hanging out with a disturbed runaway in some abandoned building and he didn't put a stop to it? And now he wanted me to help find her? Yet desperation rolled off him in big, crashing waves. He was bewildered in that way honest people get when they find themselves spinning into madness. And he had already tried the police. I suppose that counted for something.

"East Hollywood," he said. "You can follow me in your car."

I scrolled through the wires again to see what else was going on in the city. All over town, people were dying violently—shot in dead-end bars, withdrawing money from ATMs, working the night shift in liquor stores, and playing hopscotch on the corner. Usually, we waited until Sunday, when the final tally came in, then did a roundup. Unless the victims were rich, prominent, or had met their end in some horribly unusual and tragic way, they got folded into the main story as smoothly as egg whites into cake. So far the wires were at fourteen and counting. As for scheduled events, there was a Mexican concert and All-Star Rodeo in La Puente at noon. The mayoral candidates were debating at the Century Plaza Hotel. Vietnam vets were demonstrating in front of the federal building at three o'clock. It was a slow news day.

Vincent Chevalier tapped his black suede sneaker impatiently. I focused on its agitated dance. It could be a great story. I pictured the headline, strategically placed in the paper's coveted Column One slot. DANCE WITH THE DARK SIDE—BORED RICH GIRLS SEEK ULTIMATE THRILLS SLUMMING WITH HOMELESS RUNAWAYS. But if he wasn't on the level? I looked around. The other 8 A.M. reporter was just strolling in, carrying his designer coffee in its corrugated paper holder. He was a Princeton graduate who had studied with Tom Wolfe and achieved notoriety when his senior thesis, a literary deconstruction of speed metal songs, had been published to great acclaim. I had gone to a state school and jostled with 250 students in a drafty auditorium for the attention of some postdoc lassoed into teaching Journalism 101.

Chevalier was watching my colleague too.

"Is he a reporter?" Chevalier inclined his chin. "Maybe a man would be better."

That settled it.

"Can I see your ID again?" I said sweetly. Chevalier handed it over and I typed all his stats into the computer. Then I compared his license photo with the face before me. A few more lines, a certain tautness around the mouth, but it was him all right. I got his home and work phone and typed that in too, leaving a note for the early editor, who was still upstairs in the caf eating breakfast and perusing our competitor the *Daily News* to see what stories we had missed. I would be back way before noon if they needed me to cover one of the wire events. But that was all canned, predictable stuff, while the foot-tapping Vincent Chevalier was dangling some very live bait. I made a printout of what I had just typed, tucked the cell phone into my purse, and told the guards they could return to their post.

In the parking lot, Chevalier and I turned to look at each other. In the milky light of a fall morning, I blinked and wondered why I was embarking on a human scavenger hunt to find his daughter.

Chevalier fingered the bill of his tweed cap, then stuck it squarely back on his head. "I'm a single father, you know, and it's been tough since she hit adolescence. She's constantly challenging authority. I understand that, since I was a rebel myself. So I keep the lines of communication open, like the books say. I tell her I love her and I'm there for her and then I let her go. She runs away a lot. Once she was gone for three months. Don't look at me like that, she'd call. Tell me where she was, what she was up to. Tucson, Kansas City, New Orleans. It made me feel better, knowing where she was. She's always come back. Until now."

Yikes, I thought. Mister, she's a fifteen-year-old girl. She needs you to lay down the law, and instead you hand her a Kerouac novel and wish her good luck.

"We'll find her," I told him, keeping my parenting lesson to myself.

He told me to get off the freeway at Western and head north, past Santa Monica Boulevard to a side street called Manzanita. The kids squatted in an old government building that had been damaged in the 1994 Northridge earthquake and was now condemned and fenced off.

I jotted the directions down, then got in the car and pulled out behind him onto Spring Street. Downtown was empty at this hour, only an occasional panhandler and a few Latino families trudging off for a day's shopping on Broadway. I usually worked in a small bureau in the San Gabriel Valley but pulled an occasional weekend shift downtown on rotation. Today, my number had come in.

Pulling alongside, I glanced at Vincent Chevalier's black SUV. It used to be that you could tell a lot about a person by what they hung from the rearview mirror. Asians decorated their cars with golden pagodas and good luck characters. Little plastic virgins and rosary beads meant Latinos. Fuzzy racing dice, well that was low riders. But then things got all mixed up and the street-racing Asian kids started hanging fuzzy dice and Latinos began thinking pagodas were way cool. Then the white punks appropriated dragons, dice, *santos,* and *milagros* and my whole theory went south. Chevalier's windshield was as bare as the Sahara. No window to the soul there.

I let him pull ahead, then grabbed my computer print-out and looked at his car again. The plates matched. Check No. 1. Then I groped in my purse, past the squishy black banana I kept meaning to toss, until I felt the smooth plastic of the cell phone. Holding it up to the steering wheel so I could see the keypad, I punched in the home number Chevalier had given me and got a recording saying that Vincent and Isabel weren't home but would return my call as soon as possible. Check No. 2.

Now I dialed the *Times* editorial library, only to learn that the librarian on duty was working on a deadline project about campaign contributions in the mayoral race. Could I call back after nine, when more librarians came on?

Great, I thought. I'm going to end up dead in some filthy squat so that star political reporter Tony Hausman can reveal the shocking story that big money influences politics.

I hung up and considered my options, mentally tracing a path through the paper's labyrinthine corridors that stopped at . . . the copy messenger desk. Yes, that was it. Luke Vinograd could help me. He was a snarky and overgrown copy messenger who had spent years chipping away at a library degree. By now he should have been running the place, but something had stalled him, and so at an age when most people were hitting their career stride, Luke Vinograd was still delivering faxes from the wire room and ferrying over morning editions to impatient editors who had no time or desire to chat about the sixteenth-century Italian poet whose lyric couplets he'd just discovered or the fabulous French farce he'd seen the previous night.

That was a shame, because in a place that lived and died on words, millions of them each day, Luke was renowned for his bon mots, a Noel Coward type but more wickedly bawdy. Even early in the morning, he sounded as though he should have a martini glass in one hand and a cigarette holder in the other.

"I do hope you're calling to invite me to brunch," Luke said, recognizing my voice.

"Thank God you're there."

"I know this fabulous place where they throw in salsa lessons with the eggs Benedict."

"In the morning?" I groaned. "Those moves are hard enough at night."

"Dawn's early blight, eh? The trick is to extend your night through brunch."

"Then when do you sleep?"

"Sleep's for sissies. A real man can hold his yawns."

"I see. Well, see if you can stay awake for this one. I need a huge favor."

I filled him in on my concerns about Vincent Chevalier, then asked him to go online, look up Jackson

Browne, and tell me the name of the sound engineer on his last albums. Sure enough, several clicks later, I had my confirmation. It was Chevalier. Check No. 3.

"No pretender, him."

"Glad to hear it. Hey, Luke, just a couple more favors."

"Your requests always come in multiples, don't they, Eve?"

"Like my orgasms, dahling." Despite myself, I blushed. Luke always brought out the Miller's Wife in me. "Now don't smart-mouth me, it's too early," I continued. "Could you please check property records on this Vincent Chevalier?"

"Ooh," Luke said, delighted by such sauciness as he tapped away, "and who has Miss Eve been mixing it up with lately?"

We had gone out for drinks several months back at the Redwood up the street, the old reporter's bar, moaning into our beers over the peccadilloes of our respective boyfriends. Ever since, the banter between us would have made an ink-stained printer blush.

"It's all completely theoretical at this point, Luke," I told him.

"My condolences," he murmured, hands whirring on the keyboard as he recounted the latest gossip about a reporter who had sneaked off to her editor's van for an afternoon quickie. They had been caught by *Times* security guards who came to investigate when the vehicle started rocking as they got rolling.

A few more clicks onto the L.A. County Register of Voters database and Luke was reciting the same address on my printout. Check No. 4. So Vincent Chevalier checked out. He still might be a murderer, of course, but he wasn't a liar. He was fifty-four, owned a home, had a real job, and appeared to be who he said he was. I felt better.

"Next," Luke Vinograd intoned.

"Oh yeah, one last thing. Speaking of Jackson Browne, and this is very important, I need you to hum the first bar of 'The Pretender.'"

There was silence on the other end of the line, then sputtering.

"Such abuse. 'My Funny Valentine' would be more up my alley."

"That's all the abuse you get for now, dollface. *Muchas gras* and talk to you later."

I was in East Hollywood now, which had always served as the industrial back lot for the glitzy Hollywood that tourists searched for in vain at Hollywood and Vine. East Hollywood was home to prop shops and postproduction facilities. It was where wanna-be starlets rented rooms in buildings of decayed glamour and rode the creaky elevators with immigrant families whose vision of the future was no less intense because it was dreamed in Armenian, Thai, Russian, and Spanish.

Latino men lounged on the street corners, signaling with two fingers to passing cars. Crack for sale. I shook my head and kept driving. In front of me, a brown truck pulled to the curb by a large apartment building and honked. In response, black-clad women streamed out the front door, clutching plastic bags and change purses. The driver hopped out and threw open the doors to his truck, oblivious to the traffic backing up behind him.

I groaned and craned my neck to signal Chevalier to wait, but he had swerved and kept going. I cursed the vehicular gods that had stuck me in traffic behind Armenian Home Grocer. It wasn't really Home Grocer, of course, those pretty peach-and-green-colored trucks that delivered food you ordered directly from the Internet. But the concept that had been such an innovation to harried Americans was old news in this ethnic hood. In unmarked brown trucks crammed floor-to-ceiling with fruits and vegetables, pita and fresh herbs, drivers careened up and down narrow side streets where immigrants retained the vestigial memory of haggling at outdoor markets. Armenian Home Grocer didn't charge for delivery either. With traffic hemming me in, I had little choice but to watch the driver hand over scallions and curvy purple eggplants, feathery dill, and new potatoes. The women milled on the sidewalk, muttering *"che, che,"* "no, no," when he tried to sell them something extra.

Finally I saw an opening and pulled out.

Five minutes later, I stopped at a decrepit heap of a building surrounded by a cyclone fence. The place was old, dating back to the 1920s, I guessed, from the white arches and pillars. Fissures had made crazy-quilt patterns in the plaster, and here and there, chunks had fallen out to expose the lathe beneath. All the windows and doors were boarded up with plywood and festooned with yellow emergency tape. If I were fifteen and trying to get as far away from Rose Bowl Landia as possible, I might end up here too. But only if I had a death wish. With its eyeless holes where windows should be, its cracked adobe defaced by gang graffiti, and its jagged piles of plaster and glass, the building struck me as a malevolent and grinning skull.

When Vincent Chevalier walked up, I shivered in aversion. Nothing good could come from going in there. I punched in the cell phone again and got through to George Bovasso, the morning city editor, who had finally finished his cafeteria bacon and egg whites and ambled downstairs to the third floor. I explained where I was and told him to start worrying if he didn't hear from me soon.

"That was my editor," I told Vincent Chevalier, clambering out. "I was just giving him the address. He's going to call the police if he doesn't hear from me in an hour."

I scrutinized him as I spoke, watching his eyes for flinching, for turning away, for any tick or twitch or wolfish quickening that would tell me to turn back. I found none. If I refused to crawl inside the squat, I might lose the best story I had run across in a long time. I had done what I could to check out my companion, to leave a trail, and to alert the proper authorities. I had to take a deep breath, plunge off that cliff, and hope the bungee cord didn't snap.

# CHAPTER 2

S o you've been here before?" I asked.

Vincent Chevalier and I had scaled the eight-foot chain-link fence. Soon we'd be on the other side. I imagined how ludicrous we looked as we perched precariously at the top, two adults trespassing on private property in broad daylight.

"I've dragged her out of here and several other squats, but she keeps coming back. This time it's gone too far. I'm thinking seriously about sending her to one of those boot camps in Utah."

With a jingle of his pockets, Chevalier lowered himself down and I followed, glad I had worn linen pants instead of a dress. Too late, I felt the material catch, then rip. I put my hand up to stop it and only succeeded in gouging the inside of my wrist with the pointy, barbed-edge spikes. I tugged, feeling the flesh ripple as I drew blood. Christ. I had torn a big, jagged flap in the butt of my pants. I could feel my green silk underwear billowing out from the black linen. Great, so now I was half undressed and bleeding. At least it would be dark in there. I could deal with the damage later.

Sucking my wrist, I followed Chevalier onto a crumbling walkway where thorny, two-foot-high brambles pushed up through the cracks. The entrance was boarded and barred by a security door padlocked with a thick, rusted chain. "Fuck tha Police," someone had spray-painted in big letters. "The Chronic," a reference to marijuana. A large "A" with a circle around it—the anarchy symbol. "Sid & Nancy." "Sublime" and "Megadeth." More speed metal bands. Pentagrams. The usual detritus of alienated teens. I got out my notepad and wrote it all down.

"Follow me," Chevalier shouted, rounding the building. I ran to catch up. We hiked over broken glass, fast-food containers, and a faded, lumpy mattress upon which someone had defecated. It was about ten degrees colder at the back side of the building, where the sun's rays hadn't yet penetrated. Chevalier led me behind a pile of rotting wood planks imbedded with rusty nails. He pointed. Before us was another window, covered with plywood like the others. He walked up, grabbed it with both hands, and lifted it to one side. To my surprise, it came off. He clambered through and peered back out at me from inside, already half hidden in the shadows.

"You coming?"

I took a step forward. Raw sewage hit my nostrils and mingled with the earthy funk of abandoned buildings. Chevalier held out his arm to help me in.

"It's disgusting, I know, but don't be afraid, I know my way around."

I swayed there a moment, undecided, then slipped my hand into my purse, turned on my cell phone, and climbed in. I felt claustrophobic, unable to breathe the musty air, my eyes adjusting slowly to the penumbra. I looked around. We were in what used to be an office. A rusting file cabinet sat in the corner. I saw a wooden desk scarred by a thousand penknives. There were no chairs. The floor was carpeted in dirt, as if the room had flooded several times, then dried out. I followed Chevalier into a hallway. It was much darker, and I heard something click in his hand. I tensed, then relaxed as a thin beam of light came on, lighting our way. We walked to the next room and Chevalier shone his flashlight. It took me a moment to make out what I saw—two mattresses wadded with blankets, a boom box, a dead rodent nailed to a makeshift cross, porno magazines, a black duffel crammed with clothes, a bong, a smudged mirror with a razor blade, empty beer cans, and a two-gallon bottle of water. Chevalier's flashlight played along the walls, where the plaster bubbled from the damp. I saw yellow water stains and more pentagrams, scrawled snippets from rap songs, the word "Lucifer" in gang-like tagging, an upside-down cross, a rat's face with enormous whiskers and buck teeth, and, touchingly, a big red heart encircling the words "Isabel + Finch."

I'm no expert on adolescent angst, but this went way beyond garden-variety rebellion. It was self-immolation.

"My baby wrote that," Chevalier said. "This is Finch's room. They're not home."

"This is disgusting," I said. "I can't believe she comes here."

I can't believe you don't stop her, I wanted to add.

But Chevalier caught the accusation in my voice. He retraced his steps and shone the light at our feet.

"Let's get one thing straight, Miss—I don't even know your name."

"Eve Diamond."

"Thank you." He forced the words through clenched teeth. "I'm an involved parent. The two from my first marriage turned out just fine. Got college degrees and kids of their own now. Isabel was the baby and I loosened up a bit. But I know her friends. They hang out at our house. She has a curfew. But I also trust that I've raised her right. This is a phase she's going through. If I forbid it, she'll just climb out the window at night and do it anyway. But I love her and worry about her. And that's why I crawl into this crumbling sewer to drag her out. Maybe you should write about that, huh? This whole subculture of kids whose parents give them everything and yet they still seek out trouble. Not everyone who hangs out in these condemned buildings is a fucked-up runaway."

In that awful place, my pulse quickened. That was exactly what I had in mind. But I didn't say anything just yet. I wanted to find the girl first. *Cherchez la fille.*

He turned and headed off.

For a long time, our feet thudded noiselessly against a floor where the linoleum was slowly rotting and reverting to earth.

We entered a bathroom and the smell of sewage grew stronger. I breathed through my mouth and willed myself not to throw up. Someone had wrenched the cubicle door off its hinges. The toilet was overflowing with waste and wadded-up toilet paper. In a cheery domestic touch, someone had hung a roll of toilet paper on a red plastic hook.

The longer we searched, the more I hoped we wouldn't find her. Nothing good could survive here, nothing wholesome. The place was too eerie, too filthy, too desecrated. It was the underbelly of something I couldn't even name, the flip side of all those teens partying and laughing and living it up on TV and billboards and CDs. Something dark and formless and sinister. This is where you washed up when hope ran out.

We kept searching and I began to feel better. Isabel was probably panhandling on Hollywood and Vine. At Venice Beach, scoring some dope. Crunching popcorn with friends at the theater in Pasadena's Old Towne. We walked through rooms filled with more larval nests. Sleeping bags and personal effects. Skulls and crossbones. Leering devil faces. Now we were nearing the front of the building. Faint beams of sunlight shone through cracks in the plaster, illuminating the dust motes that danced in this cold, dead place.

There were no kids here. Just their crazy leavings.

"There's one more place to check," Chevalier told me.

He found the door to the stairwell and clicked his beam on high, pointing down into a basement. I shrank back at the smell.

"Do they sleep down there too?"

In a far corner of my mind, a movie loop of Isabel played. She bent to hear what a friend was saying, then laughed and blew away a strand of hair that the ocean wind had whipped into her mouth. The boardwalk was getting colder. Soon she'd be heading home. She felt guilty, thinking that she should have called her dad by now. She didn't want him to worry.

"Isabel says they do drugs down there." Vince Chevalier stared into the darkness. "She doesn't partake."

That's right, I thought. The girl on the tape loop had a purity about her, despite the punk couture. She just liked to hang out while her friends did their thing. Then she'd hold their heads while they puked. I just knew she was that kind of girl.

Chevalier began the descent, stepping gingerly on the wooden planks. Once he reached the bottom, he shone the light up. A polite gesture, so I wouldn't trip.

Holding on to the clammy stucco walls, I put one foot in front of the other, my brain riveted by the image of that little girl, tossing her head back and laughing in the fresh air. She was not the kind of girl who came to a bad end in a rotted basement. She had too much to live for, too much pluck and promise. This was just the last formality, the last place we had to look, before we could leave

this dung heap and dust ourselves off and congratulate
ourselves on a job well done.

I reached the bottom. It was a small room. The ceiling
came down at a slant, and the light was murky, like
swimming through seawater. Boxes filled with brochures
were stacked against a wall. I found a pamphlet advertising services for homeless Vietnam vets, another for a
substance abuse program. I walked farther in, making
sure Chevalier wasn't blocking my path back to the
stairs. While I imagined the laughing girl, I also imagined racing upstairs, my screams careening through the
corridors, if Vincent Chevalier suddenly lunged toward
me. I was surprised I could keep two such opposite
images so vividly engraved in my brain while continuing
to move forward into the basement, and I wondered what
that said about the kind of girl I was.

Chevalier's light flickered over the room and we saw a
storage closet whose door stood open, as in invitation.
Someone had tried to shove a rolled-up futon inside. It
was about six feet long and lay on its side, tied with thick
twine. Chevalier walked right past it, but I saw something
that shouldn't have been there, tumbling out of one side.

"Vince," I said hoarsely.

"Yeh?" His flashlight illuminated the far corners.

"C'mere for a minute."

He heard the icicles creeping up my throat. I watched
him retrace his steps. As he did, I inched closer to the
stairs and away from him.

"Down there. Check out that futon."

He squatted and the light played across what I had
seen. There was an intake of breath. He reached out a
tentative hand to stroke something, then gave a low
moan. In the light, we saw a lock of unnaturally blonde
hair, that dyed look the punk kids go for.

"For the longest time, her hair was streaked pink," Chevalier said. "She only changed it last week."

He touched it tenderly, a caress. He seemed contemplative, lost in thought, as if he was desperately trying to recollect something. I saw him tug on the hair. It did not give. It was still attached to something.

Don't unroll it, I wanted to say. Wait for the police.

But to my surprise, he didn't even try. Instead, he stretched himself out on that filthy floor, lay on his side, and embraced the futon, stroking the top part where the hair dragged in the dirt, as if he were cradling a lover or a child.

"Isabel," he crooned. "Oh, my dear sweet baby. It's okay now. Daddy's here. Daddy will save you."

It was this simple gesture that shook loose the terror inside me, the fear I had kept at bay since entering this creepy moldering building.

"No," I whispered, running up the stairs, jabbing my fingers across 911 as I ran, the crosshatch I had spent hours memorizing so I could now do it in my sleep. He was either crazy or a murderer or both, I thought. Didn't the police always suspect the one who found the body? Was that why he brought me here as a witness? And how close had I come? Down the hallway I ran, retracing my steps through this chamber of horrors, back out through the trick window and into what suddenly seemed like the brightest daylight I had seen in years.

# CHAPTER 3

B y the time the police arrived, I was in my car, writing up what I had seen. The notes would come in handy on deadline. Now I unlocked the door, stepped shakily out, and told the cops what little I knew about Vincent Chevalier and his daughter.

"I think he's lost his mind," I added, as we hiked around to the back of the building. "He's down there with the body, at least I think it's a body. There's a lock of hair poking out of the futon. It's rolled up . . ."

While one officer grilled me, another stood with a bullhorn in front of the window and ordered Chevalier to come out. A third trained her gun on the spot where he would appear. From inside came a meager shout, telling them he was unarmed and not to shoot. But when he popped his disheveled head through the window, his face tracked with grimy tears, they yanked him out by the shoulder, threw him to the ground, and searched him. Only then did they let him stand up.

"Check your goddamn phone logs," Chevalier said. "I tried to get you out here this morning but you wouldn't come. You told me she had to be missing forty-eight hours. Now there's a dead girl down there and she's . . ."

Chevalier stopped, eerily calm suddenly, and took a step forward. "My daughter," he said, as though it was only sinking in now. He cocked his head like a jay and peered at us. "Do you know that Isabel was our princess? Our miracle baby? My wife longed for a little girl. We went through years of infertility treatments, being poked and prodded and measured. From the day she was born, Isabel could do no wrong."

Lord help me but I was jotting it all down.

Chevalier was angry now. "You want to find who killed her, ask that bastard Finch. He was her boyfriend. This was his squat."

"We're sending two men in," one of the cops said. "Hold tight for a few minutes and don't jump to conclusions. It may not be your daughter. It may be some transient who crawled down there to die. It may be nothing."

Vincent Chevalier shook his head, stuck his hands in his pockets, and kicked the chunks of concrete that had once been a walkway, scattering them.

I excused myself to call Bovasso and explain there was probably a body. He told me to forget about the La Puente rodeo and stay at the scene. Then I sidled back up to Vincent Chevalier.

"Tell me more about what she was like," I said, wincing as the past tense slipped out.

He inched away, but it was a halfhearted shuffle. I stepped into the space he had just created.

"Did she like school? Have hobbies? Pets? What kind of music did she listen to?"

They weren't questions so much as memory aids, designed to jog something in his brain and loosen his tongue. I knew how profane it was for me to stand there, haranguing him at a time like this. But as a journalist, I also knew how deep grief could evoke the sacred. That was why I persisted, even though the elegies never sounded as luminous the next day, trapped in paper and ink, as they had in the trembling moment of transcendence when first uttered.

"I want to kill him with my bare hands," Chevalier said, expelling the words through clenched teeth. "I want to throttle him, watch his eyes pop out and his tongue turn purple. Then I want to pound his face into the pavement like this."

Chevalier lunged for a jagged boulder of concrete. He lifted it skyward with both arms like some pagan priest, then brought it straight down against the pavement with a full-throttle yell that culminated in a sickening thud. The concrete shattered, breaking into smaller chunks that continued to crack and crumble long after his anguished animal howl had bounced off the old industrial building and faded. Two more cops came at a running crouch, arms extended, guns trained on Vincent Chevalier.

Jesus, if this madman doesn't kill me with a chunk of concrete, the cops will accidentally shoot me, I thought, forgetting all thoughts of transcendence and putting my own arms up in surrender just in case they thought I was going to lob one next.

"It's okay," I yelled. "He just threw a rock."

They conferred, then decided to keep him in shooting range just in case. I looked at Chevalier. His last effort seemed to have exhausted him. His eyes rolled back in his head. A thin stream of spittle clung to his chin. I saw his knees buckling and grabbed his arm, easing him down onto what remained of his projectile. We sat silently. An acrid odor rose from him, mingling with the smell of wet earth from the squat, and I breathed through my mouth and waited.

"From the moment she was born, she was loved and held," he said under his breath. "All she ever heard was how beautiful and smart she was." He gave a rueful little laugh. "If only she had believed it, we wouldn't be sitting here today."

He took out a handkerchief and blew his nose loudly, then folded and slid it back into his pocket. "She went to a private school in Pasadena, Borwick Academy, but even there, she shone." He turned to me.

"Do you know she got picked to be lead prosecutor of Borwick's mock trial team, and they went all the way up to the state championships and won? My baby won."

He shook his head. "But inside, she didn't feel like a winner. She wore a dog collar to school and punked out her hair. She listened to the Dead Kennedys and X. They're good bands, I've done some work for them, but you know that song 'Sex and Dying in High Society'? She wanted to live that. I thought it was a phase she was going through. Then she started hanging out on the street. She said school was filled with boring people, but on the street she felt alive. Maybe I should have clamped down. Maybe it's all my fault. I thought I was doing the right thing. Then she met Finch. He was James Dean with a Mohawk, and I was only her dad, pleading with her to be home by ten . . ."

Chevalier broke off as we heard plywood splinter, then give. Several policemen crawled out of a broken window in the abandoned building. I hadn't said a word, afraid to staunch the flow. He hadn't seemed to notice, or perhaps he didn't care, about the reporter's notepad I had eased onto my knees.

We watched the cops report to their sergeant. A stony look hardened on his face as he headed our way.

"There's a body all right," the sergeant told us. "Young girl, wearing a black T-shirt and jeans, with blonde hair and moon earrings. Mr. Chevalier, we are going to set up some lights down there, then we are going to ask you to go back down with us and identify whether it's your daughter. After that, we'd like you to come to the station and answer some more questions."

He put a big palm on Chevalier's shoulder and paid no attention when the man shrugged it off.

Vincent Chevalier stood up wearily. "Let's go." He started walking toward the building, then stopped. "You're not considering me a suspect, are you?"

The sergeant scratched his jaw. "You are not a suspect at this time. I checked with the commander and he remembers you. My men have been here several times looking for your daughter. We have also rousted young transients who sleep in the building. Now, Mr. Chevalier, are you up to this task?"

Chevalier stared at the ground.

"Yes. Let's go."

"Can I come too?" I asked.

The policeman looked at me, as if realizing for the first time who I was and what he might read in the paper the next day and how that would affect his chances of catching his suspect, unless, of course, he was already standing in front of him.

"No press. I know he brought you out here, but your role is over. You'll have to wait until we're ready to brief you people."

My access cut off, I felt crushed, until I realized I had the Chevaliers' home address and telephone number. Sooner or later today, I'd be ringing his doorbell.

As Chevalier disappeared into the squat with the sergeant, I looked around and saw a police forensics van parked by the curb. Two burly guys were unloading industrial-strength Hollywood lights and carrying them over to the broken window, where they were gingerly lowered into the crawlspace. That would be one nasty crime scene for the police techs.

Soon the first news van pulled up, antenna unfurling. I sidled up to a policeman I knew who had just crawled out of the hellhole, shaking off grime and a smell that would linger long after his shower.

"So?" I asked. "Was it his daughter?"

He glared at me.

"Yeah, it was his daughter."

"But he's not a suspect?"

"On the record, no."

"And off the record?"

"Nothing's being ruled out," he said. "It can't hurt to make him feel we're on his side. People let their guard down, they say things."

"What about this boyfriend, Finch?"

The cop turned his head, hawked and spit. "I know that scumbag. Finch 'Mad Dog' Marino. Coldhearted little bastard, perfectly capable of a one eighty-seven. We've hauled him in for drugs, burglary, theft. Some girls usually come and bail him out."

"Girls?"

"His little groupies. He's got a whole passel feeding and watering him."

"Where can I meet them?"

"They're around."

The sergeant was walking toward us.

"So like I was saying, call later this afternoon and ask for the detectives," the policeman was enunciating loudly. "They may know more."

"Thanks," I said.

I got back in my car and took inventory. Dirt smudges on my face. A ragged cut along the inside of my wrist that looked like an aborted suicide attempt. A rip on the butt of my linen trousers. Stains on the knees. Bits of plaster in my hair. I shook it out as best I could, then looked at my watch. High noon. No time to go home and change. But I couldn't walk around like this. I checked the car trunk, found a sweater. It would have to do.

As I drove back, the clouds massed, beating back the

sun, and I thought the sky might open up and weep for fifteen-year-old Isabel Chevalier. For a lost little girl who had recently swapped dirndl skirts for black leather and traded her Pasadena mansion for a foul squat smeared with human excrement, crucified rats, and pentagrams drawn in blood.

In the *Times* bathroom, I washed my face and arms and brushed the plaster out of my hair. I tied the sweater strategically around my waist to cover the tear in my trousers.

Taking in my sorry appearance, I gave thanks that it was Saturday and barely anyone was around. Then I headed for the newsroom to talk to Bovasso. He looked at me and said something about a tough morning, then gave me twenty-two inches for a straight-ahead news story that would incorporate quotes from Dad that no one else would have. He wanted me to follow up with a news feature on the trend, if I could nail it down, of rich and middle-class girls like Isabel who caught cheap thrills and risked their lives, slumming it with homeless punks. "Dancing with the Dark Side."

"What about my San Gabriel Valley stories?" I asked.

"I'll talk to your editor and see if we can free you up. Good work, kid."

It was a word he used on every female reporter under fifty, but somehow it made me feel happy and young again.

# CHAPTER 4

Walking down the long hallway to the third-floor elevators, I ran unexpectedly into the Metro editor, Jane Sims. Even on a Saturday, she wore a trim suit. Streaky blond highlights obscured the premature gray of her hair. I felt acutely aware of my own dishabille. Jane looked uncomfortable to be trapped in such proximity to a mere suburban reporter, and gave a quick look up and down the long expanse of corridor, hoping for an excuse to flee. Seeing none, she steeled herself and said hello, asking what I was doing downtown. I told her, describing the dead girl as well as the larger story I planned to explore.

She scrunched up her eyes and fidgeted. "Hollywood? That's not exactly in your bailiwick, is it, Eve? You need to focus on the San Gabriel Valley and stop reaching so far afield. When are you going to learn that? You're downtown today, so you're doing the daily. Monday you're back in San Gabe and we put a Metro writer on it."

"But . . ." I thought about telling her that Bovasso wanted to put me on it, but I knew that would just make her more determined to override him. Better to play cocky and dumb.

"Since when do good stories fall out in neat, geographic patterns?" I asked her. "Besides, the family lives in Pasadena. That's the San Gabriel Valley. And I've got a personal line to the dad." I lowered my voice and moved closer, seeking eye contact. She edged away, clearly uncomfortable by our faked intimacy. "He won't talk to anyone else, Jane. He trusts me. We bonded over the body."

"He'll have to bond with someone else," Jane Sims said.

"It's my story. I'm already researching a larger piece. She was part of a trend." I sketched it out for her, stressing my contacts, which were nonexistent at this point.

"They'll talk to me," I told her.

Jane Sims seemed to waver. "I'm not promising anything." She frowned. "You're a hothead, you almost got yourself killed on that story about the kids last year. And what we need right now is cool, mature thinking."

She stared at my hair and I realized that whatever flakes of plaster I hadn't succeeded in brushing out probably looked like dandruff.

"Tell me, Eve, where did you go to school?"

Now what in the hell did that have to do with anything?

"Cal State Northridge."

She nodded, as if I had just confirmed some long-held suspicion.

"Well, Eve," she said with a false heartiness, "have you ever considered taking some classes at USC?"

I looked at her. She wasn't that much older than me, but she had been fast out of the starting blocks, whizzing through college and rising through the newspaper's ranks during those long years I had juggled work and school. Now I knew exactly where this was headed. I don't often chew gum, but something about that squat had left a stench in my nostrils and sent me rummaging through my purse for the Trident peppermint. Now I gathered the gum with my tongue and popped the biggest white-trash bubble I could muster.

"What for?" I asked. "I already have my master's."

Jane Sims looked pained.

"It's just that . . . they do such a fine job of teaching over there. It's a first-rate school."

I could not believe what I was hearing. Then, thankfully, I recalled a small pellet of intelligence I had once filed away on Jane Sims.

"Uh-huh. Well, I'd love to follow in your footsteps. What did you get your master's in?"

Jane Sims examined the cuff of her silk shirt, which had suddenly come undone.

"I was already halfway through the master's program in English Lit at Harvard when the *Provincetown Journal* hired me full-time," Jane Sims said, her eyes shiny at the memory. "It was a tough decision, and part of me still rues not sticking around for the diploma."

"It's not too late, Jane. I hear that USC has an extraordinary English program. Maybe we could take some classes there together."

I banged my satchel against my knee for emphasis.

"Now, Eve, that's a very good idea. I'll have to consider it." She nodded briskly up and down, then strode off, her low heels clicking on the shiny linoleum.

"Don't forget the Chevalier story's mine," I called after her, watching her step quicken as my voice trailed after her. "Those kids won't talk to anyone but me."

After grabbing a sandwich from the tenth-floor cafeteria, I spent the afternoon working the phones, calling the cops, who weren't talking yet, Chevalier's home, where no one answered, and a teen homeless center in Hollywood, where a staff psychologist filled me in on runaways.

Many were fleeing pretty heavy scenes back home— sexual abuse, neglect, beatings. Most had what they call dual diagnosis—mental health problems plus drug and alcohol abuse to dull the pain. Crystal methamphetamine was the high of choice. The shrink didn't seem surprised when I asked whether some of the squatter boys had girlfriends with intact homes and parents. It was a disturbing new trend, he told me, words that I heard in italics, picturing exactly where I'd put his quote in my story. Smack after the nut graf, I decided. The girls took their hardened street boyfriends home to shower, gave them money, bought them food, drove them around to score drugs, and sometimes squatted alongside them for a lark. The shrink likened it to setting a hungry panther loose in a cage of plump bunnies.

"They think they're just hanging out with friends, but we try really hard to tell them that this is not a safe place," the shrink told me. "They're getting used. They can get raped, robbed. These guys are predators. We try to get that message out, but the girls are living out a fantasy. Think about it—what's the twenty-first-century equivalent of the glamorous teen outlaw? A feral runaway who lives completely and permanently outside of society."

The shrink told me the kids hung out at the Santa Monica Promenade and Hollywood Boulevard, wherever they could panhandle and score. And come to think of it, I'd seen some well-fed kids scamming change recently.

I hung up and added several grafs about this phenomenon. Now I needed quotes from school friends or teachers. It was a weekend, bad timing for that. But then I remembered something. Chevalier had boasted about how Isabel had been the lead prosecutor in the mock trial. If her school had won the state championships, we might have written something, though I didn't remember it offhand. I did a database search and turned up a ten-inch story from the previous month. Then I noticed a photo caption at the bottom. "Borwick Academy students cross-examining witnesses in preparation for mock trial finals next week in San Francisco. From L to R, Antonia Chang, Jose Parilla, Isabel Chevalier, and Paolo D. Langdon."

I printed out the story, then headed to the editorial library. Luke Vinograd was on the phone, reading statistics from his computer screen into the receiver. He rolled his eyes and motioned me to wait.

"Okay, hon, call back if you need any more scintillating stats."

He hung up, swiveled in his chair, and began humming in a throaty baritone.

With a laugh, I recognized the closing bars of "The Pretender."

"Don't I always come through for you?" he said. "I have many hidden talents that you know absolutely nothing about."

"Show me one more. Can you pull a file photo?"

"Depends."

I slid the computer printout along the counter and tapped on the photo. "That one."

"You should probably get a real librarian," he told me. "They've got me chained to this stats project like a galley slave."

"Please."

Luke sighed and held out his hand. I handed it over. With a nimble roll, he wheeled over to the graphics computer and punched in a long index number. An image materialized on the screen.

"I'm coming around," I said, and let myself through the little gate into the back of the library.

I bent over his shoulder and scrutinized the photo.

Isabel was short, with freckles and unruly hair that stuck out at angles from her face. Pink streaks weaving through the natural mousy brown. She looked defiant and vulnerable at the same time, her face still rimmed with baby fat. She had been cross-examining a witness and the camera had caught her midsentence. Her full bow lips were parted.

"What a hottie!" said Luke Vinograd.

"She's dead," I said. "Besides, I didn't think you swung from that vine."

"So that's why you need the pic," Vinograd said with sudden perception. "But I didn't mean her, I meant him."

He pointed to the boy Isabel Chevalier was cross-examining. He was tall and rangy, his limbs folding into themselves on the stand. He had a high forehead, widely spaced gray eyes, and a chiseled jaw. His hair was cropped short, which only accentuated the piercing eyes and straight nose.

"He's underage. A child."

"I can dream, can't I? And besides, he's no child. Just look at his eyes."

I did. They held both intelligence and depth. You could see the gears clicking as he considered the student prosecutor's questions and prepared his answers.

"Paolo D. Langdon," Luke read. "D's short for Dellaviglia. They shortened it because they didn't have enough room. But that's Venus's son."

"L.A.'s reigning diva," I said, realizing why it had sounded familiar.

"She's enough to make a gay man swoon. And between her and her son, I'd never recover."

I studied the photo again. Everyone knew of Venus Dellaviglia Langdon. She was something of a legend in town, an Italian-born, super-socialite hostess with charm and brains whose husband, Carter Langdon III, just happened to be running for mayor. What journalist had not received a personally signed Christmas card featuring Venus, Carter, and their handsome son posed amid the ruins of Pompeii with Mount Vesuvius smoking in the background, carefully reenacting the tableau from some ancient Roman vase. There was Venus in a red velvet and black lace toga, holding up a platter of grapes and persimmons, a slightly lascivious look to her overblown features. Carter Langdon III looked more sheepish than goatish in a hand-stitched satyr's outfit, his bare, hairy legs ending in cloven hoofs, a wooden flute lifted half-heartedly to his thin, WASPy lips.

An idea was forming in my head, a way to round out the hole in my story. Venus, who never turned down an opportunity for publicity, might let me talk to her son. If the two kids had been school friends and mock trial colleagues, he'd be good for a quote. Maybe Venus had known Isabel too.

"That's perfect, Luke. I'm going to try and interview him before deadline. Print me out a color Xerox and I'll buy you a big fat puckery apple martini next week."

"Only if it's accompanied by all the salacious details of your personal life, Eve."

"I promise, just as soon as I get this nailed down."

Back at my desk, I picked up the phone to call information, then put it down. I should just go to their house. It was three o'clock. I could file the story now and call in the quote before deadline. Bovasso gave me the papal blessing to leave.

# CHAPTER 5

Now I drove back toward my part of town. The Dellaviglia Langdons lived in Los Feliz, which had always been more elegant and uptown than neighboring Silverlake, where I lived. Lately it had grown star-studded and celebrity-infested as well. But the Dellaviglia Langdon estate was old money. It sat on Via Encantada in the sere hills abutting Griffith Park. Winding my way up from Los Feliz Boulevard, I found myself on a narrow street of increasingly spacious houses built in the 1920s and 1930s. There was a Frank Lloyd Wright, whose owners opened it up once each year—probably for tax reasons—to the gawking public. There were gleaming white Spanish castles with crenellated turrets and empty moats. There were two-story Tudors with hewn timbers that provided only decorative support and Southern plantation–style mansions with rounded pillars and rolling lawns. I saw a Cape Cod house that could have been transported from New England and a Cotswold cottage whose brown-shingled roof curled low over the house like puffy gingerbread. Most jarring were the cantilevered modernist fantasies that looked like insect spaceships about to take off. A sense of winking whimsy reigned in these hills, as if the architects had rooted through a studio back lot for inspiration and come out with a polyglot style to suit their overblown imaginations. As the road curved upward, the houses grew farther apart. Finally the city street ended and a sign announced PRIVATE DRIVE, NO ADMITTANCE.

But today the twelve-foot gates that guarded the entrance thrust open in welcome. They were breathtaking, wrought of ornamental iron adorned with strutting peacocks, branching trees, and dryads. The filigreed metal evoked Aubusson tapestries more than the polluting foundry near industrial Vernon, where this thing of beauty had been forged by immigrant laborers dreaming of a better life.

Silently, I absorbed the sanctity of workmanship from fingers dead these many years. Then I continued up the private driveway. It was paved in cobblestones like the Appian Way. On either side of me, what passed for old-growth orchards in Southern California stretched out gnarled brown limbs in greeting.

I recalled what I knew about the family. Debate raged over whether Venus was the most charismatic, brilliant charmer people had ever met or a ruthless social climber to rival Machiavelli who craved pure, unadulterated power and publicity for its own sake. Venus had what society columnists and besotted male journalists referred to as a mane of cascading auburn hair and her intellectual pedigree came directly from the Sorbonne, but she was Italian, with an accent that only grew stronger and more mellifluous as the years went by. She was tall and statuesque like a Renaissance statue, curved and rounded in a town where the female ideal was a ten-year-old boy with breasts, and she spoke with her hands, laying her elegant, manicured half-moons across many a cuff-linked arm as she debated philosophy and politics. This had helped her snare a patrician diplomat husband named Carter Langdon III, who had long been considered one of the most eligible bachelors the city had ever produced. As the legend went, they had met in Italy when he had served as ambassador. Then the Dellaviglia

Langdon family, which now included a sixteen-year-old
son, had returned for good to the ancestral Langdon
estate in Los Feliz, which Venus had immediately set
about turning into a nonstop salon for her husband's
political ambitions. With family money and the best
public relations firm in town on permanent retainer,
Langdon was now launched on a bid for mayor.
Reporters considered him a bit of an empty suit. But
with Venus at his side, laughing, quoting Dante, serving
her family's treasured panna cotta recipes that imported
French maids whipped up in the designer kitchen, cajol-
ing everyone to do her bidding with a mixture of flattery
and cultural imperative, they were a team that made
many tremble with fear, envy, and ineluctable longing.
Around Venus, who spoke six languages and had mas-
tered the rare art of being a good listener, your every
utterance dripped with brilliance, your attractiveness to
both sexes jumped by leaps and bounds, and your horizons shimmered before you, unlimited. That was her
great gift, to make you believe in yourself, and thus in
her. Even for people like me, who should know better,
she inspired that kind of reverie. She was glamour and
European sophistication on a scale not seen in Los
Angeles, well, perhaps ever.

Even the benign neglect of her gardens was calculated.
But to my dismay, civilization began to encroach on the
Appian Way as I drew nearer to the house. There were
cars parked along the dirt shoulder, dozens and dozens of
them, and as I rounded the last bend, men in puffy white
shirts and tight black trousers sprinted up the driveway
and beckoned me forward.

I followed the windmill arms of one young toreador
and pulled up to the circular driveway in front of the
house, stopping my Acura Integra behind a burgundy

Bentley. A valet immediately opened my door and stood crisply at attention, waiting to help me out.

"Is this the Dellaviglia Langdon home?" I asked, afraid I had taken a wrong turn and stumbled into some Hollywood party.

"Yes, miss, right this way."

Before I knew it, I was ushered out of my stained velveteen seat, across the wide driveway, through majestic carved oaken doors and into a foyer, where I was asked to sign the guest book. I pulled my dog tags out of my shirt.

"Oh press, yes, right this way," a beaming young woman said, handing me a thick folder. On the front was a portrait of the Dellaviglia Langdons and their son, the same boy I had seen in the *Times* photo. Flipping through the folder, I saw press releases documenting Carter Langdon's run for mayor, news clippings, speeches, and his "Ten Points of Light" campaign platform. I had stumbled into a political fund-raiser.

Now an earnest young handler saw me standing there, looking confused. He steered me down a long hallway and into a high-ceilinged room filled with well-dressed people eating hors d'oeuvres and drinking glasses of wine as uniformed maids scurried around.

"The *Times* certainly doesn't stint on the reporters," he said in a professionally vacant way. He wore a name tag that said "Langdon, Man of the People" and looked like a Stepford clone, a blank-faced young man oozing Christian goodness. "There's already a political correspondent here, and one from the society pages."

He stopped, realizing the implication of his words. "And you are . . . ?"

"Eve Diamond, Metro," I said. "I'm covering the, uh, daily angle."

That seemed to satisfy him. In hushed tones, he pointed out the candidate, who was nodding as a woman in a Chanel suit held forth. Carter Langdon III was tall and slender and burned with the asceticism of a medieval monk. He wore an understated charcoal suit and had an impossibly high forehead, made even more wide and spacious by hair that was trimmed almost to his protruding skull. It gave him an odd, unbalanced look, as though he might tip over from being so top-heavy. I had never seen him in person and I found him both more intelligent-looking and alarming than in his photos. His large, gray eyes were set back deep in his face, which only enhanced the skeletal effect.

"As soon as there's a break in the crowd, I'll introduce you," my handler said, adding that his name was Skip Goodman but that I should feel free to call him Skip.

As soon as there's a break in the crowd, Skip, I am out of here, I thought, spying what I wanted in the corner by the bar, gulping discreetly from a highball glass. He wore a dark blue blazer with the Borwick Academy patch embroidered in red and gold, and brass buttons to match, and looked more sullen than he had in *his* photos. He was talking on a cell phone. Perched on the edges of his parents' crowd, he obviously would rather be elsewhere. It was my boy, Paolo. I imagined grabbing a bottle of single-malt whiskey from the mirrored bar and leading him out the door, trekking through the orchards, and settling under a grapefruit tree, where we'd talk about Isabel and forgo the glasses. I could catch Mama Dellaviglia on the rebound.

But I was only halfway across the crowded room when I heard the tinkling of female laughter and saw people repositioning themselves with subtle body shifts and head inclinations, the better to see Venus Dellaviglia

Langdon. She swept into the room on the arm of a Los Angeles city councilman renowned for living inside the pockets of developers and was promptly introduced to a young Chinese man in an ill-fitting suit.

"And this is our lovely Italian cultural pundit and hostess," the councilman said, as Venus extended her hand in a gracious drape for him to kiss. The Chinese man looked momentarily bewildered, then seemed to absorb what was required, and bent over it obligingly.

"No, no, darling, I'm not Italian," Venus Dellaviglia Langdon said with a throaty laugh and a light touch on his arm. "I am Roman. An imperial Roman."

Then she held up her wine chalice and murmured in Latin.

"Pastoral poem by Horace," whispered Skip the handler, who had materialized at my elbow again. "He was a lyric poet, 65 to 8 B.C. There's a translation in your press kit."

Incredulous, I looked at him.

"You may also want to write down," Skip said firmly, frowning at the lack of activity from my pencil, "that Venus wrote her doctoral dissertation on Horace and that it won France's Medici Prize. That's like our Pulitzer."

At this, the handler stretched out his clean-shaven neck, pressed his lips together, and adjusted his tie.

"Hey, Skip," I said, "I'm a little confused. I thought *he* was the one running for office." I pointed to Carter Langdon III, who was still deep in conversation with the Chanel lady.

"He is," Skip said stiffly. "But they work as a team." His face took on an enthused glow. "That's what's so great about this race, really, the synergy between them; you're getting two brilliant minds for the price of one. Now there's an angle for you."

"Tell it to the Southern California Living reporter," I said, then fell silent as Venus Dellaviglia Langdon's voice projected like an opera singer's in the crowded room.

"Look at this profile," she commanded the city councilman, turning her head sideways. "It is ancient, timeless. Two millennia ago, it was carved on marble temples and fired onto vases from Sicily to Gaul. Before you stands a goddess come to life."

Then, since there was a blazing fire handy and she had grown impassioned, Venus Dellaviglia Langdon dashed the dregs of her glass into the flames, watching it sizzle and hiss with pagan glee as the fire roared up. And from bended knee, the movers and shakers of Los Angeles applauded.

Pausing to obtain the full effect of this tableau, Venus gracefully accepted another Pinot Grigio from a maid in a white uniform. Then she turned back to the Chinese man.

"He's one of the student leaders of the Tiananmen Square uprising who's visiting Los Angeles for several days, trying to drum up support for democracy," Skip said, nodding approvingly. "Venus invited him personally."

I looked to see if any Chinese government officials were in the room. Invitations to Venus's soirées were prized especially because she wasn't afraid to spice up the mix. In her salon, notorious pornographers debated hard-core feminists; pro-life activists sipped champagne with Planned Parenthood honchos; Zapatista guerrillas cha-cha'd with the Mexican consul. One never knew who would show up, but it would be exhilarating and dramatic and lead to intellectual fisticuffs that would once have ended in duels at ten paces in the overgrown garden.

Now I saw for myself the spell that Venus Dellaviglia

Langdon cast on all who entered her orbit. She leaned, tête-à-tête, to the Chinese man but so that all around could also hear, saying she had recently read a novel by Nobel Prize winner Gao Xingjian but in all honesty preferred the work of Ha Jin. What did he think?

Pleased surprise rippled over the face of the Tiananmen activist that such a glamorous American knew his country's literature as well as its politics. As they embarked on a lively discussion, I knew she had won another convert. And I saw the blueprint of how she did it—bring up something that interests *them*, throw down the gauntlet with a comment that makes it clear she is well versed in a topic dear to their hearts, then draw them out, listening intently, as if they were the only other human being in the room. Finally, while they were still stunned, basking in her glow, murmur a plausible exit line—she was the hostess, after all—and move on.

It was indeed an impressive performance. Years of education, calculation, polish, and practice had gone into it. But I wondered what the endgame was for her. She already had power. Wealth. Security. Her husband's race for mayor was going well—he was polling five points ahead of his opponent, an outspoken prosecutor from the District Attorney's office. But where did Venus go from there? Did she view the mayoral seat as a jumping-off point for a seat in Congress? A cabinet appointment? A short list to the White House, where she would be the most elegant First Lady since Jackie O? For that matter, why didn't she run for office herself? Or was the game the thing, the way she played, loving every minute of every day along the way? I couldn't figure her out, and that annoyed me, but her performance was irresistible, a contact high that lasted until you found yourself waiting outside her Corinthian columned entryway, stamping in the cold while the valet brought your car and you climbed into it and the carriage became, well, if not quite a pumpkin, then a ten-year-old Acura Integra that needed new brakes. And you hated yourself in the morning but would pull whatever strings necessary to get into her next fete, telling yourself it wasn't about her, but she did manage to gather around her the most glittering orbs from both coasts, and you wanted to rub shoulders with them. And in this way, her husband inched ever closer to his goal of mayor.

From the corner of my eye, I saw Paolo Dellaviglia Langdon toss back the last of his drink, check his watch, turn off his cell phone, and slide it into his pants pocket.

"Skip," I said firmly, "I'm getting a drink, then going to the ladies' room. Can we meet back here in five minutes?"

Not waiting for his response, I moved toward the boy. He was disappearing down the long, polished-wood hallway lined with portraits of Langdon ancestors marching back into the eighteenth century when I caught up with him.

# CHAPTER 6

Hey, Paolo, I realize everybody came out here today to support your dad, but I actually want to talk to you," I said, jiggling my dog tags at him. "Eve Diamond, *L.A. Times.* Congrats, by the way, on winning the state championships in the mock trial."

He had been ready to ice me, I could tell, but when I mentioned the mock trial, something lit up in his eyes.

"Thank you," he said politely. "How did you hear about that? Surely my parents didn't tell you."

His words told me volumes about his relationship with them.

"I read it in the *Times,* actually, and that's why I'm here. Something's happened to your mock trial colleague, Isabel Chevalier. Could we go sit down somewhere and talk?"

His eyes narrowed, and he gave me a quick look, calculating what I wanted from him, what his exposure was. When his voice came, it was neutral.

"Is she all right?"

I hesitated. A tipsy woman teetered past on strappy sandals, giggling, headed to the bathroom. She wore a straw boater hat with a red, white, and blue ribbon and a LANGDON: MAN OF THE PEOPLE sign stuck to it.

"Is there somewhere we can talk?"

"You mean away from the circus?"

"Exactly."

He considered the possibilities.

"I suppose we could go out on the back porch. No one

ever goes there but the servants. Even though it has the best view."

His voice was wistful, and I knew at least one person besides the servants hung out there.

He led me through an industrial-sized kitchen with terra-cotta tiles and a hardwood refrigerator with transparent doors that I knew from our newspaper's design pages was all the rage among people who didn't mind dropping $25,000 to keep their Dom Perignon chilled.

Two maids stood at the sink, washing glasses, while a waiter wearing mitts pulled trays of crab puffs out of the brick oven and another spooned dollops of caviar over a platter of blinis.

The back porch overlooked the orchard and we plunked ourselves down on some Adirondack chairs that the weather had almost completely stripped of their green paint. Between us was a tiled table. On it sat a cobalt-blue Bauer ashtray shaped like a lily. It was filled with cigarette butts and a roach. Paolo saw me looking at it and drew my attention to where gardeners were clambering up ladders and picking persimmons. When I glanced back down, the roach was gone.

Paolo lit a cigarette and sighed. "So is Isabel okay?"

"No," I told him. "She's dead. Police found her in a squat in Hollywood this morning, wrapped in a futon."

I waited for him to digest this information.

"Oh God, that's awful."

He shook his head, blowing out smoke. His fingers picked at the cellophane of the cigarette pack. A muscle below his left eye twitched, and he wouldn't look at me. His hand trembled. I wondered what that was about.

"Did you know her well?"

He shrugged. "I'm a year ahead of her. But she's a nice kid. We hung out a lot during the mock trial."

I watched his face, waiting for more revelations. But he seemed to grow more composed, not less, as time went by.

"Did that skanky boyfriend of hers do it?" he finally asked.

"You know about him?"

"Unfortunately." Paolo's nose crinkled. "Isabel was young and impressionable. She wanted to shed her bourgeois past and thought Finch was just the ticket. I tried to convince her otherwise."

From his ringside seat above the bourgeoisie, Paolo tipped the ash of his cigarette into the cobalt lily. There was something so polished and faceted about him, just like his mother, that it was scary. But at his age, the cracks still showed occasionally.

"How old is he? Is he really a squatter?"

"Twenty. And apparently."

"Good Lord, and she's fifteen. That's statutory rape." He looked at me with mild amusement.

"I think the sex was wholly consensual. She brought him here once. Nasty fellow. Had body lice. We had to spray everything. My mother blamed it on the maid."

"Statutory rape has nothing to do with consent. But if she was his meal ticket, why would he kill her?"

Paolo shrugged. "Maybe he got bored with her."

"What was she like?"

"A bit naïve, really. Not as tough as she thought. Didn't like to be alone, so she surrounded herself with people who wanted something from her. That way she always had company."

"What else?"

"She volunteered at a suicide hot line—she'd be there half the night, talking kids out of killing themselves. She had great empathy. She was a fixer-upper, always helping people. At school, she loaned kids money and wrote their term papers. She listened to their sad stories. People trusted her. They told her their secrets. They knew she would never tell."

He looked at his watch again. "It's six o'clock. I have to go meet a friend."

"Six o'clock?" I yelped, thinking of Bovasso in the newsroom, waiting for my call. "I have to go too. But listen, can you give me your number, in case I have any other questions? Your parents won't mind, will they?"

He gave me his cell phone number and seemed unconcerned, a little too much so, at the thought of having the Dellaviglia Langdon name linked to a murder, however indirectly, just weeks before his father's election. If you ask me, he wanted to stir things up a little.

Paolo disappeared around the corner, headed for the garage, and I hiked deep into the orchard to make my call rather than face the crush of party-goers again. Amid tangled undergrowth stood rows of mature trees—persimmon and pomegranate, crab apples, kumquat, lemon, orange, and grapefruit. They were the odd, orphan fruit of the Southwest that nobody wanted, least of all millennial socialites who rarely cooked their own meals. So it splatted to the ground and rotted slowly as bees and maggots crawled through the pulpy insides, battening on the oozing flesh. A sinister still life for a warm October evening.

When Bovasso came on the line, I read him some choice quotes from Paolo about fixer-uppers and secrets. Then I watched the sun set and dusk steal over the orchard as lights blazed on in the city below. This is how the ancient Roman emperors must have felt, surveying their dominions.

As the blue air thickened to black, I retraced my steps to the porch and back into the big kitchen, which was empty now, save for a small figure at a table, hunched over a plate of *carnitas*. Probably one of the maids scarfing her dinner. As I walked past, she folded a corn tortilla and scooped up some beans. Then the shimmery, contour-hugging pantsuit and Art Deco garnet bracelet caught my eye and I looked up, just in time to see Venus Dellaviglia Langdon meet my gaze, the golden oval of corn halfway to her mouth, a trickle of emerald tomatillo sauce making its way down her chin.

She saw the reporter's pad and froze, bringing a paper napkin to her mouth.

"Who are you and what are you doing in my kitchen?" she asked haughtily, but I saw fast calculation in her eyes that her voice couldn't disguise.

"Eve Diamond, *L.A. Times,*" I said, taken aback by her hostile tone. Did this frowsy kitchen scene reveal what the real Venus was like once the curtain fell and all the party-goers went home? I studied her and saw a carefully sculpted face on which discreet work had been done. Out of the klieg lights and up close, there was something haggard about her, a reluctant awareness that her days as a sex magnet were numbered, harder to maintain with each year that passed, and that one day they would fade altogether, leaving her with only the shell, a coquettish old woman whose kittenish behavior repelled instead of attracted. And suddenly, I didn't envy her.

"I was here for the fund-raiser and stepped out back to admire your orchard," I lied, trying to figure out when would be the best time to tell her I had just interviewed her son about a murder.

"Well, what you see here is completely off the record," she snapped. "This is not to show up in any local color stories about the campaign. I did not give my permission. And while I would never accuse you of tres-

passing, Ms. Diamond," she added sweetly, "I doubt
whether you'll be able to dish up any dirt in my kitchen."

She laughed at her own bon mot, regaining her poise.
She stood up, put an arm around me, and steered me
firmly to the picture window that overlooked the now
completely black orchard and, beyond it, the glittering
lights of the city.

"It is a lovely view, and you're welcome to admire it
for as long as you like, provided you remember what I
just told you. No stories about Venus Dellaviglia
Langdon getting her grease fix in the kitchen at the end
of the day."

I didn't understand why it was a big deal but assured
her I wouldn't use it. I also noted that she had referred to
herself in the third person, an odious quirk of language
favored by the powerful and self-important. Then I confessed I had come to talk to her son.

Venus seemed relieved and didn't even blink when I
explained the murder of Paolo's Borwick Academy classmate. She must have been preoccupied by the election.

"Did you know Isabel, by chance?"

Venus threw up her arms.

"Paolo's a handsome boy, and well bred. I saw to that.
There are so many girls who come around. They bake
him cookies and ask him out. They call incessantly. I
can't remember all their names, much less their
faces. . . ."

She paused, as if realizing that she was not striking
the right note.

"It's tragic, of course, and I hope they find who did it.
My husband has vowed that if he is elected, he will support mandatory sentencing laws, even for young offend-
ers. The crime in this city is out of control, and our hearts
go out to the family of this poor, unfortunate young

woman who was friend and classmate to my son, Paolo."

There, she was back smoothly on track. Venus Dellaviglia Langdon patted down her auburn tresses, missing a grain of rice that had nestled in her hair during her hurried meal and now looked suspiciously like a head louse.

"Make yourself at home, sit and watch the stars come out on the back porch; the servants do it all the time to unwind after their shifts," she said, dismissing me as breezily as if I were the scullery maid. And then she was gone.

Puzzling over this bizarre encounter, I drove home to shower and eat. I knew I had left Los Feliz and was back in Silverlake when I saw a slacker driving a gussied-up Pacer with a sparkly lime green paint job. I had been seeing more and more of these ironic autos lately, even a pumpkin-colored Pinto with purple racing stripes. I bet it looked real pretty when it exploded. Next, they would be driving Ford Explorers with Firestone tires.

Silverlake was a funky and eclectic neighborhood populated by artists, gays, musicians, old liberals, the working poor, and new immigrants, along with a smattering of yuppies who had moved in to renovate 1920s bungalows a short hop from their downtown offices. Lately, it had gotten a little too hip for my blood. We even had a Starbucks where the lattes were slung by pierced and tattooed young employees. It had set up catty-corner to a doughnut franchise run by a hardworking Cambodian family. At one place, coffee and biscotti cost $5.00. At the other, a fiver would get you a dozen boxed pastries *plus* a large coffee. Each place had its loyal clientele, and in my neighborhood, they both thrived.

Occasionally when I drove by, I'd see two heads bent

over coffee and let myself linger over how it might feel to share space with someone. But I worked too hard and experienced the world too intensely, and reality usually came down to clobber me before things went too far. If there was such a thing as a cosmic report card, mine would indubitably say: "Does not play well with others."

Pulling up to the duplex, I let myself in. It was a modest California bungalow built on a hillside that my landlady had converted into two apartments, but its bones were as good as anything I had seen today in Los Feliz. I dialed Chevalier's number and left a message on his answering machine.

Then I called for takeout from the tiny Greek place up the street, a blue-and-white stucco box called Mykonos whose Salvadoran short-order cooks served up the garlickiest *spanakopita, dolmades,* and *tsatziki* this side of the Aegean.

"You from Mykonos?" I once asked the swarthy proprietors, brothers whose upper lips wore a permanent beading of sweat from their fretting over dropping business and rising rents.

One of the brothers had winked at me then and leaned on the cash register.

"Actually, we are from Turkey," he said, putting his finger over his lips to indicate that I shouldn't tell anyone. "Greek food, Turkish food, it's all the same, but you think we'd have any success if we opened a Turkish restaurant?"

"Pah!" his brother said. "Americans know nothing about Turkish cuisine, one of the finest and oldest in the world."

Just once in my life, I thought, I would like something to be what it seemed. After the food came, I opened a bottle of retsina, the Greek wine made of pine resin that took me back to a summer I had once spent in the Cyclades. Then I put on an increasingly crackly tape of Cretan folk music and tucked happily into my Styrofoam boxes. At ten forty-five, I brushed my teeth and toddled to bed. At eleven-thirty, the phone rang. It was Chevalier. He had just gotten home from the police station. They hadn't found Finch yet. We agreed to meet the next day at noon.

The phone rang again at 7 A.M. It was the city desk. Don't bother coming in, Bovasso said. There's been a body found, a dead female naked in the pool of a Los Feliz estate belonging to the Dellaviglia Langdons. A gardener had discovered it and called the police. No one was at home. Carter Langdon III was in San Pedro attending a breakfast meeting hosted by the Port of Los Angeles. The wires were saying he had gone alone.

# CHAPTER 7

As Bovasso spoke, I watched squirrels play tag, twirling in a Möbius strip around the branching oak outside my bedroom window, oblivious to my presence just a glass pane away.

It had been a hellish Saturday night in the City of Angels, and Bovasso said the death toll was now up to thirty-two, counting the Los Feliz body, which had yet to be identified.

"You were there yesterday, did she seem depressed? Did you notice anything weird?" he asked in his gruff voice. I could see him sitting at the city desk, fingering the knot on his tie as he spoke, flicking the tail up and down. It was a nervous quirk he had.

I thought of Venus holding court—the term might have been coined for her—a Sun Queen in her very own Palace of Versailles, perched on the westernmost tip of a swashbuckling new continent that had barely been discovered during Louis XIV's reign. I considered the baroque court games that must go on in the Dellaviglia Langdon household, where the Old World collided so ravenously with the New, of the subterranean lusts and desires that must pulse through its halls. What did such people wish for, when they already had it all? A little frisson went through me—the quickening of all predators at the scent of game. If Venus Dellaviglia was dead, that was a big story. And I intended to be in on it.

"She doesn't seem like the type to commit suicide," I told Bovasso. "But there was something off about the whole setup. The place was crawling with handlers and glad-handers. He's creepy and she's too much, and their kid was lounging around, drinking, right under their aquiline noses, and no one seemed to notice or care about what that implied for their 'family values' campaign. I saw a roach, er, a marijuana cigarette, in an ashtray outside."

"I know what a roach is," George Bovasso growled with baby-boomer indignation.

"Sorry." I paused, seeing a younger version of my paunchy, suit-wearing editor sitting cross-legged in hippie beads and a Nehru jacket, toking on a fat spliff.

"Of course you do. You probably dealt it from your college dorm. But here's what I noticed. For all her airs, there's something hollow about planet Venus. I stumbled across her scarfing some greasy food in the kitchen after everyone had gone, and she chewed me out for being there. Said it was off the record and I couldn't use it."

"You come nosing around my kitchen I'd kick you out too."

"Wait a minute," I said, remembering something. "Wasn't she featured in one of our 'celebrity workout' stories? They all swear they exercise four hours a day and eat nothing but steamed vegetables and chicken breasts."

"That's right. She freaked 'cause you busted her," Bovasso said. "Stop the presses. Celebrity caught eating greasy food."

I shrugged. "Maybe that's all there is to it. But I got a weird feeling. Anyway, I know my way around the place. Let me go back up there now and see what I can get."

Bovasso was dubious. "I don't know. I was going to send Josh."

My heart sank. It was my nemesis, Mr. Ivy League. Why should he get everything handed to him on a platter?

"Send us both. This is going to be big."

"I thought you wanted to work on your squatter kid folo."

"That's the beauty of the thing. It's connected somehow. Venus's kid knew that dead girl, Isabel Chevalier. He was cagey with me yesterday, but if I go back up there today, I'm sure I can get more out of him."

I was fully warmed up now and ready to play my trump card.

"Besides," I told him, "I live around the corner. I'll be there in ten minutes. Josh lives in Venice. It will take him an hour."

For me, the city had always been divided into two separate and unequal camps for which La Cienega Boulevard served as the demarcation point. West of La Cienega, you caught a sea breeze in the summer. The streets were free of garbage, graffiti, and junked cars. The most au courant restaurateurs and architects plied their trade. West of La Cienega was Beverly Hills, Century City, Westwood, Brentwood, Santa Monica, and Pacific Palisades. It was where movie stars and investment bankers and well-off, mostly white people lived, where the buses always ran smoothly because how else would the maids and butlers and nannies get to their jobs on time?

East of La Cienega was another story. Oh sure, there was a DMZ in the center, the regentrifying neighborhoods of Fairfax and Larchmont and Hancock Park. But somewhere east of La Brea, an invisible wave of poverty, despair, and nervous, ladder-scrambling energy washed over the streets. The buildings got dumpier, the skin tones duskier, the cars more beat-up, the languages more sibilant and guttural and singsong, the streets more crowded and alive with the kinetic force of shoppers dragging along four kids, *paleta* vendors hawking their wares, young homies lounging on the street corners while their girlfriends pushed strollers, police cars cruising by with a sharklike intensity you never sensed on the open, landscaped, and lit streets of the other Los Angeles.

There were pockets of affluence on my side of town too, old-money enclaves like Los Feliz where the Dellaviglia Langdons lived, just as there were slums like Oakwood on the West Side. But those exceptions only proved my geographic rule.

Hah, I thought to myself, imagining Josh in a hot lather, gunning it on the freeway to get to Los Feliz from his beach-adjacent loft. For once, East Side trumps West Side.

Bovasso sighed.

"Okay, kid, you talked me into it. But I want you to call in by ten, tell me what you're finding. Who knows what other mayhem's gonna break today, and I may need you on it."

"Thanks, Bovasso. I won't let you down."

The ornamental iron gates were open again, this time for emergency vehicles instead of rich political contributors, and I, who was neither, slunk past like a pariah dog. Had I seen the pool yesterday? I recalled a series of tiled steps, winding down away from the house, in the direction of the orchard, and a grotto of gleaming turquoise below, surrounded by tall banana plants. I could cut through the orchard to get there, if I had to.

As I rounded the last turn, I saw news vans and cop cars, reporters milling and police standing strategically along a long line of yellow emergency tape that blocked access to the villa. They needed to secure the crime scene,

I understood that. I made a quick U-turn and headed back down the cobblestone path and out of sight. Then I pulled onto the dirt shoulder, parked the car, and tumbled out, glad I was wearing leather flats instead of heels. Silently, I stepped off the road and lost myself under the dappling shade of the orchards. I heard the busy drone of bees and looked down, stepping carefully to avoid the rotting fruit that lined the earthen furrows. In a moment's inspiration, I reached up and picked two big hard Hass avocados and slipped them into my purse. Thieves called the fruit black gold. They rustled it from commercial orchards and sold it to gourmet markets, where it commanded up to $3.00 apiece. Maybe that made me a thief too, but I preferred to think that I was hauling away refuse. And unlike the gardeners, I did it for free.

I saw the banana plants in the distance as I picked my way through the trees, my shoes leaving deep indentations on the loamy earth. Seventy feet below, antlike figures crawled along the pool's flagstone expanse. The water was smooth and cerulean and still, and as I got closer, I saw that the body had been fished out and laid across a tarp. A police photographer was taking pictures. I was about thirty feet away now, in the citrus, and I could see the curvaceous form of Venus Dellaviglia Langdon. Yes, it was her, the same woman I had seen yesterday quoting Horace, dashing her wine into the fire, eating her solitary dinner. Her tangled hair was stiff as crusted seaweed, like Neptune's daughter come frothing out of the sea, fully formed and beautiful, Venus on the half shell, except she wasn't demurely covering her privates with one hand, long tresses shading her breasts. No, the hair was spread out like an obscene halo around her, her features waxen. How appropriate. Venus had always put on a public mask, and now in death it was welded to her. Her naked body gleamed in the pale morning light, as though carved out of Italian marble, her breasts standing straight up, saluting the sky. So they weren't natural either. What part of her was? My eyes lingered, tracing the arc of her magnificent body, pulling up abruptly at the triangle of pubic hair. It should have been auburn but it was black, a midnight coal black, the last lie before her body disappeared into impossibly long, gazellelike legs, shaped by hours on the Stairmaster, or, who knows, the lipo-surgeon's vacuum tube, but splendid nonetheless, culminating in high-arched feet curved with the grace of a ballerina's, all the way to her long, slender toes, nails enameled in bloody carmine. I didn't see any obvious signs of violence on her, no bruises or bullet holes or ligature marks around the neck. Even in death, Venus Dellaviglia Langdon was perfectly composed, hiding from view the secrets of her death.

I hiked over to the left of the hill to catch the corpse from a different angle, hoping that something new would reveal itself. I was directly above the crime scene now and I noticed steps leading off to a building that had been hidden by the trees. It was a cabana—a plaster-and-lathe mini-villa with curved arches and welcoming balconies. In other neighborhoods you'd rent it out to an entire family.

Moving closer, I peeked into a window framed by sage curtains. They opened on to a bathroom lined from floor-to-ceiling with Art Deco tile in luminous violet that I knew was original because environmental laws now banned the use of heavy metals such as cadmium that had once given California tiles their otherworldly sheen. A violet pedestal sink stood in the middle. The bath was huge and deep and violet too, with clawed feet, and I could imagine sinking into its steamy depths and never coming out. A wooden door, stenciled with a coat of arms, opened into a bedroom with a queen-sized bed topped by a lilac comforter. The bed was rumpled and unmade. There was a wet violet maillot and a man's black Speedo racing suit crumpled at its foot. Towels were strewn around, as if someone had been in a great hurry to tumble into the eiderdown.

The sheets seemed damp and rumpled. A carved wood bedside table held a wineglass with lipstick smeared across it, and a little white sculpture with odd daubs of color. The thing unnerved me. It was a skull, a gleaming white skull leaning back on a wooden stand, its empty eye sockets and mouth gaping in toothy, mocking laughter. It had a granular texture that looked familiar, but it took me a minute to click to what it was. That sandpaper feel. I could almost taste it on my tongue. Yeah, that was it. The memory of sweet, discrete grains melting in my mouth. It was a sugar skull.

Now the memory came back full-blown. It was a Day of the Dead symbol, *Día de los Muertos* in Spanish, which came right after Halloween. You could find the little sugar skulls all over the Mexican neighborhoods, sweet confections for *Día de los Muertos,* the day you remembered and honored your ancestors, visited their graves to deposit flowers and light candles and place the grinning little sugar skulls on *abuelita*'s plot, always making sure to buy extra so the children would have something to lick and savor and know that today was a special day.

I had written a story about a factory in South El Monte that cranked out hundreds of thousands of them. It was a seasonal thing, but it was part of the tradition, and while the Yanquis might think it morbid to picnic on graves and decorate homes with the grinning *calaveras*—the sugar skulls that signified our dust-to-dust passing—in Latino culture there was no such demarcation with the spirit world. The two coexisted, with no Puritan separation, no great gulf of Protestantism, and the spirits flitted back and forth, visiting the living, just as the living visited the spirit world in dreams. The Mexican proprietress of the factory had explained it all to me, her children happily licking their sugar skulls like lollipops. I had been entranced by this melding of the two worlds that in my life stood at polar opposites and left me cold and uneasy in the presence of death. But reporting had helped bridge the gap, until I no longer shrank at the sight of a corpse, realizing that the spirit had already flown, and that the body was just a shell, and that cosmic error could have put me in its place, and that coming to peace with this knowledge would make the eventual journey, the crossing over, less painful when it came, as it must to us all.

But what was a sugar skull doing in Venus Dellaviglia Langdon's private pool cabana slash boudoir? Perhaps a servant had given it to her, a tribute to the goddess? And Venus had carefully taken it out of the big house, so it wouldn't clash with her European antiques and Old Master sketches, relegating it to the cabana, where it wouldn't offend anyone. Was the cabana, hidden away from the villa, a private outlet for Venus's pent-up passions that she couldn't express anywhere else? My gaze traveled back to the unmade bed, the hastily flung bathing suit, the still life of frantic passion it evoked, and I tried to picture Venus and Carter here, reenacting the eternal Dionysian frenzy. My mind balked. I just couldn't conjure it. I looked again at the towels, in damp heaps where they had been thrown. The pillows across the bed. Then in my mind's eye I saw Carter Langdon, impeccable in his suit, running for office, running, running, always running. I tried to picture him in that racy black Speedo. Then I saw again the voracious gleam of Venus's eye in her Christmas card photo, head angled back, full lips parted, ready to devour a grape, and I knew that Carter Langdon III had not been here, on this bed, joined in carnality with his beautiful wife. In this bed, Venus Dellaviglia Langdon had whispered words of passion kindled in forbidden lust. And just minutes or hours later, she was found dead. I didn't peg her for a suicide, there was a voracious life force in her that would have precluded self-immolation. That left murder. Had her lover done it? Had her husband found them together and killed his wife in a purple crime of passion? Had she interrupted a robbery? Or had her brilliant story come to a more pedestrian end when, drunk on too much wine, she had dived in, never to surface? What tantalizing possibilities. What a great story for me. I basked momentarily in the glow of this knowledge. I imagined walking down to the dais to receive my Los Angeles Press Club prize for best breaking-news story. My speech would be modest and short, but pithy.

"What the fu——" I heard a gun cock. "Get your hands in the air. I said *now*."

I obeyed. A hand grabbed my shoulder and spun me around, and I stared into the red and angry face of a uniformed LAPD officer.

"Who are you and what are you doing behind police lines?"

"Eve Diamond. *L.A. Times.*" I dipped my chin, hoping it would point down to my dog tags. "They sent me here to cover the murder." I inclined my head down the steps. Oh boy was I in big trouble. I thought of how Jane Sims had called me a hothead. What we need right now is cool, mature thinking, she had said. Oh yes, I thought, asking the Lord to send me some.

"Richards, Mallory, check the cabana, make sure there's no one else creeping around up here," the policeman barked at some unseen colleagues. Then he turned his gaze to me.

"How did you get past the police barricade?"

"I parked along the road and walked through the orchard. I haven't been up to the house," I lied. "I was here yesterday, covering the fund-raiser, so I know my way around the estate and figured I'd head right for the pool."

"Did you go into that cabana? This is a crime scene, little missy, whether you saw the yellow tape or not. You messed anything up back there, we're taking you in."

"N-no," I stuttered, thankful that I had not gone inside. I had been planning to, that was for sure, but they had caught me first. Not that I was about to tell the cop that.

"We'll soon find out if you're lying. And if you are . . ." He leaned into me, pulling my dog tags toward him to read my name and affiliation again. His teeth were yellow, his breath laced with nicotine and sweet, stale coffee. "You'll live to regret it."

# CHAPTER 8

He hustled me along the stairs, past the windows of the cabana, where I took one last peek and saw two uniformed officers bent over the bed. We descended to the pool, and he marched me right past the body, where the other cops looked up, startled to see a civilian. Someone had covered Venus Dellaviglia Langdon's body with one of her violet sheets. Luckily, I had seen enough to add a ton of local color to my story. I hoped the cop would lead me through the big house, but we skirted alongside, all the way to the front, where he deposited me amid a pack of journalistic hounds, who immediately set up a baying as they realized I had come from the no-fly zone. Ignoring them, I slunk down the Appian Way to my car to write down what I had seen, lots of vivid, empurpled descriptions that editors would probably prune back to discreet *Times*-like prose so that subscribers could read the story at their breakfast tables without up-chucking.

I turned the car around and drove back to the front of the villa. As I got out, another policeman emerged onto the porch to brief the press mob. I saw Josh, the up-and-coming *Times* reporter who had finally made it in from the beach, arguing with a policeman who was guarding the side of the house. Josh pointed toward the pool, and I could tell he was trying to talk the cop into letting him through. It was with smug satisfaction that I saw him turn away a moment later.

Now a white limousine pulled up, tires squealing. A

back door flew open, disgorging Langdon and four handlers, natty in their black suits and already dressed for a funeral. En masse, they sprinted past the police lines and up to the front door as the uniformed officers drew back respectfully to let the entourage through. The reporters surged after them, with nervous, darting eye movements, jerky thrusts of cartilage, circling closer, tighter, waiting for the journalistic chum that would surely be dumped overboard any minute now, their mouths creased in mock sorrow but eyes shiny with such a collective shudder of schadenfreude that it's a wonder it didn't register on the Richter scale. Oh the pity and the sorrow, Venus Dellaviglia Langdon was dead.

But Langdon's party disappeared into the house. The door slammed and did not reopen. And by the time the press corps had recovered enough to protest, the police had closed in again.

My cell phone rang. I looked at my watch and saw it was 10:30 A.M.

"Thought you were going to call in at ten," Bovasso said.

I explained how I had gotten waylaid.

"So is it her?"

"Yes. It's the same woman I saw yesterday. Minus the clothes."

"Holy shit." Bovasso breathed heavily. He knew the implications for the paper. Within an hour, ten reporters would be called in from Sunday brunch in their over-mortgaged houses and sicced on different parts of this big L.A. story in which crime, celebrity, and politics had collided to create a glorious media train wreck.

I told him how I had sneaked around to the crime scene and gotten lots of local color. I told him about seeing the nude body, what appeared to be a lover's tryst in the cabana, the wet suits, the sugar skull on the bedside table.

"That's a lot of conjecture," Bovasso said. "I don't know how much of that we can put in."

"It's what I saw before the cops chased me away. Let the readers make up their own minds."

"Okay. Josh is on the scene now, he'll attend the press conference. I want you to go to Langdon's campaign headquarters and see how her death is going to affect the campaign."

"But I'm not a political reporter, I'm in suburban, I don't know anything about this race."

"Here's the address. Call me when you get something."

At Langdon's bustling headquarters, I was quickly ushered by a somber assistant into the office of his campaign manager, Alan Severin.

He told me that Langdon was in mourning and would be canceling his appearances for the next couple of days but that there were no plans to abandon the campaign. Langdon would explain why in a 2 P.M. press conference.

Severin picked up a Mont Blanc pen on his desk and ran his finger along its polished length. He wore a wedding band. Behind his desk was a photo of a smiling blonde and four children.

"His words will be unscripted, they will come straight from his heart. This tragedy, so personal and so devastating, puts Carter in unique solidarity with those who have suffered from the ravages of violent crime in this city."

Severin leaned forward, his collar cutting into the smooth, pink skin of his neck.

"Anyone can be a victim of violence, whether he is rich or poor, lives in a ghetto or a gilded mansion. That is the lesson here. No one is exempt. And that is why

Carter was so committed to tougher sentencing laws and more police on the street. The need has been brought home in a breathtakingly personal way. No, Ms. Diamond, Carter will not bow out of the race. He will fight with his last breath for justice, both for himself and the countless other Angelenos who have suffered a similar loss. We cannot relinquish this city to crime."

Was there anybody connected with these people who ever felt a pure emotion, I wondered, one that was not immediately and cynically manipulated for its spin value? I murmured some appropriate condolences, aware that we were both playing roles that had nothing to do with reality. I was nodding in sympathy, jotting things down, as if he were handing down the tablets from the Mount. He was using Venus's murder to propel his candidate, newly recast as sorrowful widower, to victory. There was a mounting excitement in Severin's voice, as if here, finally, was the grand finale to the campaign he had waged for so long, the pièce de résistance. It was a masterly stroke that could not have been dreamed up by even the most Borgia-like consigliere. And it had fallen neatly into his lap.

Severin's thin lips drooped at the corners. "Of course, we hope the police will bring this criminal to justice before the election, but they are understaffed, and while my candidate wants his wife's murderer caught, he wants no special resources deployed on this case when so many others go unsolved."

I wrote it all down.

"Mr. Severin, are you afraid some people will see this as a bald-faced and cynical attempt to exploit Venus's murder to gain sympathy and votes?"

He looked at me as if I had just said something unspeakably vile.

"How can you even think such a thing at a time like this?"

"It's my job," I told him, standing up and smiling. "And as we both know, it's yours too. That's why he hired you."

On my way out, I ran into a young kid stuffing envelopes. He wore an Explorer Scout uniform.

"Lots of volunteering today, eh?" I said.

"Yeah, earning my merit badge. I'll probably be here six hours today, filling in."

There were a lot of people around for a Sunday, but then, the election was three weeks away. I looked out through the twenty-first-floor plate-glass windows, feeling like I was inside a falcon's eyrie, scanning below for scurrying things with a warm, beating heart. I saw the Hollywood Hills, brown in the autumn air, the houses built on stilts overlooking the basin. Foolish humans. These sandstone cliffs would crumble one day like their Malibu counterparts. I had seen the damage unleashed by ferocious winter storms, the rivulets of water carving deep fissures in the earth. The sandy soil would swell until it jiggled like pudding and then the million-dollar structures would calf like icebergs, huge chunks breaking free and sliding down canyons and onto Pacific Coast Highway. It was only the very rich and very poor who built on hillsides. One out of hubris, thumbing their nose at nature, the other out of desperation and poverty.

Now my eyes moved east, where the Hollywood Hills merged into Griffith Park. Far away, the white dome of the observatory twinkled like an alien spaceship. There were no storms on the horizons today, not any wrought by Mother Nature, at least.

"Seems a shame to be stuck indoors on such a nice fall day."

"They can really use the help. They had a couple people quit last week."

The boy's pride was etched into his voice. He was being useful. More than he knew, I suddenly realized. Why had two employees quit right before the election?

"Who quit?"

"Oh, Anne Marie Ruiz and Marsha Mardsen."

"Where'd they go?"

"Dunno. All's I know is they left in a hurry."

"Hmm." That was even more useful. "Well, you take care now."

I turned and headed back to Severin's inner sanctum, but the big oaken door was closed. I knocked but no one answered. A pretty young woman with blonde curls and a pencil behind her ear walked past.

"He's gone to meet with the candidate," she said, smiling through her bloodshot eyes and trying mightily to look perky and efficient. "He'll be back this afternoon, if you'd like me to take a message."

"Maybe you can help me. I understand two of your employees, Anne Marie Ruiz and Marsha Mardsen, just quit. Do you know why?"

The forced cheeriness was replaced by a schoolmarm purse.

"That's a personnel matter. It's confidential information."

"I understand that. But what can you tell me unconfidentially?"

A flurry of confusion passed across her eyes.

"I'm sorry I can't help you," she said at last. "But I'll be happy to take a message."

She pulled the pencil from behind her ear and licked her lips in preparation.

"That's okay, I'll catch him later."

Once back in my car, I called Bovasso to fill him in. When I read back one of Severin's quotes, the words sounded even more cynical coming out of my mouth than his. I realized I would never make it as a political reporter. I felt too much outrage, wasn't evolved enough for the game. I drove back to the office and ducked into the library, asking for all the election clips on Carter Langdon III. Carefully, I made a list of every employee quoted, from Severin, the campaign manager, down to consultants, assistants, calendar clerks, and spokespeople.

Sure enough, Anne Marie Ruiz and Marsha Mardsen were among them. I called Information to get listings. Ruiz was hopeless, the name was too common. But Mardsen, with that odd slam-dance of consonants, was in the book. Since it was a weekend and she had just quit an exhausting job, she was home. Taking a nap, by the gravel in her voice.

I identified myself and said I was calling because Venus Dellaviglia Langdon had been found floating naked and dead in her Los Feliz pool.

"I'm no longer working there. Why are you calling me?" Her voice went from gravel to sharp, shiny obsidian. There was no expression of surprise, regret, sorrow.

"I thought you might want to know, that's all. I thought you might have something to say about your old bosses."

There was a harsh laugh.

"I have nothing to say about Venus Dellaviglia Langdon, either on or off the record."

"Why not?"

There was stubborn silence on the other end.

"Hey, could we meet for a bit, coffee?" I asked. "I really need some background. I could be there in twenty minutes."

Silence. Then, "What do you want me to say? I already told you I don't work for her, uh, I mean him, anymore. Sorry for that slip of the tongue. She micromanaged everything, so sometimes it seemed like I was working for her. But let's get this straight, I was on his payroll."

"Hey, now that's something. The micromanaging. Is that on the record?"

"No."

"How about if I call you a source close to the campaign?"

She thought for a moment.

"No one would ever know it's you, he's got, what, forty people working for him? Surely you're not the only one who felt that way?"

Marsha Mardsen's laugh was jagged splinters of falling glass.

"You got that right."

"So, Marsha, it's history now. How about it?"

"If I see my name in the *Times*, I'll never speak to you again."

"No problem. You're a source, you could be anyone. You could be Langdon himself, for all people know. Now how about some coffee?"

She was wary. "I'd better not."

"Darn. I could really use something else. Deep background, even. We're on deadline."

"Why don't you try Anne Marie Ruiz. She quit last week too, and she's not staying in this line of work. Gonna join the Peace Corps and go to Albania."

"Great, got a number?"

Soon, I was on the line with Anne Marie Ruiz. She agreed to meet me at 1:30 P.M. I had just enough time to scan the wires. The weekend murder tally was now up to thirty-four. The latest was an El Sereno resident named

Ruben Aguilar, twenty-eight, who had been gunned down Saturday night as he sat in his car. The details were all too drearily familiar. He had just pulled up in front of his house after returning from working all day. Poor old Ruben Aguilar, I thought. No way was he getting his own Metro story. It had happened in the barrio, where the gangs constantly shot at each other, so there was nothing unique about the place or circumstance of his death. He wasn't rich or well known. His death wasn't especially salacious or quirky or gruesome. So we would just include him in the roundup story. In the newsroom, we called it collecting string.

Then I drove to meet Anne Marie. When we sat down, I learned she was a devout Christian who had come to the belated conclusion that political consulting did not make her feel good about herself.

"But why quit now, with three weeks to go? Why not just ride it home?"

She looked at me, her glasses steaming as she sipped her macchiatto. It was one of those places.

"This is all off the record."

"What do you care? You'll be on the other side of the world."

"Off the record or I'm not saying another word."

"Can I say a former employee?"

She considered it. Revenge glittered in her eyes. She wanted this to get out. She just didn't want it to get traced back to her.

"No," she said finally. "There were only two of us consultants. They'll know."

"I can deny it."

"What if you get subpoenaed?"

Was she going to tell me something that loaded? "We talking criminal activity?"

A worried shadow crossed her face. "Oh no, I don't think so."

"Well, then what?"

"It wasn't what I expected."

"Tell me."

"Let's make it not for attribution. You can call me a source close to the campaign. If some heat gets on that bitch Betsy, too bad. She's part of the problem."

"Who's Betsy?"

"A coworker. That's inside ball. Never mind."

"Okay. I've forgotten Betsy already. Now tell me what the setup was like."

"For all the money they threw around, they weren't very professional. And Severin made me nervous," Anne Marie said. "He was always fighting with Venus. They'd have screaming matches and poor Carter would just slink into the corner."

"What did they fight over?"

"Money."

"What about money?"

"During the primary, she ordered Severin to hire private investigators to dig up dirt on Carter's opponents. People who couldn't be traced back to the campaign."

Anne Marie ticked them off on her manicured fingers—"Abortions, drug use, illegal nannies, drunk driving, sexcapades. You name it. She wanted it. Severin said no, he was worried it could backfire. They had terrible arguments."

"Backfire how?"

"I don't know. Maybe if the press found out they were up to dirty tricks."

She picked up her chocolate chip cookie and broke it carefully into bite-sized pieces, spreading them out on a napkin. Then she picked one up and examined it for chocolate chips, which she gouged out with her long nails and licked off. I distrust a woman who pays too much attention to her nails.

"Look, you're Christian. If you think something unethical was going on, you should tell me. It would never get traced back to you. And what if it had something to do with Venus's murder?"

She hesitated. "I don't know what happened with the dirty tricks. I guess all campaigns do that stuff. But Venus had something on Severin. I heard her threaten him. Said he knew what would happen if he refused to toe the line. I was working late that night and they didn't know I was there. He ran after her, saying, 'For the love of Christ, Venus, I'm a family man.'"

"What did that mean?"

"I don't know. And then she did something weird. She crossed her arms across her chest and said the whole campaign was built around family values and he'd better remember that. Then she slammed the door and took off."

I sat back in my faux-Eames chair and looked out the floor-to-ceiling window, where people were strolling. Real-life pedestrians walking in L.A.

"Put it all together and what have you got?" I asked her.

She shrugged, then went back to mining her chips. "It means that every campaign has its secrets, and that's exactly why I'm joining the Peace Corps. I applied months ago on a whim. When the acceptance letter came, I put it aside. But the in-country training starts next week and with everything that's happened, I felt God was telling me to bail. My work here is meaningless. Over there it's different. I'll be keeping people from starving, getting them basic health care and access to clean water."

I shook my head at her naïveté. "Don't you think there's corruption where you're going? The local officials are way worse than American politicians, they sell UNESCO cooking oil and tinned meat on the open market to the highest bidder while their own kids go malnourished. What's so pure about that?"

"There I can make a difference," she repeated, a mantra she no doubt whispered nightly to lull herself to sleep. "I'll be dealing with raw survival, not getting some figurehead elected. Don't you understand why that's appealing?"

I wanted to goad her, see what else she would say.

"Sounds like you hate Venus and Carter."

"I took the job because they were my idols. Venus, especially. I thought she should be the one running for office. She was the epitome of family values to me, and she had it all—a handsome husband, a career, great intellect, beauty. She could do anything she wanted. To tell the truth, I didn't want to work for her. I wanted to *be* her. But she collects people, uses them, then discards them when they've outlived their value. She isn't what she seems."

I studied Anne Marie more closely and noticed that she had the same haircut as Venus, the same tousled locks sprayed into studied disarray. I dropped my swizzle stick, and as I bent down to pick it up saw the same florid color on her toenails that I had seen on Venus's unsheathed talons this morning.

And I knew without asking that Anne Marie was one of those people Venus had used and then discarded. But now Anne Marie was extracting her petty revenge, pushing her onetime idol off the pedestal and shivering with pleasure as she shattered into a thousand pieces.

"Is there anything else you think is important, something that might help the police catch her killer?" I always say that at the end when I'm fishing.

She breathed heavily and looked out the window. Her eyes were glassy. She blinked several times.

"Were you involved with Severin? And Venus found out? Is that what she had on him?"

"What makes you think that?"

"You're so transparent, Anne Marie. You did good to get out of politics. You wouldn't have lasted long."

"We weren't having an affair, if that's what you mean. He was my mentor at USC several years ago—he teaches there."

"Did he break up with you? Is that the real reason you're going to Albania? Get as far away from him as you possibly can?"

"You've got it all wrong," she said, but her tears and snuffling told me otherwise.

"Is that why you hate her so much? She threatened to betray you? Wouldn't that give you a motive for murder too?"

"That's the sickest thing I ever heard," she whispered, shaking her head.

"Then maybe Severin did it."

She seemed taken aback.

"He's a political consultant. She was his client. That doesn't make sense."

"But you just told me she had something on him. What if she was blackmailing him?"

"Look, whatever she had on him, she couldn't very well have gone public with it, could she? Right before the election? Anything that smeared him would get her too."

I thought she had a point.

"No, Eve," she said sadly, "I'm afraid it's not so simple."

"It is complicated," I agreed.

"It was just time for me to move on." She stirred the foam at the bottom of her cup, slick with caramel syrup. "From Severin. From Venus. From politics. I found the entire business distasteful. What's that saying about sausage-making? You don't want to see how it's done. I just couldn't stand it another day. And when I looked at the Peace Corps letter again on Thursday, that was it. I didn't have any reason to stay."

"You've totally washed your hands of that world, huh?"

"You bet."

I leaned forward. "Then, Anne Marie, how about you let me use your name? You've just told me you're through with that line of work."

She reflected.

"I don't want my name in the paper. But I don't care if you tell Severin we've talked."

I leaned back. "You want to put the fear of the Lord in him?"

She sniffed. "The Lord, sadly, had nothing to do with my relationship with Severin. I now see that was the big problem."

She rose to go.

I couldn't think of anything else. "Why don't you give me your e-mail, in case I have more questions," I finally said.

She scribbled it on a napkin. I didn't tell her I was going back to her boss. But I had a few more questions about family values.

# CHAPTER 9

Driving back to Langdon's campaign headquarters, I called in the new information. When I got there, Severin had returned and was annoyed as hell to see me again after my parting comment. He had been briefing the candidate and the press for much of the afternoon, and now here I was again, pestering him for more. He was about to cut me off when I pointed to the photos behind him.

"I see you're married. Got some kids."

He sized me up. "What's that got to do with anything?"

"This is a real family values campaign, through and through, huh?"

He put down a sheaf of papers.

"That's right. I don't like the innuendo I'm picking up in your voice. A tragedy has occurred, just as we face the biggest political challenge of our lives. I'm a very busy man, so if you'll please excuse me, I've got a lot of work to do."

He saw I wasn't going anywhere, so he came around the desk and took my shoulder, steering me gently toward the door. I knew I didn't have much time and I thought that startling him might be my best and perhaps only chance at gaining any information.

"Let me give you a hypothetical, Severin," I said as we walked. "What if a campaign manager who was not what he seemed was managing a campaign for a political candidate and his wife who were not what they seemed? And the wife found out this campaign manager's secret and threatened to expose him if he didn't run the campaign the way she demanded. And that included some very dirty tricks. Would that give him a motive to kill?"

Severin had been reaching for the doorknob. Now he stood there, holding it but not opening the door, his face growing redder and angrier as I spoke. He raised his arm and I thought he might hit me, but then he lowered it and rattled the doorknob. When I looked at his face again, I saw only irritated annoyance.

"You had better watch what you are saying, Ms. Diamond. I don't know you, you are not a regular *Times* political reporter, and I shall chalk up your insolence to the fact that you don't understand how things work in this business and are grasping for melodramatic straws. But if I hear any more bizarre innuendo from you, I will be forced to pick up the phone and call the political editor and ask that you be taken off this story."

"The only bias I have is for the truth," I told him, cringing at how corny the words sounded. "And I know that Anne Marie Ruiz left the campaign suddenly for a very legitimate reason. I just spoke with her."

"You wha——? . . . Ms. Diamond, I can tell you in confidence that Anne Marie Ruiz is a troubled young woman, and we were not at all displeased to see her go."

"She seemed perfectly coherent when I had coffee with her an hour ago."

"People are not always what they seem."

I wasn't sure if he was talking about Anne Marie, himself, or the Dellaviglia Langdons.

"Yes, that's what I was saying a minute ago," I said.

"You were spouting some kind of nonsense that I won't even dignify with a response." Severin was once more an avuncular uncle indulging a young reporter. I wanted to squash that image right away.

"Why did two of your aides quit suddenly right before the election?"

"I can't discuss personnel matters."

"How'd you like the *Times* to write this up in tomorrow's paper and let readers come to their own conclusions?"

"They already folded it into yesterday's campaign story, which you obviously didn't bother to read. It was no big deal then and it's no big deal now that Venus is dead. Besides"—he shrugged—"campaign workers come, they go. It's a transient profession."

I looked at my watch and saw I was overdue to call George Bovasso.

"Thank you, Mr. Severin, if I have any more questions, can I give you a call?"

"Sure," he said, in a tone that said he was going to set up impenetrable barriers to make sure I didn't. He closed the door firmly behind him. I heard the lock click and saw one of the lines light up on the receptionist's phone. Severin was making a call.

On the way back in, I called Bovasso and went over everything again. He said we wouldn't be able to use most of what I'd gotten but he'd pass on the staff defections scuttlebutt to Tony Hausman, a political reporter who was covering the campaign.

When I hit Pico-Union, I grabbed some *pupusas* and *curdito* at a Salvadorean place, biting into the chewy corn masa dense with pork and melted cheese as I drove. At red lights, I scooped up the vinegar-and-chili-laced *curdito*—a sort of salad made with shredded carrot and cabbage—with my fingers. I was ravenous.

It was 3:45 P.M. when I got back to the office, though I felt as if an entire week had gone by. Bovasso wanted

me to write up and file my murder scene notes to Josh,
who had been deputized to write the main story. That
was the way of it at newspapers sometimes; you were
just a conduit through which information flowed. You
ran around all day, interviewing people, feeding bits to
other reporters who were amassing details from a dozen
others to massage into one comprehensive story. If you
were lucky or they were feeling generous, your name
got slapped alongside theirs. If your contribution had
been minimal, you were relegated to a tag line—*Times*
Staff Writer Eve Diamond contributed to this story.
It was writing by assembly line, and when it worked, it
rivaled the streamlined efficiency dreamed up by Henry
Ford.

At five-fifteen, while I was going over my notes to
make sure I hadn't forgotten anything, Bovasso called
me over.

"You sure about the man's black swimsuit in the
cabana? Josh says they didn't mention that at the press
briefing, just the woman's one-piece suit."

I stepped back, momentarily caught off track. Then I
saw them tangled together in my mind's eye again. How
could I have imagined that tableau of moist lust?

"Of course I'm sure."

Bovasso frowned.

"Do me a favor, call the cop shop and check it."

I hurried off, doubting myself now.

After being connected all around Parker Center for ten
minutes, I finally got a flack willing to read to me from
the police report. I sat there, fidgeting, while he droned
on. Again, there was the violet maillot, but no mention of
the black Speedo.

"Look, could I talk to one of the cops at the scene?
I'm sure I saw it. Their names were . . ."

In my mind now, I heard an echo, the angry cop who had nabbed me, yelling out instructions to . . .

"Richards or Mallory," I said.

"Just a minute."

"Mallory here," he came on, five minutes later.

I explained who I was and apologized for any trouble I might have caused that morning.

"I saw a man's black Speedo bathing suit at the foot of the bed, next to the woman's purple one-piece, but for some reason, it isn't mentioned in the police report. . . ."

I trailed off, certain that he would chime in now. But there was only silence.

"So I just want to confirm, for our story, uh, I didn't hallucinate it."

Again, I waited. "Officer Mallory, are you there?" I finally asked. "Yes," he said. "I was trying to think of what else might have been there that would have misled you."

"I don't understand."

"There was no man's black bathing suit of any kind in that cabana. Just a woman's one-piece suit."

"But I saw it." I was getting alarmed. My journalistic honor was at stake. Bovasso and Josh would know I had made a huge mistake. Or worse, that I had made it up to spice up the story, aggrandize my own journalistic skills. And sooner or later, Jane Sims and the rest of the *L.A. Times* honchos, all the people who held my career in their hands, would hear of this. Rumors would go around that I couldn't be trusted, that I embroidered, that I was inaccurate. It was the kiss of death.

"I don't know what you saw," Mallory said. "But you're mistaken about the man's swimsuit. Hold on. Let me check with Richards."

After an eternity, he came back on. "Richards says a black chiffon scarf was found near the bed."

My head was pounding. "What about the man's black swimsuit?"

"Negativo."

"Thanks for checking." I hung up and sat in front of the computer. I knew I had seen a man's black Speedo. Why had it morphed into a black chiffon scarf? Because someone didn't want the Speedo publicized. And why not? The only reason I could think of was because Carter Langdon III didn't wear black Speedos. Which meant that Venus had gone swimming with a man other than her husband shortly before she died.

I leaned back in my chair, hearing it squeak. What if the swimsuit had been discreetly removed after I had seen it but before the murder investigation had gotten under way? Because it wouldn't look good for the wife of the aspiring mayor to be discovered in flagrante delicto with her lover, right before the election, especially when he was running a family values campaign. In that case, I had just tipped my hand to Mallory or whoever had removed the Speedo. And from now on, I'd have to watch my back. What was worse, I couldn't even bring it up with Bovasso; he would think me paranoid as well as error-prone.

I saw him waiting impatiently for the answer. So with my reportorial tail between my legs, I slunk off and told Bovasso it had been a black chiffon scarf, not a man's swimsuit. Across the pod, Josh smirked and scrolled through the story to amend it.

"Don't take it too hard, kid," Bovasso said, "but don't let it happen again, either. These are the types of details that sink ships and derail campaigns, if you know what I mean."

He winked at me, but I couldn't summon up anything screwball and forties' comedy in return.

I made a few more calls on the murder roundup story, mildly disappointed to learn that thirty-five bodies—the grand weekend finale total—wasn't any kind of record. I finished writing it up and filed that too. Then I logged off, went home, and crept into bed. Tomorrow was Monday and I had to report back to the San Gabriel Valley. My Metro furlough was over.

It was only the next morning, when the alarm went off, that I realized I had forgotten to call Vincent Chevalier. I pulled myself out of bed and heard the heavy thud of the paper being delivered. Then a second, lighter thud. I got the *Times* and my landlady, Violetta, who lived downstairs, got the *Daily News,* our nearest rival. I looked at my watch—6 A.M. Too early to call Chevalier and apologize. I decided to read the *Daily News* story about Venus and see how our coverage compared with theirs.

I opened the front door and picked it up, knowing I'd have it back in a neat pile on Violetta's doorstep by the time she got up. I made a pot of coffee and sliced off a piece of Ukrainian poppy-seed cake that I got from a deli down the street. Then I opened the front page. There were three stories in the *Daily News,* and I read them all carefully. Venus had died from a bullet to the back of the head. It had lodged in her thalamus, the brain's switching station, which controls everything else. No wonder there wasn't any messy exit wound. I finished my cake and cut another slice. They hadn't mentioned the black Speedo either. But then, that wasn't surprising. According to the public record, the suit didn't exist. Well, no matter. This wasn't my story anymore. I didn't even own a piece of it. It was Monday and I was back in the valley and working squatter kids.

Still, I wanted to know one more thing. I went back

and hunted for the grafs that would tell me how Carter Langdon III had passed Saturday evening. It was after the jump, which in reporter parlance means the inside page where the story continues. He'd been busy. At dinnertime, he had been volunteering at a soup kitchen on Skid Row. Then he had given a speech. Finally, at 11 P.M., he had attended a prayer vigil with a high-ranking Tibetan lama and assorted Hollywood celebrities. With all those speechifying super-egos, the vigil hadn't ended until after 2 A.M. Then he had headed to a hotel in San Pedro to catch a few hours of sleep before his early morning breakfast meeting. Which made it highly unlikely that Carter Langdon III had been frolicking with his wife in their backyard pool shortly before her death.

*I* had barely sat down at my desk when Tom Thompson called me in.

"Remember that Mexican All-Star Rodeo in La Puente that was on the Metro budgets all weekend?"

Tom Thompson put his feet up on his desk and hooked his thumb into his belt loop. A drawl had crept into his voice. I imagined he was wearing pointy cowboy boots of hand-tooled ostrich skin.

"Yeah?"

It was Monday morning and I was wary, not wanting to get saddled with a bum assignment when I had the Isabel Chevalier folo to write. Bovasso had promised to free me up, but it was a delicate dance pleasing two masters—the twice-a-week suburban section with its huge news hole and the equally ravenous maw of Metro.

Tom Thompson laced his hands together behind his head and leaned back in his chair. I saw a ten-gallon cowboy hat atop his head, big steer horns sprouting from either side of his skull.

"It got postponed due to technical trouble."

"Bummer." I shrugged my shoulders in sympathy.

"Water blew out some generators. They got a bunch of big-wheel entertainers from Mexico cooling their heels at a local hotel. Power should be back on by the weekend."

"That's good." I nodded with relief. He wouldn't expect me to work two weekends in a row.

"So that got me to thinking." Thompson's eyes narrowed. "I want you to go out there and talk to the

folks who run that place." He rummaged in his briefcase
and pulled out a business card. "Arena La Puente. Here's
the head dude, Felipe Aguilar. He's an immigrant from
the Mexican state of Nuevo León. Came up here to pick
grapes, now he's a millionaire concert promoter. Says his
customers are starved for a little taste of home. So he
supplies it—the ranchera stars, the glitz, the cowboys,
even the goddamn livestock. One son has followed him
into the family business. I met them at the San Gabriel
Valley Chamber of Commerce breakfast mixer last
week."

This was not what I needed. What I needed was time
to work on my Metro story. Thompson must have read
my mind. He leaned forward.

"You can do it in between your folo for Metro. I'll
give you a couple of weeks," he said in a voice that
brooked no disapproval. Thompson leaned back again,
chewing his mental cud. "After your story about those
Asian kids got all that attention, I got to thinking we need
to bore into some other cultures too. Enough on the
Chinese, already. What about our Southern neighbor?
I'm sick of reading about these poor bastards dying in
the desert as they try to sneak across. All those drug car-
tel shoot-outs. How about a positive story on Mexicans
for a change?"

It was his sixties' dander kicking up. Although he was
a white boy, Thompson had worked in the San Joaquin
Valley one summer in college, organizing farm workers.
His butt was planted squarely in corporate America now,
but Thompson's heart had never left those fields. Okay,
buddy, I thought, feeling a flicker of enthusiasm at last. I
hear you.

"You thinking a business story?"

"I want you to go in there with an open mind. Do you

know that amphitheater can hold twenty-five thousand people, and every ticket last weekend was sold out, at forty-eight dollars a pop? You do the math."

He pointed his finger at me for emphasis. "And yet I've never heard about this damn place, or any of these performers. And I bet that goes for most of our readers as well."

He pulled out a piece of paper and frowned, trying to decipher someone else's handwriting.

"Vicente Fernandez. Maria Castro. Those were the headliners, but there were dozens more, plus movie stars from those telenovellas as they go crazy for. They're all madder than hornets, stuck here for another week. Except for Fernandez—he hopped on his jet and went back to Mexico till they figure it out. Private jet. You understand what I'm saying? So go check it out, then come back and let's talk. You seem to have a nose for this."

Thompson's last comment made me think of poor departed Venus Dellaviglia Langdon. Look at this nose, I wanted to tell Tom Thompson. It is a Roman nose. It is a roamin' all over this town, sniffing out news for our paper.

Felipe Aguilar agreed to see me that afternoon. He sounded nervous, but I told him not to worry, we didn't care about his technical troubles. We were after a feature. Something uplifting. We would meet at the bar of a nearby restaurant to talk. Then he'd take me to the arena for a tour.

Right before I left for La Puente, Vincent Chevalier called. I apologized for not getting in touch Sunday, explaining I had gotten stuck on another story. It took some diplomacy, since I couldn't exactly admit I had been pulled off his daughter's case to work on a murder that was considered more important, even though it was the truth. Chevalier seemed strangely unfazed and said he was trying to get several of Isabel's friends to come over to the house for our interview. I tried to cancel on Aguilar, but got his machine and realized he was probably already on his way.

Cursing, I called Chevalier back. We settled on the next morning.

"Guess that knocks out Isabel's friends. They'll be in school."

"Not really," he said. "They go to continuation school. That's where they ship 'em when they have trouble at the regular school. Setup's a lot looser. I'm sure they'd make time to talk to you."

I thought about those kids as I took the 605 freeway south, past the hulking gravel pits of Irwindale, where gray mountains of slag towered above the gouged-out earth and nothing green grew. It was a dead, desecrated landscape, bereft even of litter, and I pressed on the accelerator and stared straight ahead until I hit the 60, when I jogged east. I was moving through the southeastern San Gabriel Valley now. It was half cow town, half industrial wasteland, limned by blue-collar suburbs hastily thrown up in the post–World War II euphoria that had started crumbling even as the final coat of paint was being slapped on.

I got off at La Puente Boulevard. I was looking for a restaurant called El Charro, and soon I saw the neon-lit lasso flickering over a bucking bronc and pulled in. I was right on time.

There was no one at the bar. I ordered an orange juice and slid onto a stool. It came with a maraschino cherry and a swizzle stick.

I got out the *Times* and opened it onto the varnished

wood surface of the bar and started reading. I was on my third maraschino cherry when the bartender held up the phone and beckoned to me.

Surprised, I got up and came around the other side of the bar.

"Ms. Diamond?"

"Yes."

"This is Silvio Aguilar, Felipe's son. I'm very sorry, but something has come up and he can't make it. He asked me to convey his apologies and suggest that you call him next week to reschedule."

I was livid. Here I had driven all the way out to god-forsaken La Puente and wasted my afternoon, precious time I could have spent on my Isabel folo, for nothing.

"We're all busy, Mr. Aguilar." My voice rose an octave. "That's why we find it so loathsome when people waste our time. I just lost two hours driving out here and sitting in a—"

"Whoa, whoa, Ms. Diamond. I resent the implication. We had an unexpected death in the family. My father is very upset. I thought it would take his mind off things to talk to you for an hour, but I was mistaken."

"I'm sorry about your loss," I said quietly. "Well, I don't want to waste any more of your time and mine so . . ."

"Ms. Diamond? May I propose an alternative? Since we've kept you waiting, perhaps I can free up my schedule and meet with you in his place. *Momentito*."

He yelled something in rapid-fire Spanish that I didn't catch. I hadn't spoken it much since college, and had gotten rusty.

He came back on the line. "Everything is arranged," he told me. His voice was silky, as if he had straightened his tie, slicked back his hair, and stuck a flower in his lapel. He gave me directions, told me to park in the dirt lot adjacent to the arena and head for the trailers to the left.

Feeling slightly ashamed, I agreed. It had rained a few days earlier, which meant the dirt was pretty compact. As I pulled up, I imagined what this place must be like in high summer, with thousands of cars streaming in, making the dust rise and billow in clouds. I stepped out of my car and realized I had misjudged things badly. The surface where the sun beat down was caked and dry, but underneath, the ground was still wet, and my pointy heel broke through the thin membrane of dried dirt and sank through the crust, wobbling, into a muddy swamp.

They were purple heels, with a floral appliqué pattern, and I cherished them precisely because they were so frivolous. Now they would be splattered by mud that probably wouldn't come off. Ruined shoes was one of the occupational hazards of the job, and you couldn't exactly put it on your expense report, although one naïve intern had tried. She had been laughed out of the editor's office, left to stew with the well-worn advice rattling in her brain—keep a pair of boots or tennies in your car for emergencies. But my beaten-down tennies were in the trunk, which meant I had to walk through the muck to get them. And wouldn't I look ridiculous, walking into Felipe Aguilar's office with a tailored skirt and nasty old tennis shoes? Certainly, this was not something that White House reporters traveling on *Air Force One* had to deal with. Still, I wouldn't want their job, I thought, imagining Beltway versions of Severin and Langdon.

I stood there with the October sun beating down on me. In the distance, I heard the faint white-noise roar of the 60, the Pomona Freeway, which led only to other desolate spots like the one I had just reached, far from the nexus of power and influence that was downtown Los Angeles. Here, on the county's forgotten eastern rim, the only hopeful thing about the hard-bitten towns was their names—Artesia, named after an ancient and pure spring; Baldwin Park, a hardscrabble suburb with precious little parkland; and La Puente, which meant "the bridge" in Spanish and spanned a community of working poor and gangs.

Yet at the edge of the dirt lot, where the weeds began, I heard the whirring of hidden insects, the buzzing screech of cicadas, and I could imagine what it had looked like two hundred years earlier, when the land was all hills and plains and native foliage and Indians creeping single file on their way to the Whittier Narrows, hunting for deer and squirrels and acorns. Later came agriculture, tall fields of corn and wheat, then dairy farms. I almost heard the lowing of cattle, the grassy, welcoming smell of baled hay, the pungency of cow manure. I closed my eyes, swaying a moment, and then I did smell it. Opening my eyes, I headed for the smell.

As I rounded an old red barn, the smell of animals grew stronger, and I found myself staring at real bales of hay and cows and horses and manure. Far off, a cock crowed and chickens scratched. A dog ran up, a mangy, burr-ridden animal. I gave him a few wary pets and continued my stroll.

Off to the right was a cluster of trailers, their doors clicking shut with a sharp metallic snap as workers came and went, carrying paperwork.

I found the one that said ADMINISTRACIÓN and walked over, scraping mud off my heels before I entered. Music blared through the window. The reception area was paneled with wood and cooled by a ceiling fan. Along the walls hung gold records, posters of glamorous Mexican stars, and photos of smiling musicians shaking hands with a dignified Latino man sporting gray hair and a paunch who I figured was probably Felipe Aguilar.

A woman wearing an embroidered peasant blouse was filing papers in a steel cabinet, her back toward me, her hips swaying as she sang along to a Spanish pop song piped in from the office stereo system. *"La Mujer en el Espejo"*—"The Woman in the Mirror." The receptionist's head bounced and her foot tapped in rhythm as she shoved papers with great gusto into manila folders, matching her movements to the tempo of the song. I could just catch the gist. With much rolling of *r's,* the singer sang about how she had once been a sweet and innocent girl. But her lover had broken her heart when he left and taught her a cruel lesson. At first she thought she'd die. But slowly she recovered and grew stronger. And now that he was back, smiling sheepishly at her door, it was her turn to reject him. She didn't need his beatings and running around. She had gained self-respect. She had survived. Only one thing still pained her. When she looked in the mirror now, she saw a stranger.

It was incongruous, hearing these feminist lyric flourishes juxtaposed against the traditional ranchera tune. The postmillennial production values featured celestial blips and burbles, reverb, and fuzzy mike work. It made for a peculiar hybrid—heartfelt northern Mexican laments accented with the cool elegance of disengaged electronica. Then the refrain came around again, and this time, the woman clenched her fist and thrust it straight up into the air, pumping her arm up and down as she sang *"La Mujer en el Espejo,"* shouting out the lines of female empowerment as the singer's voice crescendoed and finally ebbed.

As the last chords sounded, I opened the door again and slammed it shut, as if I were just walking in. The girl whirled, dropping her papers, clearly upset to be caught at her impromptu Mexican karaoke.

"Sure is muggy out there," I said, wiping my brow. "Feels good to get inside. I'm here to see Silvio Aguilar."

She flushed and nodded briskly, smoothing down a flouncy skirt. Gone was the wildly gesticulating woman of a minute ago. I saw that her eyes were red. "You here to do an interview?" she asked suspiciously.

"Yeah. For the *Los Angeles Times*."

She examined my card, then shoved it deep into a pocket. "The police coming too?" Her question was casual, but freighted with meaning.

"Should they?" I asked.

She turned on the ball of her foot without answering and hustled out, leaving me alone in the office. The radio was still on, and after a rapid-fire station ID that told me I was listening to ten songs *sin comerciales* from Radio Viva 107.1 FM, I tried to catch the words, but it was mostly a blur until I heard "Arena La Puente" and *"concierto gigante"* and realized it was an advertisement for the place where I now stood. Listeners should bring their old *boletos*—tickets—to get in at the door this coming weekend.

I should listen to this shit more often, I thought, thinking of all that dead time in the car. My Spanish would improve real fast, with those motormouth DJs. But they spoke so fast, it was impossible to keep up. Why do Latinos speak so fast? I wondered, then reconsidered. Anything sounds fast when you can't understand the words. I suppose our English sounded like breakneck speed to them too.

Now my own private ranchera singer returned, and led

me into a large office. She bounced on the balls of her feet, arms hanging stiffly at her sides as Radio Viva serenaded us both, this time a Latin Bryan Ferry singing about how he wanted to drown in the blood of his lover.

She disappeared and I sat in a wooden chair upholstered in rough animal hide. Could that brown-and-white pelt have come from a cow? An autographed guitar hung on the wall, next to more gold records, newspaper clippings in Spanish and English, and a framed peso note. There were posters dating back years announcing that Aguilar Entertainment would present world-renowned singers and acclaimed stars of the cinema, from Cantinflas to Selena. On a large wooden desk, I saw a new poster of a dancing skeleton wearing a sombrero announcing a *Día de los Muertos* Festival. Day of the Dead. We had just gone through a weekend of the dead, I thought, a parade of thirty-five names once all was said and done.

My eyes wandered to a sugar skull that someone was using as a paperweight. It was white and granular, with amber eyes and rainbow-colored teeth, just like the one in Venus's pool house. It sat grinning atop a pile of bills, reminding me of the boarded-up building where I had found Isabel, which sent a ripple of irritation through me because I realized anew that I should be following that story instead of sitting here.

"I'm sorry about the confusion."

I recognized that silky tone from the phone. I hadn't heard him enter, but now I turned to shake his hand. He had hazel eyes and smooth coffee skin and masses of thick black hair he slicked straight back from his high forehead. Softness and angles vied for mastery of his features, starting with his nose, a promontory that jutted out, slashing his face in two. It was a profile I'd seen carved on temples and pyramids across pre-Columbian America. His lips were full and his face clean-shaven, which gave him a boyish air, but the impression was fleeting. His eyes were dark and swollen. The skin below was puffy and smudged. Sorrow had plowed two deep furrows between his brows.

"Welcome, Ms. Diamond. Let us sit down for a few minutes and get acquainted. I can sketch out what we do here and then we'll take a little tour."

There was no accent in his speech, just a faint whiff of Old World courtliness, something elided and baroque that played across his tongue and hinted at other cultures, other languages. It was ineffable really, but something I never caught in the speech of monolingual Americans.

Some interviews are like dancing—you let your partner lead. So I flipped open my notepad and tried not to step on his toes as he swept me away.

He threw out numbers and statistics, describing the 23 million Mexican immigrants who had made America home but still longed for the culture they had left behind. His father had seen a marketing opportunity and stepped in to fill the gap for those who wouldn't, or couldn't, go back.

As he spoke, I took in his indigo Levi's and cowboy boots, scalloped in red and cream and cut from the hide of some scaly and probably endangered species. A white shirt with red piping and mother-of-pearl buttons picked up the color of the boots. His shirt was as creased and starched as a Wall Street bond trader's, but instead of a red power tie, he wore a silver bolo studded with a rough chunk of turquoise. The shirt billowed over a small gut before disappearing into a leather belt with an engraved silver buckle that matched the tie. He stood in the room, talking and scratching the back of his neck as if he had just awoken from a nap, a full-blown Mexican cowboy.

Mexicans had lived here for hundreds of years and helped found El Pueblo de Nuestra Señora la Reina de Los Angeles de Porciuncula back in 1781, Silvio told me. In the last century, millions had come north, driven out by poverty, famine, a rigid class system, and the universal immigrant dream of a better life. In their adopted country, they had spread throughout the fifty states and become poets, bankers, politicians, and activists—and your next-door neighbors.

As he spoke, I found myself returning to the small gut above Silvio Aguilar's belt. It was barely there, really, nothing that two weeks of sweating at the gym wouldn't cure, but I couldn't stop thinking about how soft and vulnerable it was, unlike the rest of him, and I wanted to trace its promontory. And that surprised me, because I usually go for the lean ones, and this one had the sleek look of an otter. Still, I wondered what it would feel like to have that belly pressed against my skin, and something quickened inside me.

Reporter's notepads are marvelous things. They are thin paper masks, behind which I hide, hunched over my spiral lodestone, trying to capture every utterance in flattery to those I interview while my mind runs free, unfettered, a million miles away. So I nodded and smiled as a new ballad started on the radio, this one about a lover's secret tryst.

Silvio had been born here. He had grown up in the business and remembered the time when his dad didn't have an arena and his own shows, but merely sold bootleg tapes out of the back of his van. He'd set up his equipment inside nightclubs and bars and record the stars of the Mexican music circuit as they made the *El Norte* tour, singing their lungs out to patrons homesick for the *corridos* of home. Then Felipe Aguilar duplicated the tapes in his garage, meticulously typing the name of each song on the little cardboard flaps.

"My entire childhood was spent at the Azusa Mall," Silvio said. "Dad would get my brother and me up at four A.M. on weekend mornings so we'd be there when the sun came up. We didn't get back home until dark. Some nights we were too tired to eat dinner."

"I didn't realize Azusa had a mall."

Silvio's painful chuckle demonstrated some cultural gap between us.

"It doesn't have fountains and fancy lighting. There aren't department stores and boutiques and coffee bars. It's the Azusa Swap Meet. The poor man's mall. But it has everything you need. Jeans. Shoes. Pots. Soap and votive candles, hubcaps and electronic gewgaws. Fried food. There are clouds of dust in the summer and mud in the winter. Yes sir, it brings back some not-so-fond memories. Mainly of being bone-tired and having to lug back boxes of unsold tapes."

"Did your parents speak Spanish to you?" I asked, remembering my own childhood, which had been conducted in French.

"My dad went after my brother and me with a two-by-four if we spoke English at home."

Without warning, Silvio stopped his story, put his head in his hands, and said I would have to excuse him for a minute. He sat there for what seemed like a long time.

"You'll have to forgive me," he said when he raised his head. "My younger brother was killed this weekend in front of his home. He was coming home from work.

*Pinche* gangbangers—the neighborhood's getting worse and worse. El Sereno used to be nice. Now it's not so *sereno* anymore. I'm expecting a call any minute from the police."

So that explained the receptionist's query about the cops. The father who was too upset to meet with me. And Silvio's puffy eyes. He gave me a bleary look.

"Now where were we?"

"I'm so sorry. For my insensitivity earlier. Now I understand."

"That's all right. No woman likes being stood up in a bar."

The way he said it, I knew those tourmaline eyes had pierced my paper veil, intuited something beyond the sexless reporter hunched over her notepad, and that despite the grief and pain, I hadn't been wrong about him. I pictured slow, languid, undersea movements in a big white bed. I was starting to get a warm feeling in the pit of my stomach.

"Oh, forget that." I waved him away. "It's just a story."

Something came to me now, a story I had written the day before. "Aguilar's a pretty common name. What was your brother's first name?"

"Ruben."

"Oh jeez. I wrote about your brother's murder in the *Times* today."

He looked up with interest. "I haven't read the *Times* yet." He gestured to his desk, where the day's editions of *La Opinión, The Wall Street Journal,* the *Los Angeles Times, Daily Variety,* the *Hollywood Reporter,* and several regional Mexican newspapers fanned out before him.

That was a lot of verbiage to plow through, I thought, my respect for him shooting up. The music industry really was global today, crossing borders with impunity, so that a New York trader might sell stock in a Mexican broadcasting company to a Japanese bank, with intercontinental success riding on the hunched back of some sixteen-year-old *norteño* musician on the border who hadn't even been discovered yet.

"It was a roundup story. A lot of people got killed this weekend. But I remember the police giving me the details about your brother."

What I didn't tell him is that I had pegged it for just another senseless gang shooting, but that now it seemed different, with his brother sitting across the desk from me, displaying the shattered grief of a survivor.

Silvio said nothing, but slid *La Opinión* across the desk. I saw a photo of a man who looked a lot like the man before me, but more angular and tightly wound, where Silvio seemed sleepy and slow to kindle.

"Our paper did an obit." He shrugged. "My family's fairly prominent in the Latino community."

*Our* paper, I thought. That was a slap in the face to *my* paper. But it was also reality. As assimilated as he was, and as much as he read it for business, Silvio's hometown paper wasn't the *Los Angeles Times*. And it wasn't even in English. That's exactly why the *Times* had been losing circulation lately, and no one knew how to fix it.

"We're all still in shock. My brother had his own business, cleaning pools. He didn't want to get his shoes scuffed with dust and horse manure every day. Gisela out there"—he pointed to the outer office, to the woman who had serenaded me—"was his fiancée. She works for us. We didn't want her to come in today but she insisted. Said it would make her feel better."

"I'm so sorry."

I paused. "Why didn't your brother work in the family business? It sounds a lot better than cleaning pools."

Silvio squinted and looked out the window. My gaze followed his, and I saw the grandstand rising behind us.

"He was too proud. He wanted to make his own way. And his business was expanding like you wouldn't believe. He was starting to get some famous clients. And not just Mexicans."

"Another immigrant success story," I said. "Maybe I should write about him next."

But I knew I wouldn't. I was sorry I had gone off on this tangent about his brother. It was Silvio and his father I needed to focus on, not the dead prodigal with the hungry eyes.

"Yeah, he had Brad Pitt. He did his pool. And Cameron Diaz. And what's her name . . ." Silvio Aguilar snapped his fingers. "Demeter, Diana, Aphrodite, oh hell, I'm getting all my ancient goddess names mixed up. Venus. That's it. He was supposed to start doing Venus Dellaviglia and Carter Langdon. And she had promised to turn him on to a bunch of her friends."

I stared at him and chose my next words carefully. "I don't think she's going to be doing anything much anymore. Maybe *La Opinión* didn't carry a big story, but the *Times* did. She was found dead yesterday morning, right about the time the police told me about your brother. Floating naked in her very blue, very clean pool."

I watched his reaction.

He stared down at his desk and moved the papers around minutely, shifting them. He sucked air in through his teeth, then exhaled noisily.

"Christ," he said, and a muscle in his jaw twitched slowly and repeatedly. "That's too bad."

"Horrible coincidence, huh?"

He raised his eyes. "They have any suspects?"

"Not yet."

"I can only hope our city's finest will deploy as many resources to solving my brother's murder as they do to solving hers."

He smiled grimly as he said it, knowing the answer as well as I did. Then he put his palms on the desk and pushed himself into a semi-erect position.

"Well, Ms. Diamond, can I invite you back on Sunday for our Siglo de Oro concert? It got rained out last weekend. I'll get you a box seat. You can bring a friend. . . ."

There was something probing in his voice.

My brain had been feverishly working all the angles on the murder connection, and his question jolted me back to reality. I didn't want to leave right now with so many things unanswered.

"I'd rather come solo and tag along with you behind the scenes to see what you do?" Despite myself, my voice rose in that despicable way that has now been calibrated as "Val-speak." But I meant it. It would add color to my story. "How about that tour?"

"No can do. Sorry, I had to rejuggle my schedule just to see you, but I don't seem to be able to concentrate on anything except my brother's death. The funeral's Thursday. But the show must go on and I promise you'll get quite a tour this weekend though you may find some of it distasteful. Not the music, though that's an acquired taste." He smiled, as if at some secret joke I didn't get. "But the *charreada*. That's our Mexican rodeo. There's the barnyard smells. And some women don't go in for lassoing bulls and bucking broncs. We're even starting to get the animal-rights protestors showing up."

He was laying down the gauntlet—we're nothing but a bunch of country bumpkins. It's not exactly the Buena Vista Social Club.

"Perfect for my story," I said.

# CHAPTER 11

T he jangling phone woke me up the next morning. It was Vincent Chevalier, calling to confirm we were still meeting. He wanted me to come to his house. His voice was whispery on the other end, intimate and low, as if he were telling me a slightly sordid secret. The guy unnerved me.

"I'll show you her bedroom," he said. "I know reporters like to describe what dead kids put up on the walls, the stuffed animals on their beds." He gave a hiccupping laugh that ended in a snort. It was so true, what he said, but I felt again how inappropriate his comments and behavior were. It was an odd way to show grief. And I didn't want to be standing in the dead girl's bedroom with the fey, twitching Chevalier behind me, his long, skinny fingers wrapped around the doorknob, blocking the only path out.

Then I had an inspiration. We'd need photos. That meant a photographer. In the San Gabriel Valley, that meant Harry Jack. He'd grumble, of course, and complain that he couldn't fit it in on such short notice, and why hadn't I filed the photo assignment the day before, but he'd be there. Harry was seventy-four if he was a day, small and spry and remarkably fit, still shimmying up trees and dropping to his arthritic knees to get the shot. And he clung like a limpet to his job, despite the *Times*'s best efforts to pry him loose into what could no longer be called "early retirement."

Stubborn and cranky, like someone's kvetching

grandfather, Harry was a relic of a more freewheeling time in journalism when city editors kept bottles in their desk drawers, "girl" reporters were banished to the society pages, and City Hall journos moonlighted by running the mayor's reelection campaign.

The stories about Harry were legend—the time he arrived at a Times Awards Banquet with a hooker on each arm; the bar where he told off Frank Sinatra and lived to laugh about it; the day he overheard two bookies fixing a big fight and rushed to bet two weeks' pay before shooting the spectacle. Now in the twilight of his career, Harry had been shooed out of downtown and into the suburbs, where he wouldn't embarrass anybody with his frank manner or spark any sexual harassment lawsuits with his ribald tales. If you looked hard enough, you could still find forgotten characters like him inhabiting the dusty nooks and crannies of my modern, streamlined, politically correct newspaper. They were relics of a bygone time who stubbornly refused to acknowledge their own extinction. When they finally shuffled off the mortal coil that was the *Times,* they joined the Old Farts' Club, a garrulous group of old Timesmen and a few women who gathered each month at a Burbank restaurant to relive their old glory, trade gossip about the latest changes, and complain about how the paper had dwindled along with their eyesight. Yup, Harry was a true old salt, and each time I went out with him on a story, I realized anew that downtown's loss was deepest suburbia's gain.

I caught him on his cell phone.

"Aw, Eve, I'm halfway to Pomona to shoot that varsity team thing, don't make me turn around in this traffic and go back to Pasadena," his nasal voice rose in indignation.

"But this could be our only chance. Daddy-O's in a pensive mood and he's agreed to let us into the house."

Grumble grumble grumble went the voice on the other end of the phone. I stood there, torn between playing badass reporter and telling him the truth, which I knew would immediately invoke his paternal side— that Vincent Chevalier creeped out this girl reporter who didn't want to be alone in a big empty house with him.

But Harry was already wheeling his company sedan off the freeway and queuing up with all the other cattle to join the daily stampede to the city center.

"Okay, Eve, I'm turning around, but don't expect me to be there anytime soon, this traffic's a mother today. Why, I remember when . . ."

I pulled out the *Thomas Guide* to hunt for Chevalier's address.

Then I called Thompson to make sure he didn't need me. He said a brown bear had come down from the San Gabriel Mountains to take a dip in some Monrovia resident's pool, but he planned to send another reporter on it. I hung up and glanced at the front page of the *Times*. There were three stories about the upcoming mayor's race and a double-bylined story by Joshua Brandywine and Tony Hausman about the latest developments on the Venus Dellaviglia Langdon murder. There were no suspects yet, and I imagined the pressure on the cops must be severe. Then I noticed Josh had a sidebar story. To my shock, it recounted how the LAPD had lost the black chiffon scarf found at the scene of Venus's murder. Carter Langdon III had told the police that it was his wife's scarf, though he couldn't remember if she had been wearing it that day. Then it had been ticketed as evidence, only to disappear. An internal investigation was under way and several police commissioners said it was time to revamp the evidence department because of "continuity" problems.

I sat there, holding the paper, thinking that they were all missing the point. What if the black chiffon scarf had disappeared because it had never been there in the first place? Talk about a scarf would throw everyone off the scent of what really had been found near the murder site—a man's bathing suit. I had seen it with my own eyes. But what was my word against the LAPD's? I wasn't even officially on the story anymore. Besides, I had my own murder to keep me busy—Isabel Chevalier's. It might be a whole lot less glamorous than Venus's, but it was a murder nonetheless, and I vowed to make the murdered squatter kid pop into such 3-D color that people would forget all about Venus.

Harry's white, *Times*-issue sedan was parked in front of Chevalier's Georgian manor house when I pulled in. The old shutterbug was hunched over his trunk, swinging camera bags onto his bony shoulder and checking lenses. If Chevalier tried anything, I could always grab one of the heavy black things, solid as a lead pipe, and womp him upside the head. But Harry was my good luck amulet. With his reassuring presence, nothing would happen now. Besides, I was being paranoid. The poor guy was in mourning.

Chevalier met us at the door. He was wearing a blue-and-gray plaid bathrobe that ended just short of his pale, knoblike knees. He started when he saw Harry, then stood there, rubbing his hands together, as we walked in. This was one weird dude. He knew I was coming. Why hadn't he gotten dressed?

"How ya doing, Mr. Chevalier, Harry Jack here. *L.A. Times* fotog. And you already know Ms. Diamond. I'm sorry to hear about that daughter of yours."

Harry grabbed Chevalier's hands, untangling one from the other like he was separating brambles, and pumped up and down. He stepped back to appraise Chevalier.

"Looks like we caught you before you had a chance to dress. I can understand, after all you've been through. But we can't shoot you in that there bathrobe. Why don't you go put on some slacks while we set up. Eve here will be happy to iron you a shirt."

I opened my mouth to tell him off, to suggest that I'd iron the clothes if he'd fetch the coffee, but closed it when I saw his face crinkle up in a wink. Then he slapped his forehead with his palm and said, "Whoops, Mr. Chevalier, I forgot, we can't ask the gals to do that kind of work anymore. It's not in the job description."

"It never was, Harry," I muttered as Chevalier finally got the joke and broke into a weak smile. Harry was bringing him back to life. "I'll be back," Chevalier whispered.

Harry looked at the photos lining the hallway. Isabel at age three, holding up a squirming puppy, both of them still brimming with baby fat. At six in her Brownie uniform. Giggling with friends at ten. Then the punk beginning to come out at thirteen, the pink-streaked hair and the scowl. Harry shook his head.

"It's a damn shame, a man's daughter gets murdered. Looks like a sweet kid."

"She was." Chevalier was back. He had put on a long-sleeved shirt and khakis and splashed water on his face. Drops still clung to his long forelocks, tap water dew from a malevolent morning.

Harry bustled off to the bathroom, returning with a comb, which he thrust into Chevalier's face.

"Why don't you run this through once or twice, get yourself presentable," Harry said. He shook his head and reached for his cameras. "Fathers shouldn't have to bury their children. It goes against the natural order. I know. I buried one of mine too."

My head jerked up at the same moment as Chevalier's. "You did?" we asked in unison.

"Yeah, I did. I never told you that, Eve? My youngest boy. He was sixteen and the leukemia got him. They didn't know how to put it in remission like they do today." Harry Jack shook his head, then dug into his camera bag and pulled out another filter.

A small cynical voice inside my brain was wondering if this was true, or if he was just trying to put Chevalier at ease with a ghastly gray lie. Either way, it was working. Chevalier's eyes seemed to focus and he snapped to attention. Here was another man who had experienced great sorrow and come out the other side.

"How did you cope?" he asked.

Harry made a clicking sound with his mouth. "Not very well. I drank too much. My marriage broke up." He stopped, realizing that this was not what Chevalier needed to hear.

"It's a lie that you get over it," he continued, "but the grief does dull. Whole hours go by and you don't even think of it. Then one day a photo of mine got plastered all over Page One and it felt good. Only for a moment, but it was a beginning. Yeah, life's a funny thing. He would have been about your age, Eve."

It chilled me, thinking what I would have missed if my life had been snuffed out at sixteen. That sent my thoughts hurtling back to Matthew, my kid brother, whose life had ended tragically in his early teens. He had gotten drunk and fallen off a balcony at a party and been killed when his head hit the concrete of a swimming pool, while I was just twenty feet away, the older sister who was supposed to be watching over him.

So here we were, three people brought together by work, each of us nursing private vigils for our own dead loved ones. Time shimmered and broke in waves around me, uniting me with these two men who had also suffered. Then the moment passed, and we were just three people with unpleasant jobs to do.

"When did your daughter start getting into punk?" I asked Chevalier, pointing to the photo of Isabel with black-dyed tresses and a ripped shirt, a safety pin stuck in her cheek. She seemed to have changed her hair color every week.

"She was, uh, thirteen, I think. Let's ask Sophie and Caitlin. They're in her room."

"So you were able to round them up."

He was full of curveballs, this Chevalier. Here I had been afraid to come to his house alone, and it turned out that his daughter's friends had been here all along, holed up in her bedroom. But that still didn't explain the bathrobe. Didn't his daughter's friends find that somewhat unusual?

"I was about to get in the shower when you knocked," Chevalier said, reading my mind. "The girls are willing to talk, but they want to make sure you're not going to hype Isabel as some little dumb punkette who got what she deserved."

"This is the *L.A. Times,* not the *National Enquirer,*" I told him, wondering to myself what exactly the difference was anymore. But my answer seemed to satisfy him, and he led us down a hallway with a low ceiling that made me feel claustrophobic. We entered the room of a little girl who, despite the bristling aggression in her latest photos, hadn't yet had time to remake herself completely, to jettison the pink wallpaper and ceramic bunny collection so lovingly assembled in childhood. They lined a top shelf. On a lower shelf, where she had easier access, the transformation was well under way—spiked belts and Iggy Pop record covers, an empty bottle of Jack Daniel's with a half-melted red candle stuck in the neck, flyers for Nine Inch Nails, Korn, and Rancid, a skull-and-crossbones mug filled with dried flower petals. There was a poster of the Sex Pistols, Johnny Rotten's mouth twisted into its eternal sneer. Next to it sat an Algebra II textbook and an English 202 paper entitled "Rimbaud—Punk's Original Bad Boy," which had earned Isabel an "A."

Reporters were urban archaeologists when it came to compiling human portraits. We excavated ruined lives, and Isabel's was all laid out before me here in her lair, her half-finished pilgrimage from frills to barbs. I knew without looking that there was a recently discarded Britney Spears poster in the closet, maybe even girly skirts and flowery tops folded in brown paper bags ready to be donated to the Goodwill. Now her uniform was metal T-shirts, steel-tipped boots, and black jeans. In another few months, the metamorphosis would have been complete, but here, it could still be documented at odd angles.

A door burst open, revealing a pink bathroom with white tile, and two girls came out, holding tissues to their noses and sniffing back tears. One had dyed platinum hair and wore hip-hugger jeans with a big, braided leather belt. A push-up bra accentuated her bosom, barely contained in a shiny scoop-neck Lycra top. The other girl had flame-dyed hair and was tall and angular, dressed all in black. They walked over to Isabel's bed and arrayed themselves across the bedspread like divas posing for some Marilyn Monroe photo shoot. Harry, who hadn't missed a beat, started murmuring, "Fabulous, hold it right there, now turn to the right," and I heard the click and whir of his camera start up.

Sophie was the blonde one, Caitlin the dark wraith, and they pouted and posed and fiddled with their nails and asked what kind of story I was planning. So I launched into my little song and dance about filling in the details of Isabel's life and her personality and her accomplishments and her greatest yearnings and what kind of friend she was, and I soon saw that it was all a front, and that they would have talked to me no matter what I said.

"Isabel had a loud mouth, and she could piss off people who didn't know her, but she was a caretaker," Sophie told me. "She loved people and would give them her last dollar, buy them food. She gave me this stud on my birthday, when my own parents forgot." Sophie fingered a diamond that sparkled in her left nostril.

"She wrote poetry and wanted to be a lawyer so she could help poor people," Caitlin added, gathering the hair around her face and twisting it atop her head in a knot. "You should have seen her at the mock trial. She was fantastic."

I felt uncomfortable asking about her boyfriend while Chevalier was still in the room, but luckily Harry shoved a framed photo of Isabel into his hand and led him outside, to where the morning light cast its pale magic.

I decided to probe about Mr. Dad while I had the chance.

"So Isabel's parents are divorced?"

"Her mom's a hippie. Lives on some ashram in India. They split when Isabel was ten and she hasn't seen her since. But her pops, he's so cool. We all wish we had dads like Vince. We hang out here, this is the clubhouse. He lets us do what we want."

So creepy Vincent Chevalier was cool. Imagine that. Boy, was I out of the loop. But somewhere, there was a disconnect that I had yet to put my finger on. It didn't track. Neither did kids who ran away when they had a decent home life. I decided to throw out a line.

"Was Isabel a happy girl? Or was she troubled? For instance, do you think someone could have been abusing her?"

They looked at each other, then back at me.

"I don't know any teenagers who are happy," Caitlin said slowly.

"And if you mean, like, her father?" Sophie whispered. "No way. She had a great relationship with her father. Everyone loves Vince. We call him Dad. Many of us don't have fathers in the picture. So we tell Vince what's going on in our lives. None of us was ever abused. We just liked to experiment and rebel. But we had it under control."

Yeah, right, I thought. Isabel had it so under control that she ended up dead in some fetid squat.

I'm on the pale side, and sometimes my dark thoughts flicker across my face for everyone to see.

Sophie lit up a cigarette.

"I know you'd like to think that Isabel had a fucked-up childhood and that's why she ran away," she said. "Adults need that cause and effect. Two plus two equals four. Like she saw her dad run over her puppy when she was five or got raped by her uncle when she was six and that's why. It makes adults feel better when they can find a reason."

She tipped her ash into a pink ceramic tray that looked like it had been fired in a high school art-class kiln.

"But what if there's no why?" she continued. "What if it just is what it is? That scares the shit out of people. Cuz that means it could happen to your daughter. To your kid sister. Sometimes teenagers just do stuff and there's no easy reason."

I was shocked that she had articulated my thoughts so accurately.

"I understand what you're saying. But tell me something . . ."

I struggled with how to phrase my next question without offending them. They smelled nice. Their hair was shiny clean. Their heads brimmed with algebraic theorems and Enlightenment poetry. Somewhere on their desk was an application to a four-year college.

"I understand how it might sound romantic to run away," I finally said. "But what do you do when five days have passed and you're cold and wet and hungry and wearing the same stinky clothes and there's some psychotic kid puking or shooting up next to you? Doesn't that get old pretty fast?"

"Oh no," Sophie said. Her eyes went all glazed and soft. "It's exciting. Like . . . Girl Scouts or something. Learning to survive in the wilderness."

She looked at me, uncertain of her metaphor.

"But this is a dangerous urban wilderness," I said.

"Haven't you read George Orwell's *Down and Out in Paris and London?*" Caitlin asked. "Or Arthur Koestler's biography? Young people have been doing this forever. We're just doing it our own way."

What a dangerous age is adolescence, I thought. They were smart and well-read enough to rationalize their behavior. But they lacked the wisdom and maturity to see the argument to its ultimate conclusion.

"With one slight difference. Orwell and Koestler had no choice. They really were down and out. You guys aren't."

"Our lives are boring and predictable," Caitlin agreed. "So we like to challenge ourselves."

"I spoke to a youth counselor in Hollywood who said a lot of the street kids are predators, especially the guys."

"That's the exception," Sophie rushed in. "Most of them are smart and really sweet, once you get to know them. They just never got a chance. They were in foster care or had psycho parents. So they ran away. It's not their fault. They're just trying to survive."

"So you give them a second chance?" I said dryly.

"They're just . . ." Sophie said.

"Cool," added Caitlin. "It's hard to explain. They're rebels. They're not like the dweebs at our school. They're mature. They live totally outside society."

I was writing it all down. It was the age-old adolescent rebellion with a new twist, in which the ideal prom date was a homeless predatory street kid and no one lived happily ever after.

"But I wonder what that kind of life does to your psyche," I said. "I've heard a lot of these street kids are mentally ill and whacked from drugs. Doesn't all this take its toll? You guys can go back home when things get too rough. They can't. Does that cause friction?"

"No way," said Sophie, with a disarming naïveté. "We buy them food, bring them home to sleep and shower. We help them. We admire how they live."

"You don't think they'd want to trade places with you?"

"They despise our bourgeois upbringing. I don't blame them," Caitlin said fiercely. "So we try to be, like, socialist. Share what we have. It makes us feel less guilty about our privileged lives."

"You want to work off some guilt, you could volunteer at a soup kitchen. Or a home for the elderly."

I knew as I said it that my suggestion lacked one crucial element—libido. The danger and sex wrapped into one testosterone-fueled package.

"That would feel like an obligation, like going to church. This is fun. We learn how to survive on the street. It toughens us up."

"Yeah, Isabel survived real well. This Finch guy. Can you tell me more about their relationship? Why would he kill her?"

They both sat up on the bed now. "He didn't kill her," Caitlin said, indignant beyond belief.

Sophie chimed in. "He's crazy at times, really gone, but he's a fucking brilliant man, really stellar, he can recite Verlaine and Baudelaire. He's read the Bhagavad Gita. And you should see his paintings, they're like German Expressionist. I showed one to my art teacher and she said he could probably get a scholarship to Cal Arts. He's that good."

Her eyes went all dreamy again, and I saw what the psychologist meant when he had talked about how ripe these girls were to be taken advantage of.

"But he's too creative and individual to fit into our conformist society," Sophie was saying. "He wants no part of it. So he smokes his weed and tends to his squats. He's the squat Nazi."

"Squat Nazi?"

"He's the head of the squat. He makes the rules and enforces them. Anyone who doesn't obey has to leave. He's like the emperor."

"But a good emperor," Caitlin hastened to add. "When I ran away from home, Finch protected me. Made sure no one raped me. It can get crazy in the squats. But sometimes it's chill. I didn't get to stick around for too long cuz my mom found me and made me come back."

There was annoyance in her voice, the quashing of this party, her adventure. "He let me share his sleeping bag and bought me food. He's the one who taught me how to squat."

I found this black rite of passage horrifying and fascinating at the same time. Private school girl rebels by running away from home and squatting with psychopathic street kids.

"You'll never find Finch," Caitlin continued. "He's lying low cuz of all this heat. But if you want to find someone who knew him and Isabel, you should talk to Scout. She was tight with Isabel these last months."

"Scout, huh. Did she go to school with you too? Do you have a number for her?"

Sophie giggled. "She doesn't go to school, exactly. Unless you count the school of hard knocks." More giggles. "She's from Portland, came down a couple months ago to squat here. She's real spacey and skittish. I don't even know her real name. Her street name is Scout, on account of she often wears a Girl Scout uniform. She had a thing for Isabel though. Followed her around. Thought she was her older sister and, like I said, Isabel was a caretaker. She helped Scout a lot. She was talking to some agencies about finding Scout a place to live and going back to school. She knew that was important. Scout was devastated when she learned Isabel had been killed. We heard she was collecting shit for a shrine."

"For Isabel?"

"Yeah. People who knew her are going by and putting up stuff in front of where she was killed."

Harry Jack came clomping back into the room, complaining about his beeper going off. He had to get back to the office and wanted a few more shots of everyone. Submissive as a lamb, Chevalier shuffled into his daughter's bedroom. He picked up a pair of her earrings, then a David Bowie CD, scrutinizing them as though they belonged to a stranger. The girls balked at more photos. This was not what they imagined models had to put up with in fashion shoots, Sophie said indignantly.

"That's where you got it all wrong," Jack said. "Hey, girls, did I ever tell you about when I photographed Ava Gardner's fiancé at their home in Beverly Hills? This was after she and Frank broke up."

"Sinatra?" Caitlin said.

"Ol' Blue Eyes himself. Hold it right there a minute." The camera got off a few shots.

"I walk into this big mansion, and Ava is curled up barefoot on the living room couch, looking glamorous. The fiancé is playing piano. He was some kind of musician too. Caitlin, stand over there by those photos, take one down and stare at it like you're sad.

"Yeah, well, I was supposed to take this fellow's picture. But he told me, 'Don't bother, it's her they want, they'll never run my photo in the paper.' And I said, 'You do as I say and I guarantee your picture will run in every paper in America.'"

"What did you tell him to do?" Sophie asked.

"I told the guy, 'You get over there, kneel by the couch and kiss her toes.'"

"And did he do it?"

"Yeah, he did it. And you know what? That picture ran around the world. Thank you, girls," Harry Jack said, straightening up.

"Wow, have you ever shot Madonna?"

"I've shot everyone," Harry Jack said, as I got all their

phone numbers with promises I could call them again if I needed.

It was easy to see why Harry had been so successful. Now if only some of that success would rub off on me. I had a hunch I wanted to check out. So I turned the car west and headed for Hollywood.

# CHAPTER 12

Traffic was bad on the freeway, and I overshot my exit because a road-hogging, gas-guzzling, cell-phone-using SUV driver wouldn't let me over. Probably didn't even see me, flea-speck that I was, riding on his gleaming left buttock of a bumper. I got off in the heart of old Hollywood and doubled back east along the once-glamorous boulevard, past Grauman's Chinese Theater, where footprints still slumbered in the concrete, and Frederick's of Hollywood, from which angry young men had looted black-lace push-up bras and red satin teddies in the '92 L.A. riots. After years of decline, the old harlot was getting a major face-lift, and the boulevard, long abandoned to the homeless and unwary tourists, teemed with life and purpose again, as developers restored Art Deco masterpieces and erected instant classics of glass and steel. The street kids and older bums seemed more wary than I remembered, like coyotes flushed out of their habitats as civilization encroaches. I heard cranes and drill hammers, bulldozers moving earth and men yelling orders, sounds that hadn't rung out in this part of town since the 1920s. Then, as if on cue, it stopped.

Stuck at a three-way light, I watched a phalanx of construction workers in white hard hats pour out of a building site, moving in formation past the Hollywood stars embedded in the stained sidewalk. As they got the green light, they turned and streamed across the boulevard.

It made me think of a Norman Rockwell painting to see them walking so erect and dignified, steel lunch boxes clutched like a businessman's briefcase. They wore work boots, white T-shirts, and jeans that showed off muscled physiques. It had been years since I had seen construction workers like this in the middle of L.A. Most of them were white, and by their carriage alone they telegraphed that they were well-paid union workers, light-years removed from the day laborers who clustered at corners, a palpable desperation in their eyes that said, Hire me please. No job too hard—$6.00 an hour will do. And as the last of them streamed past and a car honked impatiently behind me, I realized I had just witnessed a migration of dinosaurs. Each year fewer blue-collar jobs paid a living wage. How long would it be before these men joined their *compañeros* at the corner?

I turned right on Western, then left on Manzanita. Even before I got close to the abandoned building where Isabel had died, I knew my hunch had been right. Someone was there. I drove past, casing my quarry. She was a thin girl wearing long cut-off jeans and a T-shirt that said "Korn." She had a tattoo around her bicep and a backward Lakers baseball cap covering long, dishwater blonde hair that was as scraggly as the rest of her. She crouched there, weaving something in and out of the cyclone fencing.

I parked a block away, stuck my notebook in my purse, and walked back toward her, memorizing what I saw. She didn't look up as I passed, and I went a ways, then turned around. At her feet were puddles of melted candle wax, piles of beach sand, and bouquets of sun-flowers and roses picked from nearby yards and shrivel-ing in the sun. Pinned to the fence were buttons for heavy metal and punk bands, along with a photo of the dead Isabel and little poems, prayers, and thoughts. "You're in a better place now, little angel," read one. "We miss you!" "Rock on from up high." They were signed with street names—Squeaky, Tiny, Star Girl, Finch, Scout, and Chill Bill.

I was surprised to see Finch's name. Wasn't he the main suspect? But didn't they say the perp always went back to the scene of the crime? The girl straightened, aware that I had stopped and was staring.

"Scout?" I asked.

"Who wants to know?"

She ran her sleeve along her nose.

"I'm a reporter. I'm, uh, doing a story about your friend. This shrine here, it's a beautiful testament that Isabel was loved. You loved her, didn't you? You wanna tell me about her?"

The girl put her hand to her mouth and giggled, then backed away from me slowly. I saw that her eyes were unfocused. They were blue and watery, but an unearthly light shone from them, as if something smoldered out of control, deep inside her head. She had high, plump cheekbones and tiny ears, and her stringy hair fell into her face. She could have been a young eighteen or a very old thirteen.

"I'm not going back to Mac, you can't make me," she said, swaying. Then came that strange and unearthly laugh again and I knew that the synapses of her brain had gone astray, firing in strange wild uncharted paths where I could not follow.

"Isabel promised, she promised. Fucking wicked witch. And now little Finch has flown away, seeking warmer weather. And it's getting colder by the minute, oh so cold. Ice is coming, creeping, running." The girl turned to me, shivering now, her teeth chattering, her face contorted. "And it will come for you."

The incantation chilled me, standing on that broken sidewalk on a warm fall day. But I persevered.

"Scout, what did Isabel promise you? And where is Finch? It's very important."

But it was too late. With an agility that astonished me, Scout shimmied up the fence, jumped the eight feet down to the ground on the other side, and sprinted to the far edges of the abandoned property. Then, as nimbly as a squirrel, she shot up the chain-link fence on the other side, leapt down, and disappeared into a side street. I ran to the car and tore off after her. But by the time I got there, the street was empty.

Damn, I thought. That is one crazy little girl. Something about my questions had scared Scout pretty thoroughly. What did she know about the murder? Standing there on the sidewalk, fingering the pretty ribbons Scout had woven for her dead friend, I realized that the little street kid cared about Isabel. She was drawn to this place. To this shrine. And she'd be back.

The rest of the week passed slowly as I chiseled away at my squatter kids story, methodical as a stonecutter. Sunday afternoon, I found myself unaccustomedly lingering at my closet door, trying and then discarding outfits. Who are you dressing for? I asked myself accusingly. Not for him, I answered, I just want to be comfortable. I reached into the back of my closet, dusting off a pair of old black cowboy boots I hadn't worn in years. I found a pair of skinny jeans and shimmied into them. Then I fished out a scoop-necked burgundy blouse and topped it off with a black Parisian suede jacket with a fake fur collar that nipped in at the waist and ended high on my hips. I looked over my shoulder into the mirror and nodded. Trust those French to make anything sexy.

I put on Viva as I drove down to La Puente. It seemed that every five minutes, the announcer paused breathlessly to hype the concert I was about to attend. When I switched to Super Estrella, the other Spanish-language station I had discovered, I heard the same ads. Both played too many lame pop ballads. Although I liked the edgy rock songs better, it was easier to pick up the words in the slow ones.

So I drove, moving to the groovin' as the smog hung yellow-brown in the air. Big rigs rumbled past me, their drivers bouncing in high seats. Industrial sprawl and mall outlets and cookie cutter houses grew on each side of me as I drove El Cinco, the Five, the concrete causeway east of downtown. Then I merged east onto the 60. You didn't see so many Mercedes and SUVs on this freeway, but more beat-up jalopies with lowered suspension, people driving with the windows rolled down and their elbows hanging out, the poor man's air-conditioning.

I got off the freeway at La Puente and drove north to the arena. Traffic inched along, whole families loaded down with picnic baskets, toddlers, and grandmas, everyone trying to get a good seat for the evening's entertainment. It took twenty minutes to go a half mile. When I pulled into the lot, the dirt billowed up.

This time when I walked into the office, the receptionist's desk was empty. But a Spanish-TV crew was milling around. I saw a suited female reporter with glossy hair and a red silk blouse flipping through a press kit. The cameramen fiddled with their equipment and joked in Spanish. I went past them, down the hallway and to the doorway of the inner office.

Silvio was on the phone, typing into his computer. He looked up absently as I entered, went back to his call, then looked up again as my presence registered, and then he gave me a real look, adjusting his chair for a better view. I wondered if he had looked the same way at the pretty Canal 52 reporter in the front office. Now he motioned me to wait a minute, swiveled in his chair, turned his back to me, and began typing something into his computer.

I eased out of the office, back down the hall, and took a seat with all the other supplicants.

He came out a minute later, and I saw now that he was wearing a cream-colored guayabera shirt—the dressy Mexican shirt with accordion pleats—over loose slacks, and looked like some wealthy Mexican landowner out for a stroll around his ranch.

He was immediately swarmed by the TV crew and signaled that it would be another few minutes. I decided I should write this all down, so I edged over and tried to decipher the interview in my sketchy Spanish.

I didn't need an interpreter's license to see that Silvio and the TV reporter were flirting. She was giggling at his jokes and giving him looks that bespoke an easy intimacy. They were probably lovers.

I asked a production assistant what it was all about and she explained that the reporter had asked Silvio about a controversial singer who wrote songs about *narcotraficantes*—drug dealers. Silvio was explaining that he'd never invite the singer to play Arena La Puente because the music glorified violence much the same way as gangsta rap did.

I noticed that Gisela, the dead brother's fiancée, was watching me watching Silvio and the TV reporter as their heads bent together. I thanked the production assistant and walked over to Gisela, remembering the queer way in which she had sung along defiantly to that song the other day right after the murder of her beloved.

"I'm so sorry about your fiancé," I said. "It's terrible and unjust."

Her face hardened. I was afraid she thought me presumptuous, but then her upper lip twitched and her nostrils flared and I realized she was trying not to cry.

"He was a good man. He worked fourteen hours a day. So we could have a life."

"Silvio said Ruben's business was taking off. That he had just got a bunch of new high-profile clients."

"Yeah," she said bitterly. "A lot of good it does us now."

"Gisela, did your fiancé have any enemies who might have wanted him killed? Like maybe a business partner or someone who did these people's pools before he took over the work?"

Now she turned a stony gaze on me, and it was as empty and flinty as the Irwindale gravel pits.

"What are you, the police? They asked me that too. No, Ruben had no enemies that I know of."

"Last weekend was a bad one for murder in the city," I said. "Did you know that one of Ruben's new clients, a woman named Venus Dellaviglia Langdon, was also murdered? In her pool."

"She that rich white bitch was gonna set Ruben up? I never met her, but Ruben told me some stories about her. No, I didn't know she got murdered too. That's too bad."

"What kind of stories?"

Gisela yawned. "Oh, the usual. Her kid is all fucked up. She's fooling around on her husband. Ruben talked to the gardener. You wanna know something about someone, you talk to their help."

"Who was she sleeping with? And is her kid on drugs, or what?"

"Hey," she poked me in the ribs, "there you go with

those cop questions again. He never told me nothing specific. We had better things to talk about. Like us, and how we was going to live in a big house ourselves one day, get us some servants. And now that is all blown sky-high because of some punk gangbanger. You put that in your paper, huh. Write how one way or another, the poor people always get screwed."

"I understand your grief, but I'm a little confused. I thought your fiancé's family had done real well and that you're not exactly poor."

She glared at me. "Yeah, they did. What of it? Ruben wanted to make it on his own terms, and I supported that one hundred and ten percent. He was what you'd call the black sheep. He didn't mind me working here; they been good to me, and we needed the money. But as soon as his swimming pool business expanded, Ruben was going to take me on full-time. He didn't want to depend on his parents."

"Well, hopefully you can stay on here, right? They'll take care of you, I mean?"

"The Aguilars? Oh yeah, I'll have a job here, I want it, till the day I die. I just don't know if I can stand coming to work each day now, seeing all of them, reminding me of Ruben."

Gisela studied Silvio now, who was still deep in conversation with the TV lady.

"Look at him, he got a way with the women, huh?"

"You think?"

She shrugged. "That TV reporter is my friend. For a long time, they went together."

"Oh yeah?" All of a sudden, I was fascinated by a government plaque that honored the Aguilars' contribution to Mexican culture. But from the corner of my eye, I saw the reporter reach out a manicured hand to touch

Silvio's face. From it glinted a large teardrop diamond.

I decided to play stupid.

"He sure gave her a nice ring."

"Nah," Gisela said with a hint of derision. "That ain't from him. It's not his style. He's worth millions, but he still lives in the barrio. He shops at the 99 Cent Store and eats at the *taquerias*. Wants to stay close to *la gente*."

"And tele-babe didn't care for that?"

"She was in it for the *plata*. They had great sex, but when she learned he wasn't living large, she bailed. Got herself a new *novio*."

"*Plata?*"

"*Dinero*. Simoleons. Bucks, baby. Ain't it always about the bucks?"

I looked at her and shrugged. "Not always."

She gave me a little, unfriendly push and her metallic laugh filled the room.

"Go to him, *huera*, you two would get along."

Then the reporter came up to Gisela and the two women went into the next room, chatting in Spanish. My cheeks were red as Silvio ambled toward me. Suddenly, I knew a lot more about him than he knew about me, details that were highly important for reasons that would never make it into the story.

"C'mon," he told me, "we're missing all the fun."

The amplified sound rained down on us as we walked outside, growing louder as we neared the stage. A woman who appeared to be in her late sixties, her red lipstick and rouged cheeks setting off immense false eyelashes and jet-black hair pulled into a tight bun, was singing huskily into a microphone on the bare stage. Silvio told me her name was Maria Castro. She was a smoldering legend come to life, her voice an elixir for the homesick, who had hand-carried her recordings from the old country on cassettes played until they warped and frayed. And now, to the crowd's transcendent approval, she was here in the flesh before them, a miracle reborn. As she sang, Maria Castro sobbed and berated her lover, her chest heaving mightily with each stanza, lips quivering, head lolling back, then falling forward at the song's end, as if in supplication, and there was a moment's eerie silence in the packed amphitheater until the crowd erupted with whistles and clapping and cries of bravo and flowers began hurtling onstage, heaps of roses and orchids and lilies. The diva bowed and gathered them. Spreading her arms wide, she waded into the crowd.

At her approach, parents held up children to be kissed and she clasped them to her. Men swept off their hats and placed them over their hearts. Women cried and offered small gifts. Finally Maria Castro returned to the stage, clambering aboard from several bales of strategically placed hay, seemingly oblivious to the wisps sticking now to her black crepe dress. And she launched into an encore that had the crowd on its feet, tears streaming down faces, as she transported them back to the dusty *charreadas* of their youth.

Silvio explained all this to me, and more, as I mingled with the crowds to interview her fans, then went backstage to talk with technicians, musicians, and finally the diva herself, then other musicians, until they all blurred in my brain and my notepad filled with chicken scratches. And still I dogged him backstage and front, into the barn and out among the *charros*—the Mexican cowboys.

"In college, I wanted to get as far from all this as possible," Silvio said. "I went off to UC Berkeley and lived in the dorms. I studied philosophy. After graduation, I planned to go live in a cave in the desert and come up with a unifying theory of the universe."

"And then?"

"And then my dad had a heart attack. The doc told him if he didn't slow down he'd die."

"So you came back."

"He asked me. Ruben was still in high school. He would have lost everything he had spent so many years building up."

"And how did you feel about giving up your own plans?"

He made a clicking sound with his teeth and surveyed the crowd.

"I've made my peace with it," he said. "Those years in Berkeley, they seem like a dream now. My life is here."

He pointed out a group of pierced and tattooed teens and twenty-somethings, people not so far from our own age.

"These are the children and grandchildren of our original audience," Silvio said. "They still come to hear the old standards, but they're into *rocanrol*."

"You mean like American rock?"

"Sort of. It's rock, but with a Latin sensibility and sung in Spanish. *Rocanrol*. I'm trying to get Papi to showcase some of it. He's skeptical. Wants to stay with the tried and true. But I'm telling you, it's exploding. And L.A. is the hub. There's these small clubs, they pack them in. We could do that here too."

"Take me to one of these clubs."

"I will. As a matter of fact, several great *rocanrol* bands are playing Tuesday at a club in Silverlake, Starman. . . ."

"That's near me."

Suddenly, we were on shaky ground again. My house made me think of my empty bed with its single pillow, my kitchen table set for one. Catch me at the wrong time and I can fall, oh yeah, I can fall fast. I changed the subject.

"That's cool how you tap into the Mexican community here. The, uh, Diaspora. It's like the Jewish Diaspora, really, or the Chinese."

Yeah, I thought. Millions of Mexicans have been uprooted from their homeland, forced out by financial need, if not war and revolution, though there was that too. The Mexican Diaspora. I liked the elegant way the words rolled off my tongue, giving its people a historical imperative beyond sneaking across the border. I would use it in my story.

Silvio was looking at me like I didn't get it.

"It's not exactly a Diaspora. California was part of Mexico long before it joined the United States. *Tierra Mexicana.* Two hundred years ago, this land right here," he scuffed his foot in the dirt, "was my ancestral home."

As if to illustrate his point, a thirty-two-piece mariachi band started up and an eight-year-old girl singer in pigtails, a brocaded vest, and too much makeup began to work the crowd. Silvio grabbed me by the waist and pulled me to him, then let me go.

"Sorry," he said, "I got carried away. You know us Latins. We're hot-blooded."

"Bullshit. But I didn't mind."

At 11 P.M., we went back to his office. He pulled two Pacificos from his fridge, serving them with a twist of lime. We drank the cold, musky beer and listened to the music, sitting on the steps outside the trailer. A female singer with a powerful and raw voice was now onstage.

"Hey, I know that song," I said. "Wasn't it on that album Linda Ronstadt did? When she discovered her Mexican roots. I love that album."

"La Ronstadt's voice is a little too *linda* for those songs," Silvio said.

"Why is her voice too pretty? It soared on that album in a way her pop songs never did."

"That's the problem exactly," Silvio said. "Ranchera music should be raspy and raw, and her delivery is too respectful and sweet. It's not what that music's about."

"Oh."

Would I ever get it right? Even music could be a quicksand of racial division, and I had just sunk into it by announcing my enthusiasm for half-breed Linda Ronstadt instead of a more racially pure voice.

"But enough of the ethnomusicology lesson," Silvio said. He jumped up and returned a moment later with a bag of what looked like chips. The packaging crackled as he opened it, giving off a pungent smell of lime, grease, chile, and salt.

"What's that?"

He looked at me. "If I tell you, you won't eat it."

"I'm pretty adventurous."

"*Chicharrones.*"

"Is that . . ."

"Yup, pork rind."

"You're right."

"The white West Siders have just discovered these in a big way. All those folks on the Zone Diet. High in fat is okay, but no carbs."

"I don't live on the West Side," I informed him.

"Good for you," he whispered. "Now try one."

I tried. The fat melted on my tongue, exploding in a sensation of chili and lime. I had to admit it was the best grease fix I had had in a long time.

"The guy who makes these, he's a family friend. Delivers it by the case. *¡Qué lástima!* If I could cut my habit in half, I'd lose this *pancita*." He grabbed his belly and pulled.

"I think you're fine the way you are."

"Oh yeah?" He was laughing. "Tell my ex-girlfriend. The Mexican-American princess."

"I'd rather tell you."

We sat, basking in the warmth and grease and animal smells. I waved my beer around by its bottleneck.

"Why didn't your brother want a part of this?"

"I told you, he wanted to make it on his own."

"There's got to be more to the story than that. Tell me about your brother."

"Haven't I talked enough? I thought this story was about our business."

Something shrill had crept into his voice.

"It is. But I wrote about your brother too, remember. What if there's a link between your brother's murder and Venus Dellaviglia Langdon's murder? Do the police even know that he had just become her . . . ?"

"There is no connection." Silvio was stiff and proper again, cutting off that line of inquiry before I could get started. "And I don't think it's any of your business to bring it up. Our family is devastated. You can't imagine how hard it is for me to talk about this. Please don't make it worse."

The easy intimacy of our evening was destroyed. I thought about Silvio's reticence and concluded I'd outstayed my welcome.

"I should go," I said.

He grabbed my hand. "Why? What have I said?"

"Nothing. I've just got too many stories percolating in my head."

"Till Tuesday then?"

"Yeah." I gave him my address.

"I'll pick you up at eleven."

"That late?" I realized how lame I sounded. "I could just meet you at the club."

"How about I come to your house and we'll walk down?"

I pictured a moonlight stroll along the staircase street overlooking the lake, heading down to Silverlake Boulevard and the club.

"All right," I said.

# CHAPTER 13

*I* dedicated Monday morning to reading clips about Latin music in L.A. In the last few years, the *Times* had started writing capsule concert reviews, a lagniappe tossed to our Spanish-speaking readership, but there wasn't a whole lot about the Latin music business. Good, I thought, clutching the clips greedily to my stomach. More for me.

At lunch, I drove to Pasadena's Old Towne to meet my friend Babette. She was an accountant, but the most unlikely number cruncher I had ever seen, with her high heels and glam outfits. We had known each other since high school, and she was my reality check, the one person I trusted to tell me when I was full of shit. She also served as my unofficial adviser in matters of the heart.

Now I told her about Silvio and she gave me an approving look.

"About time you started circulating again."

"It's work, Babette. I need to follow Silvio around, see what he does all day and into the, um, night. Since he's a music promoter, he sees a lot of live shows. I'm just tagging along."

"Strictly research, I'm sure. I dunno, Eve, when we do audits, we're not supposed to fraternize with the client."

"Journalism is different," I said a little too quickly.

"Yeah, right." She sipped her espresso.

"And by the way, I'm not so ready to date. But you have to go on living. There's just a little less of my heart to get broken the next time."

"Don't be silly. Your heart is the same size as it ever was. And you're wiser in the bargain. I say that in my book."

To my surprise, Babette had used her many romantic adventures and pratfalls to write and self-publish a love advice book that she hawked determinedly at nightclubs and singles gatherings. A big publisher had now snapped it up and was sending her on a book tour. Babette's theory involved scrutinizing one's previous romantic experiences for patterns and assigning them complicated equations of numbers that you could improve with motivational exercises that honed healthy behavior.

Now she turned her romance high beams in my direction.

"First Mark Furakawa. Now Silvio Aguilar. What pattern do I see here?"

"I don't know," I said. "Youth counselor and concert promoter. One's Japanese-American, one's Mexican-American. What's the tie-in?"

"You just said it."

"What?"

"Both of them are ethnic," she said triumphantly. "You go for the exotic."

That smarted. It reminded me too much of what my old flame Mark had told me. That I was only drawn to him because he was so different from me.

"First of all, Silvio and I are not dating. Second, I'm just drawing from the available pool, Babette," I said with some irritation. "This city is majority minority, so the chances are better than fifty-fifty that I'm going to end up with someone who's not of Northern European extraction."

"So if you're not dating, what's to worry? Still, pay attention. I think I'm on to something here."

I realized that my subterfuge was getting nowhere with Babette. She had seen through me right away, heard the quickening in my voice, the dreaminess in my eyes. I might as well own up.

"What if I am drawn to someone who's not like me? Should I purposely stifle that? And what a shame it would be if someone from another culture was drawn to *me* but couldn't get anything going because I had resolved on PC grounds to only date white boys."

"You're just making excuses."

Was I?

"Give me a break, Babette. Both of those guys were born here. They're Americans. Besides, the most exotic guy I ever dated was a white boy from Tulsa. His skin was pale as Irish lace and he played the fiddle real mournful, like he was channeling the potato famine through his DNA."

"Oh-ho, now you're back on that deeply rutted groove, singing the blues about your great lost love Tim Waters," Babette said. "Hasn't he receded into the mists of your romantic history where he belongs?"

Tim and I had spent four delirious years together in our early twenties. I had left him because I was young and spoiled and hungry for new experience. When it's so intense from the beginning, you have nothing to compare it to, and it's only absence that can make you realize, belatedly, what you have lost.

But Tim knew. After the breakup, he packed away his fiddle, moved to Singapore, and put his computer skills to work, riding the dot-com wave. We hadn't talked in years, but that didn't mean I had forgotten.

"He has, he has," I said impatiently. "I'm just pointing out that I do date Northern Europeans."

Babette was not swayed. "It's all that traveling you've

done, all those adventures you've had," she continued. "And now that you're back in L.A., you're treating this suburban posting at the *Times* like a foreign country, pretending you're in Hong Kong or Chiapas or something."

I thought about it. "Perhaps subconsciously. What of it?"

"Just that you should be aware of it."

"Okay, I'm aware of it. I still think Silvio Aguilar is sexy as hell."

When I got home from work Tuesday, I took a nap. I wanted to be fresh for whatever the evening would bring.

Silvio knocked at my door right at 11 P.M. and I was ready. I didn't know what to wear to a *rocanrol* show, but figured that a black T-shirt and black jeans wouldn't look too out of place. We hiked down to Glendale Boulevard, ran across, and climbed the next hill, pausing at the top of the Cove Avenue stairs to look down. Palm trees and century plants stood silhouetted against the night sky, the lake shimmering purple-black in the background, with only the occasional whir of a car's engine to remind me that we were still in a big city.

The air surged with electricity, growing heavier as we descended. It felt like ions charging before a storm. I wanted to stay suspended on this concrete staircase forever. But too soon, we hit bottom. We drifted down Silverlake Boulevard, past the dog park, empty of animals now, and several blocks to Starman, a nightclub that had grown increasingly popular since Beck had played there several years ago. Now the owner had branched out into *rocanrol* a few nights each week. "Shhhh," read a sign at the entrance, "your neighbors are sleeping."

The return to humanity from the lush stillness of the

lake snapped me out of my reverie. Music blared inside, heavy primal rock chords mixed with punk.

"This is the only club in town where they actually discourage music industry vultures from coming around," Silvio said. "The owner thinks it gives the place a bad vibe. And those cheap bastards, they have their assistants call up, demanding to get comped on the fifteen-dollar cover charge. The owner promises he'll put them on the special list. Then he charges them twenty-five to get in." Silvio laughed. "And the best thing is, the Hollyweasels always pay up."

"You're a music promoter," I told him. "Doesn't that make you a Hollyweasel too?"

He considered. "I'm a new breed. The Mexiweasel. Watch this."

Ignoring the long line that snaked down the block, Silvio led me to the entrance, where he took the doorman aside for a quick, whispered conversation. The young goateed Latino bowed his head just a fraction more than necessary, then swept back the red velvet curtain and ushered us inside and onto the club floor. Here, the sound was deafening, a sea of glorious churning noise that charged right through my rib cage and took up residence inside my beating heart.

Onstage, an androgynous singer in full makeup clung to the mike and crooned while the band crashed and clashed behind him.

"See what that guy's playing," Silvio whispered. "It's a *bandoneon,* a small, accordionlike instrument that defines tango. But he's using it for rock. That's what I love about this genre."

Women walked by wearing embroidered hip huggers and Pucci dresses, lips outlined in scarlet and magenta. A man wearing a Guatemalan vest and a knitted shoulder bag of dyed yarn sheared from sturdy Andean sheep struck up a conversation with them. Lava lamps lit the gloom. Conversations swirled in Spanish and English.

"There's no such thing as *'La Raza,'*" a beret-clad man announced to a girl in leather jeans who hung on his every word. "The culture's been injected with recombinant DNA. It's forever evolving."

"What's *La Raza*?" I asked Silvio.

"It's a term Mexicans use to describe themselves."

"What's he mean?"

Silvio pulled me to him and began to whisper in my ear.

"What exists here in L.A. isn't Latino culture anymore. It's not white culture or Mexican culture or Central American culture or border culture. And it's not a mix of those either. It's something completely new. *Fijate.* Picture some undocumented gangbanger from East L.A. who gets deported to Mexico and gets himself a little crew. But he's not in the States anymore, he's in some pueblo. The homies do some damage and someone writes a song and it gets broadcast on the border radio. And bilingual L.A. punks hear it and pick up on the polka groove and the Spanglish rap and put their own spin on it, but they grew up listening to The Germs and Depeche Mode so when they sing in Spanish, it morphs again. That's what he means about the DNA. Swap it back and forth across the border enough times and it's like playing telephone. You can barely recognize its origins."

Listening to him sketch it out, I felt plunged into a moment of history when the fabric of life rips wide open and enormous change is suddenly possible at warp speed. This dim cabaret, with its Latinized echoes of prewar Berlin, was an incubator of our mestizo future.

While the naysayers were busy electrifying the border and posting more guards, the wave was already crashing over us, utterly transforming the Los Angeles of our fathers.

"Los Despreciados," Silvio said now, pointing to the stage.

"What?" I whispered back.

"It means 'The Disdained' in English. They're going to be huge. Next time you're at Hollywood and Vine, check out the music billboard on the northwest corner. You'll see them, glowering from on high, sneering at the tourists and the traffic. A bunch of longhaired art rockers from Cartagena who sing in Spanish. They're one of the pioneers of *rocanrol*. It's one of the fastest-growing segments of the L.A. music market today. And I aim to be in on it."

A waitress appeared with two drinks and Silvio smiled, greeted her by name, and flipped her a bill folded sideways. We hadn't even ordered, so I knew he must be a regular here. Silvio handed me a tumbler and said *"Salud"* as he tinkled his glass against mine. I lifted up the amber liquid, taking fiery nips. It was some fancy tequila, anejo, I guessed. There was an energy here that was palpable, and the words crooned in Spanish by the slender young singer were making me swoon even more than the tequila.

I had brought my notepad along, but soon gave up any pretense that I was doing research on a story about Latino music promoters and just gave in to the vast sensory extravaganza that was washing over me in the most pleasurable deluge. Taking a last sip of my firewater, I turned to deposit my glass on the bar when I caught a glimpse of someone familiar, though it took me a moment to place the dishwater blonde hair and baseball cap and remember where I had seen them, in front of an abandoned squat. My different worlds were melting and bubbling together in the most unexpected of places. The intensity of my gaze must have registered, because Scout looked at us, then ducked and darted away, disappearing into the crush of people still coming through the door.

"Silvio," I said, grabbing my surprised date by the arm and tugging down until his ear reached the vicinity of my mouth. "I'll be right back."

And then I was after her, pushing through the crowds, my fingers grabbing, crushing silk and satin and suede and sequins, moussed hair and hands holding drinks, pushing, tugging, wiggling, diving through clots of people, to where I had seen her last, only to arrive at a wall and look wildly around and see no one who looked like Scout. She had escaped me again. But she had been here, was maybe still here. I now had a new venue in which to look for her—she liked *rocanrol*. Or maybe she had just come here to sell or buy drugs.

I inched my way to the front door, where I asked the bouncer if a girl with long blond hair tucked into a baseball cap had raced out, but he just gave me an incomprehensible stare and I gave up. Damn. I had lost her twice now. Deflated, I headed for the ladies' room, the tequila already working on my bladder. The rest room was baroque splendor, all brocaded chairs and gilded mirrors, with luscious-lipped women primping in their luminous light. I walked past and pushed open the door of the nearest stall, only to find a hunched figure, bent over the toilet seat, snorting up a thin white line. I could see the bleached hair and the dirty baseball cap, sweat stains on the rim, before she saw me. When she realized the door had come open, she leapt up and twirled around.

"Hullo, Scout," I said. "Pardon me, but the door was

unlocked." I grasped a side of the rickety stall with each hand, planting myself firmly in her path.

"Whassup?" She gave me a sick look, running her sleeve along her nose as she took in the blocked exit. I knew how meth worked. Soon she'd be jabbering like a jay, unable to stop. I took her wrist. "Let's have a little chat in the powder room, shall we?"

It was like pulling a paper kite behind me, she was so thin and pliable.

"Left your Girl Scout uniform at home today, did you?" I asked.

"Who are you? What do you want?"

She sniffed and rubbed her nose again, tender inflamed membrane. I pulled her into one of the clawed chairs and sat down opposite her, our knees touching. We might have been exchanging gossip about the cute bass player.

"I'm not the police. I'm not taking you back to 'Mac.' I'm just a reporter. Who killed Isabel, Scout? Was it Finch? Was it her dad? Or was it one of her rich Borwick Academy pals?"

"I didn't see nothing," Scout said, her eyes rolling back in her head as the meth connected with her synapses. Her leg began to twitch, and she scratched at her arms, gouging herself. "I wasn't there. Swear to God. I loved Isabel. She was like the sister I never had. I can't believe someone did this to her."

She shook her head violently, but long after the gesture should have ended, she was still twitching.

"Was it Finch? Did he finally snap?" I had a moment's sudden inspiration. "Is he here tonight too?"

"Finch couldn't kill anyone. And I don't know who whacked her. I dropped L that night. I'm still seeing traces."

"Is Finch here? Maybe he knows."

She looked at me, perplexed. "Nah, man, he hates this music. I grew up speaking Spanish, that's why I'm here." She was babbling now, the drug kicking into high gear. "My mama was from Guadalajara. It's only my dad who's, like, Aryan. I take after him lookswise. But he left when I was two. Then I had a lot of other dads."

She shook her head violently. "Yeah, man, I don't like all that *ranchera* shit. But this music has a vibe I can relate to."

I heard the thumping outside the bathroom walls, the rock chords. Here was the demographic Silvio had told me about, come to sniveling life. She began to twirl jaggedly. Several women came in, swarming around the mirrors, applying magenta lipstick to already perfectly bruised lips. I looked at them, my glance lingering longer than it should. When I turned back, Scout was gone. I heard the door slam. She had a head start on me, and she had the furtive cunning of a cornered animal. By the time I reached the club entrance, she was probably halfway to Sunset Boulevard.

I felt a large hand on my wrist.

"Eve, what's going on? Where have you been? I've been looking all over for you."

"Bit of business," I told Silvio. "I saw someone I needed to talk to for a story."

He stiffened. "This doesn't have anything to do with my brother, does it?"

It was an accusation. I was weary suddenly. "Not unless your brother was consorting with a Hollywood street kid named Scout. She knows something about a murder I'm covering. I tried to get her to talk. But she ran away."

He frowned. "Somehow, I don't think she'll run far. Now come, we're just in time for the second set."

I allowed him to lead me back into the crush of people. I perched on a vacant bar stool and he leaned close to murmur the convoluted romantic history of the lead singer and the guitarist. But my mind drifted as he spoke. I found myself mentally chasing Scout around the corner and down the street, following her to her hideout, where I could finally unravel the story. At 1:45 A.M., the band packed it up and we did too.

We hiked up to the lake, the spell long since evaporated. When we hit Cove, we climbed up what seemed like a hundred stairs before stopping for a breather. I sat down. Though the air had cooled, the stone still radiated a faint warmth from the day's sun. Silvio joined me and, thigh to thigh, we watched the moon gleam over the lake.

"You're a difficult woman," he said. "I thought you liked me just a little bit."

"I do. But I told you, I saw someone I had to talk to. I'm really bad at separating business and pleasure."

He laughed. "Then let me do it for you. This," he waved his arm, "is pleasure. Is that so hard to understand? We are perched here, on these stairs, overlooking a lake in the middle of the night as though we were the last two people awake in the world. Or do you see a source hiding under that agave plant?"

I had to admit I didn't. He pulled me to him and kissed me, under the Dr. Seussian century plant with its frilly white blossoms dangling over us, and his lips were soft and warm.

I leaned in and kissed him back, but it wasn't working. I kept thinking I heard scuffling nearby, breathing and whispering. I pulled away.

"I hear something."

He sighed. "I don't hear anything except your heart beating much too fast."

"There it is again."

"Okay, okay, let me go investigate."

He took out his key ring, dug into the mass of keys, and pulled out a small black tube. He pressed a button. All of a sudden, a beam of light came on. It was a god-damn flashlight. I had to laugh. I loved him for this, that he carried a flashlight; what a Boy Scout he was, he came prepared. That reminded me of Scout, which made me tense up. Had she followed us here?

Silvio stepped away from the concrete stairs and into the underbrush. I heard an intake of breath, then rapid-fire questions and the murmured response of an unfamiliar voice. All in Spanish. Now a man crawled out, sheep-ishly leading a woman by the hand. They hiked down the stairs without looking back up at us, sweeping dried leaves off their clothes as they went. We weren't the only would-be lovers to find this a perfect trysting spot, sus-pended between the moon and the black-groomed lake.

I would have to trust my instincts more.

I went to bed and slept soundly for an hour until a lovesick mockingbird woke me up.

He perched in the tree outside my bedroom window, trilling urgently. Poor fellow, with his unrequited pas-sions. He could have benefited from some of Babette's romantic advice. But after twenty minutes of trying to get back to sleep, my patience gave way.

"Shut up," I yelled.

I recalled reading that mockingbirds only sang in the spring when they mated. This one's internal clock was really off. After another half hour, my sympathy curdled into black hatred. I stumbled to the kitchen, got an ice-cube tray, cracked it open, and dumped the cubes into a bowl. Then I went to the bedroom window with my projectiles. Stealthily, I slid up the casement window. The mockingbird kept up his brave, lonely song. I cocked my ear, aimed, and lobbed. The mockingbird stopped. With a rush of wings, he flew off. But not far. Within moments, he started up again. I threw more cubes. Soon he didn't even halt in his singing. When I ran out of ice, I rummaged the fridge for more weapons. I found raw baby carrots in the crisper and threw them at the mockingbird. I heard wings flap, then silence, but just as I got back into bed, he started up again. Lovelornness was not assailed so easily.

# CHAPTER 14

*I* was sneaking up on him, armed with broccoli florets this time, when the alarm went off. I sat up and rubbed the sleep out of my eyes. My head still buzzed with mockingbirds, tequila, my pursuit of Scout, and something else. Something warm and liquid. Silvio Aguilar's body pressed against mine as he kissed me. Unlike the aborted kiss on the stairs, this dream one had been slow and sure and deliberate, delivering an unspoken promise of what lay ahead. I needed a run. Hollywood came to mind, not the seedy boulevard of Scout and Finch, but the windswept upper reaches, the serene hills of Runyon Canyon where man's dominion ebbed into something more ambiguous. I had to drive there, but traffic was scant, and soon my rubberized soles were scrunching on the dirt trails that hugged the side of the sandstone hills.

The path I trod was man-made, wide enough to drive a pickup truck along. This was wilderness as theme park, but it was reassuring for urban dwellers like me who grew uneasy straying too far from civilization. As my eyes adjusted to the patches of chaparral whose resinous oils hung in the air, I picked out faint trails, narrow paths for deer and silent, padding coyotes.

I heard a sound like paper tearing and looked up to see a hawk cutting through the air, feathers rippling in the wind as he traced figure eights. It was hard to remember that his flight was not some breathtaking air ballet but an unceasing hunt for food. If we spent most of our waking hours stalking prey, we'd all be lean and graceful too.

I hiked until I stood on a promontory jutting out over the L.A. Basin. From my perch, I could see the cracked foundations of what had once been a silent film star's estate. Time had reduced it to some kind of Ozymandiac ruin, much as silent films themselves, and I felt the pull of seasons, the burrowing insects, the creeping vine, that would reclaim us all. That had already reclaimed Isabel Chevalier and Ruben Aguilar and Venus Dellaviglia Langdon. And as I stood exposed, I thought how it was only humans who clambered clumsily across the ridges, silhouetted in plain sight for anyone with a scope rifle. Animals knew better; they traveled the back corridors and skirted the high hills. Then I hiked down.

Hot and thirsty, I slid into my car, reached for my water bottle, and saw a number on my cell phone that I recognized as Tom Thompson's. While I had been musing about eternity above the broad shoulders of the city, something had happened deep in its bowels.

Covered in a thin, sweaty film of dust, I called him back. He answered on the first ring and told me there had been an arrest in the Chevalier murder case.

"No, it's not the dad, you were dead wrong on that one, pal-o," he said. "Cops say the squatter boyfriend did it. Finch something or other. Turns out he was a Satanist; they found crucified animals down there, books on demonology. I spoke to Metro and here's what we decided. You're taking the Pasadena angle, you've already interviewed her family and friends, right? Joshua Brandywine will attend the police press conference at ten A.M. Should be a nice package. Now go."

I looked at my watch. It was 8:10 A.M. The earliest deadline would be three o'clock. I figured I had time for a shower.

Driving home, I thought about Josh. His dad was Phillip Brandywine, a newspaper legend, retired after a long and illustrious career at the *New York Times*. As a young UPI stringer just out of Princeton, Phillip Brandywine had attached himself to the Allied troops that liberated Dachau, getting the greatest and most awful scoop of his life. He had covered the Korean War and Vietnam, the assassination of Patrice Lumumba in the Congo, the French student riots of 1968. His career had spanned more than a half century. If there was such a thing as journalistic royalty, Phillip Brandywine was it. That made his son a princeling, imbibing foreign affairs and diplomacy with his mother's milk in the Third World capitals they had called home. And in the dynastic tradition that still exists in the modern newsroom, though it's rarely discussed, the son was being primed to ascend his father's throne.

There wasn't any throne to ascend to in my family, unless you counted the leather recliner in the den where my father held court each day after work. The only strings my paterfamilias could pull would have landed me a job at the L.A. Unified School District. He had worked for years there, teaching Romance languages he had picked up in a Central European boarding academy where the genteel legacy of the Austro-Hungarian Empire had survived long after the monarchy itself had crumbled.

But in America, my father was a double exile, suffused with exquisite longing for a time and place that no longer existed, except in memory. He never quite adjusted to the brawny, can-do capitalism of his adopted land, and his impassioned but sporadic efforts all ended dismally. Even when he sat with us on the beach in the bright Southern California sun, there was something spectral about my father. He was a portal into a vanquished world where we could not follow, and when he retreated to his Stendahl and string quartets, he left my brother and me pining for an American dad who would lob softballs and bring home fast food. And we grew cruelly resentful, as only children can be, when the sorrow descended and took him away from us for weeks at a time.

There were so many secrets in our house, questions we didn't dare ask and topics that were never discussed, most of which revolved around his life before we were born. Eventually I made up my own story to address what remained unsaid. In the fairy tale I concocted, my father was a handsome prince who lived in a castle and dressed in silk and jewels. One day a great scaled dragon descended with much flapping of wings. The dragon burned down the castle and slew his family, forcing the young prince to flee. Left a vagabond, he wandered the wastelands, taking shelter with kindly peasants who fed and hid and clothed him. Eventually he found his way onto a ship bound for America, where he met my mother, herself an immigrant. Then we had been born, commencing the life I knew.

One day as my brother and I crouched inside a tent we had made by draping blankets over chairs, I spun the tale for him, making his eyes goggle at the wickedness of the dragon. Feeling a muted presence in the room, I lifted a flap, stuck out my head, and found my father listening, an unfathomable expression on his face. Then he squatted beside us and cupped my face.

"You are a dear, sweet child," he said, "and yours is a valiant attempt to make sense of a world for which no rightful explanation can exist."

I had been thrilled with these words, which offered a tiny window, however barred and smudged, into my father's past. With my story, I had broken through, made some kind of tenuous connection.

"Why is there no rightful explanation?" I asked.

But he only straightened and turned away.

It was then I began to write in earnest, a seven-year-old trying to make sense of her parents' ghost world and connect it to the life around her. But my stories did little to lessen the mystery in which he cloaked himself, nor did it alleviate his depression. Our veiled communion under the blankets failed to unleash the hoped-for deluge. And in the end, it was the emphysema that got him, not the sorrow.

He lay, gasping for breath and cursing in six languages, while we petted his papery hand and explained why we couldn't fetch him cigarettes. The grave diggers lowered him into the ground two days after I turned sixteen. My mother, who never adjusted to his absence, followed him several years after that.

Later, when I cast about for a way to make a living, I realized I could recount the tales of others and get paid for it. Journalism liberated me to ask personal and probing questions of complete strangers that I hadn't dared raise with my own parents. Each time I embarked on a story, I attacked it with Valkyrie fury, sure that this time I would slay the demons that hovered over my family.

But it never happened. The great irony was this: By banishing their past, my parents had only succeeded in infusing it with a mythic intensity that life in a denatured American suburb could never match. And instead of creating the safe haven they had hoped, my parents had kindled in me a savage need to prove myself.

It was little wonder I was transfixed by Josh, who seemed to glide effortlessly through life while I thrashed and struggled. He had slid into Princeton as a "legacy"—

the child of an alum. When you added in his dad's *New York Times* career, Josh was a double legacy. And so I had teased him and called him "Legs" and the nickname had stuck. Josh assumed it grew out of his penchant for wearing shorts, no matter how cold the weather, and was a good sport about it. Or maybe it was just blue blood obliging.

At home, I ate a turkey and Swiss cheese sandwich slathered with Dijon. Murder should always be tackled on a full stomach.

Then I reviewed my notes. I had quotes from the girl-friends. Some from Vince Chevalier. Local color about Scout tending the shrine. Now I called social workers and psychologists to get stats on runaways. But I needed more details, more anecdotes about Finch. That meant visiting Isabel's friends again.

By the time I pulled in front of the Borwick Academy in Pasadena, it was 2 P.M. and classes were letting out. I felt a bit like a stalker, my car idling at the curb, hoping to see Sophie and Caitlin.

They emerged, each clutching a stack of books. Admiring how they kept it all together, I hopped out and waved. A prim lady who looked like a vice principal watched with suspicion. I was too young to be a mother, too old for a student, and not the right sex for a rapist.

"Hi, remember me?" I said. "The cops have arrested someone in Isabel's murder."

"Shut up!" Sophie said. "Who?"

I told them, and was surprised by their heated response. The cops had it wrong, they told me. Finch was no murderer. So the scumbag had bamboozled them too.

"How did they get him?" Caitlin asked. "Someone must have snitched."

Sophie stirred and looked away.

"The police didn't say anything about informants," I said, watching Sophie, who was stroking the braided leather of her belt.

Her reaction told me to go for it. "But they did say he probably had accomplices who were bringing him food and stuff."

Caitlin looked up at the sky. Sophie's grip tightened.

"You were helping him stay out of sight, weren't you?"

"No we weren't." The denial was tossed off too swiftly to be believable.

"Amazing. Your good friend has just been murdered and her boyfriend is the prime suspect. And you help him to evade the police. Weren't you scared? What if he killed you too?"

Sophie put the back of her hand up to her mouth to stifle a sob. "He wouldn't. We keep telling you. He's being framed or something. He didn't murder anyone. He loved Isabel."

"Why won't you believe us?" Caitlin said.

"Where was he hiding?" I asked.

They regarded each other dubiously.

"If he's in jail, it doesn't matter anymore."

"I guess that's right," Sophie said. "You know that old fifties' motel on PCH. The one that got hit in the mud slide last winter, they're going to tear it down?"

"Paradise Motel," I said. For months, it had sat abandoned across the highway from the beach, right under the crumbling cliffs of Pacific Palisades. The city's Historic Preservation Society had filed a lawsuit to keep developers from tearing it down. They claimed the low-slung building was an icon of postwar beach culture, whatever that was.

"Right. Finch checked in last week." She sniggered.

"He liked the rates. And the location. At night, he'd cross the highway and sit at the waterline, watching the phosphorescence. Even from inside the squat, you could hear waves crashing and seagulls crying. He wrote a poem about it."

"Did he write a poem about strangling his girlfriend too?"

"You're not listening," the girls shouted. "How can a guy who writes poetry kill his girlfriend? He didn't do it, Eve."

The unearthly light of the fanatic shone in their eyes. But a realization was dawning in mine. Here was part of the story that no reporter knew but me. Finch Marino was a Manson for the millennium, a dark, anticharismatic lord who exerted an unfathomable power on his young female acolytes. I pictured the headline: "Accused murderer on the lam helped to hide out by clean-cut Pasadena prep school girls."

"How did you know where he was?"

"He called me," Sophie explained. "Said he needed our help."

"Was it creepy inside that old hotel?"

"Not really." Her face lit up. "We brought candles and a guitar and our sleeping bags. We took walks on the beach."

"How idyllic," I said, writing it down. "Are you even old enough to drive?"

"No, but we know how. We took driver's training. No one ever stopped us. That's because we look so mature." Sophie fluffed up her hair with her pudgy fingers.

But then those fingers came down, moistly encircling my wrist.

"You can't say in the paper that we helped him."

"Why not?"

"We'll get in trouble," they wailed.

"Then why did you tell me, you know I'm a reporter?" I asked coldly, though I knew full well why. This was the wildest adventure of their sheltered lives, and they couldn't help boasting. And if Finch was in custody, they weren't revealing much.

"We'll help you find Scout if you keep it out of the paper," Sophie said.

"I already found her. Twice. But she ran away when I tried to talk to her."

"We'll get her to talk to you," Caitlin said. "She saw something that night. She never told us," the girl added hurriedly when she saw my expression. "But if Finch is in jail for murder, we have to find out who did it so he can go free."

My newspaper headline receded into the distance. For now. If Sophie and Caitlin could deliver Scout, I'd have an even bigger scoop.

But I was also suspicious.

"Why don't you go to the police with this? Tell them she knows something."

"We couldn't rat her out like that."

"Why not?"

"It wouldn't be right. They'd put her in a loony bin."

"What's Scout's story?"

"She doesn't talk much. Only to Finch. They have some kind of cosmic bond."

"Didn't you tell me she wears a Girl Scout uniform? She wasn't wearing it when I saw her."

They told me she put it on when she hawked herself on the boulevard for food and drugs. She had gotten it from the Salvation Army. It fulfilled some childhood yearning to slip into the crisp green uniform, the sash adorned with merit badges for first aid and water safety, baking and embroidery, all the skills she had missed out on. She never had to wait long before some middle-aged man appeared, drawn like a bee to the forbidden nectar of deflowering a Girl Scout.

"That's sick," I said. "Why can't someone help her?" I thought of Harper Lee's fierce little girl in *To Kill a Mockingbird,* who was also named Scout. But the Hollywood Scout had no Atticus to guide her.

They shrugged. "We've tried. She doesn't want help. She was in McLaren Hall and she ran away. She's supposed to take all these meds, but she sold them to some tweakers who needed to come down. Isabel would bring her home once in a while, give her a bath and a hot meal. But she preferred the squats. She really did."

*I'm never going back to Mac*, Scout had said. Now I knew what that meant. McLaren Hall was the over-crowded, violent juvenile hall where society's throwaway kids were dumped—those removed from abusive homes, the mentally ill, the delinquents. Everyone knew it was bedlam.

"We could go to the shrine now and leave a message," Sophie suggested. "You want to come with us?"

But I couldn't. I had my deadline story to file and was already running late. Which reminded me.

"Listen," I said. "How about if I don't identify you by name. Just quote you as two teens who squatted with Finch occasionally."

Caution and ego warred on their faces. Ego won.

I drove downtown because it was closer than back-tracking to Monrovia, thrilling as I always did in the old Art Deco elevator with the streamlined brass design. I was entering the nerve center of L.A. journalism, not my usual office—a dinky suburban bureau in a shopping center. Finding an empty seat in the third-floor editorial offices, I started typing. Metro wanted fifteen inches, which Josh would work into the arrest story.

They had us on the budget for thirty-five inches. In my cub reporter days, I hadn't known what a budget was and assumed the paper kept a tally of how much each story cost to produce. Only later did I learn it was the list of stories that ran in the paper each day.

Pulling up Josh's sked—the short description that reporters file before they start writing each story—I read that Finch Marino, a homeless street kid from Cincinnati, was in custody on suspicion of killing Isabel Chevalier, a bright prep school girl from Borwick Academy. It had supposedly happened as part of a Satanic ritual during sex. I checked the wires and they were carrying the same information. Finch was twenty, had been on the streets since he was twelve. He had a long rap sheet with the LAPD's Hollywood division starting with loitering, trespassing, urinating in public, and as he grew older, burglary, breaking-and-entering, drug use, dealing, arson, and robbery.

It was a textbook trajectory of abuse and neglect. His mother was dead, his father long gone. He had lived with relatives who punished him by sticking his hand into a lit gas burner. At twelve he ran away and dropped out of school. An aunt in Atlanta, the only decent relative the cops had found, had kicked him out for stealing her prescription pills and never wanted to see him again. But she expressed skepticism that he could have killed anyone.

As I reviewed my notes and pieced together what I had, something nagged at me. None of the crimes on his rap sheet showed violence against people. And Finch's girlie gang had echoed the aunt's defense. What if they were right? Their statements should either raise some doubt about Finch's guilt or convince everyone of what a manipulative sociopath he was.

After the first deadline, I went over to Josh's desk. He was on the phone so I dawdled, wondering if there was anything new.

"But, Dad . . ." I heard him say. He fell silent and I figured he was getting a lecture. It probably wasn't easy being the golden boy, the repository of everyone's dreams. Here at the paper, editors either fawned over him, saving him plum assignments and muscling his stories onto the front page, or else cracked down hard, berating his every tiny mistake as if he should know better just because of his genes. For his part, Josh treated everyone with the insouciance born of great privilege. They might have been mosquitoes stinging at the protective netting, never to taste the sweet blood within.

From my perch in the San Gabriel Valley, I hungrily watched as the pageant unfolded. It was hard to resist Josh's nonchalantly tossed-off stories about growing up in Delhi and Bangkok, Paris and Istanbul, paragliding in the Seychelles all summer, skiing in Gstaad come winter. Hadn't everyone watched the sun rise over Angkor Wat? Why, it was one of the transcendent experiences of a lifetime, the jungle stillness before dawn, the carved stone temples impassively greeting the light as they had for centuries. There was a whiff of glamour about Josh that rubbed off. His touchstones were the Roman Coliseum and the Taj Mahal. Mine were the Sherman Oaks Galleria and Van Nuys Boulevard.

Seeing me standing there, Josh told his dad he had to go, flung down his headset, and asked if I wanted to grab a soda.

I told him yes, hoping his talents didn't include mind reader. Our story was now in the hands of the copy desk, where up to five pairs of fresh eyes would review it for accuracy, continuity, and dangling participles.

A giddy, post-dreadline euphoria came over us as we cruised up to the cafeteria. The rush that refreshes. But tomorrow we'd be off again, chasing the next day's high.

"I heard you were taking Chinese," Josh said. "That's awesome."

"I was for six months. Then I realized it would be years before I could interview a five-year-old, so I got depressed and stopped."

On the tenth floor, we got our drinks and took them to a window seat, a term conveying a grandeur that was sorely lacking in the *Times* cafeteria. Here we were, overlooking downtown, and you'd think they would have put in big picture windows to inspire us ink-stained wretches. But no, it was dirty glass that hadn't been washed in years, probably still filmy with nicotine from when all reporters smoked. Tatty venetian blinds kept the glare out. It was not a view to inspire Pulitzer–winning stories.

"I have to admit I was a little *chartreuse* about your story on those Asian kids," Josh said. "Hanging out with all those hot Mama-sans."

I looked at him with distaste.

"Legs, uh, Josh, that girl Lily I wrote about? She was fourteen."

"I know, but maybe she has an older sister?"

"You're a dog."

"I can't help it. Wherever I am, I'm drawn to the most exotic babe, the one with the darkest skin. I'm like a heat-seeking missile."

He grew pensive. "Which is why I cannot for the life of me explain my current entanglement. She's about as WASPy as they come."

He smiled. His teeth were white and straight, ivory sentinels rounded in all the right places. Mine were pointy and crowded, elbowing each other for lebensraum.

"Anyone I know?"

Josh smirked. "I'd rather not say. It's complicated."

"From you, I would expect nothing else."

We sucked our drinks until only air bubbled through the straws, then rode down to see if the copy desk had any questions. Soon we got the green light. On the elevator out, Josh asked me to dinner. Why not? I thought.

We chose a downtown eatery on Boyd, all blond wood and exposed pipes, where you could order angel-hair pasta in a salmon-vodka infusion. Outside in the alley, those less fortunate were forgoing the salmon and penne in favor of straight rotgut sheathed in brown paper bags.

Josh sipped his Merlot and we started in on every reporter's favorite pastime—newspaper gossiping. He was having a hard time with an editor named Cynthia Snodgrass. That surprised me, since Josh rarely complained. Besides, Snodgrass had a reputation for assigning investigative stories that landed on Page One.

"She's gone off the deep end," he said. "The other day she calls me over and says, 'I've got a hot one for you. As I was driving in to work today, I noticed that the leaves are more vibrantly colored this autumn than in previous years. The reds, oranges, yellows, they're absolutely fluorescent. I want you to call botanists, climatologists, find out what is going on.'"

I put down my fork.

"No! That's too bizarre. She was pulling your leg."

Josh leaned back against the wooden booth. "That's what I thought too, so I made some snide remark but she gave me a withering look. I spent all day on the phone.

Everyone was polite, but kind of puzzled. Of course they said there's nothing unusual going on."

"Did you tell the Snod?"

"She wouldn't buy it. 'Keep digging,' she said. 'I know there's a story there.' I wanted to tell her it was only her acid flashbacks intensifying with menopause. But she's convinced we're onto the next El Niño and she's hovering over a Pulitzer."

Josh picked at his penne and looked miserable.

I asked him what he thought of Boris Johannesen, another assistant Metro editor.

"Do you notice how he always smells like chocolate and talcum powder, and he rubs his hands together a lot?" I said.

"I never get that close."

"Well, I wish I didn't, but sometimes he's on Metro rotation with me, and he comes up and compliments me on stories. Then one day he tells me how much he likes my writing and he's going to put in a good word to Jane Sims. They're friends from college. And by the way, he's got an extra ticket to the Lakers game Saturday, and do I want to go. I told him no thanks."

"You think he was scamming you?"

"Well, duh!"

"It could have been legit."

"Yeah right, he layers on the compliments, hints how well he knows my editors, then asks me out. I see a thinly veiled threat."

"Whoa, Eve, don't get all feminist on me, give him the benefit of the doubt."

I wish that someone would trace the etiology of the word *feminist* and pinpoint exactly when and why this word of empowerment metastasized into today's insult.

"Oh, Josh, you're hopeless."

After we finished eating, he asked me to come with him to a downtown club.

"But first, I've got to get a little something," he said.

"What?"

"We shouldn't have much trouble around here."

As his meaning sunk in, it struck me again how no one was who they seemed, even the princeling Josh.

"I'm not slinking down some putrid alley with you to score drugs."

He recoiled. "Why not? You're a party girl."

"Unh-unh."

"Have it your own way, but don't be so uptight." He looked at the wall, where crushed metal shards of a car had been mounted on a canvass and splattered with paint. A sort of Jackson Pollock meets Ed Keinholz. A dreamy look glazed his eyes. "It was so easy in Bangkok."

I was startled. "But you told me you haven't lived there since you were sixteen."

"That's right. But some habits stay with you. Did you know that opiates are among the safest of drugs? Even long-term use produces no organ damage. Way safer than alcohol. Look at William Burroughs. What was he, eighty-three, when he finally croaked?"

"Yeah, look at him, he was a walking cadaver. Didn't he kill his wife?"

"It was an accident. When your life is dedicated to art, things happen."

"Yeah, like death. Why don't you drop me off at the parking garage?"

He shrugged. "You're missing out."

"Pass, man," I said, rejoicing somewhere small and mean, deep inside. So the golden boy had an Achilles' heel after all.

I threw down some money and slid out of the booth,

unable to fathom how a reporter so primed for success would risk such calculated self-destruction. Or was that the problem, that everything went so smoothly you had to stab yourself with a needle just to feel alive? When you work as hard as I did just to get to the *Times*, you don't take anything for granted.

# CHAPTER 15

As I walked along the big granite bar of the restaurant, a black leather jacket caught my eye. A familiar row of blue-black curls fell over the collar and I recognized Luke Vinograd, my copy messenger buddy. The original poster boy for underemployment. He was sitting alone and I stood next to him and murmured in my huskiest voice did he mind if I joined him. He turned, recognized me, and patted the empty stool beside him. I was the wrong sex to make his night, but he seemed happy to see me nonetheless. Now Josh came over, and Luke's eyes gleamed. We had been sitting in the womblike booths so he hadn't seen us before.

"Have a drink?" Luke held up a shot glass filled with a bright red liquid that wobbled like molten lava.

"What on earth is that?" I asked.

"Jell-O shot," Luke said, tipping it back and letting it slide down his gullet.

"What do they mix it with?" asked Josh, who immediately grasped the concept.

"Vodka. It's sweet, just like Mama used to make. But gets you good and liquored."

I told him I'd prefer a Cosmopolitan.

"Oh, Eve, that's so last month. Try one of these. Josh?"

"Sorry, I have to run." Josh looked at his watch.

"I'm sorry," Luke said.

"I'll stay for a drink if you give me a ride back to the *Times* lot," I said.

Luke agreed and motioned to the bartender for two drinks. We watched Josh leave.

"So, Eve, you got something going with young Josh?"

"No way, my skin's not dark enough for him. I just like hearing about his glamorous life. How's Lance?" I asked, turning the tables.

"Lance doesn't want to be tied down. He's dating some Shakespearean actor. How can a lowly copy messenger compete with the Bard?"

Luke sucked back his Jell-O shot and ordered a third. Actually, it might have been his tenth, for all I knew. His usually acerbic demeanor had gone all lugubrious, so I figured he had been there awhile. I wondered if this was why Luke's life had stalled.

He shucked off the jacket and I checked out his gold stud earring, the tight black T-shirt, the tattoo peeking out from a well-muscled bicep—he had recently taken up fencing and competed with ferocious elegance—the moody green eyes. "You're about as frumpy as a Prada pantsuit."

"Why thank you," he beamed, lubricated by vodka and compliments. "And now Miss Turbo-journo," he said, "I have something for you."

"I'm all ears."

"Weren't you asking me for clips on our esteemed mayoral candidate and grieving widower?"

"The very one."

Luke leaned his elbows onto the bar and spoke to the ceiling.

"Well, I heard something about him the other night."

"Tell me."

"Totally libelous, of course, we could never print it. But . . ." He paused for effect. "I heard someone boasting about how he knew Langdon in a . . . shall we say . . .

carnal way. Everyone else jeered, but there was something persuasive in the way this fellow said it. He got really offended when no one believed him."

"Are you saying that Carter Langdon the Third is gay?" I squirmed, agog at the fecund journalistic earth that Luke Vinograd had just tilled for me.

"I'm not saying that. Although in certain circles, there have been rumors for years." Luke wiggled on his bar stool.

"But he has a kid, and what about his wife . . ." I stopped. The dead Venus, larger than life, more beautiful than a goddess. The perfect beard.

"Don't be so naïve. People make arrangements. We both know the importance of keeping up appearances." He picked up his Jell-O shot.

My mind was turning like one of those painted horses on a carousel. "Why tell me? Why not Tony Hausman? He's the one covering the campaign."

Luke wrinkled his nose. "I don't like Tony Hausman. He's boorish and rude. I've avoided him since the time he rushed into the library when I was doing some filing, demanding to see our clips on the city comptroller. I explained that I wasn't a librarian but he wouldn't listen.

"'Hurry,' he said. 'I'm on deadline.'

"'Don't get your knickers in a knot, hon,' I told him. 'This is a daily newspaper. We're all on deadline.' But I hopped to it and got him his precious clips. So imagine my surprise when instead of 'Thank you, Lucas,' he flipped through them, spluttered, 'What's this?' and threw them back in my face screaming, 'I don't give a fuck what other reporters wrote about the city comptroller, I want to see what *I* wrote.' Can you believe the ego on that man?"

I nodded. Hausman was notorious for it. "But he's a

great reporter," I said. "You could always go right to the political editor if you want to bypass Hausman."

"I've had it with the lot of them." Luke's arm traversed the air in a grand gesture. "Besides, like I said, it's just a rumor."

I considered how Luke's personal dislike for Tony Hausman might be cramping the flow of news, which filtered up from the street and down from on high, where chance encounters led to great scoops or could slam the door forever. When it came right down to it, satellites and videophones were only high-tech frosting. At its most elemental, news is still an antediluvian business in which two people who trust each other sit down and swap information.

"So where did you hear this rumor?"

Luke downed his Jell-O shot and grimaced, and I knew it wasn't from the sweet drink.

"A place I visit occasionally."

"A gay bar? Where is it?"

"Not a bar exactly. You couldn't get in."

My mind darted, searching for possibilities.

I saw something darken his Slavic profile, furrow his brow.

"Not a . . . you don't go to those places, do you? Aren't they terribly unsafe?"

"Baths are not unsafe. It's people who make them unsafe. Certain people. Not me, I always take precautions."

Luke's hand was unsteady now as he signaled the bartender. I could see a deep red flushing the pale skin of his throat. Telling me this had cost him a lot, and I wondered why he had done it, or whether it was just the liquor loosening his tongue. Here, for the second time in as many hours, was someone who was not exactly what he seemed. Luke, the witty bon vivant, with his love of high culture and books, his intellect and charm. Yet why was I so surprised? People were sexual beings, and the expression of that sexuality didn't always flow through the main tributaries but meandered into hidden streams and still pools.

"I'm sorry. I don't mean to pry into your personal life. I just want you to be careful. You have a lot to live for."

"You didn't just lose Lance."

"No, but I've had shitty breakups too. And I'm not playing Russian roulette with my body. But clearly you don't want to talk about that. So. This boy at the baths. Did you know him? Was he a regular? Where did he live? Where is this bath?"

Luke turned to me. "My hat is off to you, Lois Lane. Never a moment's hesitation."

"That just shows how little you truly know me. Listen, Luke. Stop going to baths. Don't have unsafe sex. It's suicide. Lecture over. Now tell me about the boy."

Luke hunched his shoulders and stared down the granite bar.

"I just overheard him boasting, that's all."

"That is not all."

"He was with a group of young Latinos, they're in their late teens. Trannies, most of them. I mean T girls. They don't like being called trannies. I heard they live under the Fletcher Drive Bridge in the L.A. River. I've seen this one a few times. Actually spent some, uh, time with Pia several nights ago. He told me his parents kicked him out when he started wearing his sister's clothes."

"*Tranny* means transvestite?"

"Or transsexual. Depends."

Something hit me. "What about you?"

He looked at me with surprise. "No way. I'm a man. A gay man."

"With a taste for trannies?"

"This kid, Pia, he—I mean she—is a mess. I'm trying to counsel her. To get a job, go back to school, get her GED. But it's not like I'm going to invite her to stay in my apartment. They're feral youth, those ones."

Luke shivered, torn between fear and longing.

"And Pia lives down by the river, huh?"

"That's what she told me. Christ, how did things get so bollixed up? Let's go back to the parking garage."

"Let's get some coffee first, then we're on our way," I said, wanting him to sober up.

We drank our espressos, then paid the bill. In the car, Luke was silent. His lips were stained red from the Jell-O, like some trannie had been kissing on him all night. We waved good-bye at the edge of the *Times* lot, with its uniformed guards standing impassively, and then in a burst of speed, he was gone into the night, chasing shadows that only he could see.

# CHAPTER 16

T he next morning, I drove down Glendale Boulevard into Atwater, where I usually caught the 2 Freeway to work. But as I crossed the Fletcher Drive Bridge over the L.A. River, I remembered what Luke had told me. And instead of getting onto the freeway, I went past it, then made a U-turn and drove back toward the bridge. It was old and lovely, with high arches and sweeping pediments. Wrought-iron street-lights stretched across its length, 1920s works of art whose onetime modernity had now ebbed into vintage glamour. But most cars whooshed past without noticing the exquisite workmanship, the white span of the bridge that stayed untarnished despite decades of sooty exhaust.

The "river" that it spanned was really a concrete culvert, its original bed paved over generations ago by city engineers who feared that low-lying Los Angeles might be flooded if the muddy banks overflowed when wild torrents raced down to the sea. Environmentalists had talked about resurrecting the L.A. River and creating parklands on either side, but people continued to dump tires and tin cans and much more toxic things into its fetid stream. Still, a funny thing had happened as years of debate dragged on in City Hall. Slowly and with great stealth, nature itself had begun reclaiming the river, as trees and bushes pushed through cracks in the aging concrete floor and frogs and herons colonized the polluted water. There was even camping of a sort, though you couldn't call it recreational. The poor souls who lived on the embankments of the L.A. River were homeless and destitute, preyed upon by criminals, beaten up by drunken youths, and regularly evicted by city officials who bulldozed their meager possessions and made them move on.

I parked on the shoulder and got out, startled to see purple lupine growing along a thin strip of dirt where the bridge reared up from the ground before soaring into the sky. The very unexpectedness of it sent a ripple of pleasure through me, succoring me in a way that carefully tended peonies in office parks could not.

I clambered over a chain-link fence whose topmost spikes had been bent over for easier ascent. It was broad daylight and I didn't feel scared, though I doubted that anyone would hear me scream with the dull roar of traffic overhead.

Hiking down, I glimpsed plastic tenting and wet clothes laid out to dry on the bushes near the river bottom. Soon I had a clear view of the entire colony—five tents and a jumble of sleeping bags. Several figures waded in the river itself, which had slowed to a bare trickle in the fall heat. From a distance, they looked like the water sprites of ancient Greek myth who had frolicked by Arcadian brooks. But when I drew closer, the haggard faces and ragged clothes revealed ruined naiads.

Not wanting to scare them, I waved my hands, holding up my notepad.

"I'm a reporter. Can I talk to you?"

They clustered together, looking up at me, shielding their eyes from the sun as I descended. Once they saw I was alone and didn't look like a policeman, the thick clot of them dispersed.

"You a social worker?" asked one she-male, hidden

behind a mint-green cosmetic mask that was hardening on her features like clay. She wore white latex gloves and was squirting a bottle of red hair dye onto the pinned-up curls of another, rubbing vigorously with her thumb along the temples to massage in color as the beneficiary held up a mirror and looked on with approval.

"No. Journalist. I'm not here to cause any trouble. Just doing a story."

There were a dozen of them in and around the water, a pack of mermaids as imagined by Oscar Wilde. Several waded in the river, wearing skirts tucked into their waist-bands. One plunged a black lace outfit into the water, then rubbed the fabric gently to loosen the dirt.

From a boom box hidden in the reeds, a soundtrack blared in Spanish, and I recognized the gravel-voiced Celia Cruz, singing about love. Every once in a while, a voice chimed in for a moment, only to fade into the bleached stones and concrete chasm.

In the middle of the river, a man propped a hairy leg onto a boulder and rubbed with soap until it lathered. He took a razor and ran it from ankle to upper thigh, leaving a smooth, brown highway. He shook the razor, sending black-flecked foam into the river. Examining his leg, he frowned and picked off a bit of wet leaf. Several more razor swipes and the leg shone smooth in the sun, expos-ing rippling muscles.

"Wow," I said. "You guys have a major camp here."

A youth wearing a miniskirt and shirt knotted above his midriff, exposing his taut belly, looked up. Above luminous cat eyes, his eyebrows arched as high as the Fletcher Drive Bridge. His hairless cheeks were rouged, his lips outlined in peachy gloss. Dozens of hammered silver bracelets dangled from his arms; leather slave san-dals encased his feet. Then he went back to his toilette.

Holding up the shiny lid of a cooking pot to catch his reflection, he powdered his jawline, where the blue shadows of manhood would eventually sprout despite his most valiant efforts, and my heart went out to him, painted gypsy of the river. He wanted to be a woman so much more than I did.

Now he slid the lid back into a handbag, slung it on his shoulder, and sauntered over, his butt swinging languorously from side to side.

"A major camp? Is that supposed to be a joke?" He put his hand on his hip and tittered, and from their perches on the rocks, reeds, and rivulets came answering titters, as if a small flock of chickadees had settled onto the riverbed.

"Bad word choice," I apologized, then stood there, feeling acutely self-conscious at my lack of makeup and ragged nails, hair pulled into a ponytail, the linen shirt and khakis that hid my own curves. Here at the edge of a ruined river, in a camp for outcast transvestites, I was struck with guilt for squandering my God-given femaleness when others worked so hard to conjure up its essence.

"I'm looking for Pia. I heard he, uh, she, hangs out here."

At the name, the painted one startled and, below me, the others moved closer, closing ranks.

"She's not here," the painted one said. "And she promised to be back by ten last night. *Mira*, see, it's her birthday, and we're having a party." I looked where the manicured finger pointed, and saw a supermarket cake etched in pink flowers and green leaves that said *Feliz Cumpleaños, Pia,* and the number *18*.

"Yeah, she turned legal today, she's an adult. She wouldn't have missed this for anything, cuz we're, like, her family, *ese,* but she had a date yesterday, someone new. She left around six P.M., saying she'd be back with some money so we could buy champagne. She should have come home way before now."

A T girl in hot pants came up.

"I told her not to go with that dude, I thought he was creepy, but Pia said she could handle him. She got in his car and I couldn't even see her wave good-bye on account of the tinted windows."

"What kind of car?"

"A Lincoln Town Car. It was black and styling, man," the hot-pants girl said. "But after a while on the street, you get a sense about the clients, which ones are gonna turn on you. This guy didn't say much, but his eyes, they were like a reptile's, man. He was tracking Pia with his eyes. He didn't want nothing from the rest of us. She came running back to me right before they did their little deal, and was all excited cuz he was going to give her double the going rate. For a private show. She said it would pay for the champagne."

A sense of cold dread washed over us then, on that bleached fall day, despite the warming rays of the sun. Prostitutes got killed all the time, and homeless transvestite prostitutes were even more at risk from johns who hated the trannies for the very desire they kindled. Yet Pia was one of the luckier ones, she had a new family to watch over her. I felt their tension. These people cared. I cared too. But underneath the dread, I was also incredibly vexed. I needed to talk to Pia and she wasn't here. And she might not return.

"Maybe the show is just taking a while. What did the guy look like?"

The hot-pants girl looked at me, then spat.

"He looked like a date. Middle-aged white guy with a

fat wallet to match his fat wife and fat kids and a few fat kinks to get out of his system."

"Did he look like a politician, by chance? Anyone you've seen on TV?" I stopped and pretended to grasp for the next sentence. "A celebrity, or someone who might be running for political office, like mayor or something?"

They doubled over with laughter. "You would not believe the dates we get, lady," the painted one told me. "Celebrities, Hollywood people, you name it."

"Ever hear about Carter Langdon the Third, he's running for mayor?"

"I think we seen him on TV; he got some stellar wife."

"Stellar dead wife," another said. "How come the police don't got no suspects?"

Everyone had been expecting such a prominent case to break long before this, but instead each day we carried a smaller story, saying how the authorities were still investigating. One particularly irreverent talk radio host had called for Langdon to come on the air and take a lie detector test.

"I wonder the same thing," I told them. "But I'm not high enough on the food chain to work on that one. So back to Pia. Did the guy in the Town Car look like Carter Langdon the Third, by chance?" I asked hot-pants.

"Naw, it wasn't him."

I opened my purse and pulled out a business card.

"Please ask her to call me. If we connect, I'll buy you girls all the champagne you can drink."

# CHAPTER 17

*I*t was 10 A.M. now, and I was late for work. But instead of heading for the office, I turned the car toward East Hollywood. As I drove, I traversed invisible frontiers between the homeless trannies of the L.A. River and the homeless punks of Hollywood. They were the new urban tribes of Los Angeles, eking out a parallel but shadowy existence on the cast-off scraps of the Internet society. I wondered whether they ever over-lapped.

Traffic was heavy on Hollywood Boulevard. When I hit Vine, I looked up just in time to see the Los Despreciados billboard Silvio had mentioned, five black-clad youths lounging in vivid oil paint. The new Spanish Conquest didn't need armadas and swords. It just needed airwaves.

Now I backtracked to Vermont, getting stuck behind a guy in a tiny purple Aspire whose bumper sticker read MY OTHER CAR IS A VAGINA. Oh great, I thought, as we inched along. Just my luck. Was he saying that he drove a vagina? That he got a lot of sex? Was the driver some twisted English teacher obsessed with synecdoche—which I recalled from tenth-grade composition meant using the part to describe the whole. As the cars surged forward, I decided I had my lit crit terms all wrong. It was a metaphor, like Bruce Springsteen singing about the "pink Cadillac."

Unwilling to obsess anymore, I jerked into a suddenly open lane of traffic. As I pulled alongside the purple car,

I sneaked a peek at the driver. He was a heavy metal monster with lank, stringy hair, jerking his head up and down to the grinding and clanging that reverbed from his tinny stereo. He shot me a gritted methamphetamine grin that exposed pointy yellow canines. I looked away, staring at the road ahead, and we drove like this for several blocks, studiously ignoring each other, until the traffic slowed again and, mercifully, vagina man peeled off onto a side street and was gone.

When I saw a burger joint, I pulled into the drive-through. Scout could probably use a meal. I bought something for myself too. As the car filled with vapors of hot grease, I turned onto Manzanita and headed for the squat. Sure enough, she was sitting cross-legged at the shrine, writing in a notepad. I drove past, parked, and walked back, carrying the food.

I was about twenty feet away when she jumped up.

"Scout, I won't hurt you. Look, I brought food. Want a burger?"

Her nostrils quivered. Her tongue emerged, probing a cold sore in the corner of her mouth.

"Yeah," came a tiny voice.

"There's plenty for both of us. Look, I just want to talk to you about Isabel. I'm not going to take you back to Mac. I'm not a social worker. I'm just a journalist. I know Sophie and Caitlin."

I walked slowly over, still afraid I might spook her. Sitting by the chain-link fence about five feet away, I laid out my offerings. Then I unwrapped a burger and began munching.

From the corner of my eye, I saw a brindled dog peer from around the abandoned building. He looked like a pit bull mix, the type people abandoned at shelters each time TV ran a breathless exposé on canine maulings. That was the best-case scenario. In the worst case, people threw them out of moving cars on freeways or dropped them off high bridges. This dog had a thin, whippet-like tail and dragged his right hind leg. He took several steps closer, then sat on his haunches and licked his chops.

"Here, the rest's for you." I pushed the bag in her direction and concentrated on my burger.

Soon hunger got the better of her and she inched her way to the paper bag. She tore it open, pulled out the burger, and began eating. I expected her to cram it into her mouth, but she nibbled daintily at it, biting in neat concentric circles across the bun.

When it was gone, she reached for the fries and ate them one by one. Then, grooming herself like a cat, she licked the salt off her fingers. Finally, she stuck the straw inside her twenty-two-ounce soda and drank that down. The dog watched impassively.

Scout belched loudly, then wiped her mouth on her sleeve. She dug into a pocket in her cargo pants and pulled out a bent cigarette. She looked at it with regret, then flicked it away. It rolled down the pockmarked sidewalk and came to a stop.

"Gotta smoke?" she asked.

"Sorry."

"Aw hell."

She walked over to retrieve the slim white stick and broke off the bent part. Pulling out a green plastic lighter, she lit what remained and the exposed tobacco crackled. She took a long postprandial drag.

I put down my notepad so she could see the chicken scrawl inside. Scout scrutinized it.

"You like, write stories?" Her voice rose with curiosity. It was the first emotion she had displayed besides fear. She rubbed her sleeve against her nose again and coughed, a deep, rheumy rumble of dissonance on this Indian summer afternoon. If she sounded this bad now, when the weather was so mild, what would winter bring? I wondered if she had TB and was spraying thousands of infectious particles in the air.

"Yup, I take notes here, then I go back to the office and type them up on the computer. I see that you write too." I pointed to the papers she had left by the shrine.

"Aw, it's nothing." She tipped her ash. "I get these phrases in my head, and they get louder and louder until I have to write them down. That's the only way I can make them go away." She scrunched up her face. "Does that ever happen to you?"

I laughed. "All the time."

"I'm trying to write a note to Isabel, but I just can't get it right."

"You mean like a poem?"

She looked dubious. "I don't write about feelings or nothing. I just say what I'm doing and what I hope she's doing. I think she became a star when she died. That's what my mama used to . . ."

Scout stopped and frowned. "I gotta go now. See you later."

She threw down the butt, ground it underfoot, and started walking away.

"Scout, wait." I was desperate to keep her talking. "I want to write a poem for Isabel too. Will you help me?"

Her back hunched, but she stopped. She turned halfway.

"We can tape it to the fence when we're done; it could be part of the shrine."

She stuck her hands in her pocket and absentmindedly blew away a wisp of hair that had stuck to her lips, shiny with grease.

"I don't know nothing about poems. I haven't been to school since the sixth grade. The only one I ever memorized went like this: 'I'll tell you the truth, don't think I'm lying, I have to run backward to keep from flying.' I like that one a lot. Cuz I've done a lot of flying."

She giggled, then stuck her hands out and began spinning like a child, twirling faster and faster on the concrete until, like a top that has careened out of control, she staggered and fell to the ground.

I ran to her. "Are you okay?"

She shrugged me off. "Whenever I didn't like what was going on around me, I would just fly away in my mind. And it worked. For a long time, it worked real well."

Scout leaned forward and retched. The food she had just eaten came out in chunks, foamy with the Coca-Cola and her spittle. From his watching post, the dog jolted alert. He crept a few feet closer, then stopped. I saw his rib cage poking through his mottled skin.

I lifted her head. With my shirt, I wiped the food-flecked spittle from her mouth. She stiffened at my touch but didn't run away, and I thought it might be because she didn't have the strength.

"It was too rich, too much," she panted, the mousy hair flopping into my face. A sour smell wafted from her. "My stomach couldn't handle it." She put her hand on her belly and moaned, and I saw her ribs, clearly defined through the thin material of her white shirt. A tremor shook her body. "Oh God, here it comes again."

Scout vomited, heaving until her stomach was empty while I held her head. Then she lay limply against me.

"I've got to get you to a doctor," I said, more to myself than to her, but her eyes opened and she dug grime-encrusted nails into my arm.

"No, don't. Promise me you won't. I'm okay. I just need to sleep it off. Then I'll feel better."

"Okay," I said, and the grip loosened.

I thought about calling 911. I thought about my editor, who would be wondering where I was, of all the deadlines I might be missing. I thought about how reporters weren't supposed to get personally involved with sources, how it was the worst thing you could do. I thought about all that, then I gathered her in my arms and tried to stand up. I staggered a bit, because despite her scrawniness she was still a teenaged girl with heavy limbs. I carried her to the car and placed her in the back, buckling her in for the ride home. As I drove away, the pit bull mix crept stealthily toward the detritus we had left behind, his nose twitching.

From the rearview, I saw Scout slumped. Her eyes were closed, their lids waxy.

My grip on the steering wheel tightened. "I'm sorry, Scout," I whispered. "I know I promised, but I have to get you to a hospital. I don't know what's wrong with you. I'm scared you might die on me."

Wasn't there a children's hospital around here? There was construction on Sunset and we inched along while I wished for some kind of emergency siren like the police used to blast through the long line of cars. Sighing, I turned on talk radio.

". . . weighing whether to file a second murder charge since the revelation earlier today by the coroner's office that she was pregnant at the time of her death," a KPCC radio host was saying. "Give us your thoughts on that."

"It does put an interesting spin on things, doesn't it, Burt?" another voice said. "Venus Dellaviglia Langdon was resoundingly pro-life, but this fetus was barely ten weeks old. Does that qualify as murder?"

My foot hit the brake and it took an angry honk to remind me to keep driving. Venus had been pregnant? Now how did that fit into the picture? And why had she apparently not told anyone? Was it because no pregnancy is for sure in your forties? Or was it because the child wasn't Langdon's?

A small moan from the backseat reminded me of my urgent errand. I decided to use Fountain as a shortcut. There were a lot of stop signs but at least you kept moving. At the hospital's emergency entrance, I parked and hopped out. Scout's breathing was shallow, her forehead wreathed with sweat. Heaving one of her arms around my shoulder, I half-carried, half-dragged her through the automatic double doors, where the cool air enveloped us. I thought a smocked orderly might rush up with a stretcher. Instead, the bored eyes of other patients examined us, peering out from bandaged heads and wheelchairs.

I deposited Scout on a stained plaid chair and was directed to the intake desk, where an older man with white hair and a sympathetic demeanor gave me a form and asked whether the patient had insurance.

I stopped. "Let me get the card," I said, fumbling for my purse.

I dug slowly in my bag as a man in surgical scrubs emerged from an office. The sign on the door said TRIAGE NURSE. He went over to Scout and lifted one eyelid. Then he laid the back of his hand against her forehead. Next he picked up her right arm and put his thumb over her wrist, all the while checking his watch.

I sifted through the contents of my purse for an entire minute before pulling out my wallet. I knew Scout wasn't covered on my insurance, but I was desperate to get her treated. When the man in surgical scrubs lowered

Scout's wrist back onto the armrest and jotted something onto his clipboard, I handed over my insurance card.

The clerk looked at me dubiously. "Is she your dependent?"

From the corner of my eye, I saw the nurse press a stethoscope to Scout's chest.

"No," I said. "But I am responsible for her."

The man handed me back the card. "In order for us to treat her, her name has to be on this card."

So much for that feeble idea.

"Then use this." I pulled out my credit card. It couldn't cost more than a few hundred dollars for the initial tests, could it? By then, I'd have figured out the paperwork to enroll her in Medi-Cal.

He took the card and punched in the numbers. Then he peered at the machine.

"It's been rejected."

My stomach tightened. I had gone over my credit limit the week before. It was some silly business with my new computer, which I had foolishly charged, never dreaming I'd need the line of credit for an emergency. I thought fast. I had money in my savings account and my credit union account, but they weren't linked. I would have to go to the Times Mirror Building and request a check, and then deposit it. . . .

"Oh please, I'm good for it, it's just that . . ." My voice trailed off. I sounded like every other deadbeat in L.A.

"She's sick." I pointed to Scout. She had curled up into a ball and was sucking her thumb. "I don't know what's wrong with her. Please. It's an emergency. And this is an emergency room. You can't just turn her away."

"Take her to County General, miss," the man said in a soothing voice. "They won't turn her away there."

"But I don't know what's wrong with her. What if she dies on the way?"

Aware that I was making a scene, I turned to the people in the waiting room, hoping they might rise up and prevail upon this administrator to treat Scout even though she had no insurance. The triage nurse was walking over.

"She's not going to die," he said. "Her vital signs are okay. Breathing shallow and depressed, pulse a little fast. They'll do tests. Believe me, miss, I did my internship at County. They'll take good care of her." He took my hand and squeezed it.

"Do you need a wheelchair to get her into the car?" he asked, rolling forward onto the balls of his feet to examine me. And something more, to decipher how I knew this girl and what our connection was. And of course to wheel her out of the Children's Hospital emergency room and off their property, just in case something should happen. They didn't want to be responsible.

"That would be great," I said bitterly. Within moments, two orderlies arrived with a chair and we were loading her back into the car. She startled when she felt the strange hands upon her and fought, scratching them.

"Where are you taking me? You promised."

One orderly chuckled. "Nothing wrong with her that a brisk shower, a hot meal, and some clean clothes won't cure."

Scout flung her head around and spit in his face. He shrieked and ran, wiping his eyes and screaming about HIV. I hadn't even thought about that. It was a sobering thought. I had Scout's body fluids all over me.

As I drove away, she asked where I was taking her. When I told her, she grew hysterical and started to unbuckle her seat belt, threatening to jump out of the car. She seemed to have recovered her strength.

"Okay," I told her. "Calm down. Maybe you're right, it was just a reaction to the food. How about I take you to my house so you can sleep and shower?"

In my brain, I heard Luke Vinograd's voice: "They're feral youth. It's not like I'm going to invite them to stay with me," and I knew I had crossed some new line. Scout slumped against the backseat, her eyes wary slits. Maybe she had crossed a line too. Or perhaps she was just too exhausted to protest. Her vital signs were okay. If she got worse, I could always call 911 and they'd take her to County.

We pulled into my driveway and she entered my house skittishly, inspecting every room. I got her some clothes and a towel and she went to take a shower.

Meanwhile, I changed out of my vomit-encrusted shirt. Then I called the office and told Thompson I had been interviewing Isabel's friends all morning and wanted to continue if he didn't need me.

"I guess I can spare you," he said. "But, Eve?"

"Yeah?"

"Be careful."

"Since when is that in the job description?"

When I walked into the bedroom, Scout lay on my bed, dressed in my white T-shirt and sweatpants, tracing lines in the air.

"How do you feel?" I asked, sitting down on the mattress.

"Better." She frowned, scooted over to the far side of the mattress, and kept up her task. Tremors shot through her arm, jolting her hand from the imaginary grid.

"Up for a chat?"

" 'Bout what?"

"Finch."

"What about him?"

"What was he like?"

She lowered her arm, then propped her head on her elbow and scanned the room.

"Are you sure you don't have any smokes?"

"Yes, I'm sure. You should really lay off those. You'll live longer."

She looked at me with incomprehension and a hint of superiority. Only fools thought about tomorrow.

"So anyway, tell me about Finch."

"Finch rocked."

"How exactly did he rock?"

"He was my guardian angel on the street."

She reached her free arm down and scratched vigorously at the inside of her leg.

"Sorry," she said. "I had an itch."

She looked blankly at me, and I realized that the thread of our conversation had unraveled and blown away. It was like interviewing a two-year-old.

"How was he a guardian angel?" I prompted.

"Who?"

"Finch."

"Oh, yeah, right. Finch. Well. He took care of me. And Isabel. And Sophie and Caitlin. They called us Finch's Angels. Cuz we all hung out together. Finch always shared his smokes with me."

It was an accusation, as though I were greedily hiding them all for myself.

"Did you have something going with him?"

Scout drew back. "No way. He was like my brother."

"I heard he and Isabel were an item. Was he the jealous type? Could he have killed her in a rage? Or in some Satanic ritual? That's what the cops are saying. They found books and crucified animals and stuff in the squat."

She laughed, the crazy laugh. "That wasn't even his, all those animals. Chill Bill did that, and Finch kicked him out because of it. Paolo was there. He saw it."

"Paolo Dellaviglia Langdon?"

"Yes, Paolo Dellaviglia Langdon." She rattled the flowery name off with ease. Then she leaned her face into mine, her eyes spinning crazy circles in her head. "Mr. Big Shot himself. You think we're such animals that some rich kid wouldn't want to hang with us? That's exactly why he wants to hang with us. That and the drugs. Once his momma even dropped him off in her stylin' Jag."

"Venus Dellaviglia Langdon dropped her son off in front of your squat to buy drugs?"

"He told her he was doing research for some school paper about homeless street kids."

"But she left him there with you guys?"

She gave me an opaque look. "If you lived like me an' Finch, just see where you'd end up. Fox News at Eleven."

"I'm sorry. You're right. I'm just surprised, that's all."

Paolo had told me he barely knew Finch, and he hadn't mentioned Scout at all. Now I understood the crossed signals I had been getting from him that night. It was because he wasn't a very good liar.

"Could Paolo have killed Isabel? Had they fought? Did he have a crush on her or something?"

She waved her arm lazily to dismiss the idea. "Only crush Paolo's got is on himself."

"What about Chill Bill then?" I asked, remembering another name.

"Chill Bill's angry at the world, but he took a Greyhound to Tucson two weeks before Isabel was murdered. He's one of the traveling kids, and there are tunnels there that they stay at."

"How could you stand being around those dead animals? That's disgusting."

"That's disgusting, that's disgusting," she mocked me in a singsong. "But it was dry and it was safe and it was home to me."

"Why didn't someone toss out the dead animals?"

"We were gonna get around to it," she told me. "It wasn't, like, priority."

"So what was, like, priority?"

"Scoring money for food. Getting high. Hanging out."

It was a brand-new Maslow's hierarchy of needs, as interpreted by a whacked Hollywood street kid.

"Scout, do you ever, um, wish you had a different life?"

"You mean like a family? Cuz I have a family."

I was saddened at the defiance in her voice. She had a family, all right, a mini–Manson family run by a crazed squat Nazi named Finch. Who served as her protector and, Lord knows, probably her pimp, and was now in jail on charges of murdering the only other person who had ever been kind to her. But what an unfair question I had posed. Of course Scout would have preferred parents who loved her and a home she could retreat to. But it would cost her too much to say so, would shatter the fragile cocoon of dignity she spun to stay alive.

"This crib ain't bad," she whispered, looking around. "Yeah, I'd take this life."

"Maybe you can," I blurted out before I could stop myself. Then I looked at her, both horrified and entranced by what I had just said. "Why not?" I nodded. "I could try to help you. Get you enrolled in school. Feed you right. We could try."

Why was it that I was so drawn to teenagers in trouble? Was it because I had narrowly escaped their fate at that age? Because I had been unable to save others I had met through work? Christ, if I felt that strongly about it, why didn't I just quit journalism and open up Eve Diamond's Reform School for Troubled Teens?

"A B C D E F G," Scout chanted, continuing to the end of the alphabet. "Now I know my ABCs, see how happy we can be. *Not.*" Her face soured. "I can't do school. And I don't want to try. Ever again. Understand? I will not go to school. I will not go back to Mac. Never. You can't make me."

Her limbs curled tight against her torso, chin and knees folding into her chest until she lay in a teenaged fetal position, rocking and humming, thumb wedged inside her mouth.

I had only the faintest glimmer of what I had done to trigger this catatonia but knew in my gut that the solution would not be as simple as health food and high school algebra. Scout was damaged in ways I couldn't even imagine. I couldn't talk about the future with her. She was here with me today, and that was as far as we could take it. Part of me wanted to console her, part of me knew I had to back off if I wanted this to work. And a third, more venal part of me chafed because I was getting so off-track. I had to get the conversation back to Finch.

"I'm not going to make you do anything, Scout. Why do you say Finch couldn't have killed Isabel?"

She lay there, glassy-eyed. I waited, watching two cabbage butterflies flutter outside the window. Slowly her limbs relaxed. I brought her some orange juice and she drank it down and told me it was awesome. Then, patiently, I repeated the question. And this time, she answered it. Sort of. But I knew we had turned a corner.

"Have you ever met Finch, dude?" she asked me. "He's like, stellar. Freaking brilliant. But gentle somehow."

"I thought he was into Satan."

"Satan, Jehovah. Kris Kringle." She giggled. "Finch is a seeker. If you met him, you'd know he could never kill anyone, except in self-defense."

There went the denial again. Scout slid off the bed, walked to her backpack, and pulled out a small amber container. She rolled out three pills and popped them into her mouth, swallowing them dry.

"What was that?"

"Something to make me sleep." Her voice caressed the words.

"What's it called?" I persisted.

She huffed unhappily. "Vicodin, okay? It just relaxes me. And all your questions are bumming me out so I need a little helper. Scout's little helper." I could see she was drifting off into her own world. But weren't three pills a lot? What if she OD'd on my bed?

"Aren't you just supposed to take one?"

"Gotta high tolerance."

"Where did you get them?"

She shrugged. "One of the daddies gave them to me." She snorted. "Well, he didn't quite give them to me. But he can always get more. More, more, there's always more," she sang tunelessly.

I knew I didn't have much time left. And something was nagging at me. "I wonder why Paolo never told me he had been to the squat?"

She propped her head up on one hand and observed me slyly.

"Why would he do a silly thing like that?"

"Because he'd want me to know how cool he is, hanging out with squatters."

She looked at me from under her anemic lashes and sucked her thumb. Then with a soft plop, she removed it.

"Not murdered squatters."

"You mean when his dad's running for mayor?"

"Paolo said he was running for something. Baby, he was born to run. Just like me."

"Do you and him have something going?"

She flicked her hair back. "Nah, he's just a drug buddy."

"What kind of drugs?"

"Meth. It makes you feel like Superman. 'O Superman.'"

"That's a Laurie Anderson song," I said, surprised she knew it.

"Paolo used to play it for us. But Finch, he was more into Nietzsche's Superman. How cool is that?" She was slurring her words.

"Whoa, Scout. You better think twice before telling people that. Nietzsche believed that his Superman could do anything he wanted because he was superior. That's pretty loaded stuff, when Finch is about to stand trial for killing Isabel."

Scout's eyes were pinpricks, spiraling into far-off nebula.

"He didn't kill her. I know he didn't cuz . . ."

She stopped.

"What, Scout?"

"Nothing. Leave me alone, I need to sleep."

"Do you want your beloved Finch to get convicted for a murder he didn't commit?"

But she just yawned and rolled away from me, exposing her back. It was a slender back, and through the T-shirt she wore, I could see the knobs of her spinal column poking out at regular intervals. Didn't she know she should never turn her back on someone? Especially in bed.

I stood up, and the mattress bounced back.

"Okay, Scout, sleep now." I tiptoed out of the room.

On the balcony, I sipped a cup of faux joe, the decaffeinated coffee I turned to when my nerves were shot. Even though it was a placebo, it still gave me a rush that was good for a few hours of thinking.

Scout knew something about Isabel's murder. She was a material witness. The cops would want to talk to her. I had promised her sanctuary, but we both knew it couldn't last forever. Would I be betraying her if I called the authorities? Yeah, I sure would. She'd be sent back into the child welfare system and would just run away again, unless they locked her up in a psycho ward. She had experienced too many betrayals already in her short life. Then there was Finch. Why couldn't she understand that her testimony might free him from a murder rap? She was the one who insisted he wasn't a killer.

"If you met him, you'd know," Scout had said.

Something clicked in my mind then. I had to meet him. It wouldn't be hard. I just had to take a little drive to Bauchet. It was the L.A. County Jail downtown, which was located on Bauchet Street. But everyone just called it Bauchet.

# CHAPTER 18

*I* sat cross-legged on the floor and called Tom Thompson, sketching out my latest brainstorm. I didn't mention that another squatter kid lay passed out on my bed as we spoke. That was more information than he needed. Thompson agreed it would make a great folo if I could get into the jail. He told me to go through the kid's lawyer.

I knew a guy like Finch had no money for lawyers so I called the Los Angeles County Public Defender's office to see if his court-appointed attorney would give me the okay.

It took the clerks a few minutes to find out who had been assigned the case, but they finally transferred me to the right PD. I laid out the facts, then pled my case.

"Absolutely not," came the response. "We are not going to try this case in the media. He'll talk to the jury, or not at all."

"But it would give him a great opportunity to recount his side of the story," I said, pointing out how I had all these other street kids and straight kids on the record, talking about how Finch couldn't have done it. But the clipped female voice on the other end of the line wasn't buying it.

"We've had a lot of media requests and we're telling everyone the same thing. You'll have to wait until the trial."

"Have you even asked him whether he wants to talk? You're supposed to be representing *his* wishes."

"No, Ms. Diamond, I'm supposed to be representing him to the best of *my* ability, and I've advised him it's in his best interest not to talk to anyone."

I hung up the phone and considered. He was a teenager. Accused of murder. Stuck in a jail cell. He'd be scared. Angry. No family to visit him. No Finch's Angels either, since minors couldn't get in without an adult. He'd be bored. Lonely. And maybe intrigued at the opportunity to talk to a stranger. It was certainly worth taking the chance.

I checked on Scout. She was snoring with her mouth open, but her color and pulse seemed good. Still, I was taking no chances. I knew that kids sometimes chased downers with alcohol, and I didn't want an OD on my hands. So I went to the liquor cabinet. There were two bottles of wine, one of tequila, and one of rum. I stuck them in my trunk. I stood there for a minute, then ran back into the house and got Scout's bottle of Vicodin out of her smelly backpack and threw that in the trunk too.

Then I drove down the hill to Sunset and headed east toward downtown. This Sunset was light-years away from the glamorous Strip. Yeah, sure, there were nightclubs on the eastern end too, but they had names like El Nayarit or Candelejas that harkened back to scorching desert or humid jungles. On this Sunset, storefront shops sold overruns from the downtown garment district. And instead of video screens displaying celebrity hotties, my Sunset had wall murals of dancing fruits and vegetables advertising the produce piled high in mom-and-pop grocery stores alongside *chicharrones* and *cerveza*, *canela molida* and dried *pasilla* peppers.

In the booming ethnic markets of Los Angeles, the shopping carts told you how long someone had been in the country. Those of new Armenian and Salvadoran and

Fukienese immigrants cascaded with greens and yellows and reds. Places like 99 Ranch Market and Jon's barely even stocked dinner entrées and packaged lettuce. Who in their right mind would pay extra for such things when there were grandmothers and great-aunts at home to cook?

But the longer they lived in the States, the more fractured the families grew. Now the shopping carts held microwavable meals and fast foods. Ironically, it was only at high-end markets that the trend reversed as educated white-collar workers gobbled up black-eyed peas, mustard greens, and cave-aged sheep's-milk cheeses at double the prices charged by the competitive ethnic stores. I knew because I shopped at both ends of the grocery spectrum.

Soon there were no markets at all and I was downtown on Bauchet, one of the city's more dismal and sorry streets, where hulking concrete buildings seemed to squash the very joy from your psyche and gray walls were stained with the tears, blood, and bodily fluids of every inmate who ever got into trouble.

Walking into the L.A. County Jail, I milled with the other visitors, most of them brown and black. In the sea of dark hair and skin, a tall, painfully thin blonde woman in a white minidress stuck out. I could only see her back, but she teetered on pale stilts that seemed too fragile to support her. Meth freak, I thought. Then she turned and my stomach flopped. Her eyes were hollow sockets, her skin ravaged. But her belly was a balloon, at least eight months gone with child.

Each time I came down here, I was stunned by all the children—infants and toddlers and sullen tweens carting Gameboys. The TV was permanently tuned to the cartoon network.

At the counter, a guard smiled and handed me a form, and I was surprised at his courteous demeanor. Somehow, I hadn't expected kindness in this inferno. Under "relationship," I wrote "friend." I was a new friend. One Finch didn't know yet. Now the form asked if I was with the news media. My eyes wandered to a placard in the room which said that providing false information was a felony. Finally, I checked off the Yes box. Under affiliation, I wrote *L.A. Times*.

When I brought it back, the guard scanned it. The smile ebbed from his face and I yearned for our earlier relationship when he had taken me for a felon's girlfriend instead of a poxy reporter. He asked for my ID, fingered it thoughtfully, then shoved his chair back and stood up, saying he'd have to check with the watch commander.

"Do you think it will take long, sir?"

I felt a slight thaw. "If the commander clears it, we'll ask the inmate. It's up to him."

"I'll be here."

I had barely started on a *National Enquirer* story about Brad Pitt when the guard said they would bring him out. He gave me a pass and I got into another line, riding the slipstream behind two teens pushing strollers and trading tips on how you held the babies up to the plastic partition so Daddy could see how much they'd grown.

We got herded through a metal detector and frisked, then entered a large room with about fifteen partitions. At each one, people were talking. It could have been a bank, but with tighter security. A warden directed me to a seat, and through the glass I saw another guard lead in a tall, skinny white guy. He had sallow skin, waxy from a bad diet and vampiric life. Blackheads clustered near the outside corners of his eyes. He had a high greasy forehead and lank brown hair. His hands were large and graceful with long tapering fingers, and I tried to imagine him grabbing Isabel's neck and strangling her. As he walked, his eyes darted around, sizing up his surroundings. Then he sat, slouched low in his chair, and crossed his arms in front of his concave chest, affecting disinterest.

I introduced myself and said I was writing about Isabel's murder. He looked away with elaborate boredom.

"So what do you want from me, a confession?"

I ignored the provocation.

"Your aunt and all Isabel's friends say the police have the wrong guy. They're convinced you didn't do it. Especially your pal Scout."

He glanced at me, and in his eyes I saw the cynicism battle with the possibility that I might be sincere. It gave me an inkling of how much he wanted me to be for real. Then the curtain of diffidence dropped again.

"Howdja meet Scout?" he asked, deflecting my probe with one of his own.

"At your squat," I told him. "She was weaving a purple satin ribbon around the cyclone fencing. There's a big shrine now. Then I ran into her at Starman a few nights later. We talked. She's at my apartment right now, recovering from a stomach upset."

Again the flicker, this time of astonishment, the veil parting, allowing me to peer inside before it slammed shut again. Oh yes, there was definitely somebody home.

"I know you didn't do it," I told him. "I know the police have interrogated you. And you've probably talked to your court-appointed attorney already and told her everything you know. But I want you to tell me too."

Something quickened behind his eyes. "Ain't no lawyer been to see me."

"Maybe not yet but they will. And I can tell you're too smart to spend the rest of your life in prison for something you didn't do."

Finch shrugged. This time, he didn't risk looking at me. "They got a lot of evidence. Bags of it. They got my books on Nostradamus, Nietzsche . . ." There was a lag, a whoosh of air. His voice changed timbre, grew whispery. "Oh yeah. They found my books on Satan, demonology."

I swallowed, remembering what the psychologist had told me about how manipulative these kids could be, how they'd charm and shock and ultimately burrow deep under your skin. Still, I wanted to give him a way out.

"Scout told me you read up on lots of religions. She said you're searching."

"I read a lot," he allowed. "The Kabala, the *Book of Sufi.* Freud. I'm interested in everything." I pictured him sitting cross-legged on the dirt floor of the squat, a candle flickering before him, reading water-stained paperbacks and cloth-bound hardcover books stolen from the library while the wax dripped down and the dark hours of the night passed, his own home-schooled version of the Comparative Religions class he had missed by running away.

"Yeah?"

His shoes scraped the linoleum. He sat straighter and crossed his legs as something kindled.

"I study the human condition. I want to figure out why people do such terrible things to each other. There's some bad shit out there. Really fucked-up folks. But it's fascinating, in a perverse way. Don't you think? Not devil worship, that's just a bunch of mumbo jumbo, but pure evil. The power it exerts over people, how it draws them in. Does that make sense?"

From across the pane of glass, he saw me recoil. I had seen the pentagrams and upside-down crucifixes at the squat, read about the eviscerated possum carcasses. And I knew that those who murdered often started out by torturing and killing animals. The police knew it too. Even as we sat in Bauchet jail, some DA somewhere was preparing the color photos as "Exhibits A through L" of the criminal docket in the first-degree-murder trial of *People vs. Finch Marino*.

"All that Satanic worship stuff they found in the squat looks pretty bad, Finch."

"I didn't kill those animals," Finch said softly. "That was Chill Bill. He's one scary dude. I wasn't there when that happened. Chill Bill had himself a Satanic teach-in and invited some punks into my home."

The pride with which he said "home" almost broke my heart.

"So how did it work there? You were the boss? The squat Nazi?"

He gave me an astute look. I knew more about his world than he thought. A stillness grew at the center of him. He seemed intent on convincing me of something.

"Yeah, I'm the squat Nazi. And when I got back, I told him to clear out with his filthy friends and take his Satanic rituals with him."

I had eased my notepad out and was scribbling surreptitiously, but he seemed not to notice or care.

"I can do that cuz it's my crib. They stay, they pay. They gotta bring home food or money or dope. And they gotta lie low. You wouldn't believe some of these wannabes; they climb in and out all day when anyone can see them, they play their boom boxes. Rank amateurs. You don't want to draw attention. That's the best way to get busted. And these little chickies like Isabel, coming 'round, wanting to hang with us, give us money, take us home to shower and eat. They got us on a pedestal. They want to be like us, but they're too soft, living in the straight world. You can't cross back and forth like that. Sooner or later, the raft is gonna sink."

"So was it Chill Bill then?"

Finch looked annoyed that I had interrupted his monologue.

"Chill Bill? Nah. He's talked about keeping girls in cages and shit, but I don't think he'd ever do it. Besides, he was in Tucson."

Scout had said much the same thing.

"Then who do you think killed Isabel?"

"You got me. I never made it home that night. Got stuck down in OC. When I came back the next morning, the place was crawling with cops, so I took off. I was living on the beach till they picked me up. Bastards."

Instinctively, I put my hand up to the plastic pane to touch him, and the oil from my fingerprints smudged the bulletproof glass.

"I want to help you get out of here," I told him. "But I need your help too."

Finch wasn't listening. He was watching a bored two-year-old run around while his parents talked across the partition.

"Dorrick, c'mere," the woman called. She got out a baby bottle and dumped in a can of cola. When it stopped fizzing, she screwed on the rubber nipple and handed it to the boy.

I looked back at Finch, who averted his eyes but not before I saw them blink rapidly.

"I never had no momma take care of me," he said,

watching Dorrick, who sucked greedily from the bottle. "Maybe if I had, things would have been different."

"Where was your mom when you were growing up?"

"It's not *even* important."

Yes it is, I thought. It's terribly important. But I also knew that with these kids, their stories, no matter how horrible, were often the only private thing they had left. I didn't push it with Finch. I couldn't ask him to bare his soul unless I was prepared to get involved. And right now, I was already about as involved as I could get with his little friend.

"So what's Scout's story then? I know she won't tell me."

Finch sized me up.

"She's at my house, for chrissakes, Finch. She's sleeping in my bed."

His head whipped up when I said that, and I saw him examining me anew. With shock, I realized what he thought. In their world, people were either predators or prey. There wasn't a whole lot of in-between.

"It's not like that," I said. "She collapsed in front of the squat after she ate some food I brought her. I didn't know what to do, so I took her to my home. She knows something about Isabel's murder. She's convinced it wasn't you, but she's too scared to tell me. If I understood where she was coming from, maybe I could get her to open up. And get her some help. She seems, well, unbalanced."

"Open up? She's spent her life closing down so it don't hurt so much."

"Tell me."

"I don't know why I'm even talking to you."

"I want to help her. And you."

"Yeah, everybody wants to help everyone. You gotta

understand that on the street, it's not cool to ask. Lotta kids just don't want to talk."

"You're not on the street anymore."

He shook his head and exhaled loudly.

"I don't know much. Her dad was a Mongol, that's a biker group, he roared out of her life when she was two. Her brother is a retard and she had to take care of him cuz her momma was usually drunk with her latest boyfriend. One of them started doing Scout when she was eight. She ran away at twelve. That's when she discovered men would pay her to do what her momma's boyfriend made her do for free."

He glared at me. Is this the dirt you want? his eyes asked.

"So why should she open up to you or anyone else?" Finch said. "She only opens up to me. I'm her family, see. Me and the other traveling kids, but me especially. I take care of her, make sure she doesn't get raped no more. I call her Lil Sis. She looks up to me."

Emotion welled like a bubble in my gut, then popped. This wasn't the boasting of a murderer. This was the boasting of a kid who recognized damage in others because he carried it around himself. And I knew I had to learn who killed Isabel before this thing went to trial.

"What about you, Finch?"

He gave me a scornful look, then shook his head. One leg pumped up and down, regular as an oil derrick.

"I don't care if it's not cool to ask. It's important."

"Why?"

"Because it helps me understand who you are, where you're from, how you got here."

Finch scanned the waiting room, searching for his idealized childhood that never was, but Dorrick and his momma had left.

"I'm from Ohio," he said, answering me literally. "My mom died when I was little and I never met my dad. Some of his people took me in, but it was only for the monthly checks. When I ran away, the county put me in group homes. I never stayed there long either."

"Why not?"

His leg jerked angrily. "Would you stay at a place where they feed you spoiled pork and there aren't enough blankets in winter, where most of the kids are always fighting and stealing?"

"It doesn't sound too good."

"It was all I knew. Then we got a new psychologist. He talked to me. Gave me books to read and shit. He let me study in his office. He'd close the door so I'd have some peace to do my homework. Then he . . . then one day I realized that . . . that what I was looking for didn't exist, and that I had been stupid to trust him."

"What did he do, Finch?"

His eyes hardened. "I deserved it, I guess, for leading him on."

"How did you lead him on?"

He shrugged. "No one had ever hugged me before."

Finch stood up and shoved his hands in his pockets. He kicked over the plastic table next to him, then began to stomp it violently yet methodically with his foot, as if to destroy it along with his memories. With each blow, the plastic table creaked and groaned against the linoleum floor.

"Finch," I said urgently. "Finch, it's okay," even though it wasn't. But he had gone beyond my voice. Two guards came running and one got him in a headlock and brought him to the ground. I stood there, helpless on the other side of the partition, my fingernails clawing the glass, watching his eyes dart like those of an animal caught in a steel trap. He seemed to reserve his fiercest looks for me. A moment later, a woman in a white jacket came striding over with a needle, shot it into his arm, and within moments, he relaxed and went limp. The last I saw was the two guards dragging him away.

Now a security officer strode purposefully toward me and I braced for trouble. But he merely took my arm and escorted me out of the visiting room.

"Don't blame yourself, that stuff happens in here more often than you would think," he said apologetically. "They'll be reevaluating whether he should have visitors."

I turned to the man.

"Oh please, I don't want to be the cause of his further isolation."

"They're not lining up to visit that one."

I retraced my steps out of Bauchet and back into the late afternoon sunlight. Pulling up to the parking kiosk, I slid my stub and $7.00 across the bulletproof enclosure to a sad African with tribal scars on his cheeks. Or was it the permanent souvenir of a police interrogation in his adopted land? He barely looked up from his U.S. citizenship textbook as he let me out.

Scout was just waking up, a little groggy from the Vicodin. It was dinnertime and we were both hungry, so we went to a little place on Los Feliz Boulevard just over I-5 for takeout.

We were on our way back, the comforting aroma of garlic and tomato sauce drifting up from the stacked aluminum containers, when Scout leaned out the window. "Could we stop there?" she asked.

I looked but saw only blue-and-orange playground equipment, a cheerful jumble of swings, slides, and monkey bars tucked into a corner of Los Feliz Park.

"You want to go to a playground?"

"Please."

I swung the car around. When we pulled up, she dashed out of the car before I could put it in park, and I wondered whether she had seen someone she knew and was taking off again. But she plunged into the sand, her sneakered feet leaving deep imprints as she sprinted for the swings. As several toddlers looked up curiously from their sand shovels, Scout hopped on, adjusted her butt in the sling, and began pumping her legs in the air. Soon she was soaring back and forth in a high arc as she gripped the metal chains tightly in her fists, a look of bliss on her face, her long hair whipping out from under the ever-present filthy cap.

"C'mon, it's fun." She beckoned me. I shrugged, then carried our takeout containers to a green picnic table. It had been years since I had set foot on a playground. Around us, dusk was falling, a warm October twilight. The playground sat at the bottom of a grassy incline on the corner of Riverside Drive and Los Feliz, one of the busiest intersections in the city. But its location shielded it from the evening traffic that rumbled and whizzed past. Here in the hollow, amid great oak trees that stretched their sheltering branches like a canopy, the real world seemed muffled and remote.

"C'mon," Scout shouted again, and I bent down and undid the laces of my shoes, rolled off my socks, and sank my pale sweaty feet into the granular coolness of the sand, feeling it scrunch under me. I padded to the empty swing beside Scout, hopped on, and began pumping. Soon I was flying over the sand, watching the slide and the jungle gym recede, then approach, recede, then approach, cutting through the air with glorious abandon.

"It's like flying, isn't it?" Scout shouted, and her voice

rang with a childlike exuberance I hadn't heard before.

"Yes," I told her, as we crossed in midflight. I tried to match my swinging to hers. "It feels good."

Lost in our thoughts, we swung. Evening settled, wrapping its velvety arms around the park. The last of the children left. It was too late for playing now, too early for gang-banging, a fleeting penumbra to be savored precisely because it was transitory.

"Does it remind you of when you were little?" I asked, hoping to draw her out.

She didn't answer.

"Did you used to go to parks a lot?"

"I remember a long time ago," she said. "My mom was pushing me and my brother on the swings. We screamed 'higher.' She wore a polka-dotted dress. But maybe I just imagined it from TV."

"What do you remember from your childhood?" I shouted as we whizzed past each other again.

"Too much shit." She shook her head. "Like scenes from a movie, crowding my head."

"Such as?"

"Bean dip. It still makes me gag. But there was nothing else in the fridge. And other kids, making fun of my clothes. The teacher, asking if everything was all right at home . . ."

She turned to me, her hair flapping in the wind.

"So I just turn it off in my brain. Click." Her hand made a turning motion.

"We're not going to eat bean dip tonight, Scout," I yelled. "We're going to have a feast."

And we did. Later that night, after Scout had gone to sleep and I was sitting on the balcony, savoring a glass of Grüner Veltliner so cold that it sweated up the glass, I heard the back screen slam.

"Can't sleep, huh? Want to sit here for a minute?"

"No," she said. "I just got up to go to the bathroom and I wanted to make sure you were still here."

"I'm here, Scout. I'm right here."

The door clicked and I saw her shuffle back down the hall and take a left into my bedroom. I stared out into the blackness for a long time, then made my rounds, locking up the house. I pulled out the futon that doubled as my living room couch, laying it flat on the thick white carpet. I got some bedding out of a closet. It smelled of dust and airless spaces. Then I drew the blankets over me and fell into a thick, dreamless sleep. In the morning, the daylight streaming in through the big picture window woke me up. I felt disoriented, and it took me a minute to remember where I was and why I wasn't in my own bed. The house was silent and empty. I threw off the blankets and ran to the bedroom, but I already knew.

I looked around the room, half expecting her to leap from behind a door and startle me like a naughty child, but the only surprise came when I noticed the top to my jewelry box standing open. I walked over, not wanting to believe, until I saw the necklaces and rings and earrings swirled into a jumbled pile. I pawed through it but failed to turn up my grandmother's engagement ring, a square-cut diamond that had been my family's only legacy to me. Also missing was a vintage garnet necklace and matching earrings an old boyfriend had given me. Dread turned to anger. Scout had wiped out my past. What about my purse? I ran to find it and noticed the wallet lying on the kitchen table, gaping open. The $200 I had withdrawn from the ATM last night was gone, but my credit cards were still there. I threw myself down in the chair, half disbelieving that Scout could pull such a low trick, half chiding myself for failing to see that I had left myself vulnerable. While I had been playing Lady Bountiful, she had been plotting to rip me off.

How could I have been so naïve? Why should she trust me? What in her short life had ever taught her that she could? I should have taken better steps to secure my valuables. We had both gotten what we deserved.

I couldn't bring myself to call the police so after brooding about it some more, I showered, ate, and drove to work. As I rounded the 2 Freeway, up where it dumps onto the 134 near Eagle Rock, I saw highway workers trimming the cactus at the freeway's edge. A job perilous to flesh and cloth. But these men wore jeans and T-shirts, not orange road crew uniforms. They straddled the spiny succulents, plastic grocery bags looped around their wrists. A man winced as a spine plunged into his brown hand. Another plucked the rich cactus fruit, smooth pink outsides cracking to reveal the creamy center speckled with black seeds. I had tasted them, knew the fruit was sweet and crunched like frozen sorbet. Was this dessert for them, these urban scavengers, a poignant treat to remind them of home? Or was it the main course? Whizzing past at sixty-five miles per hour, I couldn't exactly stop and ask.

At work, I waltzed into Thompson's office to recount my jailhouse interview with Finch. But before I could open my mouth, he told me to put the squatter kids on ice. It was storius interruptus again. He had a daily on accordion schools that couldn't wait.

"Accordion schools? Give me a break, Thompson."

"I'm serious."

"Don't tell me. The last one in the San Gabriel Valley, where they crafted the suckers by hand just like in the old country, is going out of business."

"Flip it. They're springing up like poisonous mushrooms."

"You got something against the polka?"

He thrust a wire story into my hand. "I do when the bastards rip off poor families. Here's the setup. Free introductory lesson, rave about how talented the kid is and sign 'em up for two thousand dollars' worth of classes. Sell 'em a worthless instrument for a couple grand more."

"Oh no." I pictured the miserable scenario.

"It's despicable, these immigrants, preying on their own kind. They opened up dozens of schools, recruited hundreds of students. The ringleader allegedly used the money to finance a sex change operation."

"We've got a German transsexual crime ring operating in the San Gabriel Valley? Tell me you're kidding."

I tried to imagine a florid-faced Bavarian with breasts and lederhosen demonstrating the accordion to a crowd of hopeful children.

"Nah," Thompson said. "Mexican. Every one of them was Mexican. They're nuts for polkas over there. That's why the con worked. People lost the deed to their home, took out loans they'll be paying back for years."

He shook his head sadly. "All so a guy could buy himself a vagina."

I was still trying to wrap my mind around it. No doubt about it, Thompson had me hooked. Now he reeled me in.

"It needs that special Eve Diamond touch, Ace. And be sure to get lots of sob stories from the victims. I need it by four."

He walked away and another image came to mind, a mustachioed man onstage at Arena La Puente, deftly playing the heavy instrument strung around his neck as the crowd clomped and twirled. A Mexican polka, that unholy mix of Teutonic accordion and Mexican ranchera that coalesced a century ago when German immigrants settled in the Southwest.

I decided to call Silvio for a quote about the music's zooming popularity. Talking to him thrilled me in a way that had nothing to do with journalism.

The day passed quickly. Sitting on a sagging couch in Baldwin Park listening to a shell-shocked mother with varicose veins, I realized she was more devastated to learn her sons weren't accordion geniuses than by the $4,000 loan she now owed on a Burger King salary.

Silvio gave me a good sound bite. When I hung up, it was with the agreement he'd pick me up Saturday at 7 P.M. He wanted to go to a club to check out a promising new singer.

# CHAPTER 19

*I* stood on my balcony. Above me, cotton candy clouds hung low in the sky. The air was humid, heavy, the evening still and menacing. I missed the breeze that kicked up in the late afternoon, cooling my damp skin, ruffling the tops of the palm trees. It felt like a tropical storm was gathering offshore, ready to blow in, typhoonlike. Silverlake was only fifteen miles from the ocean but it usually felt a lot farther when you were driving through the smoggy neighborhoods or stuck on the freeway. As I watched, the horizon began to change, filling with a viscous, yellow-brown haze that reflected my mood. Yesterday's accordion story had soured me on mankind, as had Scout's disappearing act. I knew I had to find her again, but I also knew that this time, she wouldn't be hanging out at the squat. The police had boarded it up so she couldn't get inside. But there were dozens of other abandoned buildings in East Hollywood that hadn't yet attracted the retro renovator's eye.

I went inside and called Sophie and Caitlin. They hadn't heard from her. I decided to ask Silvio if we could stop at Starman after the show. Scout might show up. We would be nearby, at La Playa Azul nightclub, to see a singer Silvio had booked at Arena La Puente for *Día de los Muertos,* Day of the Dead. She was way too pop for his taste, but she had a couple of hits on the radio and was going to be a star, he said. Her name was Flavia Jiménez.

My contribution to the evening was drinks. I had once

read an Ernest Hemingway biography about how Papa had favored a Cuban rum drink that sounded decadent and healthy all at once. So that evening, I bought soda water, cane juice, rum, and limes, which I squeezed for their emerald essence. Then I picked sprigs of mint that grew lush and wild in Violetta's backyard, mixed the drinks, and sprinkled in the torn leaves.

I hadn't yet washed my hands when the doorbell rang. It was Silvio, wearing jeans and a beige cashmere vest over a white T-shirt. Tonight, his cowboy boots were elaborately stitched beige-and-white leather. It complemented his white cowboy hat, which he swept off as he walked in. I saw a flash of blood red, yellow, and blue on the inside of the hat and stopped, wondering what that could be.

He saw my puzzlement and held out his hat for my inspection. Silk-screened onto the dome inside the Stetson's crown was an image of the Virgin of Guadalupe.

"Even a traditional Texas outfitter like Stetson realizes the market isn't just good ol' white boys anymore. It's good ol' Mexican boys like me. This is La Guadalupana, one of their biggest sellers. She brings good luck."

We could use it, I thought, as I handed him a drink on the balcony.

Silvio sniffed it. "Is this . . ."

"That's right, a *moquito*."

He laughed. "You sure about that?"

"That Cuban drink with rum and mint and lime that Hemingway liked," I said, pleased that Silvio would know how well read and cosmopolitan I was.

"You mean *mojito?*"

"That's it."

"Well, you just said 'snot' in Spanish. *Moquito* means snot. The drink is *mojito.*"

"Oh," I said, deflating. As a native Angeleno, I had grown up with Latino culture as a familiar and ubiquitous backdrop. And that tricked me into thinking I knew more than I did.

"*No importa*," he said. Never mind. "It's tangy and perfect for this weather."

As we walked out, I told him the bare bones about Scout and he agreed we should visit Starman on the way back. He stopped in front of an old, beat-up truck. Its panels were smeared with primer. A rusty chain lay coiled in the truck's bed. I supposed he found it useful for transporting bales of hay, livestock, and musical equipment for his dad's business. But somehow, this wasn't what I expected for a date.

"Welcome to my humble abode." Silvio held the door open for me. It was humble, all right. The dashboard was cracked plastic with aluminum knobs. He got in and started the truck, which roared to life with surprising ease. Then he pressed a button. From either side of the instrument panel, a gleaming walnut and chrome shell descended over the cheesy dash and clicked into place. I was now staring at the instrument panel of a luxury car. Luminous dials and gauges of a stereo system winked at me.

"What would you like to hear?"

But I was still figuring out his car. "Wow, so that's just a front."

He smiled and pulled away from the curb.

"I wouldn't be caught dead in a Mercedes or a Lexus," he said. "It's an invitation. Yoo-hoo. Criminals. Over here. I have a fancy car. Rob me."

"You can rest easy, slick. Ain't no one gonna jack this ride." I laughed and inspected him anew. He was full of layers, like an onion, this Silvio, not a rube at all.

But the smile had disappeared. "Do you have to talk like that?"

"Like what?"

"That substandard English. It makes you sound so . . . uneducated."

I was astonished.

"Actually, I'm quite overeducated."

"But people who hear such language don't know that."

"I don't give a shit what people think."

Silvio stared at his gleaming luxury dashboard. "Well, I do. Because of where I'm from, it's important to make a good impression."

"You're from the same place as me, Jack. El Lay."

He ran his finger thoughtfully along the fine-grained wood.

"Yes, but you're . . . I don't have the luxury . . ."

I got his drift.

"You mean people will assume you can't speak proper English because you're Mexican-American so you want to show them up by speaking only King's English?"

"Precisely. And you know what?" He winked at me. "It's been a very successful strategy."

"In that case, I'm surprised you deign to be seen in public with an uncouth Valley Girl like me."

"Perhaps next time we'll stay home."

This titillated me but made me nervous too. I steered the conversation back to cars.

"I like the idea of an urban camouflage car, it's brilliant."

"I'm a concert promoter," he said. "When I listen to music, I want to really hear it."

He pressed another button and great waves of audiophile sound crashed into the cab. I felt more than heard the horns kick in, the maracas shiver, the beat shimmer and swoop as Marc Anthony moaned, sweet and urgent, in "I Need to Know," a torrid paean to lust. But this was in Spanish for the home audience, the words more raw and molten than the English version. It gave me a funny feeling in my lower belly. I closed my eyes and gave myself up to the sensation.

"I like this," I said when it ended.

"Nothing but ear candy. Unlike this."

Silvio popped in a CD and a new male voice came on, cooler but no less urgent, the silvery ballads of long ago.

"Who is it?"

He flipped me the CD. "My parents' music. But I'm partial to it."

"Agustin Lara," I read. The singer leaned into the camera, dressed in a suit and hat from another era, a man with a pencil-thin mustache and a melancholy air.

Lara's voice drifted over the speakers, crooning with the big band behind him, transporting me to a Mexico City nightclub circa 1955. I felt a sense of dislocation, listening to this music as I bounced around millennial L.A. in a primer-splattered pickup with this man, born in the same city as me yet heir to a legacy that straddled two worlds. Where did I belong on his crowded stage?

All too soon we were pulling up to the club. Silvio whisked me inside, all the way backstage, where Flavia Jiménez was getting ready. She sat at her makeup table, the big lights illuminating her face like a halo. She fluffed her curls and applied eyeliner and eye shadow. She licked her thumb and smudged the corner of her eye, adding charcoal gray, then midnight blue. All the while, she kept up a heated debate with a reporter who wore dog tags that said *La Opinión*. It didn't seem to be going well.

Flavia saw us in the mirror and her demeanor

changed. She whirled her chair around and greeted Silvio effusively. He came on like liquid fire, murmuring into her ear, kissing her on each cheek, telling her she looked gorgeous. Finally he introduced me.

Now an assistant hurried in and began lacing up a corsetlike vest. Flavia leaned forward, examining her face in the mirror and wincing as the laces were pulled tight to give her the matador waist her public wanted.

"Some critics say your songs stir up trouble between men and women," *La Opinión*'s reporter started in again after the introductions had been made. "You tell women to stand up for their rights."

"And what of it?" Flavia said. "Should they put up with scum who beat them and drink up the paycheck and chase other women?"

Slyly, she took in the reporter, a well-coiffed professional woman wearing heels and a pantsuit. "Would you put up with that from your man?"

The reporter considered. "Well, no, but I wouldn't be with such a man in the first place."

Flavia gave her a knowing look. "Oh, you're so sure of yourself, you're too smart and educated. Well, let me tell you, baby, love doesn't always come in neat little packages. I've been there, and I know."

Flavia tossed her hair and pursed her lips to examine her lipstick.

"I didn't write that song for women like you, I wrote it for women like me, who have felt the heel of oppression grinding into their cheek, who know the salt taste of tears, of blood pooling in their mouth from a cut lip. And who still go crawling back. *Claro que sí.* I was that woman in the mirror, and if my song can save just one woman from getting hurt the way I was, then I feel proud."

"You feel proud you're breaking up marriages? You feel proud you're assaulting traditional Mexican values? The wife should obey her husband, not rise up against him."

Flavia looked at the reporter in disbelief.

"You reporters are all alike, trying to create conflict when none exists. I'm not saying she should rise up and kill the bastard, just that she should leave him. That is usually punishment enough, as the man is the weak one in the relationship; he abuses her to make himself feel better. But when she leaves, his power evaporates." She threw her manicured fingers up into the air. "By the way, I'm donating the proceeds of tonight's show to the Battered Women's Shelter of East L.A. Put that in your paper. And why don't you go and interview some of those women if you want to hear real horror stories."

"Don't tell me how to do my job," snapped the reporter, as we slipped away unnoticed.

"Flavia's a real firecracker. She'll go far," Silvio said. "This is just what the listening public needs at this point in the emancipation of the Mexican woman. A woman who will sing to their fears, their tears, their empowerment, their *poder*."

"You agree with her then?"

"But of course."

"You gonna do the dishes?"

He leaned in to me. "For that, we hire a housekeeper."

There was something thrilling and intimate about the way he said it. What exactly did he mean by "we"?

I was hoping we'd sit at one of the front tables that said RESERVED but Silvio led me to the back of the club where the smells of perfume and sweat mingled. He stood with his arms crossed as Flavia Jiménez emerged to wild applause, studying her, gauging how her voice projected, the reaction she elicited from the crowd. Eavesdropping on conversations, he asked patrons what they thought of her and listened carefully to the response. Although he bought me a drink, Silvio sipped from a highball glass of soda water. What was play for most people was work for him.

Flavia Jiménez sang for almost three hours without a break, and Silvio noted that too, admiring her stamina, her charisma. When she announced she was taking a short break, Silvio checked his watch and said he was done. I was surprised to find his arm around my waist at the darkened entrance to the club. We walked to the car, the sweat clinging to our skin in the humid air, and we drove back in silence, each wrapped in our own worlds. My eardrums rang pleasantly from the music. As we neared my house, the storm that had been gathering all night broke, cascading until the wipers couldn't keep up. Water gurgled all around, chugging along the gutter, coursing downhill, sweeping up the sediment and dried leaves and empty fast food containers. We parked and sprinted to the front door.

Then we were inside, our hair hanging in limp, dripping strands and our bodies clammy and slick.

"This is like the Yucatán," Silvio said. "Every afternoon, the sun goes behind the clouds and the market vendors gather up their wares and the streets empty and the storm gathers and then it rains, pours for two hours, while the people are inside, having their lunch and then their siestas under the whirring fans. It's the hour of making love, the long afternoon, and then by five the sky clears and the puddles steam in the sunlight and the market starts up again and the shopkeepers throw open their doors for a few more hours before dinner. And then the next day it happens all over again."

His voice was intimate, infused with the hallucinatory quality of dreams. I felt I had been there with him already and had just invoked the memory. Be careful, my heart, I scolded, as I fell from a great height.

"I'm, uh, going to change out of these wet clothes," I said.

"I should be going," he said, but he didn't. I stepped back toward him.

"How about a drink? Or some hot tea? To take off the chill."

"Tea," he said. "And then, I must go. Really. It's late."

I boiled some water and brought over two mugs, spoons, tea bags, cut lemons, honey, and blackberry jam.

"My grandmother always said tea with honey and jam and lemon wards off colds."

He dutifully spooned in the emollients.

"To grandmothers, *las abuelas*," he said. He drank his tea in great hot gusts, then put the ceramic mug back on the saucer, making it groan in protest.

"I'll be going now."

He stood up. I stood up too.

"Good-bye," he said.

He raised his hand, as if to shake mine, then let it stray to my face. He tucked a lank strand of hair behind my ear. His fingers were warm from the heated mug. I imagined we were in the Yucatán, in a pension with wrought-iron furniture and orange adobe walls, a ceiling fan whirring above us, and the sounds of the rain pelting down on a tin roof while the street emptied and the shadows played.

He put his arm around me and pulled me toward him. Then he tipped my chin with his hand and traced my features. I closed my eyes. At some point, I no longer felt his warm fingers, but his lips. Pressing softly at first, then with insistence. We fell against the couch. But something was missing. It was as if he was possessed. In a dark fugue. I felt blackness emanate from him, a deep sorrow smoldering. He moved blindly, as though exorcising demons that had nothing to do with me. And I let him, awash in the throes of something deep and atavistic myself, spiraling up with him as the lightning flashed and the thunder growled and shook the earth around us, stone giants heaving boulders in a crescendo that matched our own.

When it was over, he sat up and hung his head in his hands.

"I'm sorry," he whispered.

"It's all right." I traced his smooth flank.

"I promise it will be different next time. This blackness. I can't shake it. My brother . . ."

But all I heard was "next time."

"It's okay. I understand."

"No one can understand," he said, and as he turned to look at me, his eyes were empty, haunted pools that reflected no light. I sensed subterranean currents that could drag him and anyone close to him under, to suffocate and drown.

"This isn't how I wanted to . . . I didn't plan . . ."

"Ssshh." I pulled him to my bed and he did not resist. I drew the comforter over us and we lay holding each other for a long time, watching the water slap against the window, while inside the steam rose from our warm bodies, fogging the view.

# CHAPTER 20

*I*t wasn't until morning when I woke to find the sun shining through the window and Silvio sleeping next to me that I realized we had never gone to Starman. Where had Scout found shelter from this unseasonal tropical storm?

Silvio stirred. Rolling over, he touched me and we made love again and this time it was sure and measured, incandescent white where the previous night had been swathed in deepest black.

Spent from our exertions, we needed sustenance. I thought of a Caribbean place in Santa Monica that made *chilaquiles*. I got wolfish cravings for those tortilla strips, coated with egg and cheese and chiles and cooked into a molten sculpture, creamy and spicy on the outside, but crisp when you bit down. Served on big, oblong, faux Fiestaware platters with violently yellow rice and black beans. Oh yeah, a big platter of *chilaquiles,* a poor man's food, was just what I needed after such a night. Then we could walk along the beach. It would be peaceful. We showered and I stuck his shirt and jeans in the dryer because they were still damp. He would have to forgo the cashmere vest.

But Silvio was wary of my idea. "I don't do too well on the West Side. I've lived too long in six-two-six."

"You mean you don't want to leave your own area code? Don't worry. I'll protect you from the big bad three-one-zero'ers."

Finally he agreed, and shrugged back into his now-dry shirt and jeans. Finding a baseball cap in his truck, he stuck it backward on his head to tame a cowlick. We left my duplex and drove past brown hills daubed in color, here a festive mauve house, there a lime green one, saffron picket fences setting off pumpkin adobe walls, all the vibrant colors of the Southwest that blazed anew for me as I drove with this man in his urban-camouflage car. The rain had washed away the smog and nervous tension we had once felt around each other. The sky was crystalline blue and I was at peace. Los Lobos was blasting on the stereo, a live, sloppy version of "Volver, Volver," Cesar Rosas promising to return to his lover's arms, a vow that took on added poignancy because it wasn't just drink and other women that sundered families these days, but fortified borders and financial necessity.

"It makes me happy to see all those colors," I said, as we passed an electric blue house trimmed with persimmon. "Do you know that in some new subdivisions, there are covenants saying people can only paint their houses white or tan?"

"Not a bad idea," Silvio grunted. "All this color is garish and in bad taste."

His vociferousness surprised me.

"Just so you know, I don't sing and dance, either. We're not all a happy, joyful people."

I slid down in my seat and watched the painted houses flash by like a kaleidoscope, but now they brought me no joy.

"Well, pardon me, *señor,* but you're certainly in the singing and dancing business."

He stared at the road. "I can't help what I was born into."

I wanted to tread carefully. He was such a complex

character, steeped in the chivalry of an old country he knew only from stories. But he also ran a thriving U.S. business that anticipated the next trend percolating up from Latin America while charting the evolving tastes of American-born Latinos. Indeed, the only thing Silvio's business acumen could not resolve was the duality of his own existence as he grappled for an identity that kept shifting beneath him. But the fact that he wouldn't give up endeared him to me. I recognized the armies of self-loathing and pride that clashed in his soul, buttressed by instinct and ego, fueled by equal parts insecurity and intelligence, because they raged in me as well. But how to tell him that?

"It's pretty obvious you're passionate about music. You're a walking encyclopedia of Latin singers and bands, and you weave it back into culture and demographics and racial politics in a way I've never heard before."

Silvio gripped the steering wheel tighter. "I overintellectualize it. But that's my nature. I know I listen with the wrong organ. But my brain won't shut down. Now my brother, he let his heart lead, and look where that got him."

His lips clamped into a frown.

"What do you mean?" I asked in what I hoped was a casual voice.

"He did everything on impulse, without thinking. Ever since he was a kid that was his MO. His feelings drove him. And eventually that got him killed."

I thought about this as we drove. "How?" I said finally. I was excavating with a scalpel. It wasn't about a story anymore, it was about him. And me. And whatever came next.

"My father would have laid the business at his feet,"

Silvio said. "Ruben was the golden child, so talented, so like our father. He was a *huero,* light-skinned like our grandmother. I just got her eyes. Life came easy to Ruben, and he never learned its value. And when you don't know the worth of something, it's easy to squander it. People opened their hearts to him because his was always beating so nakedly before them. He had big ideas, big plans for the business. He had a little-boy-lost quality that made people want to help him. They loaned him money. He made promises. Then it all went to shit. My father caught him embezzling. He was ready to forgive him but Ruben lied. And that my father couldn't take. He kicked him out. And Ruben never forgave him. He vowed he'd show our *papi.* He started scouting new talent. For a while he was grooming some kid from El Monte who was supposed to be the next big thing. Couldn't sing, but it was the words and the attitude that counted. Nothing but trouble. Each weekend there were knife fights and threats and *drogas.* Drugs. So Ruben started his own business with the pools. It was taking off. Then he made another stupid mistake."

"What was that?" I asked, wondering if Silvio was capable of murder. It seemed to me that he was.

Silvio's jaw twitched. "The one that got him killed," he said with finality. "But we all make mistakes. I made a huge one recently, and I'll be paying for it till the day I die."

"You want to talk about it?"

"No."

I sighed. "Fair enough. I thought Ruben got killed in a drive-by shooting."

"Yeah," Silvio said, as if remembering something. "That was the bullet that got him, in the end."

"Silvio, if there's something else that you're not

telling the police . . . don't you want his murderer apprehended?"

"Justice will be served," Silvio said. His voice chilled me. It echoed with blood feuds and ancient ways of solving things that had nothing to do with a court of law.

"How did we get on to this lugubrious topic anyway?" he said, reaching for my hand and squeezing. I squeezed feebly back, then let it lie in his like a dead thing.

We drove west on I-10 and got off at Fourth Street. A few more turns and we were standing in front of Cha Cha Cha, waiting with a bunch of other people until a table opened up. Another couple pulled up to the curb in a red BMW roadster with Björk blasting out of the stereo. I don't know about Silvio, but I always feel like an Eastern European peasant when I venture into the marine layer. It's that West Side vibe. Everything is so shiny and rich and perfect and high-tech. The people in the car had that glossy sheen too. She was petite, wearing clingy workout clothes. His long blond hair was topped with a woolly cap in the reggae triumvirate of red, gold, and green. A Chinese dragon tat rippled across his buff shoulder. When he shifted the car into park and pulled up the emergency brake, the grating explosion of metal made me jump. They got out and walked toward us. The man held his car keys out to Silvio.

We stood there for a minute and nobody said anything. Perhaps he thought I had looked at his car longingly, and was now offering us a ride? I wanted to say, no thank you, but his expression wasn't right. His arm was still outstretched. He dangled the keys, then thrust them forward. Finally he said, "Here you are, my man," and jingled them a bit.

Comprehension dawned, and now all I could think of

is how embarrassed I was for this couple and how bad I felt for Silvio at the same time. I glanced at him. He was staring at the ground, shaking his head slowly, as though he had been let down by someone he shouldn't have trusted and now had only himself to blame.

I wanted to scream at this perky couple, "Hey, *pendejos,* the valet's over there," and point to the little booth where rows of keys glittered in the sunlight. The parking attendant's stool was empty.

Then at last, Silvio spoke, and I was surprised at his civil, almost conversational tone.

"Are you such an ignorant American that you assume every dark-skinned person exists to serve you?"

There was a taut edge to his voice, disdain mingling with hauteur that said, You are an insignificant worm, and I would grind you under the heel of my boots but they are too expensive, and it would just sully the leather.

"C'mon, Silvio, let's go," I said. This being L.A., I was afraid the hipster would pull out a gun and shoot him.

From the couple came only jumbled sounds that strangled in their throats. "Hey, man, I'm awfully sorry," the blond guy finally blurted out, rubbing his goatee as he looked at Silvio for the first time and really saw him. "I just figured . . . aw hell, lemme buy your meal, send over a bottle of champagne. Something." He turned to his girl-friend. "Jeez, DeeDee, I feel so bad. I didn't mean . . ."

Silvio's mouth tightened. He pointed to the valet, who was coming around the corner at a jog, hands out-stretched for the next set of keys.

"Here's the man who's going to park your car. Why don't you give him a tip large enough to ease your conscience."

Silvio walked away before he could respond, and I

scurried after him, to where we had parked the pickup, by ourselves, because Silvio didn't believe in wasting money for valets unless it was absolutely necessary, and I agreed.

"C'mon," he told me. "We're going to have breakfast at the Grand Central Market."

"Do they have *chilaquiles?*" I asked hopefully.

The Grand Central Market downtown was a cacophonous Old World–style bazaar where hundreds of merchants offered produce and spices and sundries from all over the Latino and Asian world. It was bustling and crowded, brimming with the friendly and impersonal exuberance of hungry shoppers who know their appetites will soon be sated.

Silvio had found a place that served *chilaquiles* and we had now pushed our empty plates away and were contently sipping *café con leche* and nibbling *churros,* the fried twists of dough sprinkled with cinnamon sugar.

"Much better," Silvio said.

"That guy was scum."

Silvio shrugged, as if it served him right for going to the West Side.

"What made it especially galling was his 'we are the world' vibe. Like he's so enlightened."

Silvio examined his coffee.

"Don't you get mad sometimes?" I asked. "You're allowed, you know. It's not a breach of etiquette."

"It's a breach of my etiquette. That's the way some folks are. They assume things about other people. You do it too. You're intrigued by me because I don't conform to your stereotypes about Latinos."

What could I possibly say that wouldn't get me into more hot water today? That I had been intrigued from the first by his sleepy sensuality? By the painful contradictions I sensed in him? By his wry intelligence, which hid some subterranean darkness I wanted to plumb?

"If you did, you'd be a lot less trouble," I told him. "But since we're on the subject, why are you here with me?"

He picked up his *churro,* lifted it to his lips, and bit down, chewing reflexively.

"You were alluring. All that energy. I wanted to get inside of it. You were familiar enough to be comfortable, yet different enough to be exciting. A challenge."

Alluring, I thought. No one's ever called me that before.

"Okay, so we're both guilty," I said. "Whew, I'm glad we got that out in the open. Now we can both get on with . . ." I stopped. For some time now, I had been feeling an itchiness that had been growing stronger and more discomfiting because of where it was located. I realized I could put it off no longer. I pushed my chair back, stood up, and excused myself to go to the bathroom. As I did so, I scratched unconsciously at my inner thigh, then caught myself and blushed.

Silvio was watching me.

"What's wrong?"

"I don't know," I said. "I'm feeling terribly, well, itchy."

A look of shock crossed his face.

"Me too."

"You are?" A nasty thought was dawning. "Is it like, focused in one particular place?"

"Yes."

I clamped my legs shut. "Oh, my God."

Silvio's face was frozen in a wince.

I was realizing that I barely knew this man. And that I

had slept with him. And that there was sometimes a price to be paid for such foolhardy spontaneity. We had passed something communicable between us. This fact dawned on Silvio too. We studied each other more warily, and I realized that each of us was thinking we had gotten it from the other. Why had I had unprotected sex? Especially after my lecture to Luke Vinograd the other night? I knew how important it was to take precautions, had written so many stories about AIDS, but when it came to my own behavior, I was as guilty as the lonely gay boy who succumbed to a hunky stranger in desperate animal need. Homosexuals made me think of Carter Langdon, which made me think of the missing transvestite Pia, which made me think of another missing street kid, Scout, who had been sleeping in my bed just the other night.

My bed. I had forgotten to change the sheets, and we had tumbled heedlessly into them last night. I remembered Paolo's lip curling upward with distaste as he talked about how Finch had body lice. Which meant Scout probably did too.

"I'll be right back," I told Silvio. I ran to the bathroom and pulled down my pants and underwear and saw something moving. Disgusting! So it was true. But what horrified me most was not that I had body lice but that Silvio might think I had given it to him, that I was somehow unclean.

I zipped up my jeans and walked back to the table.

"I think I can explain," I said. "Remember that girl Scout I told you about?"

"Yes," he said slowly. I sketched it out for him, how she had passed out, how I had tried to take her to the ER, how I had finally brought her back to my apartment.

"We can get something for it at the pharmacy. It's a

lotion and you have to apply it several times and launder all the sheets with bleach."

"How do you know these things?"

I could see him wondering what kind of woman he had hooked up with. For all our differences, I realized that Silvio had led a more protected life than I had.

"A photographer friend of mine got crabs once at a tawdry Russian hotel."

He looked at me with disbelief.

"It can happen," I said. "You don't have to have sex to get it. Honest. Ask your doctor if you don't believe me."

"I could never ask my doctor such a thing," he said stiffly.

"Well, then look it up on the Internet." He still had a frozen look on his face. "You think I gave you crabs?"

"No," he said, "I suppose not. It's just . . . every time we're together, something unexpected and strange happens. I just start thinking how nice things are going, and then boom. La Fiesta."

"La Fiesta?"

"A wild party careening out of control."

"Welcome to my life," I said.

I insisted we go to a drugstore outside my neighborhood where I wouldn't run into anybody I knew. Luckily the pharmacist seemed nonplussed and we were soon walking out with several bottles of medicine and soaps guaranteed to get rid of our unwelcome guests.

We took turns in the shower. I decided to throw out the sheets, knowing I could never sleep comfortably in them. I was busy vacuuming all around and swabbing the walls and the mattress with bleach and rubbing alcohol when he came out of the shower.

"No good deed goes unpunished," he said, putting his arms around me and kissing my forehead.

I laid my cheek against his chest. I could feel the pectorals surge and ripple beneath the flesh. A strong, alkaline scent rose from him. I knew I smelled of it myself. "I just imagine that poor little girl, going from squat to squat, crawling with body lice. No one should have to live that way."

"You tried to help her," Silvio said. "There's only so much you can do."

The way he said it, I knew he was thinking about his brother again. Then, even though he was in my arms, I felt him move far away. He stepped back and told me he had to go. As we said good-bye, I wondered what he had been like before the tragedy, and whether there was a heaviness about him that had nothing to do with his brother's death.

I sat at the kitchen table, thinking about how horrible it was to have crabs. Yet for me, it was no more than an inconvenience. I thought of the lucky accident of fate and class that had made me who I was. And I knew that Scout was right—if I had been cast adrift by an addicted, alcoholic mom, if I hadn't known my father, if I had been molested as a child, I could be like Scout today. Or perhaps I'd be like Isabel. Dead. And she had a parent who seemed to care for her, even though he was creepy. I still hadn't gotten to the bottom of that.

It was Sunday afternoon. I had nothing to do except recover from body lice. I turned on the radio and got a Celia Cruz song. Where had I heard that recently? The L.A. River. The meeting with the trannies fresh in my mind, I ran to my old leather briefcase and rummaged around. There was a loose end I had failed to follow. My talk with the L.A. River denizens had raised more questions about Carter Langdon III. And they were questions that campaign manager Severin wasn't about to answer.

Pulling out the fraying napkin with Anne Marie Ruiz's address on it, I fired up the computer and clicked on my e-mail. It was extraordinary how you could send a note electronically to someone in a tiny backward nation with a barely functioning grid.

From: Eve Diamond [eve.diamond@latimes.com]
To: Anne Marie Ruiz [PraiseHim@gloryb.org]
Subject: Venus Dellaviglia Langdon
Hi Anne Marie,

I'm that *L.A. Times* reporter you met in a coffee bar right after you left your job. I'm still investigating the murder of Venus Dellaviglia Langdon [I lied]. I know the police are exploring whether she might have been having an affair and was killed by a jealous lover. Not that I believe that for a second myself. But what if Langdon was having his own affair? Perhaps a scandalous one that might threaten his political career?

Cheers,
Eve Diamond, *L.A. Times*

Let her read between the lines. I sent the missive hurtling into cyberspace. Checking every hour, I was excited to find return mail that evening.

From: Anne Marie Ruiz [PraiseHim@gloryb.org]
To: Eve Diamond [eve.diamond@latimes.com]
Subject: No he's not a sodomite
Dear Eve,

If you're hinting around about whether Langdon was gay, that's an old rumor that even his opponents didn't dare to bring up. The libelous tale, just so you know, was that not only was he gay but that he liked male transvestites and would pick them up on Hollywood Boulevard. Sheer, utter, unsubstantiated hooey. Severin spent a lot of time trying to find out who was responsible for these vicious lies, to no avail.

P.S. I cannot tell you how glad I am to be away from all that mind-numbing banality. Tirana is beautiful in an undeveloped, Third World way. Everyone here is committed to positive change.

Warmly,
Anne Marie Ruiz


From: Eve Diamond [eve.diamond@latimes.com]
To: Anne Marie Ruiz [PraiseHim@gloryb.org]
Subject: Stork won't be calling

Thanks for clarifying that. Did you know the autopsy showed that Venus was ten weeks pregnant? Poor Langdon, he lost both a wife and a child.


Again, she wrote back quickly.


From: Anne Marie Ruiz [PraiseHim@gloryb.org]
To: Eve Diamond [eve.diamond@latimes.com]
Subject: That baby is in heaven

That is sooooo tragic. Poor man. Now I understand a conversation I overheard a couple of weeks ago. He was telling Severin he had to take care of the baby. At the time, I thought it was code for something they were hatching up. Now I realize that Severin knew all about it and they were just keeping it under wraps until after the election.

From: Eve Diamond [eve.diamond@latimes.com]
To: Anne Marie Ruiz [PraiseHim@gloryb.org]
Subject: Blackmail?

So much for keeping it under wraps. Now everyone in L.A. knows. I just need to ask you point blank, so you never saw any sign that Langdon had a thing for transvestites, or anyone other than his wife? You never found any lipstick-stained clothing or bras or sex magazines? There was no one trying to blackmail him?

She must have been sitting there at her desk in Tirana the same way I was sitting in mine. Was it morning there? I pictured the Adriatic sunlight shining in through her window, illuminating the tile roofs, or whatever they had in Tirana.

From: Anne Marie Ruiz [PraiseHim@gloryb.org]
To: Eve Diamond [eve.diamond@latimes.com]
Subject: They will reap what they sow come Judgment Day

We used to get anonymous letters sometimes. They were handwritten and full of misspelled words. They accused him of un-Christian acts. Severin put them in a locked desk cabinet. He said he intended to file a lawsuit if we ever learned who was playing these dirty tricks. Another time, someone planted a tiny glass bottle in Carter's staff car to make it look like he was using drugs. It was about an inch high with a wide neck and had a strong chemical odor. I know because I found it. Severin snatched it out of my hand and I never found out what it was. I've seen crack vials, and it wasn't one of those. I didn't place too much importance on it.

\* \* \*

Now we were getting somewhere. I e-mailed her back, thanking her for the information. She seemed awfully chatty, but I guessed she might be lonely and glad to hear a voice from home.

I printed out the e-mails and reviewed them. Then I called Luke Vinograd at the copy messenger desk and was gratified to find him there. Describing the vial from Langdon's car, I asked if it sounded like anything he'd ever heard of.

"Amyl," Luke said at once. "Well, butyl, now. Butyl nitrite. Amyl's hard to find. Also known as poppers."

"What's that?"

"It's big in the gay community. You inhale the fumes, and it gives you an instant rush. Lasts about forty seconds, feels like a whole-body orgasm. Lots of gays use it to enhance sex."

"Any idea how such a thing could end up in a mayoral candidate's official car?"

He laughed. "Yeah. Somebody got careless during sex and it rolled under the seat. If I see it, I can tell you for sure. Maybe it's even got hizzoner's prints on it."

"Nope," I told him. "It's all anecdotal. The campaign manager may have it, though; he snatched it out of my source's hand when she picked it up."

# CHAPTER 21

*I* read the e-mails carefully a third time, then took a yellow marker and highlighted one line:

"He was saying they had to take care of the baby."

This was not the boast of a man about to become a father again with his beloved wife. It sounded more like a problem to be dealt with. Was he pressuring her to have an abortion? Had he killed her because she refused? No, it didn't make sense. Even if Langdon wasn't the father, why couldn't he just play proud papa? Becoming a father while in office had worked wonders for Tony Blair. I had to do more digging. I called the library and asked them to pull the clips on Carter Langdon III.

"Didn't we already get you those?" the Sunday librarian asked me.

"Just the campaign ones. I want them back all the way to '85, when the electronic database starts."

"Okay, they'll be on the counter. Or you want me to e-mail them?"

"Nah, I like the feel of paper crackling between my fingers. I'll be in shortly."

I went and brewed a pot of strong Cuban roast coffee. *"Para el gusto Hispano,"* the can said. The Hispanic taste. I thought of Silvio and felt myself flush with warmth. In the car, I drove too fast, listening to Super Estrella and humming along with a bouncy song about a lovesick vampire who came back to haunt his human lover once night fell. Next came an *L.A. Times* commercial, telling listeners that the paper's classified ads could help them land a job.

I parked and scurried through the street into the *Times*. Catching the elevator just as it closed, I saw someone inside. Tony Hausman. The song was still echoing in my brain, and I realized with a start that I had been humming the refrain.

"What're you singing?" he asked, surprising me. He was a hard-nosed political junkie attached to Metro's City-County Bureau who didn't go in much for small talk. But while I couldn't share his obsession, I appreciated that he had one. As for his monumental ego, he had never been rude to me. And now he was actually making an effort to converse.

"Oh, just some bouncy pop song from Super Estrella. That's one of the Spanish-language stations I listen to in the car."

He nodded. "When I take the surface streets to work, I turn the salsa station up pretty loud when I hit Pico-Union," he said. "It can't hurt for them to know the white guy in the Mercedes likes their music."

The smile froze on my own face. I looked at him afresh, and saw a jowly, middle-aged man secure in his power. His face was a slab of raw pork. He had an overly manicured beard, and I bet he used one of those round whirling devices to shear excess hair from his ears and nostrils. He beamed at me now, as if we shared a secret bond, and I stepped away to shatter the illusion. Did he really think a few timbales and horns would make him one with the 'hood? That it would keep a railroad spike from hurtling through his tinted windows if someone decided they wanted his car? But then I wondered what people thought when they looked over and saw me listening to the same music. As I left the elevator behind

Tony Hausman, who waved and said he'd see me around, I concluded that most people were too busy cursing the traffic and their bills to give me a second thought and that I was spending way, way too much time worrying about it.

Walking down the third-floor hallway to Editorial, I passed the photo department and was surprised to see Harry Jack standing there, hands in his pockets. I tapped on the glass and waved. It wasn't often we ran into each other downtown.

He raised one hand in weak salutation, staring right through me. I opened the door and walked in.

"What am I carrying, the plague, that you look so happy to see me?"

One corner of his mouth twitched.

"That's it for me," he said.

"What are you talking about?" I was getting an unpleasant feeling in the pit of my stomach. Had the doctor given him some bad news? He had mentioned a checkup.

"Friend a mine gave me the word just now. I'm on the list."

"What list?"

"They're putting together another list and I'm on it."

"You mean a . . . oh no, Harry, not another buyout list?"

Every few years, the *Times* culled the herd. Oh, they softened the blow with severance packages, career counselors, and reeducation stipends, but what did a seventy-four-year-old guy with more than a half-century of newspapering under his belt stand to learn from a career counselor younger than his grandson? Guys like Harry didn't give a hoot about their generous "package." For them, the job was the thing. They mainlined on the adrenaline rush of journalism and needed their daily fix or they would die. Harry had escaped the velvet executioner for a long time now, but it seemed that his number had finally come up.

"How can they do this?"

He crammed his hands deeper into his pockets, hunching up his shoulders. Then he put his trembly lips together and began to whistle "Taps."

"It isn't right," I said fiercely.

He finished and shrugged. "Ya gotta go sometime." For him, I realized, it was exactly like contracting a fatal disease. One that would wither you slowly, sapping your energy and will as it progressed.

"I'm sorry," I said. "It's a damn shame."

"You got that right," he said. "I'll catch you later, Evie. I'm going home and swim. Gonna do forty laps today instead of my usual twenty. I'll show those bastards."

We walked back into the hallway together and said good-bye, and I turned to watch the bent, wiry frame of Harry Jack dwindle and then disappear. I had heard vague rumors about more buyouts but ignored them. I was young and strong and not collecting a fat-cat salary so I figured I was safe. I thought about the injustice of Harry's fate for several more minutes. Then, I'm ashamed to say, I grabbed the sheaf of papers the library had left for me, started reading, and forgot about him altogether.

Five hours later, I looked at the clock in the editorial library. It was 1 A.M., and the third floor had long ago emptied. I wondered what Silvio was doing. By now he was probably in bed. I imagined him sliding between the sheets. Was he naked? Was he thinking of me?

I picked up my computer printouts again and fingered

them. For all the dreary stories about Langdon and his wife chairing philanthropic committees and blue ribbon panels, the crisp white sheets of paper had yielded no revelations. Crisp. White. These printouts dated to 1985. What if what I was looking for had happened before 1985?

In the deserted library, I scanned the neat rows of steel cabinets. Soon I found it. The newspaper clipping files. Pre-1985. From back when every *Times* librarian wielded a pair of flying scissors each morning to cut out every article from the paper, folding and tucking them away into thousands of little manila envelopes that bulged with inky newspaper print.

Quickly, I found the LA–LI cabinet. I pulled out a huge file labeled Carter Langdon II and a thin file labeled Carter Langdon III. I opened the thin file and removed its contents, unfolding and reading clip after clip. Langdon returning home from Rome with his beautiful new Italian wife. Hosting parties. Raising millions for pet causes. Here was one for Planned Parenthood that Langdon and his wife had cohosted. Hmmm. I had thought they were antiabortion. Clearly, they had changed sides. I read more closely. Carter Langdon III was talking about world overpopulation. How he had done his share to curb this global threat. Carter Langdon III had undergone a vasectomy.

I sat there, holding the faded, yellowed clipping, a relic of an earlier age in journalism that would soon crumble into dust. After the birth of his first child, Carter Langdon III had gotten himself fixed. He couldn't have children. He couldn't be the father of the child Venus was carrying when she died. And this little nugget lay buried deep in fifteen-year-old society pages that no self-respecting Metro reporter would ever read because it was flowery and self-congratulatory drivel chronicling blue-blood society.

I ran to the city desk, where the computers always stay on, and looked up the Metro overnight note, in which the night editor lays out for the morning city editor what stories need to be followed. I quickly scanned to see where the mayoral candidates would be Monday morning and learned that Carter Langdon III was holding a rally at a nursing home at 7 A.M. to demand reforms. I could go home, grab a couple hours of sleep, then shower, apply my damned crabs lotion, have some coffee, and drive out to the nursing home. I'd intercept him there, hit him with the question. In some part of my brain, I knew I should lay this all out for an editor, and not go off half-cocked, but it was terribly late and I was exhausted and perhaps not thinking straight, and slightly itchy, which distracted and maddened me like all hell.

As I pulled into my driveway, I wondered whether the red light would be flashing on my machine. Had Silvio called? I willed my heart to slow down as I ran to check. A big red digital zero.

In my mind, I replayed our time together. The electric languor. Sweat on my skin. The contours of his body pressing against mine. *Next time,* he had said. I clung to that phrase like a lifeboat, painfully aware that words uttered in passion don't always hold up to scrutiny.

The bed was cold and vast, its white expanses screaming with emptiness. I wrenched my thoughts away from Silvio, considering how clever it was for Langdon to stage a big rally at a nursing home. Everyone knew how wretched those places were, and he could play directly to the home audience. If he had been running for state or federal office, he'd have to worry about offending lobbyists of the nursing home industry, among the most powerful in the nation. But in Los Angeles, all he had to do was recite some of the abysmal statistics about bedsores and malnutrition, restraints and improper medication, wheel out a few sympathetic white-haired victims of greedy nursing home operators, and he'd have the crowd cheering.

The next morning, I drove to the nursing home. It was in El Sereno, east of downtown L.A. Where Ruben Aguilar had been killed in a gang shooting. If it had lain a few miles north or east, it would have been part of the San Gabriel Valley, and then the suburban reporters would have been crawling all over it. But it was too close to downtown, an area none of the Metro reporters really covered, so a lot of good stories slipped through the cracks. When I got there, I saw only a few English broadcasters, though the Spanish media were out in force. Then I spotted Severin.

"As always, Severin," I murmured, sidling up to him.

He looked at me with distaste, but spun me anyway as Carter Langdon III emoted from the front steps of the nursing home, his long skinny arms tracing paths in the air.

"The mayor-elect has made this a lifelong cause," said Severin, who had an annoying habit of referring to Langdon as though he had already won. "His own father was in a long-term-care facility for several years before he died of a stroke. A better one than this, of course," he added hurriedly. "But my point is that Carter speaks from personal experience. There is a gravitas about him that is compelling."

"Gotta love that gravitas," I agreed. It was the political *mot du jour,* applied indiscriminately to presidents and two-bit candidates, especially those not previously known for their acumen.

The speech ended and Langdon walked down, surrounded by his staff. I caught him at the foot of the steps as he posed for pictures.

"Eve Diamond, from the *Times* San Gabriel Valley edition, and I think it's great you're tackling nursing home reform," I told him. "Could you explain what first inspired you to get involved in this worthwhile cause?"

Langdon beamed. This was exactly what his handlers had rehearsed him for. He launched into his speech. I took cursory notes.

"That sure shows your commitment to the elderly," I said when he finished. "Now perhaps I could ask you about the very young. We just recently found out that your departed wife was pregnant. Could you talk a little about that, how the loss of that child has affected you personally?"

He looked startled. I wasn't playing fair. He had already addressed that in earlier speeches, he said with a piercing look, and I knew that he was registering me an opponent to measure and watch.

"I know," I told him, "but we're talking about the beginning and the end of life, and I just wanted to ask you to draw a parallel."

He looked momentarily confused about the nonsense I was shoveling up, then said how the murderer had robbed him of not only a wife, but a child. That thought automatically triggered his impassioned "get tough on crime" speech.

I doodled in my notepad as he spoke. "Could you give us your stand on some other important issues?" I continued. "How about family planning? I was doing some research on you, Mr. Langdon, reading old clips, and I noticed you had a vasectomy back in 1984 after your son was born. So I was wondering. In light of that. How did your wife get pregnant?"

Carter Langdon III's eyes narrowed. He took a step backward. "Severin," he called. "I need you here right away."

Severin's dark blue suit glided over. "What can I do for you, Ms. Diamond?" His voice was an oil slick spreading over clear water.

"Ms. Diamond is wondering how, uh, with the vasectomy that I underwent fifteen years ago, Mrs. Langdon was able to get pregnant."

"Carter, you never told me you had a vasectomy." Severin's thick eyebrows raised. Then he looked at me.

"What does this have to do with the campaign? I've warned this reporter once already about insolent insinuations." His voice caught fire. "Ms. Diamond, surely you know that vasectomies aren't foolproof, and that the severed, uh, veins can, uh, fuse back together and that pregnancies can happen," he said, nodding vociferously, "yes, and sometimes do, and that what we were seeing develop and grow was a miracle baby, a symbol of the love that Venus and Carter shared between them, which makes it all the more tragic, yes, reprehensible, even, that two lives would be snuffed out on that tragic day instead of one."

I had been writing it all down, knowing there would be no second chances, that they would now close ranks and get their stories airtight, and that I was witnessing one of the few unscripted moments this mayoral campaign had seen.

Now I lobbed my last grenade.

"By the way, have you heard from Anne Marie lately?" I asked Severin.

"Of course not," he snapped, then a guarded look came into his eyes. "Have you?"

"As a matter of fact I have," I said blandly. "We've been e-mailing."

He seemed to regain his composure. "And how's the weather in Tirana? I hear the rebel activity is moving down from the hills. It's a dangerous place."

He sipped from a paper cup of coffee.

"I'm sure she's taking all precautions. Unlike when she was working for the campaign," I added over my shoulder as I walked to my car. Then I drove to Monrovia, where I blurted it all out to Tom Thompson. He looked first incredulous, then proud of my chutzpah, then finally aghast as I read back my notes. He said he'd talk to Metro and they'd review the information and run it by the political desk and get back to me. When he called me back in, he sounded irritated.

"Metro wants it. They've budgeted a twelve-inch story on Langdon's vasectomy and his wife's subsequent pregnancy. They say it's an interesting sideline to the mayor's race. And Jane Sims says be sure you get some stats from medical experts about how common or rare this is. And get the cops on the record about whether this changes anything in their murder investigation. If not, Sims wants an LAPD quote saying no one is suggesting this gives Langdon a motive to murder his wife."

"But if the child isn't his, that's exactly what it does," I said. "Can't they do a DNA test or something?"

"I'm sure they will. But meanwhile, I hope you didn't approach your interview of the candidate in this way."

"Don't worry."

I sulked off to write my small Metro story. I knew there was a big story here, and that I had just unearthed an important tidbit of information. I just couldn't prove it yet.

# CHAPTER 22

*I* was still sulking two days later when Thompson buzzed me in.

"The Aguilars are having a wake for their murdered son this afternoon and I want you there," he said.

I looked at him in surprise.

"Don't worry, they haven't been keeping the body on ice," Thompson said. "But Grandma missed the funeral, she was in the hospital, and now she wants a proper wake."

"You want a story on a wake?"

"Maybe just color for your family business story. Maybe a sidebar. It's your call. In retrospect, Metro should have done an obit on old Ruben. The family's well known in the Mexican community. But at the time, who knew?"

Just three days ago, I had slept with the dead man's brother. My body still tingled each time I thought of him. So how could I blithely show up at the house today, ready to interview his family? Still, it would give me an excuse to see him again, if only to reassure myself that I hadn't imagined our time together.

"Shouldn't we back off, let them deal with their grief in private?"

"They won't mind," Thompson said. "I saw the father at the Chamber of Commerce meeting and he said we're welcome to send a reporter. You'll pick up some good details. I don't want a cut-and-dry business story anyway. These people aren't selling widgets, they're selling culture. Nostalgia for the homeland. And here in their adopted land of *El Norte,* they fall victim to the same violence that haunts us all. Yet still they persevere. They bury their dead and keep going."

"You got such a handle on it, why don't you write it?"

"Editors don't write. We only shape and mold."

His hands dipped and curved, like he was kneading a lump of dough.

"I think you need a little less yeast, Thompson, or that bread's gonna explode."

Back at my desk, I thought of the Faustian bargain I had made. There was a huge conflict of interest in writing about someone I was sleeping with. I should hand the story over or stop seeing Silvio until it was published. But did one night constitute romantic involvement? What if it never went any further than that, even though I wanted it to? I would have given away a great story for nothing. Thompson didn't know about my entanglement. Nobody knew, not even nosy Jane Sims. So for now, I'd keep reporting. Then I'd turn my notes over to a colleague who could write it up. That way no one could accuse me of bias.

I called Silvio. I wasn't sure whether I wanted to warn him, beg his permission, or apologize. He wasn't in the office and he didn't answer his cell. He hadn't given me his home number and he wasn't listed. I didn't want to spring this on him unannounced, but it looked as though I had no choice.

After filing my twelve-inch story on Langdon's vasectomy, I left. The wake was at Silvio's grandmother's house in Alhambra, which lay just south of affluent San Marino. The demarcation line was Huntington Drive. Those with maids and chefs lived north of the broad thoroughfare. Those who worked as maids and chefs lived south. North of the boulevard, housing covenants had historically prohibited non-WASPs from settling and zealous local police still pulled over ratty cars with dark-skinned drivers. There was no reason to be cruising past the leafy baronial estates, since most of the streets dog-legged and dead-ended into the Huntington Gardens. With its rolling acres of roses, Shakespearean herbs, and Japanese pagodas, the gardens were a rich man's pastoral fantasy built by one of America's most legendary rail-road barons—Henry Huntington—but its location and $10.00 entry fee discouraged pilgrimages by the poor as surely as a castle guarded by dragons. Even the area parks had cleverly limited traffic by requiring fifty-dollar advance permits for parties and ballgames. This was L.A. discrimination, millennial-style.

South of Huntington Drive, the houses were less grand, the lawns more sun-baked, the school scores lower. As you drove south, bars and taco stands and auto body shops and furniture-stripping businesses prolifer-ated until finally you hit the railroad tracks.

Yet the Latinos who had historically lived south of Huntington built their own dream palaces. The area was full of nice two-story Spanish houses, and Agrippina Aguilar owned one of them.

Pulling up, I saw tall banana palms framing a leaded-glass picture window. The yard was overgrown like a jungle. I went to the door and knocked, a feeling of dis-may gnawing a hole in my gut.

Silvio opened the door, and before the mask crashed down, I saw a serenity in his face, here in his dominion, bathed in the warmth of his family, inside these walls suffused with memories of childhood. I caught a glimpse of heavy wooden furniture and arched rooms, boisterous relatives to whom he would always be a fierce, precocious little boy. But all that was wiped clean when he saw the barbarian at his gate.

"Eve?"

Then, remembering his manners, he opened the door wide. "What brings you to my grandmother's house?"

I hesitated, feeling like a carrion bird.

"My editor sent me. To cover the wake and learn more about your family. I didn't want to come."

He frowned. "This gathering isn't open to you as a reporter. But I invite you as my friend."

"Well, your father apparently told my editor we could send a reporter so, voilà, here I am," I said with a weak curtsy.

"*Quien es,* Silvio? Who is that?"

A older man sailed into view, his paunch preceding him. He wore suspenders and a starched linen shirt and looked debonair and patriarchal. I recognized him from the photos in Silvio's office. It was Felipe Aguilar.

"Ah, the reporter," he said. "Yes, come in, my dear. I've been waiting for you."

He took me by the elbow and I threw one last look at Silvio as I half-stumbled into the flagstone entryway. The thick adobe walls were whitewashed and cool as a wine cellar.

Silvio's lips tightened, and I could tell that he was furious. His dad obviously didn't know about us, and I was being made to choose between a budding romance and work. Silvio strode off, leaving me alone with his father.

"So you are writing a little story about our family business?"

"Yes, I am."

"*Bueno.* Please make yourself at home. Silvio will tell

you everything you need to know. I have delegated him to handle this in light of . . ."

His voice trailed off. He groped in his pocket, pulled out a creased white handkerchief, and blew loudly into its linen depths.

"Excuse me. Great paper, the *Times*. They've been very shrewd to buy half of *La Opinión*. Now where did that boy go?"

Aguilar *père* led me into a huge living room whose ceiling was held up by stenciled wooden beams. A large, wrought-iron chandelier hung from one of these beams. It was in the shape of a huge wagon wheel with thick metal spokes radiating out from the center, its lights meant to evoke half-melted candles. I felt the weight of history, of guilt, upon my shoulders.

A group of somberly dressed men and women stood beneath the chandelier, and Silvio's father introduced me and asked if I'd like a glass of wine. I don't usually drink on the job, it's a bad policy, and the opportunity rarely presents itself anyway, but this time, my nerves jangling like the blond hipster's keys at Cha Cha Cha, I said a grateful yes. He left and I stepped up to the circle, listening politely as a nattily dressed older man complained about changes in the neighborhood.

"They're buying up all the businesses," he said. "Did you see what happened to Rocio's Auto Body Shop? My boys went to school with Rocio's kids. He's been there forty years. Then last week I drove by and there's a new sign that says 'Hang Li Auto Repair.'"

"*Los Chinos!*" a woman with hair pulled severely back into a bun chimed in. "They're pushing north and west from Monterey Park, south from San Marino, pricing us out of our own neighborhoods. Chinatown's spreading east into Lincoln Heights, El Sereno, Alhambra."

"Where are we supposed to go?" another man asked. "East L.A. is too crowded. We don't want to move to Palmdale or the Inland Empire. For generations we've raised our children here. Buried our dead. This is our valley too. Our barrio."

There was a murmur of appreciation and much clinking of glasses. It wasn't surprising that they felt they had somehow lost out. The same generation that had seen integration, ESL, and the end of official racism was now witnessing the erosion of those gains as Latino communities in the western San Gabriel Valley shrank and the tidy stucco houses and small businesses changed hands, often for cash, to Asian newcomers.

You could chart the sea changes in our newspaper coverage. For decades, the *Times* had written Christmas stories about La Posada, the Mexican nativity pageant that proceeded down San Gabriel Valley streets as residents reenacted Mary and Joseph's search for an inn in Bethlehem. Then one year Baby Jesus and his parents disappeared. Soon a new set of equally enthusiastic residents danced down those same streets, wearing dragon costumes and banging drums to usher in the Chinese New Year.

There was a historic continuum to all this that struck me as inevitable. Hadn't the Gabrieleno Indians—a peaceful and seminomadic people who gave their name to this arid land—been swept away 150 years earlier by the Spanish land grantees, whose beautiful daughters were in turn assimilated through intermarriage with WASPs from the Eastern Seaboard? What goes around comes around.

I remembered interviewing a UC botanist who wanted to restore California flora to the days before the Spanish Conquest. He had devoted his life to stopping the spread of non-native grasses and plants that had colonized the valleys and hillsides. But you could no more halt the spread of palm trees and lantana than you could the immigrants who came by ship, car, and plane.

"*Los Chinos*," someone whispered in my ear. It was Silvio, returning with the glass of wine that Aguilar Senior had promised me. "You should know that when they talk about *los Chinos,* they mean Asians in general, not just the Chinese. For instance, there's a nice Filipino family that moved next door to my *abuelita,* and she gets along with them just fine, but I cannot get her to stop calling them '*los vecinos chinos,*' the Chinese neighbors."

"You seem to have recovered from the shock of finding me on your doorstep."

"I decided to make the best of it, maybe even flirt a little to distract you from your task. I didn't realize my father had approved this."

The way he looked at me belied his light words. I wanted him to lead me down the hallway and into some unused bedroom and close the door, already unbuttoning his shirt as he turned the lock.

He shrugged. "I must be a dutiful son. Especially in *abuelita's* home. You must meet Agrippina."

Then he would walk over and pull up my skirt.

"Your grandmother's name is Agrippina?" I said. "How extraordinary. Wasn't she a Roman empress or something? The mother of Nero?"

He laughed. "You get an A in ancient history. There were two Agrippinas. One the mother of Caligula, the other, yes, of Nero. Our Agrippina didn't sire any bloodthirsty tyrants, but she is definitely a force of nature. It's the fault of my great-grandmother. She was an illiterate housemaid from Guadalajara. As she cleaned, she eavesdropped on the children's tutor and was so taken with his descriptions of these Roman ladies that she named her first daughter Agrippina."

I laughed too, leaning against a carved wood table to steady myself. My legs had begun to feel rubbery. "This colonial Spanish furniture is amazing," I said, running a hand along the sleekly oiled wood and wishing it were the curve of his hip. "And those nineteenth-century paintings. It's so great you've kept those heirlooms in the family, they're priceless."

"Ah, yes, heirlooms," he said. "My father bought this house for *abuelita* with the first real money he made and she immediately set about collecting the trappings of a landed-gentry past. She knew what she was looking for too; she had grown up dusting and polishing it. It took her twenty years, scouring old shops and Mexican flea markets. With her peasant cunning, she paid a pittance for pieces that are worth a fortune today. Come. Let's see if she's awake."

He took my hand and my X-rated fantasy dissolved into a G-rated reality. I felt like a child sneaking down a secret passageway. One that smelled of lilac perfume in stoppered decanters and lavender sachets. I marveled at how you could buy a past and fit it snugly over your old life. After enough time elapsed, did you simply become what you had once yearned for?

"Wasn't she just in the hospital?"

"She had some gallstones removed," Silvio said. "But she's a spry old bird of eighty-two. Dramatic as hell. Took to her bed with much lamentation twenty years ago when she learned my *abuelito* had a mistress in Pico Rivera. Refused to speak his name. We didn't care. We'd perch on her bed and beg her to tell us stories about witches and devils and talking animals."

"I bet you were her favorite."

He hesitated, and my insensitivity washed over me. Why had I brought up ancient sibling rivalries at a time when his family had gathered to mourn Ruben?

"She wanted my energy," Silvio said. "I wanted her wisdom. I always felt closer to her than to my own mother."

"So she's just stayed in bed for twenty years?"

"For ten. The whole time I was growing up. Then my grandfather, who was always the robust one, we thought he'd still be carousing in his nineties, had a stroke. He had great genes but one bad blood vessel felled him."

"Did he die?"

"No. But he couldn't walk or talk. And here's the real miracle. The day of his stroke, *abuelita* rose from her sickbed to care for him. *Dios la bendiga,* God bless her, she nursed him for five years while he sat, mute and drooling in the corner with a serape draped over his knees. Finally I put my foot down and hired an orderly. But she wouldn't let him do anything. She floated through the house at all hours, a set of keys tied to her skirt, all the neurasthenia and maladies gone. It's like *abuelo*'s stroke gave her a new reason to live. She had a great and noble cross to bear—the long-suffering wife, a role that appealed much more than the wronged wife. I used to think that if he recovered, she'd take to her bed again. But he died five years ago. And Agrippina has slowed down too. But she still goes out shopping every morning. There's a Safeway around the corner, but no, she has to drive to El Sereno and find the Mexican butcher with the best *carne asada*. She pinches every chile. I tell her to send the housekeeper, but"—he lowered his voice—"*abuelita* doesn't trust her to bring back the change."

It was modernity scoffing fondly at antiquity, both

thinking they knew best. I sensed the empty spaces in my own heart, the lack of older relatives fussing, their dentures clacking, the smells and complaints of age. Most of mine had scattered and died a continent away, before I had been born. Perhaps that's why I craved this connection to the past, even if it meant fastening on to the memories of others. A big, boisterous multigenerational family like Silvio's. I wanted to slip inside his world for much longer than one night.

He stopped before an arched wooden door and knocked, then stepped back and waited attentively, hands clasped.

I heard the sugary clearing of an aged throat, then the words, *"Pasa, pasa."*

Silvio pushed the door open and we entered a room dim with candles. An old lady lay in bed, propped up by embroidered pillows. Dressed in a violet peignoir that set off her alabaster skin, she reached a trembling, jeweled hand to pat the filigreed silver combs that held the hair away from her face. It streamed down on either side, white and feathery as goose down. Her eyes were a cloudy green.

*"Buenas tardes, m'hijo, ven aca."* Come here, she said in Spanish. She peered at me, her eyes glittering like a jeweled scarab's. "Who's this? You didn't tell me you had a new girlfriend."

I blushed and waited to hear what he would say. "This is Eve," he said, pulling me forward. His thumb stroked the inside of my palm. I stepped up and shook the stiff, bony hand. A diamond set in platinum glittered on her ring finger, a bracelet of amber beads clanked coolly at her wrist. She had pierced ears, the holes slashing almost to the bottom of her lobes from years of wearing heavy dangling earrings.

*"Bienvenidos,"* she murmured, tilting her head graciously.

Looking around the room, I saw an old-fashioned dressing table. On it sat a sugar skull. It rang an uncomfortable bell. Agrippina saw me looking at it.

"Isn't it lovely?" she said. "Gisela brought me that, she remembers how I like my sweets. Ruben had them made for *Día de los Muertos,* to hand out to his clients. It will remind me of my dear grandson," she said. "Gisela's just gone for my tea."

"Well, *abuelita,*" Silvio said, "we don't want to tire you with too many visitors. We'll come back."

"But you just got here," the old lady said querulously as he bent and kissed her powdery cheek. Silvio straightened up and tugged at my hand, but my mind was still buzzing around the sugar skull, darting into the eye sockets, through the gaping nose, popping out of its ears like some kind of frenzied djinni. I had seen the same sugar skull on Venus's table in her cabana. So? This was Los Angeles, and Day of the Dead was around the corner.

"Eve is just learning about this custom of ours, *Día de los Muertos,*" Silvio said. His manner, too, had changed. There was something tense, brittle about him, and I didn't know why.

"I know about Day of the Dead," I said stiffly. I didn't want to be condescended to. "How could I not, I've lived in L.A. all my life."

Silvio raised his eyebrows and began to lead me out of the room.

"Oh, wait for Gisela," Agrippina said, then clasped her hands in pleasure. "Here she is now."

The young woman from Silvio's office walked in, carrying a tray with tea things. She wore a black crepe dress, medium pumps, and a little hat with a rhinestone-studded veil, and looked every inch the bereaved widow. But her demeanor, so different from the last time I had seen her, had something of a costume-ball quality to it, as if she had studied old movie stills before getting dressed that morning. She stopped when she saw Silvio. Then her eyes turned to me.

"Oh, hello," she said, her eyes lingering on Silvio's hand, frozen in mine. As she watched, he twisted away, withdrawing it.

"The *Times* reporter," Gisela said. "I didn't expect to see you at this family gathering." Her eyes probed mine. "Are you here on business?"

"Yes," said Silvio, just as I blurted out "No."

She clicked her tongue in disapproval.

"Well, get your act together, which is it?"

"My father invited her. To gather material for the story. But she knows it's a sensitive time. She will be discreet."

Discretion is my middle name, I thought. Gisela walked past us to Agrippina and placed the tea service on her bedside table. When she bent over the bed to fluff pillows that didn't need fluffing, the crepe dress cupped her behind.

"You've forgotten the lemon," Agrippina scolded. "Silvio, please be a dear and get some lemon for my tea."

"C'mon, Eve," Silvio said with forced heartiness. "I'll give you a quick tour of the rest of the house while we fetch the lemons."

"No, thank you," I said, my erotic scenario gone for good. I sensed some tension in Gisela that I wanted to probe while Silvio was out of the room.

Silvio walked out. With a clack of her heels on the hardwood floor, Gisela jumped up and followed him, saying she would be right back. So much for my bright idea.

I pulled up a chair next to Agrippina.

"I never got a chance to meet Ruben," I told her in halting Spanish, "but I heard so many good things. I bet you were really proud of your grandsons."

The old lady gave me a shrewd look. "Ruben and Silvio," she murmured. "Silvio and Ruben. They were inseparable as children. But they tore at each other. They fought for their father's attention. One dark, the other light. Both strong-willed as bulls."

"Tell me what they were like," I said eagerly. I wanted to understand Silvio. He had told me so little about himself and there were shadows that needed illumination.

She patted her hair again and settled back against the pillows. It seemed we were embarking on one of her favorite topics.

"Silvio was the eldest, the dutiful son," she said. "He was a strange child. Pensive and melancholy. He spent hours writing in secret journals. No matter how much his father urged him, he had no interest in sports. He spent his days with me, with the *tías* and *tíos*. He never tired of our stories. We called him an old soul, but none of us knew whose spirit animated him."

So it was true, what Silvio had started to tell me.

"What about Ruben?" I bowed my head to indicate respect for the dead.

"Rubencito was the opposite. He took after his father. Both of them were loud and physical, always clowning around and slapping friends on the back. My son, God help him, loved Ruben best. He thought his youngest could do no wrong, and he ignored the son who worked tirelessly to please him. It was Silvio who built the family business and brought in new acts, raising the profile of Arena La Puente until it was known from Los Angeles to Mexico City."

"Was Ruben a good businessman too?"

The old lady shook her head. A comb fell out and she carefully replaced it before continuing.

"No, *desgraciadamente*. Unfortunately. And when his plans failed, Silvio covered for his brother so their father would be spared the shame. But still the father loved the younger one best. And it broke the older one's heart. He would do anything to get his father's approval. And it was always withheld from him."

She lay back on her bed, tired from so much talking.

"It must have grieved him so much," I said, as Gisela came back, smoothing out the layers of crepe as she sat on a brocaded fainting couch.

Gisela had caught my last words. "We're all grieving," she said. She turned to Agrippina, who had dozed off in that way the very old drift in and out of consciousness. We sat and watched her breath emerge in synchronized puffs of air, and I realized I had another opportunity here. Silvio didn't want to talk about his brother. But Gisela might.

"Tell me about Ruben," I begged her. Gisela looked dubiously at Agrippina. But people love to boast about their loved ones, especially when they're dead. Convinced finally that the grandmother was truly and deeply asleep, Gisela said, "Silvio wasn't the only innovator in the family, you know. Ruben had ideas for Arena La Puente too. But no one wanted to listen to the younger brother, even though his singers would have brought in a lot of money."

"What kind of singers?"

"In Latin music today, you have to tread carefully. You've heard that Miami Cubans won't play on the same bill with Castro Cubans? Well, a lot of Mexicans turn their noses up at the *corridos pesados,* the 'heavy' ballads that recount the macho tales of drug smugglers. They're also called *narcocorridos."*

"Of course," I said, though I hadn't a clue.

"It's the sleazy backwater of the Latin music business. At first the mainstream record labels wouldn't touch it. Now they're making millions as kids who used to listen to Snoop Dogg and Eminem discover their roots. Working people love it. It's got heroes and villains. Loyalties and betrayals. Guns and violence and quick money. It's dramatic, like an action movie."

"Sounds like where rap was fifteen years ago," I said, picturing a gritty outlaw subculture and another good story materializing before my eyes.

"Before the kids got on board, the traditional *corrido* was in danger of dying out. It was considered old people's music. Now you got guys playing in barrio bars from San Fernando to Santa Ana. *Puros corridos perrones*. Nothing but badass ballads. Ruben wanted to break out the scene, give the singers a bigger stage. He said people would pay to see them perform in arenas. He had one guy he was grooming. From El Monte. Not a great singer, but *muy valiente*. He played a lot at El Bronco Negro. Could have been a big star. But Silvio and his dad closed ranks on Ruben. They said it would be an insult to all the honest, hardworking people who came to their shows."

"We've been through this before," said a measured voice. "We are not going to ennoble criminals and sully the family name by booking that kind of music."

Silvio stood in the room, holding a porcelain plate painted with violets and etched in gold. On it lay a mountain of lemon wedges.

Gisela jumped up, eyes glinting.

"But it's okay to bring in a bunch of homosexuals to sing *rocanrol* because that's your idea?" she said.

I stood, spellbound, as the argument ricocheted between them, the second generation of a music promotion dynasty, each with their own clear ideas about what kind of Latin music to bring to the masses.

Silvio inspected the plate. He pushed the citrus wedges around until they formed a circle. "They can sleep with sheep for all I care, so long as they don't do it in the arena. Have you forgotten Chalino?" he asked softly.

"Who's Chalino?" I asked. Was this some more buried family intrigue?

They both looked at me, as though surprised I was still in the room.

"Only the greatest *narcocorrido* singer who ever was," Gisela said in hushed tones.

"Don't forget dead," Silvio said.

"He was killed for his art," Gisela said with reverence. "A martyr. In death, he became a legend. His songs are more popular than ever. Now others write ballads about him."

"He wrote songs memorializing the exploits of drug dealers," Silvio explained. "Turned the dealers into Mexican Beowulfs. So that their sagas lived on, even after they were betrayed by treachery. As Chalino eventually was."

"Chalino shouldn't have named names and places. It pissed off rival drug lords. But you know what they say, Silvio. It was men in Mexican police uniforms who took him away after that show."

"He was performing in Sinaloa," Silvio told me. "His body was found the next day on the highway outside the capital. *Los asesinos,* the assassins, often borrow uniforms. The truth of what happened will never be known. But the music is bad news all the way. In Mexico, some states have even banned it. And Gisela here wants us to bring this filth into our arenas."

"Porfirio is more careful," Gisela insisted.

"He glorifies their lifestyle, and this we can never allow. Arena La Puente is not some barrio bar. We have families, small children, what about them? Is this family entertainment the Aguilars can be proud of?"

That reminded me of Langdon and his family values campaign. But whereas the mayoral candidate spoke in platitudes, there was a plaintive urgency to Silvio's voice. He truly felt responsible for setting standards in his community, and I was touched by his gallantry. I wondered what Langdon and dear-departed Venus would think of what the *narcocorridos* belted out each weekend night in Mexican juke joints at the eastern end of Sunset. Places just down the hill from their Los Feliz villa but light-years removed from their gilded universe.

"Los Angeles is changing, Silvio. It's not the city of our parents anymore. Ranchera and salsa will always sell, but if we want the new generation to shell out fifty dollars, we need to offer music that grabs them. And that's the *corridos pesados*. Don't barricade yourself into a barrio of the mind."

"I told this to my brother, and I'll tell it again to you," Silvio said. "It's gangster music. Foul-mouthed, swaggering, drunken tales of murder and mayhem, set to a Mexican hillbilly beat. Just because radio plays it now doesn't mean we have to follow. But you're right, Spanish-language stations are exploding in California; each year more stations switch their format. And in two of the biggest, what do you hear? Not *corridos*. You hear

Maná. Jaguares. Aterciopelados. Shakira. Café Tacuba. Fabulosos Cadillacs. The kids are ravenous for this stuff, and I want to give it to them. I know we have to evolve or die. I just want to maintain some class as we do it."

Gisela folded her hand into a fist and turned it over to examine her painted nails.

"Oh yeah, Silvio," she said. "You know a lot about class."

He stared at her, furious, and I sensed a chill undercurrent in what remained unsaid.

A gentle rumble came from the bed, followed by a clicking swallow and feathery intake of breath as Agrippina roused suddenly from her nap. *"Hablen Español, por favor,"* the old lady chided. Please speak Spanish.

"Oh, it's nothing, *abuelita,* we were just leaving," Silvio said. "Now if you'll excuse us, Eve and I have to pay our respects to my father."

In the hallway, he said, "As you can see, Ruben and Gisela disagreed with me about what music to bring to the arena. It caused a lot of conflict. But we've got to all hang in there together as a family."

"Speaking of which, what did she mean by that comment about class?"

"I don't know," he said, turning away.

# CHAPTER 23

**W**e stood there silently for a minute. I noticed he had gotten a haircut. Unlike many men, his hairline was as smooth and precise as a geographer's map, curving away from his exposed nape. I longed to trace its contours. Instead, I asked, "Do you think Ruben's death might have been connected in some way with the *corridos pesados?* That maybe he crossed the wrong person? As Chalino did?"

He gave me a piercing look. "Ruben wasn't a singer, Eve. He was a manager."

"But if he hung out in those bars, with the guys who sang those songs? Silvio, will you take me to one of those bars? I think those singers would make a great story for the *Times.*"

"The underbelly of Latin music? Here I've spent so much time and energy trying to block that music from my arena, and you want to zero in on it. Give them some more salacious press. Why are journalists always drawn to the lowest elements of society?" he asked in disgust.

"Because often the best stories are found in the gutter," I said. "That's the unfortunate truth. So will you take me?"

"No. You don't know what you're messing with. You don't know that world. Stay away from it."

"You're right. I don't know it."

"Are you going to write about our arguments over which bands to book?"

"The *narcocorridos?* It's fascinating. I'd like to."

He gave a short, tight nod. "My father and I disagree on this. I'm very private, I'd rather not talk to the press. He thinks it will be good for business. So I must defer to him."

"Talk to the press? You're sleeping with the press."

A small imp was pulling up the corner of his mouth.

"As a matter of fact, I'm feeling rather sleepy right now," he said.

"What a coincidence. Me too."

"Silvio? Silvio? Ah, here you are," said his father, bustling up to us.

Felipe Aguilar saw me and smiled.

"Well, my dear, is he giving you everything you need?"

I looked at Felipe Aguilar.

"He's just given me a taste," I said, "and I'm overwhelmed. The deeper I get, the more there is to learn."

"That's my boy," Felipe Aguilar said, slapping Silvio on the back. "Always the perfectionist. He's slow but thorough. You'll be begging for mercy before he's done with you."

"I hope so." I lowered my eyes.

"Sorry to drag you away from the interview, Silvio, but we need to talk a little business," Felipe Aguilar said.

"That's okay," I said, "I was just leaving."

"I'd like to continue this conversation later, Eve," Silvio said. "Shall I call you?"

"Of course," I said, as Felipe Aguilar threw an arm around his son and led him away, their two heads bent together. Oh yes, I thought, anticipating the lessons that Silvio would teach me. That would be just ducky.

It was late afternoon by now, and I was much closer to downtown than the San Gabriel Valley office, so I drove to Times Mirror Square. When I logged on to the system, an e-mail flashed across the top of my computer.

"Please see me right away. [Sims, Jane]"

Oh dear, I thought, wondering which of my faux pas Jane Sims had uncovered. Could someone have told her about Silvio and me? Damn it, I should have recused myself from that story a long time ago. I was just too greedy. But on the other hand, Jane Sims had a terrifically annoying habit of leaving cryptic messages that hinted darkly at errors that would involve retractions, libel lawsuits, and other journalistic hobgoblins. Then, after you had dropped everything to run to her office, heart pounding, she would smile thinly and say you had forgotten to sign up for the weekend Metro rotation.

I tried to walk in nonchalantly, as though I had been strolling past and the sight of her glass cubicle had reminded me to drop by. She saw me coming and rolled her office chair over to a file cabinet alongside her desk. She bent over it, running her nails along the plastic tabs with a loud flutter. She pulled one out, placed it on her desk, and smoothed it flat with her palm.

As I sat down, I realized it was my personnel file. And that this was not the month when merit raises were doled out.

"Eve, how *good* to see you," she said, her voice waggling and stretching the word until it meant something completely different. She blinked, pursed her lips, and continued.

"We've had a complaint." She folded her two hands demurely over the manila file in front of her. "Would you like to take a wild guess?"

I thought it out. If I confessed something she didn't know, she would seize upon it and demand a full explanation. If it was the Silvio conflict, we would get to it soon enough. I decided to let the white queen make the first move.

"Haven't the faintest." I crossed my legs and looked at her. I knew from the twitch in my right cheek that I needed to work on the no-affect look at which she was a master.

"I thought you had learned your lesson," she reproached me. "And now this." She tapped on the file with one enameled nail.

"And now what?"

"You know exactly what. You dug up an interesting tidbit on our mayoral front runner. Hurray for you. But there's no conspiracy. So what exactly gives you the right to be rude to Alan Severin and question the paternity of Carter Langdon the Third's murdered child? Perhaps you haven't noticed, Eve, but the *Times* expects its reporters to hew to a high level of professionalism."

My knee-jerk relief that she didn't know about Silvio quickly morphed into a sickening feeling that I was well and truly screwed this time. If anyone knew how to besmirch the opponent, it was attack dog Alan Severin. But perhaps it was because I was homing in on something he'd rather keep under wraps.

Jane opened the file and sifted the papers, pulling out a page from a yellow legal pad that was covered with handwriting. Hers.

"I took notes on our conversation." She scanned the page. "Here it is," she said with satisfaction. "Mr. Severin called you 'a hyena with a notepad.'"

"I'll take that as a compliment."

"Don't."

"Check the raw copy I filed on him, Jane. There's never been any insinuations."

"I'm not talking about what you filed. I'm talking

about what you said. You're a loose cannon. We can't have you mouthing off to him right before the election. If this got out, the paper would be accused of bias. You are hereby prohibited from talking to anyone in the Dellaviglia Langdon camp until this election is over. And that includes the son. I'm taking you off that squatter kids story."

The top of my brain felt like it would explode. She couldn't be serious. I was so close.

"Alan Severin told me you've been interviewing Venus and Carter's son, trying to draw some imaginary link to Lord knows what. You are harassing the family, Eve, at a time when they're traumatized, and you're flirting mighty close to slander as well."

"I'm just trying to interview as many people as I can, cover all the angles and be skeptical of what everyone tells me. Isn't that what reporters are supposed to do? Besides," I added, "there's no malice aforethought."

What libel was to the published word, slander was to conversation. If you called someone a murderer, they were free to sue you. But in order to collect damages, the aggrieved party had to prove, number one, that you had lied and, number two, that you had malice aforethought, which meant that you knew it was a lie and said it anyway in blatant disregard for the truth.

"That's not what Mr. Severin says. He says you've got a shitty attitude." Jane Sims crossed her arms over her chest and stared at me. "I've got to agree with him on that one."

"But—"

"No buts," Jane interjected. "You're off the story and that's final. Turn your notes in to me. A more seasoned Metro writer will be assigned to it. Josh Brandywine might be good. Now there's a reporter who's going to go far. And now, if you'll excuse me, I have to call my husband to tell him I'll be late. I have a speaking engagement this evening. It's something I do for the community."

For a long time, I sat in front of my computer. I had just seen my career crash and burn. I was a hothead. I wasn't professional. I wasn't objective. I had slandered a well-known politico, a pit bull in a human suit, who spent so much of his professional life smearing shit all over everyone that it was a wonder his hands weren't crawling with flies.

"Hey, kid," said a voice. "Want to earn some over-time? I've got a little story brewing and thought I'd send you if you're up for it."

It was Bovasso.

"What is it?" I croaked, realizing it might be the last Metro story of my career.

"The cops are cracking down on counterfeit goods sold at concerts, and they're staging a raid tonight at Staples Center. I want you and a fotog to tag along."

"Oh?" I brightened a little. I had never been to Staples Center, hadn't been to a concert in years. "Who's playing?"

"Band by the name of Limp Brisket."

Despite myself, I laughed. "It's 'Bizkit.'"

"What?"

"Limp Bizkit. It's white-trash speed metal. Kind of misogynist, slap-my-bitch-up kind of music. Yeah, okay, I'll go."

Bovasso's fingers groped nervously at his tie. "Slap-my-bitch-up music? That one of the new *Billboard* categories?" He snapped his fingers. "Oh, I got it. Like Eminen." He looked up, pleased with himself. "You think I don't got it going on?" He swizzled his hips a little and then stuck out his arms to steady himself. "I read Richard Milbourne."

Milbourne was the *Times*'s sixtyish rock music critic who took a lot of shit for being a dinosaur.

"Yeah, except Eminem is a compelling storyteller, regardless of whether you like what he's got to say. Not so with Limp Bizkit. Pray your kids never buy the CD."

"Well, make sure you put in the story about how this band hates everyone but relies on the Man to nab counterfeiters so they can make millions more on their T-shirts and posters."

Bovasso stopped and hiked up his pants with a worried look. "Does limp biscuit mean what I think it does?"

"Yeah," I told him. "In need of Viagra."

"Hard-ons," he snorted, hiking his pants one last time, adjusting his tie and walking away. "Guess they don't know how to spell either."

I drove over to a Chinese joint in Little Tokyo for dinner. It took me longer to drive the six blocks and park than it would have taken me on foot. But it was probably safer. If nobody walked in L.A., even fewer people strolled downtown after dark.

My work predicament couldn't be worse, and I didn't see any way out this time. My brain swirled with angry images of Jane Sims morphing into Severin's oleaginous face, then into something more hopeful. Silvio. So he felt it too. I wouldn't be home if he called tonight, but that was okay. I didn't want to be sitting around waiting for the phone to ring. At 7:30 P.M., my belly full of pickled cucumber and scallion pancakes, I got back in the car and drove a few more blocks to Staples Center, a huge state-of-the-art arena on downtown's southwestern boundary. I was supposed to meet

Harry Jack outside the main gate. Weaving my way through the sea of parked cars, I saw Harry standing by the entrance, taking in the pierced, tattooed, and torn crowd with a practiced eye. After more than half a century on the beat, there was nothing that shocked Harry Jack anymore. I mourned the fact that I wouldn't be working with him for much longer, but didn't want to ask if he knew any more about his fate while we still had a job to do. I was afraid he'd turn into a sad sack again.

We were able to sweet-talk the security beefcake at the door into letting us through. Once inside the Staples Center security office, we watched a bunch of LAPD officers shove guns into their fanny packs, because you never know, the fans might get agitated and start yelling "off the pigs" or some such millennial equivalent, and it would turn into a melee. In which case we'd get a better story than we bargained for, I thought blithely.

Then we tagged along with a posse of officers from the counterfeit crimes division as they caught a merchant ringing up a counterfeit T-shirt to some punk with his arm slung around a date. Her khakis were way conservative for this crowd, but I could see the guy's blue-black hair sticking straight up from his head. His hands were adorned with rings of skulls and dragons. The policeman showed the vendor his badge and asked him to step aside. "What did I do?" the vendor repeated, handing the girl her shirt.

"Hey, Eve," said Harry Jack. "Why don't you ask that gal there if she feels ripped off. Then, when she turns around, step out of the way and I'll get their photo holding the T-shirt and looking surprised."

That sounded good, so while the cops led the salesman away, I inched up and said, "Excuse me, miss, I'm a reporter with the *L.A. Times* and we're doing a story on counterfeit merchandising. Did you realize that the T-shirt you're holding is a fake?"

She turned and Harry Jack's flash went off, disorienting me momentarily. When I was able to focus on the low-cut purple-and-black top that read "Good & Plenty" and the thick black eyeliner ringing her eyes, my jaw dropped. It plummeted even more when I saw who her date was.

"Jane?" I said. "Jane Sims? Josh? What are you guys doing here?"

"Nothing," a meek female voice answered. And with that she was gone, pushing through the crowd that had gathered to gawk at the police activity.

I stood for a moment, staring at Josh Brandywine, who was looking at me with a sheepish expression. So this was his "complicated" love affair with some unlikely WASPy babe, I thought, recalling our earlier conversation. I wanted to stay and get the whole story, but then I realized that my true quarry had just fled. I could catch up with Josh anytime.

"Wait," I shouted, darting into the crowd to catch Jane Sims, the counterfeiting story all but forgotten. It was her. It was the *L.A. Times* Metro editor. And I was ready to bet that she and Josh weren't here on assignment. Somehow, improbably, I had stumbled on to their secret life: Married Jane Sims was having an affair with her underling Josh Brandywine, the golden boy of journalism who had once goosed the New York publishing world with his witty critique of metalhead lyrics. He must have talked her into coming here for the Limp Bizkit show, knowing how unlikely it was that any *Times* people would be here. Sure, there was the music critic, but the *Times* often used stringers to cover these things, and even if they sent a staffer, he'd be in a private skybox near the front, not mingling with the hoi polloi on the floor.

"Jane," I screamed, scampering after her. "I want to interview you. Don't run away. It won't work anyway. Harry Jack took your photo with Josh. Tomorrow it will be all over the paper."

I saw her hesitate. "Don't be a loose cannon," I yelled out. "*Times* staffers have to hew to a high level of professionalism."

Her shoulders sagged and she stopped running. I caught up with her. I was breathless, capering with glee. "So is this your speaking engagement, Jane? Were you and Josh going to stroll onstage after the opening act? Urge everyone to subscribe to the *L.A. Times?*"

Jane Sims's lower lip trembled. She sniffed and blinked, then caught herself and straightened her back. "Josh and I are here doing research on an investigative project that I can't disclose to you right now," she said. "In fact, this is just between you and me, I warn you."

Even now, she was trying to pull rank. Who would have suspected that uptight Jane Sims, the colorless Metro editor, had such a delicious secret. And with a reporter she supervised, my own pal Josh. That was grounds for demotion, even termination, at the *Times,* where the honchos were terrified of impropriety that might lead to sexual harassment lawsuits. And as for her personal life, I knew Jane was married, with children. No one is who they seem, I told myself again. *Yo no soy la mujer en el espejo.* I'm not the woman in the mirror. I'm someone else, someone other than you think, someone you can't even conceive of. Perhaps I was the only one who didn't know the rules, who wore her secret inner life as outerwear. Is that why Jane Sims despised me? Because she saw in me the part of herself she kept hidden and fed secretly, ravenously, with younger men like Josh?

"It's between you, me, and the *Times* photo lab," I told her.

She pinched her nostrils together with her fingers as though she might cry. I looked at her and saw that she was scared. Jane Sims was scared shitless. And that was an emotion I could put to good use.

"Harry Jack is my good pal, Jane. Do you know what I mean? He'll do me a favor if I ask him. Which means I can get you that photo. The neg too. We'll just snip it right out of the roll. It will be like it never happened. And I will never breathe a word of this to anyone. Even Josh. But it's going to cost you."

Jane Sims put a hand to her pale throat and shrank back from me. "What will it cost me?"

I looked long and hard at her. "I want you to tear up Harry Jack's retirement papers. Don't look at me like that, he told me. Someone slipped him the list. He knows he's getting the ax. And you may not know or care, but it would kill him. He lives for this, Jane, and unlike you, he doesn't have any secret hobbies to distract him. He's been here more than fifty years. He's the institutional memory of this place. You and your yuppie buddies ought to be ashamed. Except now you don't have to be, because he's not on the list anymore. It was a clerical error. Pffft. Gone." I snapped my fingers.

She gulped. "Okay, he's off the list. Now can you please get that photo for me and promise to keep this to yourself?"

"Not so fast. There's one other thing. I'm back on the squatter kids story. Our conversation this afternoon never happened. You got that?"

Jane Sims cast wildly around for someone to rescue

her from this abomination, but Josh was nowhere in sight and the lobby milled with trolls, not white knights.

"And then I get the photo and the neg?"

I nodded. "And then you get the photo and the neg. I will personally deliver them to your house tomorrow. What's your address?"

"You're going to come to my house?"

"Would you prefer an alley at Fifth and Main?"

She grimaced with distaste.

"No. Come to my house. I'll have to spend the morning cleaning, it's a mess."

"Don't go to any effort on my account," I told her as I left. I still had a story to file. But I also had my secret scoop, and for once, it was better than seeing my name on the front page.

# CHAPTER 24

O n the way to work the next morning, I stopped in the Glendale foothills near the Brand Library to meet Jane Sims. I had never been to that part of town before and it looked pretty idyllic—mothers pushing strollers, people riding bikes and jogging. The gardeners you see in nice suburbs. I watched them work, wondering if they were so tired when they got home that they hired other gardeners to mow their lawns? Or did they live in apartments that didn't have lawns? Or did they pave over their own lawns with concrete? I was surprised to see Japanese gardeners, small, wrinkled men with bent backs and skin stained brown as betel nuts from years in the sun. Their assistants were taller, huskier, and younger Latinos, and I knew that I was seeing a historic changing of the guard as elderly Japanese throughout Southern California handed over their lawn-mowers and leaf blowers and battered pickups to a new generation from another culture. They had no one to pass on the family business to—their college-educated kids wanted jobs that paid more and ached less at the end of a long day. The Japanese themselves had only gone into gardening because whites wouldn't hire them after the war and a gardening business required minimal investment. Soon, they would be but a sepia-toned memory of the city's more intolerant days.

As I drove, I thought about what I had told Harry Jack the previous night after we finished interviewing and photographing people at the concert and returned to the paper.

Even though the *Times* now had photo techs who did most of the grunt work, Harry still developed his own rolls, a habit he had held on to since the old days. Before he could scan the photos into the computer, I asked to see them. Sure enough, there was Josh, fingers entwined with "Good & Plenty." She had one arm up, blocking half her face, and looked like Bambi's mother caught in the forest fire.

"Harry, I need that photo."

"Why's that?" He took a closer look. "Hey, isn't that Brandywine? But who's the gal with him? She's not exactly a babe, now, is she?"

"No, she isn't. I have to ask you a favor. Can you give me that photo and the neg? I don't want them scanned into the computer. I want you to pretend you never took them."

"Is she a friend of yours? Funny, that dame looks a little like Jane Sims. What I can see of her. But I don't think she'd be at a concert like that."

"Jane will be happy to hear it. And no, this gal isn't a friend, exactly. But it has something to do with a story I'm writing. And if it works out, we'll both be happy campers."

"All right. Makes no difference to me. With her arm in the way, I doubt they'd use it."

"That makes it even better."

He handed over the photo and the neg and I slipped them into a manila envelope and sealed it.

Now I was knocking on Jane Sims's door. She answered right away, looking like she'd been waiting up all night. She wore a button-down broadcloth shirt and

Smith & Hawken gardening clogs. Walking in, I saw some Diego Rivera–esque oil paintings and heard old Amadeus on the stereo.

"What, no Limp Bizkit?" I asked.

She looked at me with alarm. "My husband is due back in town with the kids any minute. He doesn't, uh, know." She led me into a study and closed the door. "Where are they?"

I handed her the envelope, and she fumbled with the clasp, then pulled out the photo and the neg. A small moan escaped her.

"Don't I look ridiculous," she said, as if she were talking about a stranger. "You're sure there are no more copies?"

"I can only take Harry's word for it. He's a gentleman from way back. But he'll be expecting you to keep your word too."

"Of course."

Her face fell. "But how can I be sure you'll keep this to yourself?"

"Because I'm a gentleman too."

She looked at me, sizing me up, and realized the situation was out of her hands. She didn't like the idea of trusting me, but she had no choice.

"All right," she said briskly. "Now let's go outside. I want to burn this and bury the ashes. I was just digging a hole for something else."

"Love letters from Josh?"

"Can you stop already?"

We walked outside. I couldn't believe how the tables had turned.

"One other thing," I told her. "I want full freedom to investigate the squatter kids story wherever it takes me."

Her eyes shifted. "But what do I tell the political editor if we get another complaint?"

"Tell him you're looking into it. Then let me know."

"Okay," she whispered. She marched to the back of the large yard. Under an oak tree was a hole.

"I have to do this," Jane Sims told me. "So Mandy doesn't catch me in flagrante delicto."

"Who's Mandy?"

"Sshhhh."

What a bucketful of secrets Jane Sims balanced inside her head. No wonder she always looked so pinched.

"Mandy," she looked around conspiratorially, "is our housekeeper. A dear lady. She gave me these," Jane Sims indicated a plastic bag full of wrapped bundles, "and I have to bury them."

"Is it drugs?"

"Tamales," Jane Sims said grimly. "Filled with pork and lard. What am I supposed to do with that?"

"How about you try eating them," I said, taking in Jane Sims's two-dimensional physique.

She looked as if I had made a disgusting joke. "I am not going to touch those heart attack packs, and I can't throw them away because Mandy will find them in the trash, which she takes out. So I have to bury them on her day off. And I have to make sure the gardener doesn't try to plant anything here for the next six months, because he's Latino, so he'd be insulted too." She stabbed at the ground.

"What kind of a name is Mandy, anyway?" I asked. "That doesn't sound Latin."

"I suppose her real name is Maria or Ana or something. We've called her Mandy for longer than I can remember. She was always saying 'mandy, mandy,' each time we asked her something, so the kids started calling her that, and it stuck."

She tossed in the plastic bag, then brought out a container of cayenne pepper and sprinkled it on the half-buried tamales.

"So the dog won't dig them up," she explained. "It would probably give her diarrhea for a week."

She stomped the reddened earth with her shoes, then pulled out a fancy silver lighter and clicked it on. She pulled out the photo and watched the celluloid curl as the flames licked greedily. She dropped the blackened remnants onto the tamale grave. Squatting close to the ground, she now did the same with the negative. Then she filled up the hole.

"Jane," I asked, "how did you get together with Josh in the first place?"

She stared moodily into the branches of the oak tree and my gaze followed hers until it settled on the acorns. I have always loved acorns, the way they grow in clusters, little riparian soldiers with tiny green hats and shiny brown bodies.

I wasn't really expecting an answer, but she surprised me.

"It should never have gone this far," Jane Sims said. "I suppose he reminds me of some boys I knew in school. The ones who wouldn't have looked twice at me back then, because my mother was a waitress and I was on scholarship."

I held my breath. Everything I knew about Jane Sims was dissolving as a new person materialized. Someone more like me than I might have guessed.

"He's brilliant, and it's so effortless for him," she said, her sharp features softening. "At first I told myself I was just mentoring him. Then one evening after work we went out for coffee. He wanted guidance on a story.

Away from the office, I felt less like his boss and more like a woman. In a way I no longer felt after fifteen years of marriage to Mel, God bless him. So it started. I told myself it was just an affair, but somehow it didn't feel tawdry. Mel would just die if he knew."

I was completely, perversely fascinated by every word that tumbled out of Jane Sims's mouth. At the same time, I was struck by my own audacity, amazed I could stick it to her when I too was transgressing, sleeping with Silvio while writing about his family business. Not a sin of her caliber, to be sure, but actionable nonetheless.

"So how long ago was that?" I asked.

Her eyes snapped from the acorns to me, her underling, who she realized had been busily collecting nuts. Big blackmail nuts. For what might be a long journalistic winter. She grew peeved, as though I had tricked her.

"Why am I telling you this?"

*Because you have a burning need to confess your secret life to someone. It's been driving you crazy. And I'm a sympathetic listener. I draw people out. Get them to say things. It's something intuitive that has nothing to do with J school. Or master's programs. Or the Ivy League. Which is something you'll never understand.*

I shrugged. "Because I'm here," I told her. "And because I already know, so it's not like you're incriminating yourself. People have affairs. And where do they meet people? At work."

She stood and stared at the freshly turned earth for a long time. Then she scuffed it with her foot.

"But I'm older and I'm married. Happily married. Worst of all, I'm his supervisor."

I was glad she had said it, not me.

"It can't go on, of course," she continued. "But I'm not ready to let go just yet."

"So don't. What if he's your soul mate and you're denying a piece of yourself?"

She looked at me, and the vulnerability of a moment earlier was gone.

"We should all practice self-abnegation more often." She turned on her heel. "And now, you'd better go. As I told you, Mel will be home soon, and we're expected at the Music Center."

That night, Silvio called. I apologized again for showing up at the wake. He said it was okay. Then I recounted how I had trumped Jane Sims, mighty Metro editor. As I got to the part about her burying the tamales and the burnt negatives, I doubled over in laughter. But Silvio was more interested in the housekeeper.

"So she always said 'mandy' when they asked her something?"

"Weird, huh?"

"I think she was saying '*mande*.'" Silvio pronounced it with the proper accent and liquid consonants of Spanish, and all of a sudden my laugh choked in my throat.

"Oh no."

"Oh yes."

I remembered that in Spanish *mande* was the polite response to a request.

"It literally means 'command me,'" Silvio explained. "For the family to pick up on that and start calling her 'Mandy,' that's like a white family nicknaming a black servant 'Yessum.'"

"I'm sure she has no idea," I said, put in the uncomfortable position of defending Jane Sims. The way our

conversation was going, I didn't think Silvio and I would
end up together that night. "She doesn't mean ill by it.
She's got Latin art all over her walls."

"I'm sure she does. Cultural appropriation is big these
days. Poor 'Mandy,' putting up with that insult all these
years, on top of having her tamales buried like cat poop.
What's wrong with some people?"

# CHAPTER 25

*I* went to sleep alone and had uneasy dreams. I was locked in a cage in the basement of an airless squat. I banged, screaming to get out, but nobody came. I woke up, my limbs rigid—1:49 A.M. The banging continued. At first I thought it was my heartbeat, but once that slowed down, I realized it was my front door.

I threw on a robe.

"Who is it?"

"It's Scout," came a mild voice. "Do you think you could, like, open the door?"

"Scout, is that you?" I called stupidly. What if it was some rapist masquerading as Scout?

"Yeah, it's me. Isabel's friend."

I recognized the befuddled quality of her voice and the sniff that followed.

Undoing the dead bolt, the chain, and the regular lock, I opened the door. She stood there shivering in a black Iggy Pop T-shirt, hugging her elbows. A cigarette dangled from her fingers.

"Trick or treat," she said. She stared down at my welcome mat, the letters embroidered in pretty violets. Then she flicked the cigarette into the damp earth and stepped over the threshold and into my life again.

I stared at her, torn between pity and loathing.

"Halloween's still a few days away, *chica*," I told her. "And you've already played the trick. Now comes the treat. Where's my jewelry and my money?"

"I pawned your stuff," she said, rummaging in her pocket and pulling out a stub. "Here."

"Did my cash run out that fast?"

"I'm sorry," she muttered, but it was just a formality. She walked to the wall and ran her finger along the crown molding like she was doing a white glove test. "Lights, camera, action," she said as she came to the picture window and looked out over the glittering jewels of nighttime L.A. She yawned. "I had a little too much action tonight."

I leaned against the wall and watched her. I had decided that befriending Scout was like trying to cuddle alligators.

"So now you're back to steal some more? Make a fool of me twice. Wrong-o, pal."

"You can get it back."

"Oh great. I can pay to get my own jewelry out of hock."

Wearily, I put it on my long list of things to do. Then I thought of something else. "You've got body lice, by the way. You gave it to me and this guy I . . . uh . . . my boyfriend."

A ludicrous impulse had washed over me to shield Scout from the fact I had slept with a man I barely knew.

Her head cocked, then pivoted. "I didn't know you had a boyfriend. You never talked about him. So who is he?" She walked up to me, stuck her face close to mine, then sang, "Evie's got a boyfriend, Evie's got a boyfriend."

"He's just this guy. And he got crabs. From this bed." I pointed at the mattress and box spring. "I hope he doesn't hold it against me."

She shrugged. "Why would he?"

"Because people don't . . ." I stopped, frustrated. I had been about to say that in my world, people don't take kindly to such a thing. But then I considered her world.

"So what do you want now? A place to crash?"

"It's not what I want from you, but what you want from me," she corrected. "Sophie and Caitlin said you want to talk."

"And you thought two A.M. was a fine time to jaw?"

"Huh? Oh, sorry. But they said I was late. For a very important date. With you. It's about Isabel. They said I should tell you about Isabel."

"I thought you already told me about Isabel." I wasn't making it easy for her.

"No, man, I'm not talking about how she lived. I'm talking about how she died."

She wound a strand of hair around her finger, examining it, her arm doing a palsied Saint Vitus's dance.

"So how did she die?"

"That's a profound question."

"Scout," I said with irritation. "Are you just putting me on again? Because if you are . . ."

I stopped. I listened to myself. I took a deep breath.

"You can stay here tonight," I said. "Here." I tossed the shivering fool a jacket. She shrugged it on, and the long sleeves gaped, empty and eyeless from her thin arms.

"Do you want a cup of tea? A meal? I could heat up some quiche and a baguette."

Even as I said it, I thought how puerile my foodie terms must sound to someone whose sommelier was the night clerk at 7-Eleven.

"Kewel. I could eat."

I led her into the kitchen and she ate most of a spinach

quiche and an entire baguette and drank two glasses of milk. I was afraid she might get sick again.

Then she stepped onto my balcony to smoke. I watched her impatiently but didn't say anything.

"Don't get mad at me for leaving the other night," she said after she came back. "I can't help it. Isabel used to say I wasn't domesticated. She tried to get me to stay in one place too. But I can't think so good with walls around me."

"I suppose that's not surprising, considering what you've been through."

Her mouth tightened.

"I don't know why people make such a big deal about stuff. The shrinks always tried to get me to talk about it. They said it would help me 'heal.'" She snorted with derision.

"I'm sure it's painful to think about. But if your mother's boyfriend abused you, he's probably done it to twenty other little girls. You could still file charges. There's special statutes of limitations on child sexual abuse."

She looked away and her lip trembled.

"How do you know about that?"

"Finch told me. When I went to visit him in jail."

"You know little Finchie?"

"Don't you remember? Well, maybe not, you took those Vicodin."

She licked a finger and pressed it down on her plate, collecting bread crumbs. Then she raised the finger to her face, examined and carefully licked off the crumbs.

"Lots of people get abused. They get over it. It hasn't affected the way I live my life."

Right, I thought. Not one little bit. I felt sad and tired and not angry anymore.

"I'll leave when you do in the morning," Scout was saying. "I'm not gonna steal nothin' this time. Caitlin and

Sophie told me you're trying to help catch Isabel's killer and get Finch out. I give you props for that."

"Scout, how about we go to the police in the morning? They need to hear what you know."

"No way, man. They'll put me back in Mac." She shuddered and her eyes darted.

"You'll get a lot of attention if I write a story about it. We could get you placed in a good foster home. I'd come visit. Promise."

"No way. That's not the way they do things. I tell you, then I split. That's the deal."

"As soon as my story runs, the cops will be here wanting you to confirm what I wrote. Don't you want Finch out of jail? He's being set up for a murder he didn't commit."

"I know," she said in a tiny voice.

"The cops found Finch, they can find you too."

She got a crazy gleam in her eye. "They can't play hide-and-seek good as me. Besides," she added coyly, "I don't know what happened. I left Isabel at the squat and went up to the boulevard to get some money. I never made it back that night."

Oh, Christ, I thought, wondering how I was ever going to unravel the true story.

She saw the look on my face.

"That's the truth. Swear."

I scrutinized her. She regarded me blankly. She knew something. It was a matter of triggering it.

"Okay, you weren't there. But something happened. Maybe earlier that night? Did Isabel seem upset about anything?"

"Yeah."

"What?"

"She saw something maybe she shouldn't have."

"What was that?"

Scout fidgeted. She hummed a few lines of a Grateful Dead song.

"What did she see?"

"Well, me and her were up to Paolo's that night."

My hands tingled.

"Paolo Dellaviglia Langdon?"

"I went to deliver some L."

"Acid? Yeah. Go on."

"And he wanted to test it out. Even though I told him it was primo."

"So did you?"

"We each dropped a tab. We were in his orchard, coming on, and it was frigging stellar. Then Isabel decided to go for a swim. They got this pool there, smooth as glass on a summer night."

"I know the one."

"Paolo and I passed. We couldn't move. I felt like a plant, pushing roots deep into the ground."

"Then what?"

"Paolo had to go and ruin it."

"How?"

"He scammed me. I was pretty high, but not enough to go for it. So I pulled up my plant roots and walked farther into the orchard. That's how I ran into Isabel."

"What was she doing?"

"She was running the other way. I asked her what was wrong, cuz she was tripping me out, she looked scared."

"What did she say?"

"Fucking grown-ups." Scout shook her head. "And they think *we're* fucked up."

"What happened?"

"Well, if you've been to Paolo's place, you know the layout."

"You mean how you hike up to the cabana, then down the flagstone steps to get to the pool?"

"Yeah. Well, the cabana lights were on. Isabel wanted to see who was in there. Everyone says L makes you paranoid, but it makes you fearless too."

"Go on."

"So when she looks in, she sees Paolo's mom and some guy going at it. On the bed."

I looked out of the kitchen window, saw the lights of downtown blinking like a Christmas tree. Here came my present.

"Was it Paolo's dad?"

"Nope. He was younger. Isabel said he was buff, man."

"So she saw them having sex."

"Yeah. He was being rough, you know, throwing her around, putting his hands on her throat, but it was just fooling around, Isabel said."

"How could she tell?"

"She said Paolo's mom was squealin' an' moanin', begging for it. And he'd just throw her against the wall again and laugh. Then they got down to it."

"And she winds up dead, floating in her own pool, not long after that. I wonder if the sex got too rough," I murmured. "Or if her husband found out and had her killed. Maybe he learned that Isabel had seen them and had her killed too."

Scout didn't seem to hear me. She was bent over her plate, hunting for more crumbs. Here, finally, was proof that Venus had been having an affair. Which undoubtedly had something to do with her murder. There was only one problem, and I was staring at it. Why would anyone believe a homeless, mentally ill, substance-abusing, larcenous teen survivor of child sexual abuse over the impeccable and illustrious Carter Langdon III?

"Then what happened?" I asked.

"Check out the cool pattern on my finger." Scout held up a crumb-encrusted thumb. "Doesn't it look like a star?"

"Scout, you were telling me how Venus and this guy were having sex. What did Isabel do when she saw that?"

"Look, Eve."

"Oh for God's sake." I grabbed her hand and held it up. "Yeah, I see it. A star."

"It's my lucky star. Isabel should have had one that night."

"But she didn't?"

"She didn't," Scout echoed. "L can make you goofy too, see, and Isabel thought Paolo's mom and the dude looked pretty funny going at it. I mean, they were old-sters. So she giggled."

"Did they hear it?"

"Yeah. The dude asked what the hell was that and Paolo's mom said it was probably a possum but she's going to investigate. So she comes out, and she's, you know, naked, and Isabel tries to run down the stairs but she's stoned and so she falls. Venus grabs her. Isabel tries to squirm away but Paolo's mom holds on tight.

"Then Isabel says she's sorry and Mrs. Langdon says, 'You will be sorry.' She's so frigging angry. She says she was taking a nap and asks Isabel what she saw in there. Nothing, Isabel tells her. And Paolo's mom calls her a lying little bitch and slaps her. That's pretty messed up. I'd a cut her, she tried that shit with me."

"You mean with a knife?" Suddenly Scout didn't seem so small and defenseless.

She reached into her pocket and pulled out a switch-blade. "Never leave home without it."

I looked at the ugly blade and realized Scout could

have killed me in my sleep the last time she was here. I was glad I hadn't known about it. She pressed the tip of the metal into the pad of her forefinger until the skin broke. Then she watched, hypnotized, as blood pearled.

"Sometimes pain can be good," Scout said. She wiped her finger on her jeans. "There. Now I can put it away."

She snapped the knife shut and shoved it deep into her pocket. I reconsidered what I knew about Scout. From the beginning, she had seemed like someone who could help unravel the murder of Isabel. But what if I had it all wrong? There was little doubt that Scout was unbalanced. She professed her love for Isabel, but what if she hated her too, hated her for the idealized image she represented? Because even as she slummed with Scout, Isabel was the little street girl's exact opposite. She had a future. She had a home and a family, even if it was creepy old Vince Chevalier. Had Scout killed Isabel to remove the glittering image of what she could never be? Or did she feel Isabel was betraying her by trying to get her off the street?

"Why are you looking at me like that?" Scout asked.

I jolted back into the present.

"I guess I just don't like knives," I said, wondering how I would be able to sleep.

"Neither did Isabel."

"So Isabel didn't have a knife?"

"She didn't need one. Until that night."

"Why did she need one that night, Scout?"

"Well, for when the murderer snuck up on her, of course," she said with exasperation.

"Any idea who that might be?"

"Nope," she said, and her hand slid into her pocket, fingering the metal.

"No one who had a motive?"

"What's that?"

"A reason to kill her."

"Uh-uh."

I sighed and decided to cut back to the chase.

"So Isabel is standing by the cabana and Venus slaps her. Then what?"

"I should have stayed with her that night. Then she'd still be alive."

It sounded like what a loyal friend would say.

"What did Isabel do after Venus slapped her?"

"She swore she wouldn't tell anyone. Not Paolo or anyone else."

"And?"

"Mrs. Langdon laughed, which was weird, and said Paolo was the least of her concerns. Her lipstick was all smeared and her chest was splotchy red. Paolo's mom said that if Isabel told anything, she'd call the cops and tell them about the drugs. She said she knew Paolo did drugs with his friends in the orchard and that the cops would put Isabel in jail."

"That wasn't too bright of Venus," I said. "Because if Isabel got arrested, Paolo probably would too, and that wouldn't look so good right before his dad's election."

"Whatever," Scout said. "So when Paolo's mom let her go, Isabel ran back into the orchard and that's when I found her. We hiked back to Paolo and told him to take us back to the squat."

"So he drove you. Was Finch there?"

"No."

"And then what?"

"I already told you. I went up to the boulevard."

I still wasn't sure I believed this.

"Do you think it was wise to leave your friend there alone when she was so scared?"

Scout shrugged. "She was crashing. I figured Finch would be along soon."

"And you never saw her again?"

"Right."

"But sometime after you left and before nine A.M., Isabel was murdered in that squat."

"I guess," she said. "I wasn't there. Honest. You need to go find Pia if you want to know anything else."

"Pia?"

"She's a trannie. We know each other from the boulevard. I ran into her that night. She had been up for two days at some party. She asked if I knew a place nearby to crash and I told her to go down to Finch's."

With a start, I realized it was the elusive Latino boy from the L.A. River. So the lives of these two had intersected after all.

"You think Pia went there that night and saw something?"

"Yeah, maybe. Can I go to bed now?"

"In a minute. Where can I find him, uh, her?"

"At the river, probably. I haven't seen her in days."

I thought back on what Scout had told me. A sense of urgency had been growing in me ever since I learned that Isabel had caught Venus with her lover. Someone didn't want that news to get out. And they wanted it badly enough to kill.

"Scout, if I write what you told me, it could put you in danger."

She gave me a streetwise look and patted her pocket. "I can take care of myself."

"Don't be a little idiot. The killer knows your world. Isabel was murdered in a squat. They'll find you. Why don't we go talk to the police together? They can protect you."

"That would be a first."

"I'm worried about you."

"We had a deal."

I looked at her in despair. I knew I needed to talk to Tom Thompson to figure out how to proceed.

"Okay, Scout." I stood up and put away my notepad. "You've certainly sung for your supper."

I handed her my toothbrush to tackle her jagged and discolored teeth, knowing I'd never use it again.

"How about giving me that knife until morning? I can lock it in my car."

"What for?" She looked at me with suspicion.

"Because it makes me nervous."

"It's for my protection."

"I don't want weapons in my house."

"It's not like I'm going to use it on you."

"There's no need to sleep with a knife in my house."

Finally, she agreed. We walked outside and she watched me tuck her knife under the passenger seat. Then I threw some sheets on the futon for her. She wasn't sick anymore, and she wasn't sleeping in my bed this time. I grabbed my purse and when I got into my bedroom, I slid the lock across.

# CHAPTER 26

E ven with the knife safely stashed, I found it hard to sleep. I thought about poor stoned Isabel, leaving her nice Pasadena house to play squatter girl in Hollywood. Huddling in her sleeping bag waiting for Finch to arrive. Eventually falling asleep. And waking up to find someone strangling her. I pictured Isabel looking into the eyes of her killer as she took her last breath. Had they been familiar eyes? Eyes of a friend? A lover? What secrets did Isabel know how to keep? Did they have anything to do with her father? Had another vagrant stumbled across her warm body and killed her? Or did her murder have something to do with what she had seen at the Dellaviglia Langdon estate?

Friday morning, true to her word, Scout retrieved her knife, grabbed her backpack, and began trudging down the hill, cigarette in hand, as I headed off to work. I pulled alongside her.

"You're welcome to stay with me a few more nights. I don't bite."

She blew smoke in my face. "No thanks."

"Can I give you a ride anywhere?"

"Naw," she muttered. "I'm still working on a plan. My brain is so sporadic. Too much random shit. Maybe I'll go to the shrine. I miss Isabel."

"I can take you."

"It's okay."

"Here," I said, handing her some cash, even though I realized it would probably go up her nose. "You'll need this for food." She took it wordlessly. In my rearview mirror, I saw her turn left on Glendale Boulevard and head toward Sunset. At the office, I recounted Scout's tale to Tom Thompson, leaving out none of the lurid details.

"Now I'm playing devil's advocate here, mind you," he said when I was done, "but who's going to believe a word of it? The lot of them were on drugs. The Chevalier kid could have hallucinated the whole thing. And what did she see anyway? Mrs. Langdon indulging in a little rough trade? Both the kid and the contessa are dead and there's no sense dragging out dirty laundry."

I opened my mouth to speak, but he threw me another curveball.

"By the way, you could have called Children's Services as you drove in. They would have found her."

"I could, but she needs someone she can believe in. Maybe that could be me. She'll be back."

He raised his eyebrows. "You walk through this office, there's only room for one hat on your head. It says reporter. Leave the bleeding heart at home."

"Will you at least ask Metro if they want the story?"

Thompson placed his feet on the desk and leaned back in his chair. "You betcha," he said, adjusting his headset. "They need to know every vile rumor out there. Just don't hold your breath."

I walked over to the lunchroom and found Harry Jack standing by the coffee machine as a new pot brewed. One day, scientists will discover that it fills more slowly when people watch it.

"Yo, Harry, heard anything more about that list?"

His shoulders slumped. "No, I haven't. But I'm girding my loins."

I ambled back to my desk and found an e-mail from

Josh flashing on the computer screen that said, "We need to talk. Call me."

I picked up the phone, considering the delicious things I might say, when I felt Thompson looming over me.

"Metro's interested."

"Great," I said.

He held up one hand. "Not so fast. They want you to check Scout out thoroughly first. Call DCS, the cops, probation. See what you can get on her. And track down this Pia critter. Find out if she was there that night, what she saw. Then let's see what we've got."

"That could take days. This has to come out now, before the election."

Thompson's eyebrows beetled. "What has to come out?"

"Well, how his wife was having an affair."

"It's exactly because the election is in a few days that we have to move cautiously. Carter Langdon the Third has the city's deepest sympathy. I'm not so naïve as to think the upper crust doesn't screw around and kill each other. But we need proof. Otherwise, the pope himself could accuse Venus of adultery and it wouldn't mean shit. None of this has any bearing on Langdon's ability to govern the city."

"Unless he killed her," I said.

He pointed a finger at me. "That's exactly what we don't need around here. Crass speculation. Leave it to the *Enquirer*. Now get out there and harvest the facts like you're paid to do and no more of your back-sass."

I saluted. "Yes sir." Then I drove to the L.A. River and hiked down the embankment. I remembered the fear Pia's friends had displayed when she hadn't returned from her date. But I hadn't read anything about a murdered Latino teen transvestite turning up in a Dumpster either.

This time, one of the trannies told me Pia had shown up several days ago but had split again. I left an urgent message for her, knowing how futile that might be.

I drove back to the office and started calling around about Scout, saying I needed the information in connection with the murder of Isabel Chevalier. As I feared, the L.A. County Department of Children's Services wouldn't tell me anything because she was a minor and juvenile records are sealed for the kids' own protection. Ditto for the LAPD, whose flack referred me to Juvenile Court. They wouldn't tell me anything either. In desperation, I called a source at LAPD who took pity on me and agreed to look into it. An hour later, he called back, saying he had checked with a friend at juvie and could find nothing on her. Even that meager information was off the record.

I had just hung up with Deep Tonsil when Harry Jack came up.

"Say, Eve," he began, "funny you shoulda asked about that early retirement. They just posted the list, the bastards, they wait till the end of the day, but anyway, I'm not on it. I guess my friend was wrong. He swears he saw my name. Says they musta taken me off at the last minute. I been razzing him about his eyesight."

My face split into a hemispheric grin and I threw my arms around him. So Jane Sims had kept up her end of the bargain after all.

"Harry, that's great news. That's the best news I've heard all month."

He looked at me, surprised by my outburst.

"Gee, Eve, I didn't know you cared that much."

"Of course I do, Harry. Of course I do."

I spent most of Friday evening driving up and down Hollywood and Santa Monica Boulevards, asking street kids and hustlers if they knew a transvestite teen named Pia. Most of them assumed I was the heat and just walked away. Others told me politely they had never heard of her, though several times I saw recognition flood wary eyes. At midnight, I gave up and went home.

The red light on my answering machine was blinking with two messages.

"Hey, uh, our friend from the other night told me about your little deal," Josh's nervous voice began, "and I just want to say thanks. Mum's the word, and I owe you a big one, Lois Lane."

Don't I know it, I thought as the receiver clicked and the second message came on.

"It's a pity you're not home," Silvio said, "because I'm feeling awfully sleepy again and I wanted to describe in great detail all the things I intend to do to you the next time we're together."

Blood rushed to my face. I looked at my watch. Damn. It was too late to call him back. I slipped into bed, thinking carnal thoughts, and it took a long time to get to sleep. I was eating granola and checking out the paper the next morning when the phone rang. I hoped it was Silvio. We could have all day together.

"Are you sitting down?" asked Tom Thompson.

"Yes."

Why was he calling me on Saturday? Had I won some award?

"They just found a body behind a boarded-up building at Alvarado and Sunset," he told me. "She was wearing a Girl Scout uniform. She had been raped and stabbed with a switchblade. The cops think it's your friend Scout."

# CHAPTER 27

I t took a few moments to sink in. With it came the horrifying possibility that my inquiries had somehow triggered Scout's murder.

I had been so suspicious and sarcastic when she knocked on my door, angry that she had done what came naturally after a life on the run. Yet I knew that in her own twisted way, Scout had loved Isabel and Finch and wanted to see justice served. Instead, she too was now dead, probably killed with the very knife she assumed would protect her.

Stunned and numb, I took a shower and then drove in. Thompson was waiting for me. I followed him into the office and closed the door.

"I want you off this story," he said. "I know you were in front of the cops, and I was excited too when you pranced in with what you'd found. But you're too close to it. Everyone has your best interests at heart. Write up your notes and file to me. Metro is putting Josh Brandywine on it."

I was too upset to protest. Returning to my desk, I stared blindly at the screen until Thompson told me the LAPD was on the phone. They wanted me to go to Parker Center and tell them everything I knew. Thompson said it was up to me and that I could claim reporter's privilege if I wanted. But as far as I was concerned, the cat was already out of the bag. I would tell them whatever I could dredge up so they could find Scout's murderer. Everything except Pia. I might be off the story for the *Times,* but I was now launched on a personal vendetta. I had to find her and talk to her.

After an exhausting afternoon answering the questions of a good cop, bad cop duo, they let me go. I called Silvio but hung up when I got his machine. I went to bed early, stuffing earplugs into my ears and pulling up the comforter to muffle any sound.

The next day was Halloween. The *Times* had a story by Josh about how police were looking for Scout's killer. It was short and stark. There was no mention of her passion for swinging. Her shaky grasp of Nietzsche. A poem she had once memorized. Such frivolous details would only have disturbed the flow of facts.

I threw the paper down and drove to a Japanese place, where I got a plate of cold soba—buckwheat noodles—in a spicy peanut soy sauce. By all rights, it should have tasted like straw, and I felt guilty that I could enjoy it. But in some weird way, eating helped me focus, which allowed me to concentrate on the ever-expanding puzzle that I was convinced had now claimed Scout's life.

As a reporter, I knew that seemingly disparate lives were often interwoven far more closely than anyone might imagine. On the streets and in the high-rises and old-money villas and homeless encampments and immigrant enclaves of L.A., people collided daily. And no one kept track of their couplings, friendships, grudges, and linked degrees of separation unless they died unnaturally. Then the job began of tracing the invisible web of connections. That's where I was now. Sipping barley tea, I sketched out what I had.

VENUS DELLAVIGLIA LANGDON
Rich, adulterous, beautiful socialite, married to leading candidate for mayor who has ruthless cam-

paign manager with his own secrets. Shot to death
and found in pool in her Los Feliz villa. Was pregnant, probably by a lover, not by her husband, who
might be gay. Her son, Paolo, knew the murdered
girls Scout and Isabel.

ISABEL CHEVALIER
Upscale Pasadena prep school kid. Fifteen years
old. Friend of Venus's son, Paolo. Found strangled
in abandoned building in East Hollywood. Her
homeless squatter boyfriend Finch now charged
with the murder. But friends say he didn't do it.
Isabel's father, Vince, who led me to the body, is
one weird dude but not an official suspect.

RUBEN AGUILAR
Black-sheep scion of Aguilar Entertainment, the
firm that owns Arena La Puente. I'm dating his
brother, Silvio. (At least I think I still am.) Ruben
feuded with Silvio over musical direction of arena.
Wanted to bring in *narcocorrido* singers with possible ties to Mexican mobs. Left behind a fiancée
who works in the family business. Owned pool-
cleaning firm at time of his death. Venus was one
of his clients. She was going to "set him up." Was
he the mystery lover? Killed in front of his house
in El Sereno. No suspects. Police have written it off
as a gang shooting.

SCOUT
Troubled Hollywood street kid who befriended
Paolo and Isabel. Was with both of them on the
night of Isabel's murder. Was the last known person
to see Isabel alive. Before she was killed, Isabel

told Scout she saw Venus having sex with her lover in the cabana. Scout was found murdered behind an abandoned building after I started calling around to the cops and social service agencies, inquiring about her.

There was a common thread here, and as I reread what I had written, I saw it more clearly than ever. It was Venus. Even dead, she was the center from which these spokes radiated, the nexus through which all cultures and classes collided. Each one of them knew Venus Dellaviglia Langdon.

It was too late to ask Venus to connect the dots. Severin and Carter, the next most logical choice, weren't talking. I would have to settle for the son. Unfurling the scrap of paper on which I had written Paolo's cell phone number, I dialed. It rang and rang. I tried all afternoon to no avail. I also called Silvio, telling him I had played his phone message back until the tape squeaked. He wanted to see me that evening but I told him I had to get in touch with a source. We agreed to meet in two days. I tried Paolo again and he answered on the first ring.

"Yeah?" His breathing was heavy.

"Paolo?"

"Yeah." Palpable disappointment. He wasn't waiting to hear from me. I chose my words carefully. This kid had just lost his mother.

"It's Eve Diamond, the *Times* reporter. I'm so sorry about your mom. Do you remember me? We met at your parents' fund-raiser. I was working on a story about your schoolmate Isabel Chevalier."

"I already told you everything I know." Diffident. Dismissive. Don't bother me.

"I know you did, but I still have some questions. I could come by right now."

"I can't."

"Then when?"

"Maybe tomorrow. I gotta hang out here for a while." A sniff, and I heard him wipe his nose on his shirtsleeve. It reminded me of something.

"How about later this evening?"

"No, man, I told you, I'm busy. It's Halloween. I'm going to a party. Besides, I don't know anything more. I barely knew that chick who got offed. I mean I'm real sorry and all but . . ." He trailed off. He was elsewhere. He was also lying.

"What's your schedule like tomorrow? How about noon? At Fred 62?" I thought this green boîte on Vermont with the deconstructed fifties' diner food might appeal to him.

"Call me in the morning."

I hung up. I thought about it. The evasiveness. The sniffing, which I realized reminded me of Scout. Drugged-out dead Scout. The flat affect when his mother and a classmate had just been killed. The conflicting stories about how well he knew Isabel and Finch. And I knew that here was my missing link. I got in the car and drove to Los Feliz. Halloween or no, I was willing to bet that Paolo was home. He was waiting for his dealer.

Sure enough, the gate was open. I drove in and pulled over. I turned off the engine and was sitting in the car, wondering whether to hike or drive up, when I heard someone whistle.

It was him. He sat, arms wrapped around his knees, halfway up the hill. He was going to meet his connection right here, at the gate. He stood up and hiked down, displeasure brindling his features.

"I told you I'm busy."

"Paolo, we need to talk. I realize this is a tough time for you, with what's happened to your mom, but it's important. There's a killer out there."

He rolled his shoulders dismissively. "There are a lot of killers out there. I don't know anything. Now will you please go away so I can wait here in peace." He was shivering.

"You call this peace?"

"I will have peace as soon as you leave."

"What about peace for Isabel, Paolo? And Scout? Don't they deserve that?"

He sighed and grumbled. "I don't know what else I can tell you."

I patted the bucket seat next to me. "Why don't you come in here where it's warmer."

I threw open the passenger side door, but he just stood there, staring dubiously at the pile of papers on the seat. I gathered them up and went to put them in the trunk. When the lid flew open, we both were startled to see the bottles of booze inside. I had forgotten that I had collected them from my house and stashed them in the car so Scout couldn't get too loaded. Now Paolo's eyes gleamed.

"I guess we can sit and talk awhile." He pulled out the tequila and settled into my car, propping the square bottle on his lap. He took a long chug, then shuddered as the alcohol went down.

I got into the driver's side. I didn't like where this was headed. Here I was, sitting in a car on someone else's property while a teenager drank my liquor and told me things I wanted to know. I felt I had just crossed some poorly marked border. Behind me was ignorance, but safety. Ahead was a dangerous no-man's-land of manipulation and compromised values. But also the glittering grail. If I sprinted past the shadows, I just might reach the golden light.

"Why don't you give me back that bottle now and I'll put it away."

"I'm so cold. I got chilled sitting there. Just a little more to warm me up."

I turned on the engine and moved the "heat" lever to high. A blast of *rocanrol* came on.

"Turn that shit off," he said with distaste.

I obliged. This was his party.

"It should warm up soon." I hoped I was right. My Acura was a decade old, and the heater didn't exactly crank.

"What do you want to know?" he asked, his hand clasped around the bottle's neck, his eye on the driveway in front of us, killing time while we waited for his man.

Shutting the door firmly on the feeble protests inside my head, I said, "For starters, I want you to tell me if you saw Isabel the night she was killed."

"Naw, man."

"C'mon, Paolo. Scout told me."

"What'd she say?"

"She said you and her and Isabel dropped acid in the orchard that night."

"She told you that?" He snorted. "Little bitch."

"So is it true?"

He took a slug of tequila, coughed, and wiped his mouth on his sleeve.

"Yeah, it's true. What of it? I didn't kill her. They were here. We got high. First Isabel wandered off, then Scout. Then they show up together, saying they have to get back to the squat and meet Finch."

"You remember that pretty clearly, do you?"

"I only took one hit. I wish I had taken three."

"So if you remember, then tell me how Isabel seemed to you."

He gave me a loopy smile. "Like she was frying."

"She look shook up about anything?"

"Hard to say."

"Did you ask what was bothering her?"

"It was none of my business. She might have been paranoid from the L. It happens. I drove them to Finch's place. Home Sweet Home."

It was a distasteful word. "You mean the squat?"

"Like I said."

"Paolo," I said with frustration, "you have a home. This is a home. An awfully nice home. Scout and Finch, they had a disgusting cave. So, you dropped Isabel off too?"

"Yeah."

"And the next morning she was found murdered?"

"I guess." He looked bored, was sneaking looks around. Where *was* that guy?

"What time did you drop them off?"

"Oh, must have been ten-thirty or so. Cuz I came back and watched Letterman."

"And did you go inside the squat with them, like, you know, walk them to the, uh, entrance, to make sure they got in safe, a couple of girls?"

"What do you think I am, a creep? Of course. I waited till they crawled in the window."

"Both of them?"

"Yeah."

"But you didn't go inside. So you don't know if anyone was in there? Waiting for them?"

"I assumed Finch was there. He usually gets back around that time."

"But you didn't check."

"No."

"Do you have any idea what happened between the time you dropped them off and the next morning? Scout said she went up to the boulevard. She didn't come back until the next morning. They had already found Isabel's body by then and sealed the place off."

"I assume that Finch found her there and he tied her up and they had some rough sex and that he got carried away and he strangled her. Isn't that what the police think?"

There was an evasive quality to his voice.

"Yeah, that's what the police think. So the next morning, just twenty-four hours later, your, uh, mother is, uh, found in the pool at your house. Could there be any connection?"

He took a long swig now; I heard it chugging down his throat. Something caught and he gurgled and made wet, choking sounds. He leaned forward and spewed tequila and saliva all over my dash.

"I'm sorry," he said. He snuffled and rubbed at his eyes, which had grown suddenly wet.

I leaned over the gearbox to put one arm around him while the fingers of my other hand closed around the tequila bottle. I tugged, felt some resistance, and increased the pressure. The bottle gave way, squeaking from the wet of his hands.

"I think we've had enough of this," I said, stashing it in the backseat while my other hand continued to pat awkwardly at his back.

He looked at me now and his eyes were bloodshot and haggard. "Do we have to drag my mom into this?"

"I'm sorry," I whispered, "for the loss of your mother. I can only imagine the horrendous pain you're going through right now."

He shrugged. "It's not like we were close."

They were harsh words. Perhaps they could only have come from one so young, who still lived in the realm of absolutes.

"She was your mother, nonetheless," I said. "But if you can bear it, I would like you to tell me something."

"What?" His eyes had grown flat and dull, as if we were discussing someone else's life.

"Was your mother home the night Scout and Isabel came over and you guys dropped acid in the orchard?"

There was a long pause. He looked into his lap, saw that the bottle was gone, and frowned into the darkness.

"Yeah, she was," Paolo said. "She was meditating in the pool house. She likes privacy when she does that. Burns incense and shit. I learned a long time ago to leave her alone."

His voice was bitter.

"Was she alone?"

"Of course she was alone," Paolo snapped. "Who else would be there?"

"Your dad?"

"Nah. He was doing something for the campaign. He's going to win, you know?" Hope pooled in his eyes. "He has to. It would be too awful if he didn't . . . after all we've gone through."

He shivered worse than when he had knocked back the tequila. Inside my car, the fan blew tepid air that only chilled us further.

"I'm sorry to ask all these questions at a time like this, when I know you're struggling to come to grips with—"

"It's not like we were close," he repeated, too eager to convince. "She had her life, I had my life. It's just so . . . unexpected. I mean, she was my mom."

"She loved you, Paolo. She was so proud of you. The

night I met you, I ran into her in the kitchen, and she was boasting about you," I lied, wanting to make him feel better.

He perked up. "Really?"

"Yup. You want to honor her memory, you stop doing this shit." I pointed to the backseat. "You got your whole life ahead of you."

"Yeah." He stared gloomily into the night, like it was an interminable sentence with no pardon in sight.

We heard the faint growl of a car. It was doubling back over the turns, the sound carrying up. Paolo's dealer.

"You'd better go now." He fumbled for the door handle, let himself out, and hopped from one foot to the other, waving me away. I could see him clearly because he stood silhouetted in a pool of light as a car pulled up, its beams illuminating us. There was a logo on one side. Two guys in uniforms jumped out. One held a baton and a flashlight. The second carried a baton and a clipboard. They wore shiny badges and advanced slowly. I put my hands in plain sight. They were young, beefy Latinos with clean-cut faces. One stuck his flashlight against my driver's side window and let it play across the front seat. Then he tapped at my window and motioned for me to get out.

I turned off the ignition and opened the door. As I stepped out, the guard made a gagging noise.

"*Como huele a whiski,*" he said. How it stinks of whiskey. It's tequila, I wanted to say, but held my tongue. I could read their badges and see that they were with a private security company. The other guard was frisking Paolo.

"Hey, *señores*, take it easy," Paolo said. "I was just sitting here with my friend. Really, it's okay. *No hay problema.* Everything's aboveboard."

As he spoke, he scanned the grounds nervously. Meanwhile, the other guard walked back to my car and shone his light into its recesses. With a cry of triumph, he pounced on something in the backseat and pulled it out. It was the half-empty tequila bottle.

"Hey, Fuentes."

Officer Fuentes looked from his partner to Paolo, taking in the dried spittle on his chin, the wet shirt. He leaned in and sniffed the boy's face, but Paolo recoiled and yelled, "Get away from me, you little faggot," and would have hit him had the guard not twirled away, satisfied. He grunted, then began to write something on his clipboard.

Paolo was incensed. "My father is Carter Langdon the Third and he's the guy who hired you bozos to patrol our property after my mother's murder, okay? And he will have you fired if you don't knock it off and leave immediately. There's nothing wrong here. You are wasting your time. How are you supposed to ever catch any bad guys when you're harassing me?" His voice rose with petulance.

Paolo turned to me. "You can go now, Eve. It's okay, I'll handle this. These guys work for my dad."

Now both the guards shone their lamps into Paolo's thin white face.

"That the Langdon kid?" one of them asked.

"Damn straight," sputtered Paolo, shoving an ID into their faces.

"The photo checks out," the other guard said, with more hesitation than he had previously displayed.

"Look, Officers," Paolo said. "Let's be reasonable. Your job is to patrol the premises, and I appreciate that, so I'm going to forget about this and let you be on your way."

They stood, uncertain of what to do, but growing more sheepish. They probably made minimum wage and had families to support. They didn't want to cause any trouble. Once again, money and power would win. For once, I was glad. I was relieved they hadn't gotten my name or asked what I was doing in a car at night with a half-drunk boy and an open container of alcohol. I said good-bye and coasted down the hill, headed toward home. It was Halloween, and the air was thick with ghosts jostling and keening, pleading for blood justice. "Soon," I whispered. "It won't be long now."

# CHAPTER 28

*T*uesday morning, I woke up early and drove to my polling place. It was November 2, the day Angelenos would vote in a new mayor. But it was also a day when the past weighed heavily. Today was All Souls' Day. And in the Mexican community, it was *Día de los Muertos,* when the living paid homage to their dead.

In the privacy of my voting booth at the Silverlake Home for Boys, a scruffy, county-run place where counselors tried to turn around young delinquents, I cast my ballot for the female prosecutor running opposite Carter Langdon III. I firmly believed that every vote counted, and I was voting not so much for her but against Langdon, whom I considered the worst kind of hypocrite.

At the office, Thompson sicced me on a *Día de los Muertos* school pageant and I learned that "Day of the Dead" was a bit of a misnomer, since the holiday actually stretched over two days—babies and infants were honored on November 1, adults on November 2.

At 5 P.M. I left the office, glad to be on my own clock again. Dusk was settling and I had big plans. I had reconsidered what Paolo and Scout had told me and knew I had to find Pia. The real missing link. I figured she'd be out partying tonight. First I planned to hit the homeless encampment on the banks of the L.A. River. Then I'd head for Hollywood. I drove to the bridge and parked on the shoulder, feeling almost like I was visiting old friends. But it was nighttime now, dark and clammy as I hiked through the rushes. From the nearby hills, I heard faint hoots and howls, people celebrating Halloween and Day of the Dead, three days of partying and drinking rolled into one. Daylight savings had just ended, and with a moonless night it might have been midnight instead of 5:45 P.M. If I hadn't been so frantic to find Pia, I would have been a lot more scared. But my sense of purpose propelled me forward.

It was hard to see in the dark, and I wasn't sure if the trannies were still there or had been chased away by Department of Water and Power workers or the cops. These encampments were so transient. I felt pretty safe hiking down to a camp of homosexual transvestites, but what if someone more volatile and predatory had set up housekeeping? What was I doing here by myself at night, on Day of the Dead? A good day to die.

I heard a rustle in the reeds, then breaking glass. Hands grabbed my arms, jerking them behind me. Cold jagged glass pressed against my throat. Carotid artery, I thought. Slice it and you bleed to death in minutes.

I hardly dared to breathe. I had to get those vitrine fangs off my neck. Lord, how stupid I was. No one even knew I was down here. I'd be just another broken body found in the L.A. River, Jane Doe #105, until they identified me. Then everyone would wonder why an *L.A. Times* journalist had been skulking around the L.A. River at night.

"Speak, *gringa,* who are you and what do you want?"

My captor tightened his hold, yanking me backward. He pressed the glass tighter. Four shadows crept from the bushes. They held upraised pipes and rocks. As they drew closer, I thought I recognized two of the bathing gypsies.

"I—I'm that reporter who was here the other day," I

stuttered. "Maybe you don't recognize me in the dark. Please let me go. I won't hurt you."

Someone laughed. "Got that straight, girl," a voice said. "We the ones be doing the hurting."

"I need to speak with Pia. It's important. She knows something about a murder I'm investigating."

There was a whispered discussion in Spanish. The beam of a flashlight played across my face. *Dejale,* somebody said, let her go. Hands released me and I fell backward. Sprawled on the ground, I felt my throat for cuts. Just a scrape. Thank God. Pushing myself back up, I turned and saw them clustered around me, adrenaline dilating their pupils. Perhaps they had mistaken me for a passel of gay-bashing frat boys.

"You want something, you come back in the ayem and don't you never come creeping around here in the dark."

"I'm sorry I scared you. But it's urgent."

"You lucky we didn't kill you."

Now a man-woman dressed in a blue sweat suit stepped up. It was the transvestite I had seen shaving his legs in the river.

"Pia isn't here," he said. It was the voice that had ordered my release. He remembered me, I could tell.

"Do you know where I can find her?"

"Why you wanna know where she's at?" someone asked.

"She's in danger."

Behind me, someone snickered. "She always in danger, she like it that way."

"Can anyone help this young lady?" the sweat-suited transvestite asked, and I knew he was on my side. At his words, they surrounded me, explaining that they had bought a birthday present for Pia and a girlfriend. Concert tickets to a *Día de los Muertos* show.

"Where?" I asked.

"Arena La Puente," one told me. "It's the hottest ticket in town."

So the road was leading back to Silvio and his family. I told them thanks, dusted myself off, and hiked back to the car. On the freeway, I drove like a gusting Santa Ana. East on I-10, then south on the 605, then east again on the 60. The suburban hinterlands. The show had started at dusk so the La Puente streets were empty. The parking attendant was surprised to see me, such a late partygoer, wearing my reporter costume instead of a skeleton mask. He put aside his steaming *carnitas* and *limonada* long enough to make change for a ten-dollar bill.

I hurried through the line of cars and up to the front, where I charged a ticket to my Visa. I smelled the hot, sweet grease of *churros* frying in oil. With an *"uno, dos, tres,"* a band launched into a raucous set. I felt a surge of impatience. Grabbing my ticket, I hurried through.

The floor of the arena thronged with revelers in costumes, their faces hidden behind masks and obscured by preposterous hats. A volatile energy surged through the masqueraded crowd. Concealed by draped fabric and rubber eye slits, people hooted and jostled those around them. Dozens of huge skull balloons floated above us. I pushed farther into the crowd, where garishly painted clowns danced around a skinny burro tethered to a stake as small goblins and rouged princesses waited in a crooked line for their turn at a ride. Behind a food stall, a man wearing pirate attire retched violently, then cursed as his hat fell. He stooped to pick it up but lost his balance and tumbled to the ground, where he lay in a heap, crying softly. A woman in a frilly blouse nudged him aside with one pointy shoe, then stepped over him, all the while smiling and handing out samples of Mexican cheese on tiny plastic spoons.

The crowd propelled me forward. I washed up at a stall where copper-colored men with skin furrowed like the pueblo hills sold woven cowboy hats with plaited leather coiled around the brim. There was no sales pitch here, just stoic silence. Then they were gone too, and I was shoved against a raised dance floor where costumed couples pressed together, swaying to the beat. The kaleidoscope shifted again and I found myself on the outskirts of the pitched tents. In the shadows, I saw two figures in the dirt, one moving atop the other in rapid jerks. I turned to run and landed among teenagers wearing baggy pants and white singlets. Each had a blue-black teardrop tattooed under his eye. Were they gangbangers, or merely Catholic schoolboys who had exchanged one uniform for another tonight? I didn't stick around to find out.

In this roiling mass of people, how would I ever find one slender Latina transvestite named Pia? All I knew is that the river denizens had bought her good seats near the front and that she was dressed as a mermaid and wore a blond wig.

But what if she wasn't in her seat? I dodged madly in and out of the crowd, *pardon, por favor,* excuse me, pushing, squeezing, shimmying, scanning for yellow tresses. There couldn't be too many of those in this dark-haired crowd. The crowd surged and threw me against devils with pointy horns and mummies wrapped in bandages. They grabbed me and ran their hands up and down my body as they pretended to set me on my feet. I yelled at them to cut it out but my voice was lost in the roar of the crowd.

Now a half-naked *chupacabra* smeared with red paint appeared before me and shoved his leering, fanged face into mine. The blood-sucking vampire, which is to rural Mexico what the Loch Ness monster is to Scotland, began a contorted dance, stomping and twirling ever closer while revelers closed in, forming a circle that trapped me inside. I stepped backward but hands pushed me forward. Voices jeered and hooted. The clapping grew louder, the *chupacabra*'s dance more frenzied as he whirled closer. I searched for an exit but saw no break in the chain of party-goers, smirking and gesticulating, siccing the creature on me anew. I could smell its beery breath, body odor mixed with oil-based paint on its sweating skin. Then with a piercing shriek, it threw itself upon my neck. Moving up and down, it ground its slick body against mine, sucking and slurping.

"Get away," I yelled, but my hand skidded off a painted bicep and smashed only air. I panted now, mad to escape, and my fear only aroused the mob to greater cries. With one last desperate effort, I pulled my leg back and cocked my knee, bringing it up hard in his groin. The creature gave a sharp yelp and fell away. The crowd roared, thinking this was part of the act, and in that moment of freedom, I flung myself at the crowd, knocking two of them down like bowling pins. Kicking and punching, I sprang up and away, running until I was sure they couldn't drag me back.

Above me, a ten-foot *calavera* danced its skeletal can-can, oblivious to my plight. I wasn't sure exactly what had just happened. Had I imagined a darkness that wasn't there? Should I have laughed off the *chupacabra?* Perhaps my naked fear had ignited something malevolent in the masqueraded crowd. Feeling violated and humiliated, I took a deep breath and moved on.

Now I was in the amphitheater stands. My eye caught a roped-off section near the front where the sound engineers worked. As I watched, a ghoul with a gaping, Edvard Munch scream-face stood up and stretched. He walked over to a girl sitting by a bank of speakers. She looked up and smiled. He peeled off the rubbery mask, bent to kiss her, and whispered in her ear. She laughed. There was something about both of them that looked familiar in that off-kilter way things do in dreams, but it wasn't until he turned and started hiking up the stairs that I recognized him: Vince Chevalier. His hair was plastered to his temples, not unlike the day we had met. I let him get right up to me before I called out his name.

"This is a far cry from Jackson Browne," I said shakily, feeling like I had plunged down a surreal rabbit hole. What was he doing here tonight and where did he fit into the puzzle?

"Oh, hey." He smiled vacantly, running his hand through his hair. Now he cocked his hand like a gun. "Eve Diamond," he said, shooting me with his thumb and forefinger. "Took me a minute. You're out of context."

"So are you." It came out colder than I intended.

"Gotta go where the business is, and these days, it's not folk rock, it's *rocanrol, corridos*. I just follow the money."

"I forgot," I lied, "you're a sound engineer."

He smiled that vacant, creepy smile, then exhaled noisily.

"Yeah, running the boards here tonight. Well, nice seeing you, I've gotta get a drink, been sweating like crazy under this mask."

"Wait," I said, but he had cleaved a path through the crowd and disappeared. I stood there, torn between running after him and risking a second encounter with the *chupacabra* or continuing my hunt for Pia. I scanned the crowd and caught another glimpse of the girl Chevalier had kissed. With both hands, she pulled the hair back from her face and twisted it into a knot atop her head in a gesture I recognized. Where had I seen it? At Vince Chevalier's house in Pasadena. When I was interviewing Isabel's friends. It was Caitlin.

So my gut feeling about him had been right. He was a major creep with a big secret and Caitlin, for all her assumed worldliness, was more troubled than she let on. I remembered the girls saying how "cool" Vince was. I imagined myself in Caitlin's shoes but couldn't see what she found so enticing. Worst of all, Chevalier hadn't even had the decency to look ashamed when he had run into me.

I wanted to go down there and tell Caitlin they were busted, but a flash of platinum hair bobbing below me changed my mind. I made my way down, only to find a Madonna clone instead of a mermaid. I decided to camp out and wait for Pia to return. Maybe she had gone to get something to eat. It was hard not to get buoyed up and carried away by the crowd, and I fought to stand still. Finally I saw a creature descending the stairs, regal as an undersea queen, hand on her hip, aware of the spectacle she made, whispering something to her young friend, another trannie dressed as Dorothy in *The Wizard of Oz* and carrying a stuffed Toto. It had to be her. She wore a tight, sequined bodysuit of iridescent green fish scales and a shell bikini top that exposed as much flesh and curves as she could, set off by red lipstick, blue eye shadow, and a silver crown on her long, flowing blond wig. Most real women didn't try that hard.

I stood still as an usher, waiting for her to sashay on down.

"Pia," I said as she approached, trailing a cloying perfume.

Her almond eyes flickered over me, taking in my lack of costume.

"I'm a friend of Scout. The squatter girl from Hollywood. I need to talk to you."

Pia tossed back a lock of hair and adjusted her crown.

"It will have to wait, honeybun." She began to edge past me, doing a little slip-glide into the aisle. She couldn't move too fast with that tail of hers.

Desperate, I grabbed her by the fins and braced my legs against the concrete.

"It can't wait. Scout says you saw something at the squat the night Isabel was killed. You have to tell me. You're in danger while this killer remains loose."

She kept moving, only to stop as her tail stretched taut. She gave it another tug, then looked behind in annoyance to see why it had caught.

"Let go."

"No."

She gathered up the base of her tail in both arms and pulled, and for a moment, we were caught in a surreal tug of war. People were starting to laugh and point.

"For God's sake," she hissed.

"Scout's dead. They found her several days ago behind a building in Hollywood."

Pia stopped tugging. She looked at me with disbelief, which changed slowly to fear when she realized I was telling the truth. Her hands fell to her sides, then lifted up to her cheeks.

"Oh that poor little girl."

"Poor little dead girl. And you're next, Pia. You and Scout knew something worth getting murdered for. You have to tell me before they find you."

Beneath the makeup, Pia was turning an unpleasant shade of gray.

"You the man?"

"No, I'm a reporter. Eve Diamond. I came looking for you at the L.A. River a few days ago and they said you'd gone off to, uh, get some money. Happy birthday, by the way."

"This concert is a birthday gift from my friends."

"You have loyal friends, Pia. They're worried about you. Talk to me. Tell me what you saw."

"I didn't see anything."

"Scout told me you did." I inhaled the sticky scent of perfume. Opium, I thought, picturing the red, black, and gold bottle. What useless information my brain dredged up in times of high anxiety. I touched her bare shoulder. It was soft and brown and rounded.

"The killer knows someone was there that night," I lied. "The killer is looking for that person. The cops told me. Your life isn't worth shit until the murderer is behind bars."

Pia's lip twitched scornfully.

"My life ain't worth shit anyway. But tonight I'm a star. Like I'm in showbiz, everyone looking at me. Miss Thing. Until you came along."

"I need your help."

"Why should I tell you anything? What's in it for me?"

"Isabel was murdered that night. Now Scout's dead too. You think they're happy about that? Tonight's Day of the Dead. You want them to come back and haunt you? They're angry. They want justice. That's what's in it for you: justice."

"Ain't nobody ever given me no justice."

"That's why you've got to break the chain. Tell me what you saw."

Pia looked out at the sea of faces like she was trying to find the answer in the crowd.

"They deserve to rest in peace," I said.

"Let's go sit down somewhere," she finally said.

Pia turned to say good-bye to her friend, only to find that Dorothy had already melted into Oz. We hiked up the stairs to a food stand and sat at a table.

"You're doing the right thing," I told her.

"I'm only telling you this because I don't want no ghosts coming after me. I got no money for the *curandera.*"

I heard a shaking of maracas and a wild whoop. Far below the stands, we saw the *chupacabra* leap in front of a new victim and begin his pelvis-thrusting dance as the crowd began to close around. The girl raised her arms above her head and stepped in closer, matching her movements to his. The knot of revelers surged out of sight and I heard shouting and laughter.

"Is she going to be okay?" I asked. "That guy chased me earlier and I barely got away."

Pia caught the quaver in my voice. "He can smell your fear."

"What?"

"Chill, girlfriend. What do you think this is, *Heart of Darkness?* Give us a little credit."

I flushed, realizing I had made a fool of myself. Why did everything seem so macabre and surreal tonight? I wanted to ask Pia more about the *chupacabra,* but her impatient eyes told me there was no time. I pulled out a miniature tape recorder and put it on the plastic table.

"What's that?"

"A tape recorder."

"Put it away. It makes me nervous, all shiny black and nasty."

"Don't look at it."

"Put it away or I'm not saying another word."

I clicked it off and thrust it deep into my coat pocket. "There. Now what did you see that night?"

"Like I told you, I didn't see anything."

"Okay, what did you hear? Or smell? Or touch? Or taste?"

Pia patted down her hair. She licked the tips of her index fingers and smoothed them over her plucked eyebrows. She looked around. Then, satisfied that no one was listening, she began.

"I ran into Scout on the boulevard that night. I was fading fast. She told me to go down to Finch's. Isabel was already there, waiting for him. Those places can be nasty. So I was real quiet going in. Then, sure enough, I heard a voice. I hid behind a pillar. It was a lady cursing. Such profanity. Really bad. Stuff my mom used to wash my mouth out for, stuff I had almost forgotten. I haven't heard it in years."

"Could you see her?"

"Only the silhouette. It's dark down there. She was dragging something."

"What did it look like?"

"It looked like a damn futon. I thought she was one of those loony tune bag ladies."

"What was she saying?"

"It was a rant. She was muttering to herself. Something like, 'You're not going to fuck things up now, right as my life approaches supernova perfection. The timing was all wrong for you, *chiquilin'*—that is a term of endearment in Spanish, my mama used to call me that. Then she said, 'Sweet dreams, my pretty. You shouldn't forget that those who live in the gutter will also die there. That's not me. Oh no. I will be . . . immortal.'"

Finally, the circle begins to close, I thought, scrawling it down as the mermaid sang her siren song.

"So then," continued Pia, "I knew she was crazy. All that shit about being immortal and sweet dreams, when you're talking to a futon. It's frigging freaky. I took off."

"And you never wondered where Isabel was?"

Pia shrugged. "She was waiting for Finch. I figured he showed up and they went up to the boulevard. It's not like they have a curfew."

"And you never wondered what might be wrapped up in the futon?"

"I just wanted to get out of there."

I was exasperated by her lack of concern.

"Well, did you see any signs of a struggle?"

"You mean like blood and shit? No."

"Okay, then what?"

"Then I split. That's all."

Something occurred to me.

"Pia, what language was she speaking?"

"Spanish."

"Are you sure?"

"I didn't even learn English till I went to school. They put me in those *pinche* ESL classes. I think I know my native tongue when I hear it."

It had gotten all quiet as we talked, and I realized that the band was taking a break. Now the crowd broke into frantic clapping and screaming and moments later, I heard Flavia Jiménez's throaty, low voice start up, that song I was hearing all over the airwaves, that I was even singing along to—"Woman in the Mirror."

"That's it, that's all I know. I gotta get back now, that's my anthem," Pia said, pushing up off the table and swaying into a standing position. "That woman is a goddess."

"I like it too," I admitted. "No, really," I added, as Pia gave me a disbelieving look.

We walked to one of the landings and Pia shimmied

off. I stopped to watch the Mexican diva onstage, clutching the mike as she sang. But instead of the Rubenesque Flavia, with her big hair, scarlet lips, tight ranchera suit, and stiletto heels on the rough, wood-plank stage, I saw a more slender figure, lifting a clenched fist and swaying in the office of Aguilar Entertainment as she sang out the same words.

# CHAPTER 29

Leaving the stands, I made my way through the brightly lit amphitheater toward the office trailers of Aguilar Entertainment at the edge of the property. I had to talk to Silvio. Flavia's words from the nightclub rose up and echoed in the dimly lit air.

"I'm not saying she should rise up and kill the bastard . . ." Flavia had said.

But somebody had. Somebody had done just that.

Silvio's office was closed but light pooled in a crack under the door. He was there. I raised my arm to knock but realized he wouldn't hear me with the band playing. Then the music stopped. The crowd clapped and whistled for more before slowly subsiding.

From behind the door, a woman spoke.

"You know I adored him."

The voice was husky, crackling with emotion. And loud, as if she were still shouting over the music to be heard.

"Then why?" I heard Silvio say.

"Why what?"

"You knew he was like that, Gisela. It's in the blood."

It was Ruben's fiancée. The Aguilar receptionist.

"I couldn't stand it anymore. God, how I loved him. I would have died for him."

"How ironic, then."

I shrank into the darkness of the hallway. I could barely hear their voices over the percussive din of my own heart. Slipping my hand inside my jacket pocket, I pulled out my tape recorder and placed it against the crack at the bottom of the door. Then I squatted. Soundlessly, I depressed the lever and watched the tape inch forward.

"He betrayed me," she said, and I heard muffled sobs. Then her voice rose. "With that Ital—— huh . . . with that *puta,* that whore. He wanted to be fancy, did Ruben. He thought she would be his ticket. I confronted him and he denied it. That night, he said he'd be home early. We had fought and he was going to make it up to me. We'd have dinner and then go dancing. Just like the old days."

"He never could keep a promise."

"Then he called and apologized. They were drawing up a business plan and it was the only time she could meet. Don't be angry, *querida,* he told me, I'm doing this for us. He was so persuasive, I almost believed it. But I had to see for myself. So I went there."

"How did you get the address?"

"Who do you think does his goddamn books? They were in the back, by the pool house. Ruben had taken me up there when he first got the job. I crouched under the window. The blinds were closed. But I heard them."

"Maybe it was someone else."

"It was him all right. He was saying stuff. Words he uses when we're in bed. She called his name."

"You shouldn't have gone."

"I wanted to curl up and die and they could find me. If I had a gun I would have shot myself. Swear to God. And that got me thinking. We have guns at home. You know how Ruben buys them off people."

"He tried to sell me one a few weeks ago," Silvio said. "I guess I should have bought it."

"Wouldn't have made a difference," Gisela said. "He's got five more lying around. Next thing I remember, I'm

standing in our bedroom with the barrel in my mouth.
But I couldn't do it. I took it out and wiped it off on my
shirt and thought, why should I be the one to die? That
would just make it easy for them. Then I knew what I had
to do. I was turning off our street when he drove up. So
I went around the block and cruised back up real slow.
He had the window down. He smiled when he saw me.
That was what did it. Him coming home smiling, with
her stink still on him. I shot the smile off his face. Then
I drove to Los Feliz."

"So it wasn't a drive-by shooting." There was something weary and resigned in Silvio's voice.

"You could still call it that," she sniffed.

"Why didn't you come to me?"

"I was too ashamed. I didn't want anyone to know. I
know now that I wasn't thinking straight. But at the time
there was this weird logic to it."

"So you kill my brother. That's real logical, Gisela."

"He ruined my life."

"No, you ruined your life. And you took two people
down with you."

Gisela seemed not to have heard. Her voice took on a
dreamy quality.

"She was standing by the pool, ready to dive, when I
got her. Back a the head. She fell right in. I waited to
make sure she wasn't moving, then I left. It's pretty iso-
lated up there—anyone heard it, they probably thought it
was a car backfiring. On the way home, I wiped the gun
off and threw it in a Dumpster in East L.A. Trash day
there is Monday."

"Jesus Christ, Gisela. You're insane."

"You'd be insane too. He forced me, humiliating me
like that. I'm only human."

"No one will buy it."

"You're going to help me, Silvio. After the other night, we're in this together, aren't we?"

There was a silence and I wondered what she meant.

"We should go to the police."

"No," she said.

"Tell them straight. Explain that it was a crime of passion."

A mouse squeaked in horrid pain somewhere near me, and I started and looked around, only to realize the sound was coming from the black box at my feet. The micro-cassette in the tape recorder had chosen this moment to freak out.

I heard a sudden intake of breath.

"What was that?" Gisela asked, her voice suddenly low, barely audible.

I heard Silvio murmur something and sprang to grab the damn thing and sprint down the hallway and out the door before they could catch me. The evidence. I needed the evidence. I heard footsteps, then the door trying to open, but holding fast until someone realized it was locked from the inside. I was halfway down the hall, visualizing my escape and how I would burst outside and keep running.

Then strong arms grabbed me and forced me around. I found myself staring back at Silvio, his eyes goggling with disbelief.

"Eve. What are you doing here? What did you hear?"

"Let me go," I said, but he only squared his jaw and dragged me back into the office. He led me to the chair made out of spotted cowhide and shoved me down into it. Then he strode back to the door, locked it again, and stood in front of it. I saw Gisela, white streaks running down her face. She shot me a look filled with hatred. Then she walked to Silvio's desk, threw herself into his chair, and swiveled to face me. A blank look came over her, extinguishing all light, but not before I saw something flicker deep in its recesses. She was tiny, sitting in that man's chair, dwarfed by the huge desk, a little girl playing in her daddy's wood-paneled office.

"Now what do we do?" Silvio asked the room.

"We'll have to kill her too," Gisela said. She removed one hand from her lap and waved it laconically. Her engagement ring glinted in the lamplight.

She made me want to laugh, did Gisela. But she infuriated me as well.

"Speak for yourself, Gisela," I said.

I looked at Silvio, who was edging away from the door and toward Gisela.

"I heard the whole thing," I said. "You killed them both. Silvio had nothing to do with any of this. But what I can't figure out is why you killed that little girl. You just couldn't stand to have anyone knowing the truth about your beloved Ruben, is that it?"

Her eyes glinted and Silvio's took on a watchful air.

"I didn't kill no little girl, what are you talking about?"

"Isabel Chevalier. She was a friend of Venus's son and she saw your fiancé and Venus having sex the night before. You were there that night too, weren't you? Spying on them. You didn't tell Silvio the whole truth. It wasn't a crime of passion at all, it was textbook premeditated murder. You were afraid Isabel saw you and you didn't want any witnesses. So you followed her back to the squat and killed her."

She regarded me like I was a grease stain on her silk shirt.

"Stop talking trash," she screamed. "There was no little girl."

"Shut up, Eve," Silvio said ominously.

"Why should I shut up? I know you were at the squat," I told Gisela. "Someone overheard you speaking Spanish, saying how you weren't going to let her destroy you, how you had big plans."

"You're wrong," Silvio said. "Gisela didn't kill that girl."

I wondered how he was so sure, and my voice faltered.

"You tell her, lover boy," Gisela said. There was a knife-edge gleam to her voice that could slice a hair in two.

"Our relationship has nothing to do with this," I said, blushing.

"I'm not talking about your relationship. I'm talking about our relationship. Him and me." She pointed at Silvio.

Something that had only hovered wraithlike in my darkest shadows now took shape. I stood up and stepped forward.

"W-what do you mean?"

Gisela laughed. "Tell her, Silvio."

Silvio froze in his tracks. "Eve, she's crazy. Don't listen to her."

Gisela whipped around in the chair. "I'm crazy?" she said, in a deadly quiet voice. "Crazy with grief maybe. Is that why you thought you could take advantage of me?"

"Gisela, I . . ."

"Tell her, Silvio. You owe her that, at least."

"Tell me what?" I said.

Silvio opened his mouth but didn't say anything. A bead of sweat trickled down his temple.

"Tell her how you consoled me the night your brother died."

"Eve . . ." he said, low and urgent, but there was no more. He blinked once, ran his hand through his hair, and shifted from one foot to the other. "I . . ." He shook his head.

"It's true," Gisela said. "He came over soon as he heard. Waited with me until the police came. Said he didn't want me to be alone. After they left, he asked if I was okay. I told him to go home, get some sleep. We said good-bye. I kissed him on the cheek but he turned his face. I got his lips. And well, he stayed."

"Silvio," I said. How could he have done this, with the heat from his brother's limp body still warming the asphalt twenty feet away? How could he have slept with her? This common tart, but worst of all, his brother's fiancée? And then only days later, done the same with me? And yet, on another level, I could understand the impulse that sent him reeling to the primal warmth of another's arms, even if it was his almost sister-in-law. I had felt his terrible need, his bottomless animal grief myself that night.

Now I knew why Silvio looked at me with haunted eyes sometimes, why he loathed Gisela. They were locked in some Greek tragedy of incest and fate, hatred and lust. And each time he saw her, he was condemned to relive that night.

"Then afterward he said, 'What have I done, oh Lord, what have I done?' And I told him, 'It don't matter, *querido,* it was meant to be.' And that's why you have to go," Gisela continued. "We could have waited a decent interval, then announced our own betrothal. Who else knows how to run the business? And we could be even bigger if we book guys like El Chaparrito who do the *narcocorridos.* I would have worn Silvio down over time."

I was stunned at her audacity.

"No matter what happened that night, Silvio would never marry you. He doesn't love you."

"And who does he love? You? Who would take him away from his family, his culture?"

I looked at her. "You're crazy," I whispered. "Plumb loco."

She reached into the top drawer of the desk and pulled out a gun. She cocked it and pointed it at me. "And you're dead," she retorted. "Tell her, Silvio."

"Silvio," I whispered, not daring to look at him. My only hope was to keep them talking as long as I could. "Tell her how sick she is."

"I wish I could," he said.

Now I did look at him. He stood with hands clasped and shoulders hunched, unable to meet my gaze. A shadow played across his face.

"What?"

He ignored me. Instead, he walked closer to Gisela, putting his arms out. I saw a satisfied look in her eyes and she made a small, mewling sound. I thought I would be sick.

"Didn't I warn you in the beginning, *huera*, that he had a way with the ladies? But you didn't want to listen." Gisela gloated.

I knew then I had made a huge mistake in dismissing her as a pathetic bit player. And what about Silvio, who had wooed me so assiduously, and yet hidden a black inner core from me? Did I have it all wrong? Had they conspired to kill Ruben?

"So now you'll get the answers you want," she said. "Tell her, *querido,* how you were just playing with her."

There was a shrill insistence to her voice, as if a small part of her needed to be reassured of this too. But all I felt was a blanket disbelief that Silvio could have betrayed me this way. And at how easy I had been to fool. I had thought I was dealing with a clear-cut family business, when in reality, I had gotten sucked into a clan of modern-day Borgias, as sticky-red with fratricidal blood as a Renaissance painting.

Silvio had almost reached the desk. At her words, he stopped and faced me.

"Who do you think you are, barging into our lives, showing up at my brother's wake, expressing complete disrespect for our family, our traditions?" Silvio said in the same scathing tone he had used to flay the ignorant West Sider who had mistaken him for a valet. "We were too polite to tell you. But you kept forcing it, coming around, asking more and more questions, getting closer and closer to things better left unspoken."

I blinked back the salty oceans pooling behind my eyes.

"Silvio, I . . ."

"Shut up," Gisela said. "We don't want to hear your sniveling." Her eyes were glittering, lit from within. She was stark, raving mad. Couldn't Silvio see that?

"But now I've figured out what to do with you too," Gisela said. "It just took me a while. There's going to be another crime of passion here tonight."

"Oh yeah? What do you mean?" I tried to look curious and keep the terror out of my voice. My entire existence was concentrated on the gun. So long as I engaged them, it wouldn't go off.

"A suicide. You walked in on Silvio here, putting the moves on me. And you were so distraught that you killed yourself. *Que loca, esa gringa!*"

"I don't own a gun, Gisela."

"But Silvio does. Got a permit and everything."

"It will never fly, Gisela. The cops will be all over it. Especially with Ruben's death three weeks ago. It's too much."

"It is too much. Poor Ruben."

She brought her other arm in to steady the gun. At the same time, Silvio reached her, and his arm came down, knocking it out of her hand. The gun discharged into the floor.

# CHAPTER 30

Something jelled in my brain then, and I ran, not to him, but away from them both, unlocking the trailer door, running down the hallway and into the crisp evening air, grateful for the crowd cover. I darted in and out of families carrying balloons and beer and paper plates of steaming food as a throaty roar went up from the crowd and Flavia Jiménez strode back onto the stage for a fifth encore and the opening bars of *"La Mujer en el Espejo"* kicked in again.

I thought I knew what had just transpired in there, but I wasn't taking any chances. I ran to the edge of the arena and called 911. I gave them the address, then hung up and sprinted all the way back to my car. I started it up and headed back to L.A., the scene in Silvio's office playing like a broken record in my brain. He had been faking it, hadn't he? Playing along with her? But they had slept together too. I saw it in his sad, haunted face. I heard it in Gisela's taunts. How sure she was about bringing Silvio around to the *narcocorridos*. I saw her swathed in mourning at the wake, playing the grieving widow to the hilt as she extolled the talents of the kid from El Monte who played at El Bronco Negro.

Silvio's anger that day was key to something I still wasn't getting. Maybe if I heard this music, talked to the singer, it would shed some light on this family and their battles. Maybe then I would finally understand. I looked at the green freeway signs. I was still pretty far east. Pulling out my cell phone, I called 411.

"El Monte," I said. "El Bronco Negro." There was no listing. I hung up and drove for a while, thinking things through. The Black Bronco. Was it a coded reference to drugs, or perhaps to SUVs favored by drug traffickers? I redialed. "Los Angeles," I said this time, repeating the name. Bingo. It was located at 1051 Sunset Boulevard. That was low-rent, Latino Sunset, where it snakes west from Chinatown. I checked my watch. It was 9 P.M. on *Día de los Muertos*. By the time I got there, El Bronco Negro should be in full swing. I gripped the steering wheel and allowed myself a faint smile.

Soon, I saw the clustered spires of downtown. I curved past them onto the Hollywood Freeway and took the first exit. But it wasn't until I had parked and walked a few blocks on Sunset, thick with strolling families and mariachis, that I had second thoughts. What was I going to do in there? Still, I paid my twenty dollars and walked in. The room smelled of cheap cologne and beer and sweat. A banner announced Porfirio Lopez, better known to his fans as "El Chaparrito."

On the tiny stage, a young man with a shaved head and a slim-fitting suit lifted his head back and sang his lungs out while a band played behind him. His eyes were closed. He held a cigarette in one hand, a tumbler in the other. His voice was nasal, almost tuneless. But I was struck by his wolverine intensity as he began to prowl the stage. I heard the cheering, the bellowed demands for old favorites. I saw the tribute tossed onto the stage, pesos and dollars, flowers and cigarettes. It occurred to me that Gisela and Ruben hadn't been wrong about this guy.

Now he launched into a song about a young dealer from a poor pueblo who goes into the drug business because he needs money to get medical treatment for his beautiful wife, who has been struck by a mysterious illness. A drug lord takes the young man under his wing and makes him a trusted lieutenant. Soon he is wealthy beyond his dreams, but it can't save his wife, who dies swathed in diamonds in her gold-plated bed.

People's eyes filled with tears and they sucked noisily on their long-necks. Tough young women who reminded me of Gisela hung on to their men, plaited hair shimmering in the light.

As El Chaparrito left the stage, I sidled into the dressing room. No one stopped me. They just winked. Another female fan come to worship at the feet of El Chaparrito. It meant "shorty," a term of affection in Spanish, but even the lifts in his shoes and the tall hats he wore couldn't disguise the fact that he was only five foot six, though he sang like a much bigger man.

He was pouring another drink. When he saw me, he straightened up in surprise. My clothes weren't skimpy enough for a groupie. I introduced myself, flashed my ID, and told him I wanted to do a story on him and the whole *narcocorrido* industry. Suspicion mingled with pleasure on his face.

"Why do the readers of the *Times* want to know about this? Will they buy my albums?"

"Yes," I assured him, though I had no idea. "Or perhaps some Hollywood producer will read about you and want to use your music in a movie."

El Chaparrito had an hour to kill before his second set, so we walked down to a taco stand that did hefty business once the clubs closed and people staggered out, their bellies crying for something to soak up the booze.

Sitting in wooden chairs under the fluorescent light, I saw that El Chaparrito had a large mole above his lip. From it grew three long black hairs. He spoke Spanglish, with the singsong accent of those raised between two worlds, the dipping cadences, the elongated diphthongs, the *eses* and *miras*. He had dropped out of high school at fifteen, *it was too tough, ese,* and at twenty-two already had a wife and four kids, all of them crammed into a one-bedroom apartment in El Monte. But he was gonna make it, he knew it, there was a buzz about him, if only his manager hadn't been killed. But he would find another one.

"Ruben Aguilar?" I asked.

"You really done your homework."

"I wrote about his murder."

We ordered drinks and tacos. *Birria* for him and *lengua* for me. Goat meat and tongue. Wouldn't find those at Taco Bell. Polka music blared from the tinny speakers mounted on the wall.

"I like it here," El Chaparrito told me. "I gave them my tape and they play it late at night."

The song ended with a blast of horns and the DJ came on to say that the election results were coming in. A Latino candidate had won a state Senate seat on the East Side. Pomona had voted to allow a casino within its city limits. And Carter Langdon III had blasted away his opponent, becoming Los Angeles's new mayor with a whopping 62 percent of the vote. Even with absentee ballots uncounted, his victory was assured. Damn. I knew he was wrapped up in this and I just hadn't managed to unravel things quickly enough. Now, like an engorged tick, he would be more difficult than ever to dislodge. Worrying about Langdon's victory focused me on the conversation at hand.

"I'm also writing a story about the Aguilar family business. Arena La Puente."

"Those are some bad folks."

"Bad as in good?"

"No, they're bad, man. Way bad. They didn't want nothing to do with me on account of I sing about the *narcos*. Ruben was the only one; he told me, just wait, I'll bring the family around."

I took a sip of my *horchata*. The mixture of pounded rice, sugar, and cinnamon soothed my nerves. "How was he going to do that?"

"He had plans, bro. He and that Gisela Lujan."

"What plans were those?"

"All I know is they were gonna make me a star."

"He never talked to you about that? Think hard."

I didn't want to tell him what had just gone down at Arena La Puente. He could probably read tomorrow's *Opinión* to learn that.

"No, man. He said leave it to him. He'd come with his styling girlfriend. She had some *chi-chis* on her. All that long red hair."

"Gisela has brown hair, actually."

"No, man, this was his other girlfriend."

I put my elbow on the Formica counter and leaned my head into the crook of my arm.

"What do you mean, his other girlfriend?"

"His midnight lover. *Muy secreto*. The dude's dead now, so I guess it don't matter. Me, I got the ball and chain. Not that I don't catch a little on the side, but I got kids. He was flying free."

"What was her name, this secret girlfriend?"

"We just called her 'Flame.' She really dug my songs. And she could put it back. She was gonna bankroll me."

"Really?"

"She'd even come here without Ruben some nights. Bring a strange energy in with her."

"How so?"

"She'd walk into the club and a bottle of champagne

would appear at her table, just like that. Dudes would get into it. She'd watch and laugh. Like it was a human cock-fight and she had money on the winner."

"You think she was two-timing Ruben?"

"Hard to say. I know one of my *patrones* took a shine to her. They say she spread it around. I told her save some for El Chaparrito. She was gonna take me up to her crib. Said she'd disguise me as the gardener. I told her no thanks. Take me up there as I am or forget it."

"Did she listen to reason?"

El Chaparrito just winked.

"You talked in English?"

"Yeah, but she spoke Spanish too."

"How well?"

"Like a native."

"Don't you remember her name?"

He took a sip of his brandy and rubbed his stubbled chin. "Naw, man. I just know she hasn't come around lately and I miss her."

# CHAPTER 31

**W**e finished our tacos and he went back to the club. I stayed and ordered a *tamarindo,* a sweet soda made from tart fruit.

Then I called Silvio on his cell phone. He picked up right away.

"Thank God you called," he said, his voice flooding with relief. "I have so much to explain. But I'm at the police station right now, being, uh, questioned."

"Save it," I said. "Just tell me this. Remember those sugar skulls that Ruben gave his clients for Day of the Dead?"

There was a bewildered silence before he spoke.

"What about them?"

"Did he give them to all his clients?"

"Just *La Raza.*"

"You sure?"

"Yeah. He was worried his Anglo clients might find it morbid. Like he was wishing death on them or something."

"Thanks," I told him.

"What's that got to do . . ." He broke off. "Are you at home? Can I call you back when I'm through here?"

"I'll call you," I said, not sure that I would.

Now I punched in the city desk and asked the desk assistant to look on the Metro budget and see where Carter Langdon was celebrating. She checked and told me Langdon was at the Biltmore. It was one of the grand old dowagers of downtown hotels and had recently been renovated. As I drove, I turned on the news radio and heard a quick recap of the election battle and how Langdon's standing in the polls had surged with his wife's death. His stoicism in the face of the tragedy had made Langdon a hero and his opponent had never recovered.

Maybe so, but silly me, I still had a bone to pick with Hizzoner. I parked in the Biltmore's underground lot and took the elevator up to the ballroom. Inside, everyone was dressed for an inaugural ball. Carter Langdon III was onstage, thanking those who had made his victory possible. He walked off to loud applause. I showed my press pass and joined the well-wishers waiting in the wings. Soon Langdon walked by, leaning on Severin's arm, looking gray now that the stagelights no longer lit him, his pale, craggy face more skull-like than usual. With Skip the handler bringing up the rear, he disappeared into a suite of private rooms. I arrived just as Skip slammed the door in my face. Behind me, I heard guffaws. I turned and saw Tony Hausman, the *Times*'s political reporter, leaning against a pillar.

"Don't even bother," Hausman said. "He's already given his spiel to the press. What are you doing here, anyway? Those damn editors should keep me informed."

He looked at his watch and yawned. "It's way past deadline, even for election night. You'll have to come back tomorrow to learn which designer is going to dress him and what interior decorating firm is going to remodel the mayoral mansion. You working up a feature for Southern California Living?"

I gave him an inscrutable smile and knocked. Hausman knew damn well I wrote for the same section he did. I knocked again, louder this time. The door opened. Skip stood there, bristling like a surly Cerberus at the Hadean gate.

"He's not doing any more interviews tonight," Skip said, closing the door.

Behind me, Tony Hausman snorted.

"Tell him," I said, wedging my foot in the doorjamb and lowering my voice so no one else could hear, "that I found his black Speedo."

From the two-inch crack, Skip raised an eyebrow. I told him it was urgent and he'd regret not doing it. He looked at me impassively. I stared back, radiating authority. I saw the idea rotating behind his eyes. Did he risk interrupting his masters? That's the thing with slime-bucket operations. The underlings know dirty tricks can sometimes backfire. Plus they're terrified of pissing off the boss, so they're always second-guessing themselves. That gives people like me valuable leverage.

Skip's caterpillar eyebrow descended. He told me to wait and shut the door. Within moments he returned. This time, he smiled and ushered me inside. I couldn't resist looking over my shoulder as I stepped across the sacred threshold, and my expectations were gratified as I saw Tony Hausman's face crumble before the door closed once more.

Skip led me into the adjoining suite.

Langdon was on the phone, nodding and promising something. Severin strode over, greeted me, and whispered that the new mayor was talking to his son. Paolo. I had almost forgotten about him. Good, I was glad to see some father-son bonding going on, even over the phone lines.

I sat down and waited. When Langdon hung up, Severin approached, murmured something in his ear, and they went to a table near the window and beckoned me over. Good psychological ploy, I thought, forcing me to walk over like a supplicant. Let them enjoy it while they could.

I sat down, and then came the first surprise.

"We've been waiting for you."

"You have?"

Severin's cold fish eyes regarded me.

"Yes, we have. And since you are resurrecting this slanderous nonsense about a black Speedo on the eve of the mayor's great victory, we figure it's time to be forthright with you."

Do you ever let the mayor talk for himself? I wondered, looking into Langdon's alarmingly large, gray orbs.

"That would be a novel approach," I said.

"We have something we believe will help you understand the big picture," Severin said, ignoring me. "But these documents are confidential. For your eyes only. Understood?"

This was not at all what I had expected. But it was brilliant of Severin the Smear King to deflect any criticism of Langdon by revealing something dirty about someone else. Because surely that's what he was about to hand me. Still, my inner Brutus wanted the information so badly I didn't care who was about to be betrayed.

"Understood," I said.

He pushed across a pile of stapled papers. I grabbed them eagerly, scanning the top. They were police reports. LAPD. It took me a moment to make out the name in the top box.

It was my own.

Disbelieving, I read on.

Supplying alcohol to a minor. Trespassing. Open container.

I didn't have to read farther to know where these charges came from. Paolo drinking tequila in my car. The tequila that, ironically, I had tried to hide from Scout so she wouldn't get loaded. Scout, who was now dead. I remembered Paolo telling me to go home, that he would handle it. Oh yeah, I thought, you handled it brilliantly. Probably insulted those guys so much that they reported the incident out of spite. I steeled myself not to show any emotion. I didn't want to give the sadist the pleasure.

"Paolo told his dad what you were up to the other night," Severin said, watching me closely. "The mayor came home two days before the election and found his only son reeking of tequila, so drunk he couldn't walk straight. The poor boy had fallen into a Regency mirror and cut his forehead. There was blood everywhere."

Severin clasped his hands together on the desk in preternatural calm, but his eyes danced.

I shook my head. "He wasn't drunk when I left him. He had been drinking, but he was quite coherent, cussing out the guards. He must have kept going after I left and he went back up to the house. Or maybe he took some downers. That intensifies the effects of the alcohol."

"I'm sure you speak from personal experience, Ms. Diamond. In any event, after they got back from the emergency room"—Severin looked at me from under his brows to make sure I understood the significance of such a visit—"and the boy sobered up, Carter threatened him with military school unless he came clean. Which he eventually did. He wasn't eager to tell us your role in all this, but I'm happy to say that reason prevailed. The security guards corroborated Paolo's story. A copy of their findings was forwarded to the LAPD, who wrote up their own report. And here you have it," Severin concluded.

I sat, aghast. I had known I was crossing a line back in the car the other night, but only in my most horrendous nightmares could I have imagined how it would come back to haunt me.

"I didn't give him the booze. He grabbed it out of my trunk."

"It was your liquor. Why didn't you ask him to give it back? You know he's only sixteen."

"I did," I whispered wretchedly. Yes, I had, but not forcefully enough. I had been seduced by the promise of a break on the murder story. And in my heart, I knew I would have gone a lot further to get it.

"We talked. He was upset about his mother's death. I gather Dad wasn't around much to provide solace."

I glanced pointedly at Langdon, who sat watching Severin with mild distaste. He had not said a word.

"With the election around the corner," I continued. "I mean, what's more important? But I wasn't trespassing. Paolo invited me. And we weren't driving. We were sitting in my car."

Severin tapped on the police report with a plump, manicured finger. "It says here the car's engine was going."

I groaned, remembering Paolo shivering as he rocked back and forth in my car. "I started the engine because the boy was cold. So I could put on the heat. Huge crime, that."

"I'm afraid the report speaks for itself. Carter turned these private security reports over to the LAPD, and they recognized your name. Said it wasn't the first time you had trespassed. They caught you sneaking around the day after Venus's murder too and were furious you had the temerity to do it again. They were ready to arrest you. But Mr. Langdon, out of the goodness of his heart, talked them out of it. The police did it as a personal favor, you understand. It came from the chief himself."

"Why would the chief of police do Langdon any favors on my behalf?"

Severin chuckled. "It had nothing to do with you. You are a nonentity, an insignificant mote of dust. But the chief of police was very happy to have the leading candidate for mayor in his debt. Surely you've heard that it's better to give than to receive. It's a way to cement friendships. And we have many friends among the men in blue."

"So your blue friends removed the black Speedo too?"

Severin rolled his eyes.

"Nobody removed anything. But here's a news story that may interest you. Officer Thomas Mallory, a fifteen-year veteran of the LAPD, will be heading up security for Mayor Langdon as of tomorrow. In this day and age, and after what happened to his wife, we are taking every high-tech precaution with the mayor's personal safety."

"Oh, so that's it," I said, unable to believe what I was hearing. "Mallory 'loses' the black Speedo and gets a hundred-thousand-dollar promotion. Amazing. And what about the black chiffon scarf that disappeared from the police evidence locker? You guys just made that up to explain what I saw in the cabana, didn't you?"

"You're wrong, of course. But clever. Too bad we can't offer you a job with the new mayor."

I looked at him, beginning to suspect the endgame.

"What do you want from me?"

A smile twitched across Severin's lips.

"Nothing, Ms. Diamond. We want absolutely nothing from you and we have no plans to do anything with this." His fingers closed around the police reports and he pulled them back across the desk. The staple rasped across the wood grain and I hoped it had left a scratch. Severin cleared his throat.

"There was no black Speedo. Just as there was no bottle of tequila, no providing alcohol to a minor. It doesn't exist."

Unless I fail to keep up my end of the bargain, I thought, completing what was left unsaid.

"You're all in on it," I whispered. "Everyone owes everyone because everyone's implicated. Police, mayor, you. Now me. It's like some spreading disease."

"And highly contagious," Severin said. "We've just won a big victory tonight. We couldn't let anything derail that, could we?"

I knew now that they hadn't killed Venus. But I thought there were other things they might reveal if I got them riled.

"That's why you killed her, isn't it? She was pregnant with another man's child, and wouldn't listen to reason. You had to silence her."

"That's preposterous," Severin sputtered, angry and aggrieved. It was the performance of an innocent person, and I had to remember that this man was a master actor. Yet perhaps for the first time in his long and black career, Alan Severin was telling a reporter the truth.

"You have a vivid imagination," he continued, "but I'm afraid it isn't anchored to reality. It's an insult and a slander to suggest we had anything to do with Venus's murder. She was worth much more to us alive. And let me assure you that our friendship with the police chief does not extend to the sanctioning of murder. The LAPD has thoroughly investigated both Carter and myself and cleared us of any involvement. At the time she was murdered, we were in a hotel, where Carter was speaking to an auditorium full of longshoremen. We have two hundred and fifty witnesses. The alibi is ironclad."

"So big deal, you have an alibi. You hired someone to do it for you."

"We did nothing of the sort. This is character assassination, tabloid journalism at its worst. And should you take any steps to spread such libels, we won't hesitate to go to your editors."

"It will never work," I said. "It looks way worse for you than it does for me."

"And this time," Severin smirked, ignoring me, "it will not just be with a polite request that you be reined in. It will be with these police reports in hand. We've researched your history at the paper, Ms. Diamond. If this gets out, your credibility will be destroyed, your career ruined. But we are willing to overlook this and do nothing. And that is all we ask of you in turn. To do nothing. Are we perfectly understood?"

He was right, of course. No matter which way I turned, it looked really, really bad. I imagined the headline: REPORTER BRIBES CHILD WITH TEQUILA TO TELL STORY. Or would it read REPORTER FIRED IN GROSS BREACH OF ETHICS? But getting fired was only part of the problem. It would also keep me from confirming who had killed Isabel and Scout. And I was so close. The answer lay right here, in this office.

"You got me," I told Severin, eyes downcast.

He scrutinized me, probing for insincerity.

"You are young, Ms. Diamond, and don't yet understand the complicated ways of the world."

"I'm grateful to have an expert like you initiate me into its secrets."

He glowered at me. But truly, he was awesome. A breathtakingly conniving, manipulative, amoral creature.

"In fact," I said, "I owe you both an apology."

Severin harrumphed. He walked to the dresser and opened a drawer. Now he came back with two Cuban cigars. He placed one in front of Carter Langdon III, who stared at it and rolled it along the table with one long finger but made no attempt to light it.

Severin bustled about, undertaking the ritualistic tasks that accompany the smoking of a fine cigar. He opened a leather case, extracted a tool, and cut off the end of his cigar. Then he lit it, puffing until it kindled. The victory celebration was on.

"Yes," he said, leaning back, "I believe you do owe us an apology."

"Mr. Langdon, Your Honor," I said, turning the conversation back to the new mayor, "I'm sorry I accused you of killing your wife."

At my words, Langdon picked up his cigar and gripped it tightly.

"Thank you," he said.

Severin exhaled noisily. "Bravo, Ms. Diamond."

"You didn't do it. And here's how I know," I continued. "The story of what went on that night begins with a witness who saw Venus having sex with her lover."

There was a muttered oath as Severin dropped the lit cigar onto his lap. He scrabbled at his crotch. As he captured the fat brown cockroach, I smelled burning cloth. Just a few threads, but it was enough. The suit was ruined. Pity.

Severin threw the cigar into a dish, then gave me an odious look.

"I thought we had an agreement, Ms. Diamond. Do we have to go through all this again?"

"Severin . . . I, uh," interrupted Carter Langdon III.

"Carter, for God's sake, you don't have to answer these ridiculous allegations. Throw her out now and we'll put the plan into motion tomorrow."

"No, Severin," the mayor said.

Carter Langdon III gazed at his campaign manager,

his eyes somber, and I got the feeling that for the first time in his life, he had taken command and would not be dissuaded. He looked at me in a kindly manner.

"Please go on."

"You aren't murderers," I said. "But a crime has been perpetrated here. A venal one, to be sure. A pathetic and decades-long attempt by someone to maintain a fiction about themselves." *Yo no soy la mujer en el espejo,* I thought. "Venus wasn't who we all believed, was she?"

Something surged in Langdon's dead gray eyes.

"What nonsense. Of course she was," Severin snapped.

But Langdon looked mournful and even more weary than before.

"How did you . . . ?"

"Carter," said Severin sharply.

"Alan, you know full well that nothing I say here makes any difference," Langdon said mildly. "She is dead, I am mayor, and this reporter understands that silence is a virtue."

He turned to me. "Tell me, dear, how did you find out?"

"By chance," I said. "I was researching a story totally unrelated to you, about a Mexican-American family that ran a music promotion business in the San Gabriel Valley. You've never heard of them, and there's no reason you should, they don't move in your circles. They don't even speak your language at home. But it turns out someone in their family got murdered the same night Venus did. A twenty-eight-year-old named Ruben Aguilar. At first I thought it was coincidence. Lots of people got whacked in L.A. that weekend, including your son's friend, Isabel. But the more I looked into it, the clearer it became that all three were connected. In that totally improbable L.A. way that brings people together across

lines of class and race and money, especially when
secrets are involved. Ruben Aguilar was your pool boy,
Your Honor. He and your wife were having an affair."

Carter listened to me, a pained look spreading across
his taut face.

"I don't know about that, she didn't talk to me about
those things."

"Seems there's a lot she didn't talk to you about. Let
me fill you in."

I told him more about Ruben and his family, including
the jealous fiancée. I told him about Venus scarfing fast
food alone in the kitchen and threatening me when I
caught her. I told him about the sugar skull gifts to *La
Raza*. I told him about El Chaparrito, waxing eloquent
about Ruben's flame-haired girlfriend at the club who
spoke flawless Spanish, down to the curses. It was all circumstantial, and it took me a long time to lay it out. But
when you put the pieces together, it explained everything
so perfectly that it didn't make sense otherwise.

"And then she got pregnant by Ruben," I said, watching Langdon flinch. "That was the tipping point. She
would never have run away with him, of course. She was
too much in love with her life, her position. But he awak-
ened something in her, something that had long lain dor-
mant. And that was the first crack in those fortified walls.
Soon it would all splinter. But tell me, Your Honor,
what's the big deal, in this day and age, about admitting
that Venus Dellaviglia Langdon was Mexican?"

Langdon was hunched over the table now, rolling the
unlit cigar back and forth with the palms of his hand as
if he were flattening dough. He didn't raise his head.

"Ah, but it wasn't this day and age," he said. "It was
almost a quarter century ago, and things were different.
There was prejudice. My own family wouldn't have

accepted her. And I guess that on some level, I was ashamed too. I couldn't admit I had fallen in love with a poor illegal Mexican. Italian sounded so much more romantic."

He cleared his throat. "So you see, it wasn't just her, it was me. We were in on this together from the beginning."

"But times have changed," I said. "It would have been such a useful campaign tool to have your gorgeous Mexican-American wife reaching out to this city's huge Latino population."

"Now you are thinking like a politician, Ms. Diamond. But not enough of one. Venus couldn't have done that without admitting she had been lying all along. Believe you me, we had discussions. Yes, she could have reached out to them. But think what an insult it would have been, to be so ashamed of her heritage that she had denied it for decades."

I thought of Jane Sims, nursing her secret affair. I thought about the street kids, each with their own horrible secrets. I thought about Silvio's grandmother Agrippina, claiming a wealthy heritage she herself had concocted. I thought of Silvio and Ruben and their twisted relationship. I thought about Gisela's facade. And I realized that they had all been stepping-stones, leading me here to the grandest and most beautiful hologram of them all—Venus Dellaviglia Langdon.

"Why don't you tell me the whole story?" I said. "As you pointed out, I'm too compromised to reveal it."

Langdon gave the cigar a fierce push and it rolled across the table and onto the floor, where it spun momentarily, then was still.

"Carter," Severin said hoarsely. "As your manager I would strongly advise you to . . ."

Carter Langdon III ignored him.

"When I met her, she was an illegal Mexican immigrant named Maria Cruz, a ravishing, ravenously ambitious little wetback who had her whole life mapped out and lacked only the vehicle to take her there."

Once he said it, it somehow slid so easily into place. Venus's life had been so overripe and operatic from the beginning. My mind skittered again to the day I had stumbled into her kitchen and caught her eating beans and rice, scooping it up expertly with a rolled-up tortilla, eating as though the food were life itself. I recalled her anger, as if I'd caught her in some secret ritual that laid her bare before the world. And here I'd assumed she was upset to be caught lying to the *Times* celebrity workout reporter.

"How did you meet?"

Langdon cracked his knuckles.

"In college I made a name for myself, campaigning for nursing home reform," he said. "All I had to do was describe the appalling conditions of those places, the bedsores and drugging, the malnutrition, and people got angry and opened their pocketbooks to support me." He shook his head and his voice rose. "If they treated dogs and cats in shelters the way they do old folks, people would be up in arms."

Even now, he couldn't help winding into a spiel. It was the way he was wired.

"But animals get adopted from shelters. No one adopts old people from nursing homes. Anyway, at one of these horrible way stations for death, I met a nurse's aide pushing around a patient. She was a vision in her surgical scrubs, jet-black hair pulled back to expose those cheekbones, those lips. She earned two dollars and sixty-five cents an hour, changing catheter tubes and swabbing the butts of big, elderly babies."

"Venus," I breathed.

Langdon nodded.

"I stopped to talk to her, just for a minute. Soon we were having coffee. I began dropping by weekly, ostensibly to check up on the place but really to see her. We got to know each other. I urged her to sign up for classes at the local community college and helped get her enrolled, even though she wasn't legal. It was easier then. And she was so thirsty to learn. Voracious. Anything I gave her, she flipped through it once and could recite it back. Poetry by Horace. Shakespeare. Borges. She was brilliant. And so driven. You could see it in her face, before she learned to hide it.

"At first, I was happy playing Breakfast at Tiffany's. She had such a keen mind. An extraordinary facility with languages. And she was beautiful. Soon I was in deep. Who doesn't want an icon on their arm, and she played the part, seducing me with words, with stories she wove about what we'd do together. I told her my plans, my dreams, and she listened. She asked smart questions. She didn't know who I was. But she cared. And I learned how she grew up in rural Mexico, the illegitimate daughter of a rancher who wouldn't acknowledge her. She swore she wouldn't end up like her mother, gnarled from arthritis and sleeping on a dirt floor like an animal. When she was twelve, she shot up and filled out and suddenly the men stared as though her body held secrets. And she realized she could use that body to escape. She worked full-time to pay tuition at a second-rate college. She studied English. At nineteen, she learned where the *coyotes* hung out and bargained her way into a trip across the border. It was only sex, she said."

"Jesus, Carter, this campaign has really shot your nerves. You're going off the deep end," Severin muttered.

Then in an aside to me: "These are the hallucinations of a sick man who is having a breakdown after months of campaigning beyond his physical limits."

Langdon ignored him. Far from having a breakdown, he spoke like a man in full possession of his faculties who was finally telling the truth after years of living with lies. I felt I was hearing his eulogy to her, the real one that he had been unable to give at her flower-and-celebrity-drenched funeral.

"Once across, she ditched the *coyote,* who had fallen in love with her. She found another man to take her to L.A. She was living in a room in the Rampart district when we met. He would hit her, and she laughed off the bruises and covered them with makeup. But there was a desperation in her. I wanted to save her. And she could offer me something too."

As he spoke, I began to feel sorry for this man, his choices, his masquerade. They had both been living a lie.

"Your lovely Roman wife," I said slowly. "Whom every man desired and every woman desired to be. Isn't that what they said about her? Every man except you?"

He straightened his tie.

"You're wrong. I did desire her. I wanted her as my life partner. There were no secrets between us. I told her I was attracted to men and she said she didn't care, she just wanted to be with me. She talked about how money meant nothing to her. We shared a spiritual bond. All my life, I've been surrounded by people who want my money. I know what that smells like. And she was on a whole other level. She said together we'd be invincible. So we concocted this story that she was an Italian orphan. She picked out a new name and identity for herself. And with lighter hair, better makeup, and couture clothes, she didn't resemble the girl from the pueblo anymore. She stopped being her.

I don't know how to put it; she inhabited her new self so completely that sometimes even I forgot she wasn't a Roman aristocrat by birth. And she should have been born to that," Langdon said. "She deserved it."

He really believed it was only an accident of birth that had made her a landless Mexican peasant. And I saw that even cuckolded, widowed, and unmasked, he still worshiped her.

"What became of her family in Mexico?"

"She sent money to her mom until the old lady died. That was her business, I never knew exactly where she was from or who she still knew there."

"Does your son know?"

Carter winced. "No."

"Didn't he wonder why on all your trips to Italy he never met any family?"

"Italy's a big, modern place. You think anyone in Rome cares what village you're from, so long as you have the lire to back it up? And in the villages, well, Venus would say she wasn't sure of her family's origins. In each region, her accent was just a little off, her facts a little skewed, so she'd sigh and say she must be from another part of the boot."

"I bet that's why Venus was one of the few Angelenos who didn't have a Latina maid," I said, remembering how impressed people had been that she imported her help from France. "She was afraid they'd guess her secret."

"Only the household help," Langdon said defensively.

"She might have been better off hiring an Italian pool cleaner too. You think she was faithful until Ruben?"

He waved me off. "That wasn't part of the deal. She had men. Who could blame her? A woman has needs. But she was faithful in her own way. She was discreet.

She was the perfect wife. But somebody discovered her secret. Perhaps that's why she was killed."

"Your wife was killed, Your Honor, because she shacked up with your pool cleaner and that didn't sit well with his fiancée, a woman named Gisela Lujan. The police will be briefing you soon. By this time," I checked my watch, "Gisela should be in Sybil Brand, locked up on suspicion of killing both her fiancé and your wife."

I paused. Langdon was shaking his head and mouthing no, but no sound came from him.

"But here's the thing. The night before Venus was murdered, someone else got killed. Her name was Isabel Chevalier. She was fifteen, a friend of your son's. The two of them got together with another girl in your orchard that night and dropped acid."

Langdon lifted his head. "My son doesn't do drugs."

"Save it for your adoring public," I said. "So Isabel is high and decides to take a dip in your pool and she happens to look into the cabana and sees your wife and Ruben in bed. Venus hears a noise and goes out to investigate and catches Isabel. Your wife made the girl promise not to reveal what she saw. Then she let her go. But with the election so close, she decided not to leave anything to fate.

"Later that night, she followed Paolo as he drove Isabel and her friend back to the squat where they were going to spend the night. She recognized it because she had taken Paolo there before."

"My son . . ." Carter Langdon III began, but stopped when he saw the look on my face.

"Your wife followed Isabel into that squat and waited until she fell asleep. Then she strangled her and rolled her body up in a futon. She probably hoped it wouldn't be discovered for a while. But there was another kid in that abandoned building, and he overheard your wife talking."

Langdon's mouth twisted like he had bit into an unripe persimmon.

"Go on."

"Venus thought she had taken care of things. But the next night, someone else saw her and lover boy trysting. Gisela Lujan came looking for her errant fiancé and found them in the cabana. She would have killed them right away, but she lacked a weapon. So she drove home and got a gun. When her beloved Ruben pulled up, she shot him in the face, making it look like a drive-by. Then she drove to Los Feliz and killed Venus."

Langdon sunk his face in his hands.

"How sordid," he whispered.

Something in his reedy voice made me want to defend her.

"No more sordid than going to the baths for anonymous sex."

A low moan escaped him.

"You can never know the—"

"Carter," Severin shouted. "I will not stand by and let you commit political suicide."

Langdon fell silent. I wanted to tell him that people who live their lives in the closet will be suffocated by it. But it wasn't my place.

"Your sex life is your business, Your Honor. But an innocent boy is about to stand trial for a murder that your wife committed. This squatter kid Finch, who was Isabel's boyfriend. We've got to clear the record."

There was an agitated gleam in Langdon's eye.

"There is nothing in your story to link this girl's murder to Venus," he said indignantly. "My wife wasn't capable of taking someone's life. The police probably do have the right guy. Either that, or she was killed by some other demented street person. In fact, Venus had a saying, 'Live in the gutter and you'll die in the gutter.'"

He had done my work for me.

"Well, Mr. Langdon, that's exactly what the woman in the squat said as she lugged around the futon with the dead girl inside. And what's more, she said it in Spanish. In her hysterical state, Venus had reverted to her native tongue."

"I don't believe it."

"My source says the woman was babbling that she had pulled herself out of the gutter years ago and had no intention of going back there. She said she was . . . immortal."

Langdon blanched. "Venus used to joke about that."

"Put it together, Mr. Langdon. Who else would even have a motive? Your wife was starting to crack. She was under terrible pressure, helping you get elected mayor and maintain the facade. Meanwhile she was pregnant with another man's child. A younger man who was awakening an identity she had suppressed for so long. It made her reckless. She was hanging out in bars with him, speaking Spanish, rediscovering her own culture even as she disintegrated. Ultimately, she became desperate enough to kill."

"You'll never prove any of this."

"Proof will be up to the police."

"There's nothing to be gained. You'd destroy the legacy she spent her entire life creating. And my mayoralty. No, I can't risk that."

"This girl Isabel had a father, Your Honor. She had friends, people who loved her. They deserve to know. There's a boy in jail who needs to be set free."

"Yes," said another voice. "Let's speak about the

truth. Are you ready to throw yourself on the Dellaviglia Langdon funeral pyre for good measure?"

It was Severin, somber as an undertaker in his sleek black suit. He stepped closer and his bulky frame obscured the mayor. I had little doubt who would be running the city.

I waited a decent interval. "No," I said finally. "I suppose I'm not."

A carnivorous smile crossed his face.

"I thought you would choose the wise path," Severin said. "And that being the case, Mayor Langdon would like to give you the first exclusive interview of his new administration. We know you're doing a story about street kids, Ms. Diamond. You'll be happy to know that the mayor plans to donate three million dollars of his own money to build a drop-in center for the city's street kids. He will seek matching funds from private and public sources. This will be his first act as mayor, and he's been inspired by his son, a close friend of the murdered girl Isabel Chevalier, whose young life was destroyed within twenty-four hours of his beloved wife's. Isn't that right, Carter?"

The new mayor of Los Angeles stepped forward and cleared his throat, banishing the cautious, grief-stricken husband of moments ago.

"That's right. In my late wife's honor, it will be called the Venus Dellaviglia Langdon Center for Troubled Teens."

The mayor paused. He couldn't think of anything else to say. But Severin jumped in with the spin.

"For our new mayor, who has suffered the most extreme violence in his own family, this is a way to reach out to all victims, to make the circle come round in a beautifully symmetrical way."

I stared, speechless at their audacity, their way of turning a horrible thing to their advantage and ensuring the past would stay buried. I couldn't stand to be around them for another second. They beamed at me, convinced of their invincibility.

"Wonderful," I said, stumbling for the door.

"Remember our agreement," Severin called out.

I threw the door open, stepped out, and saw Tony Hausman crouched in the hallway.

"What the fuck was that about?" he asked.

"Puce," I mumbled. "Puce and gold. Those will be the colors of the administration. Make sure you get that down, Hausman," I said. "No one else knows."

# CHAPTER 32

**B**ut of course, I didn't choose the wise path. I had never planned to. Langdon might have already won the election, but I still had to redeem my tarnished conscience. Plus I had to get Finch out of jail. The evidence against him was all circumstantial, and now I knew why.

My resolve strengthened as I drove home. If I let Severin blackmail me, Finch would be convicted of a murder he hadn't committed and they would forever hold power over me. I had to face it on my terms, no matter the consequences. I owed it to the squatter kids.

So the next morning, I came clean. I told Tom Thompson what the new mayor of Los Angeles held over my head and how it had come down. And I told him who had murdered Isabel Chevalier, Venus Dellaviglia Langdon, and Ruben Aguilar, and how I knew. I produced the tape recorder and played it back for him and, wonder of wonders, there it was, right up to the mouse-torture squeaks that had almost gotten me killed. Then I explained about Venus. Thompson listened, slack-jawed, then shut his trap enough to scold me about how the end never justified the means. Then he made me repeat my story, first to the assistant Metro editors, then to Jane Sims, then to the managing editor, and finally to the Times Mirror corporate lawyers. There was broad disbelief and much shaking of heads. Jane Sims appeared especially rattled. Other editors edged their chairs away like I had some contagious disease. And I faced a two-week suspension for what I had allowed Paolo Dellaviglia Langdon to do in my car on Halloween night.

"How am I going to write the story if I'm suspended?" I asked, only to be met by looks of pity.

"You still don't understand, do you, Eve?" Jane Sims said, in a much kinder voice than I might have expected. "You're not writing the story. You're part of the story."

To my chagrin, I was relegated to the sidelines as my colleagues hunted down former nursing home coworkers, old boyfriends, and plastic surgeons who might have known Venus two decades ago as Maria Cruz. Tony Hausman himself hiked down to the L.A. River to talk to Pia, who confirmed what she had told me. And Gisela, who was mounting a defense of temporary insanity, repeated in a jailhouse interview that she had found Venus and Ruben in bed and killed them both. Her fancy private lawyer—hired by the Aguilar family, go figure—was spinning the tale as a crime of passion that pitted the white haves against the brown have-nots. He wanted to expose the hypocrisy of the very wealthy and didn't mind trying the case in the press.

Once the *Times* had marshaled its forces, Hausman called the mayor's office to go over the facts and Severin screamed bloody murder. But it was too late. The story laying out Venus's decades-long masquerade and raising the possibility that she and not Finch had killed Isabel ran all over the front page, next to a sidebar about yours truly. Yes, I'm horrified to admit that my own paper laid out my misdeeds with Paolo that night as well as my entanglement with Silvio and reported my suspension.

The LAPD was quoted as saying it was still evaluating whether I had committed any crimes and should be arrested.

The day the story ran, all hell broke loose. Severin and Langdon denied everything, but once the Mexican press got hold of it, their story collapsed. A Guadalajara reporter found Venus's remaining family. It turned out that Langdon had lied to me, he knew exactly where they were and was still sending them money, a revelation that surprised me and made me like him more. With so much new information casting doubt on Finch as the killer, the prosecutor dropped murder charges. But the kid is still in jail on old theft and vandalism warrants.

The media feeding frenzy had produced all sorts of seedy revelations about Langdon's wife. But to my utter disbelief, it didn't make a damn bit of difference. The mayor's ratings only surged. The public didn't care. If anything, they felt even more sorry for him.

As for me, I was shell-shocked and lonely. There was so much I wanted to talk to Silvio about. But the Times Mirror lawyers had forbidden me to contact him, saying it might compromise Gisela's murder trial, in which we would both have to testify.

Silvio, who was apparently under no such edict, filled up my answering machine with plaintive messages. He also showed up at my house several times when I was gone. Finally one night, my luck ran out and I came home and found him camped on my doorstep in a beach chair, typing into a laptop.

"Eve," he said, jumping up. "Why are you avoiding me?"

A warm feeling shot through me and I didn't trust myself to speak.

"Forgive me for what happened that night. It was the

only way. I had to lull her into thinking I was on her side so I could get to the gun."

"I'm not supposed to talk to you. The Times Mirror lawyers . . . Gisela's trial . . ." I trailed off. He stood there, forlorn and miserable, and I realized it was because he cared. Remembering something he had once said, I smiled.

"Do you think that I am such a shallow and ignorant person that I took it personally?" I said. "It was brilliant. The more cruel and disparaging things you said to me, the more Gisela would believe you. That's not why I haven't called you back. The lawyers . . . and something else . . ."

He looked ashamed. "I know. But I had to apologize."

"Accepted," I said impatiently. "But, Silvio, how could you? With your brother's fiancée? She wasn't lying about that."

He squirmed miserably. "I have no answer for you," he said. "It was wrong on every level, and yet, at the moment, it seemed like the most elemental thing two people could do to comfort each other. She could have been anyone."

"But she wasn't," I said, staring at the *Billboard* magazine, the *Opinión*, and the open computer on my front porch. The tools of his trade. "She was your dead brother's fiancée. And his murderer."

"Gisela had come on to me for years. She would taunt me. Walk around half-dressed. You know how she was. And she was there every day. That night, the dam just broke."

So had my heart, I thought.

"It was wrong of me to pursue that story so soon after your brother's death. It showed a lack of respect. Then we got involved, and things got even more murky. We've gone through the whole arc of a relationship in three weeks. And honestly, I'm not supposed to talk to you. Until this is over. It could be years."

"We can start over," he said, ignoring me. "Take it slowly. How about if I call you in a few weeks?"

"The *Times* says I can't," I said, hiding behind the edict.

"Don't write me off for what happened before I met you, Eve. It wasn't like I was being unfaithful."

"Except to your family. And the memory of your brother."

He winced. And began to gather up his papers. I watched him walk to his beat-up truck and something tore inside of me. Yet it wasn't meant to be. I turned to walk into my house. He had forgotten a newspaper on my porch. From the pages of *La Opinión*, Gisela Lujan stared up at me. It was her mug shot, the paper chronicling the latest details of the murder case. She looked defiant. Disheveled. And insane. I thought of what Silvio and his family must be going through, having their private lives scrutinized and dissected and dragged through very public mud. Yet still they were taking care of one of their own.

Carefully, I folded the paper and recognized what a coward I was. I, who was so willing to take chances for work—foolish, dangerous chances even—was unable to face even the slightest risk when it came to my emotional life. Instead, I hit delete.

Still clutching the Spanish-language newspaper, I chased after Silvio.

"You left this."

At my voice, he turned, an expression of hope then defeat crashing across his face when he saw what I held.

"Thanks," he said mechanically, then moved off.

"Silvio?"

"Yes." His voice was weary. He just wanted to get going.

For a moment, we stood there, avoiding each other's eyes.

Slowly, I forced myself to look at him.

"When this is over, I'd like to see you again."

*O*n an overcast November day exactly one month after Isabel Chevalier's murder, I picked up Paolo Dellaviglia Langdon outside his wrought-iron gate and we drove to the abandoned building in East Hollywood where Isabel had lost her life.

I had been shocked to hear from him. But it turned out that Venus and Carter's kid had some class after all. He had read about my suspension and called to say he was sorry. He hadn't escaped unscathed either—Langdon had taken away his wheels. We make awkward small talk, then he invited me to a memorial for Isabel. He might have been angling for a ride too, but I didn't care. The last few weeks had exploded his world more than any human being deserves. His mother was dead, as were two of his friends. His very identity had been ripped from him, switched overnight from scion of Italian nobles to son of an illegal Mexican immigrant. Oh yeah, and his dad now ruled Los Angeles.

A song by Jaguares came on the radio. *"Asi como tu"*—just like you—sang Saul Hernandez, the band's moody front-man poet.

I reached to change the station.

His hand stopped me. "Leave it."

"I thought you didn't like *rocanrol*."

He stretched long crane legs. "I figure I owe it to my mom to at least listen to this stuff before dismissing it."

"That's a fine idea."

"Besides, I've got to brush up on my Spanish. My dad's against it, but I'm planning a road trip to Mexico over spring break. I want to meet my relatives."

Well, what do you know? I thought, as Paolo sang along to the refrain of *"Asi como tu."*

"That's way cool," he said. "He's singing about a love so strong it can take away life as well as give it."

"Or a lover," I said, flashing to Venus.

"I think I'll download that when I get home."

"Could you make me a copy?" I asked.

Soon we were sitting cross-legged on the sidewalk in front of the boarded-up squat with Sophie, Caitlin, and some of Isabel's other friends. On the chain-link fence surrounding the property, a large photo of a smiling Isabel watched over Manzanita Street. Her eyes were young, yet knowing. She wore black lipstick, a nose ring, and a spiky dog collar.

In the weeks since her death, friends had brought bouquets of dried flowers and votive candles. Ocean shells. Punk rock buttons. A newspaper clipping of Isabel at the mock trial, looking tough and prosecutorial. An Eminem poster and a Borwick Academy banner. An orange pumpkin that said, "Happy Halloween, Isabel. I love you and miss you, Dad." A black-and-white dancing skeleton inscribed with *"Día de los Muertos."* A rusty can opener. Two balloons with "Happy Sweet Sixteen Isabel" in purple script. Her birthday would have been November 7.

In the murky light, we sat amid the puddled candle wax. They smoked cigarette after cigarette and reminisced about Isabel and Scout. The lost girls. They had found only one photo of Isabel's little sidekick. She was dressed in her Girl Scout greens, glaring at the camera and flipping the bird. A few days earlier, the cops had arrested a mentally ill transient with a record as long as your leg and he had confessed to Scout's murder. But I still felt that I had failed her. And I wanted to make it up to her, to all of them.

Now we laid fresh flowers. We lit scented candles.

They told stories that made everyone laugh and Caitlin affixed a poem by John Donne called "Song" that began "Go and catch a falling star."

"We had our time here, and it was the best time in the world and the worst time," Caitlin said.

They spoke with disdain of the new generation of girls who wanted to be squatter groupies. They'd seen them in Hollywood and at the Santa Monica Promenade.

"Don't you just want to run up to them and shake them and say, 'Go home'?" Caitlin asked.

I placed a candle near Caitlin's knees and leaned in to light it.

"I want to tell them not to date their dead friends' fathers," I said quietly. "Dirty old men who are just using them for sex."

She radiated shock and surprise. How did you know? her eyes asked.

"But there will always be little girls," said Sophie. "Squatters are interesting. They're rebellious. That's attractive when you're fifteen."

"People are going to say that we were just like those little girls," Caitlin said.

They waited to see if I would agree, but I was busy laying down my last offering. One that had led me to Isabel's killer. A sugar skull. So they debated the issue and concluded they were different.

"Would you have listened to me anyway?" I asked.

"No," said Paolo, speaking for the first time. He touched the sugar skull. Then, absentmindedly, he put his finger to his mouth and licked it.

"Kids don't listen," he said. "They have to make their own mistakes and hope they survive."

# ACKNOWLEDGMENTS

I would like to thank Rick Barrs, Jack Cheevers, Susan Goldsmith, and the staff at the late, great *New Times,* Los Angeles, who gave me the freedom and space to write freewheeling and far-ranging stories.

Thanks go to the Silverlake Fiction Workshop for their thoughtful critiques and encouragement—Kerry Madden-Lunsford, Judith Dancoff, Donna Rifkind, Diane Arieff, Marlene McCurtis, Lienna Silver, Diana Wagman, Sakae Manning, and Natalie Smith Parra.

Thanks to Donna, Kerry, and Ellen Slezak for reading the entire manuscript and providing valuable comments.

*Merci* to my lovely and gracious agent, Anne Borchardt, who makes good things happen and feeds my soul with our literary talks.

Thanks to my fabulous editor, Susanne Kirk, who inspires me to live up to her high standards.

Thanks to copy editor Estelle Laurence for her careful reading and close eye.

Thanks to Kelly Kervik, M. K. Laughlin, Sarah Knight, Dena Rosenberg, Sarah Turner, Erik Wasson, and the rest of the crew at Scribner. Henry Sene Yee, you are an artist of the highest degree.

Thanks to the numerous journalists in town whose stories over the years have provided extraordinary snapshots of Los Angeles and sparked my imagination.

Thanks to the librarians and the booksellers who took me to their hearts on my maiden voyage.

Thanks to Kim Dower.

Thanks to Noelle, Marc, and Roberta for your enthusiasm and support.

Thanks to Adrian and Alexander, my patient boys, who are now writing their own stories.

And finally I would like to thank David. Without you, none of this would be possible or meaningful.

SCRIBNER HARDCOVER
PROUDLY PRESENTS

Denise Hamilton's
next Eve Diamond novel

# LAST LULLABY

Available in hardcover April 2004
from Scribner

Turn the page for a preview of *Last Lullaby*. . . .

*L*ook lively, here comes Flight 1147."

We pressed our noses to the one-way glass and the parade began. A trickle at first, businessmen wheeling suitcases, cell phones already pressed to their ears. Then young couples in glitter platform shoes, bopping to Walkmans. Well-heeled families carrying duty-free bags, squinting into the fluorescent light to read the signs and line up in the right queue.

Then a pause in the traffic, empty spaces stretching out like ellipses. I scrutinized what the airplane's belly had disgorged, scanning for stains under silk armpits, restless eyes, hands clenching bags too tightly. They said even a preternatural calm was suspect, since it was normal to be frazzled after fourteen hours in the air, even if you had the patience of a Buddhist monk. Speaking of which, here came five of them, girded in saffron robes that ended in sandaled feet.

An elbow nudged my arm.

"Plenty a' room for contraband inside those layers," U.S. Customs Supervisor William Maxwell drawled lazily, watching the monks plod past.

I fingered my notepad, thinking that the monks looked more dazed than surreptitious.

"Don't you have dogs for that? Sniff out drugs and explosives and stuff?"

I realized as soon as the words left my mouth that bombs were a threat for those boarding, not getting off. If you were going to blow up an airplane, you'd do it in midair.

"One day they'll invent robo-dogs that sniff out jewels, cash, and illegals, but for now we still rely on good instincts and bad paperwork," Maxwell said, scanning the crowd.

His eyes shifted to an Asian woman walking behind the monks, and I wondered if his interest was professional. She was tall, with a heart-shaped face and freshly applied lipstick. She wore a pantsuit of raw raspberry silk and carried a slumbering little girl over her shoulder. Behind her came the husband, pushing an elephantine cart heaped with luggage. Balancing precariously on top was a large bag that said, "Tokyo Disneyland."

"You really think those monks are carrying?" I asked, more to make conversation than because I thought so.

"Prayerbooks, maybe," he said evenly. "But skepticism is a virtue. We caught some grief last week for pulling apart a Mexican grandma's wheelchair. She and the granddaughter got on their cells, jabbering to the consulate about their rights being violated. Had no idea what was packed inside those hollow metal tubes."

"Granny was a drug mule?"

Maxwell snorted. "My black homegirl was hitching a ride."

I thought I might be missing something because we were both staring out the window while trying to carry on a conversation.

" 'My black homegirl?' "

Now some businessmen moved past in trench coats. Tall and blond, with glacier-blue eyes and the slanted cheekbones of the Russian steppes. Behind them sauntered two young Asian men, elaborately casual, their hair iced up. One had a camera around his neck. The other clutched a map of Hollywood. *Props,* I thought. Way too obvious. Here's a pair I would watch. I looked to see if Maxwell had noticed the same thing, but his gaze swept right past them.

"Heroin," Maxwell said. "Ten kilos of uncut tar. It's black and sticky and La Eme moves a lot of it across the border. Worth an easy five million on the street. They call it "My black homegirl" to throw off the FBI phone intercepts."

La Eme was the Mexican Mafia. From the letter *M*. I knew that much from growing up in L.A. La Eme's tentacles snaked through the barrios and prisons of California and they laundered their money through juice bars and video stores.

"What about those guys?" I pointed to the Asian punks. "There's something off about them. Like, if they're so cool, why are they clutching all that tourist stuff?"

But he was watching three Asian women stroll past, big rocks on manicured fingers, strands of pearls, designer handbags. They were young but stout, in elegant, loose-fitting dresses and matching jackets.

"How much you wanna bet they're Korean and ready to pop?" Maxwell said.

I studied them. What crime slang was he lobbing at me now?

"Preggers," said Maxwell. "And loaded. They fly over here to give birth so their babies will be U.S. citizens. Big-time status. Shop and play tourist, stay at a fancy hotel till they drop the kid. Then skedaddle back to Seoul. There's no law against it, but still . . ."

"You mean they don't want to stay?" For some reason, I was insulted on behalf of my country. Wasn't this the Promised Land?

Before he could answer, a large clot of tired humanity poured into the room on the other side of the glass and began to sort itself into lines. This was the last layer of the plane to be excavated, and it revealed the pitiless archaeology of overseas travel. First had come the rested countenances of first class, airplane royalty from both sides of the Pacific. Then the still-groomed, monogrammed, and pampered business class. And now the flying rabble, the pack I joined when I flew, we of the plasticine food and cramped leg space, the great unruly masses of economy—cranky, disoriented, and sleep-deprived.

My gaze lingered over a swarthy man with black hair. His clean-shaven face bore the unmistakable imprint of the Levant. The plane had originated in Beijing, with stops in Seoul and Tokyo with a final destination of LAX, where I stood now. *Would he be pulled aside automatically?* I wondered, getting an inkling, for the first time, how difficult it must be to look at people's papers and faces and make split-second decisions that could affect national security.

Not that I was here on anything quite so exalted. I was a reporter for the *L.A. Times,* and after the terrorist attacks of September 11, inquiring minds wanted to know how the government screened passengers. So U.S. Customs had set me up with a high-ranking official named Maxwell. I was shadowing him for a day before demystifying the process for *Times* readers. And there would be plenty of art. My star fotog, Ariel Delacorte, was out there among the disembarking passengers, shooting away. Weighed down by cameras and the shapeless khaki vests that all shutterbugs love, Ariel still managed a casual elegance, her posture erect as a ballet dancer's, her wavy black hair cut smartly to her sculpted jaw.

I turned to ask Maxwell about the Middle Easterner but he was halfway out the door, speaking into a crackling two-way radio.

"Yeah, that's them," he said. "Pinkie and the luggage coolie. Remember, it's hands-off. Send them through with a smile. I'll be right over."

I took two steps after him. "Stay here," he said. He pushed me back, and I saw his hand go to his belt. "I won't be a minute."

The door closed behind him. By the time I recovered enough to run and yank it open, the hallway was empty.

I turned back to the one-way glass window. One of the blond businessmen was gesticulating to a U.S. Customs inspector. He dug into his bags and pulled out some papers, which he threw down. The inspector shook her head.

The man looked around, as if enjoining his linemates to commiserate. People were packed in tight, blocked by suitcases and carts, restrained into orderly lines by shiny black nylon ropes, children running around.

Then without warning, he pushed through the crowd, elbowing other passengers aside. At the same time, I saw lights flash and felt the glass rattle in sharp staccato shivers. Someone out there was shooting.

As bodies crumpled to the floor, I wondered whether they had been shot or were just taking cover. The crowd surged and shoved as people tried to break loose of the Immigration holding area. On the other side of the glass, a jeweled hand rose up, vermilion nails clawing two inches from my face, before sinking back into the roiling mass. I saw a flash of raspberry as the smartly dressed Asian woman and her husband floated past, propelled by the mob. They slammed momentarily into the other blond businessman, then bounced apart. I noticed the woman no longer held her child.

On the other side of the glass, people were stampeding past the kiosks as security guards sought to push them back. One guard brandished a gun, then got down on one knee, sharpshooter style. *Good Lord, they can't shoot into a crowd of people, it's going to be a massacre,* I thought. The glass rattled again, and I ducked instinctively, hoping it was bulletproof as well as one-way.

Now here came one of the Asian punks, doing the Olympic high hurdles as he sailed over mounds of luggage and passengers, shielding their heads in 1950s duck-and-cover style.

The second Asian punk came into view, running for the exit. He had a gun, and was yelling something. Nobody paid any attention. People pushed through the door, faces contorted in terror. After the July fourth

LAX massacre at the El Al counter, no one was taking any chances.

I realized I had been crouched at the window, peeking through my hands like a frightened toddler at the pandemonium on the other side of the glass. But I was a reporter, I needed to get in there. I ran to the door, threw it open, and stepped into a corridor, only to find a mass of people fleeing toward me, wild-eyed and disheveled.

"No," a man panted, grabbing my arm. "Go back. Terrorists. Shooting."

Ignoring him, I ran the way he had just come. Bursting through a set of double doors into the large room I had just been observing from the one-way glass, I saw a middle-aged man with blood on his face and a dazed expression. A teenaged girl sobbed and knelt on the dirty floor by a woman who looked unconscious. Sirens split the air, and a recorded voice calmly urged passengers to keep moving in an orderly manner.

On the other side of the room, I saw several crumpled bodies. I recognized the Slav man who had bolted. He lay on the ground with one arm outstretched, as if felled while playing tag. A morbid curiosity propelled me closer. Bright red blood matted his flaxen hair. One cheek was pressed against the linoleum, and I noticed grayish gumk splattered across the pale skin and clinging to his suit lapels. With a start, I realized it was the man's brains.

Five feet away, the second Slav businessman lay in a tangle of limbs and blood, entwined with the pretty Asian mother. It looked as though they had collided while trying to flee. The front of the woman's raspberry silk outfit was spotted with blood fibers charred where the bullets had gone in. My eyes flickered over to the man. An explosion had detonated on his chest. I forced myself to stare, to record every detail, ignoring the prickles of fear radiating outward from my spine. The 'bolt' reflex was coming on strong. More than anything, I wanted to flee, to run out of this terminal, back to my car, and out of the airport. What if at this very moment someone with a dirty bomb was preparing to detonate it? Part of me *did* run screaming out of that airport, shaking with fear and babbling incoherently. I let her go. Then I stepped forward. I had a job to do.

Where was the little girl this dead woman had been carrying just moments earlier as she stepped blithely toward Customs? I prayed she was still alive. There were more police and security now, their bodies beginning to block the carnage, but as they moved and space opened in odd geometric angles, I looked for a snub nose. A tiny arm. A head I could cup in one palm. And saw nothing.

"Thank God," I murmured. My fingers hurt from gripping the pen so tightly. Unclenching them, I jotted down what I had seen. First impressions were important, even scattered and disjointed ones. Later, we'd unravel them for clues. Something teetered in the upper corner of my vision and I flinched. But it was just Ariel, who had climbed atop a pile of suitcases for a better shooting angle. As the machine-gun patter of her film advanced, people dove behind luggage and covered children with their bodies until they realized that the noise came from a camera.

On the other side of the room, Maxwell was screaming into his two-way. I walked over and saw that his men had the Asian punks on the ground, hands cuffed behind their backs. They writhed on their bellies, heads cranked sideways, jaws gaping as if they were some weird pupa begging to be fed. Seeing this, Ariel leapt off her luggage mountain and ran to photograph them. This seemed to enrage the men, who hollered at her to stop, and averted their faces.

"Three dead," Maxwell was saying urgently into his radio, "Asian female and two Caucasian males. We're checking. Yeah."

There was a long pause. Part of me expected Maxwell to blow his whistle any minute now and announce that the emergency preparedness drill was over. Then the "bodies" would get up, dust themselves off, strip off the shirts with the paintball blood, and go back to their usual business.

"Don't know about the males," Maxwell said into the radio, "but Interpol Tokyo alerted us about the family. I called INS but then all hell broke loose. And now Mom's dead and Crypto-Dad's MIA."

"Are you charging them with murder?" I asked, looking at the guys on the ground.

Maxwell ignored me.

He listened as a faint voice crackled on the other end of the two-way. His lips drew together into a thin line and he seemed to whiten under his L.A. tan.

"Son of a bitch," he said softly. He hooked the radio back onto his belt, turned slowly, and glared at the captives. Then he shook his head.

"Help these gentlemen up," he ordered, drawing the word out with a sneer.

"Are they terrorists or what?" I asked.

I knew al-Qaeda didn't just recruit Middle Easterners. The South Asian archipelagos were said to be awash with Muslim fundamentalists.

Maxwell focused on me. It looked as if he was trying to remember who I was. He scratched an ear.

"We are in the middle of a triple-murder investigation as well as two undercover-criminal operations. You'll have to leave. And you," he turned to Ariel, "will have to hand over that film."

Ariel Delacorte removed the camera from her face. Her eyes were a deep, translucent green. She slid the camera into her shoulder bag, tucked a strand of hair behind her ear, and said, "You'll get their names for the captions, won't you, Eve?" Then she turned on her booted heel and strode out the door without a backward glance.

"Fine," Maxwell yelled after her. "We'll let the lawyers duke it out."

He turned back and I nodded, eager to appear more sympathetic than frosty Ariel. I would never do such a thing.

"What happened back there?" I asked, shifting nervously as the Customs police roughly hauled up the two Asian men. They wore a look of angry vindication that confused me. Here I was, a reporter, an eyewitness, but I had no idea what had just gone down. All I knew was that suddenly the place had exploded into gunfire and chaos.

Maxwell regarded the men.

"Let 'em loose. Yeah, that's right," he told his startled colleagues. "You heard what I said."

One of the freed men brushed off his jacket, took a step forward, and jabbed the air with a forefinger.

"That was fucked-up, Customs," he said. "Real fucked-up. Your career is over. Starting tomorrow, you'll be lucky to find work as a six-dollar-an-hour rent-a-cop."

Maxwell jeered. "That's your future, G-boy, not mine. Bigfoot blew it bad."

"These guys," he said wearily, turning to me, "are not terrorists. They are not murderers. They are undercover agents for the FBI. Fucking feds were tailing two mobsters from Vladivostok who are now lying here dead, and they neglected to inform us. Little lack of interagency communication by Bigfoot. Who doesn't care who they stomp on so long as they get theirs. Meanwhile, we're doing our own tail, some nasty folks out of Bangkok traveling with a kid. Couple weeks more and we'd a' taken down the whole operation. But these cowboys," he hooked a thumb at the FBI men, "blew everything sky high when their guys tried to run. And now one of my little chickens is dead and the other's flown the coop. Goddamn it!"

He swept his cap off his head and hurled it onto the linoleum floor with a slap that made me start.

A heavyset woman in a white uniform wearing a name tag walked toward us. She was holding the groggy toddler with the designer clothes who belonged to the dead raspberry lady and her missing husband.

The child couldn't have been more than two. Her pale cheek lay against the woman's blouse and she observed us with slack eyes. Her breathing was thick and rheumy. When she coughed, her thin frame shook and her plastic diaper crackled. But that was the only sound. Separated from her beautiful and dead mama, witness to the massacre that had just erupted, held tight by a total stranger, the child didn't cry. She didn't wail. She didn't utter a word. One impossibly small hand curled around the woman's neck. In the other, she clutched a teddy bear.

"She'll have a Japanese passport, but my guess is she won't speak a word of Japanese," Maxwell said. "Her papers will show she's traveled widely in the last six months, but never stayed anywhere long. She jets around with loving parents who give her anything that money can buy, but she don't look too happy to me.

"Who are you, little girl?" he asked softly. "And why did they leave you behind?"

# Visit
❖ **Pocket Books** ❖
## online at

······························································

# www.SimonSays.com

······························································

Keep up on the latest new
releases from your favorite
authors, as well as author
appearances, news, chats,
special offers and more.

SIMON & SCHUSTER
A VIACOM COMPANY
www.SimonSays.com

Pocket
Books